P9-ELV-258

HAPPY HOUR
IN
HELL

A Bobby Dollar Novel

TAD WILLIAMS

DAW BOOKS, INC.

DONALD A. WOLLHEIM, FOUNDER

375 Hudson Street, New York, NY 10014

ELIZABETH R. WOLLHEIM
SHEILA E. GILBERT
PUBLISHERS

www.dawbooks.com

First printing, September 2013
1   2   3   4   5   6   7   8   9

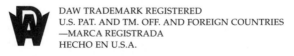

The first Bobby Dollar book was dedicated to my dear friend David Pierce. Since Dave left us, several other people I really care about have also departed—Jeff Kaye, Peggy Ford, and Iain Banks, to name just a few.

I'm glad Dave's got such good company, but it breaks my heart they didn't all hang out with the rest of us a bit longer.

ACKNOWLEDGMENTS

As always, many people were involved in the making of this book other than me (although I did a lot of the writing).

My wife Deborah Beale is always there for me with words of wisdom, calm consideration, and the occasional necessary kick to the fundament. My partner.

My agent Matt Bialer is another indispensable partner, except without the smooching stuff. (But he's still fun.)

And my beloved editors, Sheila Gilbert and Betsy Wollheim, put a huge amount of work and concern into this book. Blessings also upon Mary Lou Capes-Platt, who had a lot to do with shaping the final version. In fact, many thanks to all of the DAW folk.

Lisa Tveit continues to anchor me in cyberspace and to help me in a zillion different ways, for which I am ever grateful.

And a shout-out to Sharon L. James, for help with Classical Greek, and of course to all the Bobby Dollar Army and the other wonderful folk, readers and friends—especially Smarchers, on my webpage, tadwilliams.com, and Facebook (*tad.williams* and *AuthorTadWilliams*), not to mention the kind folks on Twitter who mostly see me after I've been edited by my wife (*MrsTad*) so that I sound smart.

Oh, and thanks to King Solomon, Hermes Trismegistus, and the authors of the *Malleus Maleficarum* for help chasing angels and wrangling demons.

Many gratitudes, my droogs.

prologue
welcome mat

A MOMENT COMES in pretty much everyone's life, or afterlife in my case, where they can't help but wonder, *What the fuck am I doing here?* I have more of those than most people (a couple a week, on average) but I'd never had one quite like this before. See, I was just about to walk into Hell. Voluntarily.

My name is Bobby Dollar, or sometimes Doloriel, depending on the company I'm keeping. I'd arrived at this ugly spot by elevator—a long, long ride down that I may or may not tell you about at some point. I was also wearing a body that wasn't my own, and all my information about the place came from a rogue guardian angel whispering in my mind while I was sleeping. Not that I had learned much useful stuff from her. In fact, most of it could be summed up with the simple phrase, "You can't even guess how bad this is going to be."

So there I stood, just outside Hell, at the foot of the Neronian Bridge, a featureless, flat span of stone that stretched over a chasm so deep that, if we had been on ordinary old Earth, the hole would probably have gone all the way through the planet and out of the other side. But Hell isn't on ordinary Earth and this pit wasn't bottomless—oh, no. See, at the bottom, impossible miles and miles below me in the darkness, the *really* bad shit was going on. I could tell that because of the faint sounds of screaming. I couldn't help wondering how hard those folks had to be screaming to be heard that far. Also, what exactly was being done to them to make them scream like that? Already I was asking questions with answers I didn't want to know.

Just in case all this isn't weird enough for you, here's another interesting fact: I'm an angel. So not only was I headed to the worst possible place anyone could ever go, I was doing it as a spy and an enemy. Oh, and I was going there to steal something from one of the cruelest, most powerful demons that ever existed, Eligor the Horseman, Grand Duke of Hell.

What was I trying to steal from Eligor? My girlfriend, Caz. She's also a demon and she belongs to him.

Oh, and when I said I was an angel, I didn't mean the avenging kind with wings and the Lord's Righteous Fire to wield against my enemies. No, I'm the kind who lives on Earth, pretends to be human most of the time, and advocates on behalf of human souls at judgement. In other words, I'm pretty much a public defender. So what I brought to the conflict was just enough information to know I was in serious trouble. Me against a Grand Duke of Hell on his home turf—great match-up, huh?

I was in what was, without question, the biggest enclosed space I'd ever seen—that anyone had ever seen, probably. All those medieval artists who'd pictured the place, even the really inventive ones, had never thought big enough for this. A wall of rugged stone surrounded me, extending straight up beyond sight. It seemed to be ever so slightly curved on either side, as though the vast cavern itself was the casing of a monstrous engine cylinder. Presumably there was another wall in front of me on the far side of the bridge, the piston inside that bigger cylinder and the point of my visit, the endless tower that is Hell. The bridge itself was narrower than my arms could stretch to either side, a walking surface only about a yard and a half wide. That would have been plenty, except for the fact that beneath the narrow span lay nothing but emptiness—a pit that extended down farther than I could see or even understand, with just enough flickering hell-light to let me know how very, very far I'd be falling if I took a wrong step.

Trust me. Like any sane being, I would have rather been anywhere else, but as I'll explain later, I'd worked hard to get even this far. I had learned how to get here, found an entrance nobody remembered to guard, and I was even wearing a brand-new demon body (because that's the only way I could travel safely in Hell). I might have been an unwanted guest, but I had already paid quite a bit to take this ride.

As I approached the span I gulped a deep breath made gritty by sulfur smoke and the faint but unmistakable tang of crisping flesh. A stone skittered away from my foot and bounced into the pit. I didn't wait to hear if it made a noise, since there wouldn't have been much point. You can only stall something terrible so long before all the courage just leaks out of you, and I knew that things would only get worse from here. Even if I made it across this whisper-thin span and managed to sneak into Hell, the whole place was jam-packed with creatures that just plain hated angels in general and me in particular.

The Neronian Bridge dates back to ancient Rome, and it's named after the Emperor Nero, the one who supposedly fiddled while Rome burned. Nero wasn't the worst emperor Rome ever had, but he was pretty much of a horrible bastard anyway, and one of the ways we know this is because he had his own mother murdered. Twice.

His mother Agrippina was the sister of another, even nastier little bastard you may have heard of—Caligula. He married one of his other sisters, but he humped them all. Still, despite all the creepy stuff with her brother, after Caligula was stabbed to death by his own guards Agrippina was rehabilitated and eventually married Caligula's successor, old Emperor Claudius. Somehow she even managed to convince Claudius to put aside his own beloved son and instead make Nero, her son by a previous marriage, his heir. Once Nero was the emperor-designate, she bumped off poor Claudius by feeding him poisoned mushrooms.

Clearly grateful for his mother's assistance in becoming the most powerful man in the world, Nero promptly turned around and ordered her killed. He first tried to do it with a trick boat that was supposed to break apart so she'd drown, but Agrippina was a tough old bitch and made it back to land, so Nero sent some of his guardsmen over to her house to stab her to death with swords.

Family values, Roman Empire style.

Nero did a lot of other pretty terrible stuff during the rest of his reign, including burning a buttload of innocent Christians, but that isn't the reason he got his own little highway project in Hell, the bridge I stood in front of now. See, what Nero didn't realize is that his mother's coup in getting Claudius to marry her and raise Nero above his own son was the result of a little bargain she'd made with one of Hell's more influential inhabitants, a powerful demon by the name of Ignoculi. Now, Ignoculi and his infernal pals didn't give a (literal) damn about Nero killing his mother—in fact, they rather admired it. But they did expect him to live up to the terms of the bargain his mother had made to put Nero on the throne of the Roman Empire, because Hell had big plans for Rome. But Nero refused to play along. To be honest, he probably didn't realize how big an operation Hell really was—the Romans had a different religious picture of things, Pluto and the Elysian Fields and all that stuff. It was probably a bit like that movie producer in the *Godfather* who thought he could tell Don Corleone to fuck off, then woke up to find a horse's head added to the bedroom decor.

Pissing off Hell is not a good idea. Things went downhill rapidly for young Nero, and within a short period of time he found himself off the throne and on the run. He eventually wound up committing suicide. However, the real surprises were still waiting for him.

Ignoculi, like most of Hell's executives, was extremely good at bearing a grudge. When Nero arrived in Hell it was to discover a special entrance had been built just for him. Yep, the Neronian Bridge. A thousand demons dressed in the finery of Roman imperial guardsmen were already there, waiting to accompany Nero across it in the splendor to which he had become accustomed in life. The great procession set off in single file across the abyss, drums pounding and trumpets tootling, but when Nero reached the other end his retinue abruptly vanished, leaving only the emperor and the one who was waiting to greet him—not Ignoculi himself, but Nero's late mother, Agrippina.

She must have made a pretty awful sight, crooked and broken and soaking wet from Nero's first attempt on her life, streaming blood from the sword-thrusts that killed her. Nero, suddenly realizing that he was going to receive something less than a hero's welcome, tried to flee back across the bridge, but now Ignoculi himself made an appearance on the bridge, a huge, quivering glob of eyes and teeth that blocked the ex-emperor's retreat like a ton of angry snot.

"*Caveat imperator,*" the demon reportedly said. In Hell, bad puns are considered a particularly ripe form of torture. Then Agrippina grabbed her son in her bloody, mangled fingers and, with strength she'd never had in life, dragged him shrieking through the gate to Hell and the less-than-imperial fate prepared for him. And of course, from what I've heard he's still there, probably down at the bottom with the rest of the screamers.

After that, the Neronian Bridge was largely forgotten until I got there, just another monument to why you never, never, *never* get one of hell's high rollers mad at you—something that I had already managed, big time. Do you think the universe might have been trying to tell me something?

I stepped onto the bridge and started walking.

I had been putting one foot in front of the other for what seemed hours when I noticed that the screams wafting up from below seemed to be growing louder. I hoped that meant I was finally nearing the center of the bridge, but it might just have been that lunch break was over downstairs. I looked down, steadying myself against a dizziness that wasn't just physical but existential. Perspective turned the flames issuing from cracks in the pit walls into shrinking, tightening rings of concentric fire like a burning bull's-eye.

Leathery wings flapped past my face, startling me badly, and I realized how close to the edge I was standing. I moved back into the middle of the bridge and began walking again, still in the wrong direction by any sane standard. The winged thing fluttered past me again, brushing against my skin, but the light was too faint to make out what it was. I don't think it was a bat, because it was crying.

Hours and hours later, the smoldering bull's-eye was still more or less right beneath me. When you're crossing a Hell-moat that could be as wide as South Dakota I guess the idea of "near the middle" is fairly relative, but it sure was depressing.

But this was all for Caz, I kept reminding myself, for the Countess of Cold Hands, the beautiful, ruined young girl trapped in an immortal body and sentenced to Hell. No, it wasn't even for Caz, it was for what we had together, for the moments of happiness and peace I had felt lying in bed with her while the infernal hordes harrowed the streets of San Judas looking for me. Yes, she was one of those infernal minions herself, and yes she had all but told me that I was turning an incident of straightforward battlefield sex between two enemies into some absurd, juvenile love story . . . but oh my sweet God, she was lovely. Nothing in my angelic life had made me feel like she did. Even more, my time with her had showed me that my existence up to this point had been hollow. If it hadn't been for that, maybe I could have believed it was all demonic glamour—that I had simply been seduced, that I'd fallen for the oldest trick in the Adversary's book. (There was another reason I didn't think I was simply being played for a chump. It had to do with a silver locket, but I'll tell you more about that later.) Anyway, if what I felt for Caz was just a trick, an illusion, then nothing else mattered, either.

Love. Tired old jokes aside, a real, powerful love does have one thing in common with Hell itself: it burns everything else out of you.

Hours in, hypnotized by endless, flickering shadows, it took me far longer than it should have to realize that the spot of darkness on the bridge ahead of me was not simply another shadow or a floating spot in my vision but something real. I slowed, squinting, my dreamy half-life suddenly cracked into pieces. Was it waiting for me? Had Eligor found out I was coming and prepared a welcome for me, something like that horned Babylonian nightmare that I had barely managed to survive back in San Jude? The only thing that had stopped the last one was a precious piece of silver, Caz's locket, but I didn't have anything like that now. My new demon body was naked and I didn't have a gun. I didn't even have a stick.

As I got closer I saw that the shape wasn't standing erect like a man but was on all fours like an animal. Closer still and I could see that it was crawling *away* from me, which gave me my first moment of relief since I'd stepped onto this bloody bridge. Mama Dollar's baby boy is no fool, though, or at least not in the obvious ways; as I began to catch up to the solitary crawler I slowed down so I could examine it.

It was manlike but unpleasant to watch, like a blind, clumsy insect. Its hands were clubbed and fingerless, the body distorted, and even by the standards of that miserable place it reflected very little light: it seemed less like a solid thing and more like a smudge on the surface of reality. I was right behind it now, but it seemed unaware of my presence, still crawling like a crippled penitent, drawing itself along as though each movement was miserably difficult. The very slowness of its progress made me wonder how long it had been on the bridge.

I didn't want to walk around it, not on that narrow span. Just because it looked slow and stupid didn't mean it wouldn't turn on me. I considered simply jumping over it, but I didn't trust the footing either.

"What are you doing?" I said. "Are you hurt?"

The sudden noise of my new, raspy demon-voice startled even me, but the crawling thing gave no indication it had heard. I tried again.

"I need to get past you."

Nothing. If the crawling thing wasn't deaf, it was sure acting like it.

Frustrated, I finally reached down and yanked on its leg to get its attention, but although the man-shape looked solid, it was as brittle as a dessert meringue. The entire limb broke loose underneath my fingers in flaky shards, leaving nothing below the knee. In horror, I dropped the substantial piece of leg. It broke into pieces, many of which bounced slowly over the edge of the bridge and vanished into darkness. The thing finally stopped crawling long enough to turn toward me, and I caught a glimpse of a gray face with empty hollows for eyes and an equally empty hole of a mouth stretched wide in surprise or horror. Then it tilted to one side as if the loss of the leg had overbalanced it and toppled off the bridge without a sound.

Shaken, I stepped over the greasy flakes that remained and walked on.

Whatever the crumbling horror might have been, it was not the only one of its kind. I caught up with the next gray thing before too long, another man-shaped blob creeping toward the still invisible walls of Hell. I tried to poke this one gently enough to get its attention. It seemed as fragile as sea foam, but just the feel of it on my fingertip made me queasy. How could something with no substance hold a shape, let alone crawl forward with such blind determination?

But this is Hell, I reminded myself, *or at least the suburbs.* Nothing normal applied here.

I poked it again. Like its predecessor it turned, but this one reached for me with its shapeless hands; in fear and disgust I stepped back and kicked at it, catching it square in the hindquarters. With a whispering crunch it broke into several large pieces. I waded through them, though they were still slowly squirming, and kicked several of them into the abyss. I didn't stop to watch them fall.

As hours passed, or would have anywhere else, I encountered more of the hideous things. I'd given up any idea of communicating with them and simply kicked them out of my way, wading through the sentient scraps. When I had crushed several of them I began to notice an odor on my skin, like faint traces of lighter fluid in the ashes of a barbecue pit. The things were slow and mindless as dying termites, and disgusting in a way I can't even explain. I wanted to grind each one of them to powder, to scatter their very atoms to the void. In fact, I was losing what little remained of my mind.

What saved me, strangely enough, was Hell itself. After fighting my way through an entire squirming pack of the things, showering myself and the emptiness on either side of the bridge with ashy fragments, I bent over in a cloud of the last swirling bits and realized that the bridge no longer narrowed to nothingness in front of me. The terrible span had an end point, something I had only believed because I had to. Now I could see it ahead of me, a wall of broken black stone with a titanic gate of rusted iron in the middle of it, tall as a skyscraper. But thousands of the gray, mindless things still squirmed between me and that gate.

I'm betting that some of you can't imagine what was so bad about having to fight through things that offered no resistance of any kind, that collapsed under my touch like fireplace ash. Try thinking about it this way: there might have been nothing left of them but crude shapes, like the dead of Pompeii preserved in the fiery ash that spewed from Vesuvius, but they had all been people once.

You see, as I came up that last span, fighting my way through the creeping shapes, making a storm of floating, powdery fragments until I couldn't see my own feet or the bridge, I finally realized what they were. Not damned souls—that would have been bad enough. These weren't prisoners of Hell, they weren't trying to get out, they were trying to get *in*. The shapes were souls who had been sentenced to Purgatory, the essences of countless human lives—failed lives but not irreparably evil. And for whatever reason, these things, once men and women, were so consumed by self-hatred that they crawled forever toward the place where they felt they truly belonged.

I should have pitied them but understanding only made it worse. As I neared the walls of Hell the things flocked as thickly as insects swarming around a hot light bulb, driven by a self-destructive urge they couldn't understand. I was too exhausted to say anything, but inside I was screaming. I thrashed through the clotted mass as if I were swimming, until everything I was and had ever been dissolved into a madness of greasy flakes and swirling, kerosene-scented dust, until I no longer knew where I was, let alone where the bridge was—the only thing between me and oblivion. The fact that I did not fall is the only testament I will ever need that something or Someone bigger than me wanted me to survive.

Grunting, gasping, I stopped to suck in air and realized abruptly that nothing stood before me now but the massive, rusty entrance and bare black stone: I had reached the shadows beneath the gate. The swarming crawlers were now behind me, confined to the bridge as if by an invisible fence. The pathetic, self-loathing things didn't belong in Hell, they just believed they did. They would not be admitted.

But Bobby Dollar? Apparently I was different. No guards and nothing to keep me from walking in but the good sense I had surrendered a long time back. By Hell's charming standards, they'd pretty much put out the welcome mat. But I don't think I'm giving away too much when I tell you it wasn't going to prove anywhere near as easy getting back out again.

one

pillow talk

WE ONLY had one night together, really. And I remember every moment of it.

"So what's it like, living in Hell?"

"Oh, it's great. We drink ice cream sodas all day and play pool and smoke cigars and never, ever turn into donkeys."

"That sounds more like Pleasure Island, from Pinocchio."

"Shoot. You got me."

"Come on, woman, it was a serious question."

"Well, maybe I don't want to answer it, Wings. How's that for serious?"

We were both naked in Caz's secret hideaway and had just made love for the first (well, technically first, second, and second-and-a-half) time. Her head was on my chest and her legs were clamped around my thigh like a bivalve mercilessly trying to compel surrender. I stroked her hair, a gold so pale you could only tell it wasn't white in direct sunlight.

"That bad, huh?"

"Oh, you beautiful, stupid man, you can't imagine." She lifted herself on one elbow so she could look me in the face. She was so gorgeous that I promptly forgot what we were talking about and lay there staring like I was brain damaged. By any normal standards I must have been, because otherwise why would a minion of Heaven be making naked squishies with a tool of Satan in the first place? "Not just bad," she told me. "Worse than you could possibly imagine."

I kept wondering how anyone, even the lords of Hell, could want to harm that radiant beauty. The official version would be that she had a face like a Renaissance angel, beautiful, delicate, full of lofty thoughts. But the truth was that she looked like the most innocently wicked graduate of a very, very expensive private school. If I hadn't known for a fact that Caz had been around since before Columbus sailed, I'd have been feeling very, very guilty after all the things we'd just done. I was beginning to believe I was in love with this woman, but of course she wasn't actually a woman at all, and she came from Hell. Think about that a little and you'll probably understand why I didn't want to consider our situation too closely.

"I'm sorry. I shouldn't have said anything . . ."

"No! No, thank your lucky stars that you don't know, Bobby. I want you to stay that way. I don't want you ever to know what that place is like." And then she suddenly hugged me so tightly that for a moment I thought she was trying to crawl through *me somehow and out the other side. Her small, hard body seemed both the most real and the most vulnerable thing in the world.*

"I won't let you go back," I said.

I thought she laughed. I only realized later that the noise had been something else, something far less simple. Her legs tightened on my thigh; I could feel her wetness pressing against me. "Of course you won't, Bobby," she said. "We'll never go back, either of us. We'll stay here and drink ice cream sodas forever. So kiss me, you dumbfuck angel."

Have you ever had somebody you loved die on you? All that stuff you feel, and you're *still* feeling it, but they're just gone? You carry that around with you every moment—all the things you failed to tell them, all the ways you were stupid, all the ways you're missing them. It feels like holding up a huge, collapsing wall, as if you were some hero in a movie waiting for everyone to get to safety, but you already know you're not going to get away yourself. That eventually the weight will just crush you.

Ever had somebody leave you and tell you they never really loved you? That you're a loser, a waste of time they should have known to avoid? You carry that one around too, but instead of an insupportable weight, it's more like a horrible burn, nerve endings fried and stuck on jangling alert, a pain that occasionally subsides to a bitter, itching ache, but then flares up into agony again without warning.

Here's one more: Ever had somebody steal the thing that mattered most to you? Then laugh in your face about it? Leave you helpless and seething?

Okay, now imagine that all three things happened at the same time, with the same woman.

Her name was Caz, short for Casimira, also known as the Countess of Cold Hands, a she-demon of high standing and about the most mesmerizing creature I'd ever seen. When we met we were on opposite sides in the ancient conflict between Heaven and Hell. We became lovers, which both of us knew was an extremely stupid, supremely dangerous thing to do. But something drew us together, although that's a pretty damn bland, vanilla way of putting it. We made sparks—no, a raging fire—and it still blazed inside of me, long after she'd gone. Some days it seemed like it was going to burn me to ashes.

Caz belonged to Eligor, one of the Grand Dukes of Hell. After our affair, our fling, whatever you want to call it, she went back to him. She even tried to make me think she'd never cared about me, but, see, I didn't believe that. I was certain she felt something too because, if not, then I was wrong about *everything*. I'm talking about *up is down, black is white, the world is really flat after all* kind of wrong.

Call me stupid if you want, but I wouldn't believe that. I couldn't. Beside, I had a more practical reason for thinking that she really cared for me. Don't worry, we're coming to that soon.

Anyway, now Eligor hated me because I'd messed with his "property" (okay, also because of some other stuff, like shooting his secretary, getting his bodyguard eaten, and generally interfering with his plans). The power imbalance between us was ridiculously skewed in Eligor's favor: he was infernal royalty, and I was a minor mid-level functionary who already had a bit of a negative reputation with my superiors. So why wasn't I dead? Because I had *the feather*—a golden feather from the wing of an important angel that marked an illicit bargain made between Grand Duke Eligor and someone in Heaven whose identity I still didn't know. Eligor definitely didn't want that feather going public, and as long as I had it stashed safely away I felt sure he would leave me alone. On the other hand, Eligor had Caz, and he'd taken her back to Hell, far out of my reach. Stalemate. At least that's what I'd thought when the whole thing started. As it turned out, I had built a house of cards out of the flimsiest set of assumptions possible.

Oops. Getting ahead of myself a little. A lot of things happened before I even heard of the Neronian Bridge, and I should probably tell you about some of them before we return to Hell.

The latest episode of the ongoing craziness that is my afterlife started with what normal folk would call a job review. Except normal folk wouldn't be reviewed by a group of pissed-off celestials who could literally destroy an immortal soul with a single word. Even the poor bastards who work for Trump don't have to put up with that.

two

five angry angels

I'D BEEN called to Heaven, specifically to the Anaktoron, the great council chamber I had visited once before, an astounding architectural impossibility with cloud-high ceilings, a floating table of black stone and a river running right through the middle of the floor. My archangel, Temuel (sort of my supervisor) brought me into the mighty building and then discreetly retired. Floating on the far side of the stone table, as if someone had jerked away a candelabrum and left the candle flames burning in midair, were the *ephors*, my five special inquisitors.

"God loves you, Angel Doloriel," declared the filmy white flame that was Terentia. "This Ephorate welcomes you." Like the first time I'd met them, Terentia seemed to be the one in charge, although I knew that Karael, the warrior-angel beside her, was about as high as anyone can get in the hierarchy of the Third Sphere (everything to do with Earth and its inhabitants). Beside him hovered Chamuel, a mist that gleamed from within, and next to Chamuel was Anaita, a childlike presence that I knew from unpleasant experience could be as coldly formal as Terentia. At the edge of the group was Raziel, a being of dim red light who was neither male nor female. All of these important angels were Principalities, the judges of the dead and the living. There is no higher rank among the angels in our sphere.

I returned Terentia's greeting, trying not to look like I was waiting for my blindfold and cigarette. "How can I serve you, Masters?"

"With the truth," said Chamuel, but almost kindly. "These are great matters in which you have been caught up, Doloriel. Dangerous matters. And we wish to hear of them from your own lips."

Yeah? And what would you know about lips? I wondered, since Chamuel's form was indistinct as a rain cloud. I'm not entirely stupid, though, so I only bowed my head. "Of course."

And so the ephors asked, and I answered. I tried to tell the truth when I could (it makes keeping track of the lies easier) but there were just too darn many things I didn't dare mention, too many laws of Heaven that I had stomped all over while trying to get to the bottom of the whole mess. They knew that my demon-lover Caz had given me information but they definitely didn't know what else had happened between us, which was good, because I was pretty sure fraternizing with the enemy was a capital offense in the angel business, and I had gone a lot farther than "fraternizing." They also knew that my buddy and partner Sam Riley, aka Advocate Angel Sammariel, had been secretly working for a group that hijacked souls belonging to either Heaven or Hell and offered them instead a "Third Way" that both sides of the ancient struggle were pretty eager to obliterate. They also knew Sam had escaped, but luckily they hadn't found out it was because I'd let him go. (They also didn't know that he'd had offered to take me with him to the Third Way's new-minted afterworld. I still thought about that sometimes.)

As I think I said, I've never just stood up and lied to Heaven before. I've kept many a not-very-angelic thought to myself, of course, but I always told the truth about what I was doing and whom I was doing it with. But the last couple of months had changed all that: truth was no longer an option. If my bosses found out what I'd done I'd be sentenced to the nastiest pits of Hell or, if I was lucky, I'd just have my memory wiped and start over again, another fledgling angel learning how to keep his robe clean and sing Hosanna. So I lied and kept on lying.

". . . As for the last part, well, it's all in my report."

"Which we have absorbed with interest," said Terentia. "But we have called you here so you can relate your experiences again, and perhaps, with our help, discover details which were inadvertently left out of your report."

How could a guy resist such thoughtfulness? "Well, as I said, when the monster attacked me in the abandoned amusement park, Angel Sammariel took advantage of the distraction to escape. I didn't see where he went. By the time the *ghallu* was dead, there was no sign of him." (Fighting the monstrous ancient demon—and almost being swallowed by it—had definitely happened, I promise you. It was the oops-Sam-got-away part that hadn't.)

Raziel's dark light grew darker for a moment, like a thunderstorm starting to roll. "But both you and Angel Haraheliel were together after the creature of the pit was dead, or nearly so. He says he was struck by one of the creature's death-throes, but before he was rendered senseless he confronted Sammariel. These conflicts confuse us."

A silence fell between the boss angels; I had the disturbing sense of things flying past above my head, of conversations I couldn't hear but which would determine my fate whether I liked it or not. Haraheliel was the real angelic name of rookie advocate (and company spy) Clarence, and trying to make the kid's report jibe with my invented recollections was one of my major challenges.

"I'm sorry, Master," I said quickly. "You're right, of course. When I said 'attacked,' I meant the creature's last movements. I thought it was dead. It lay still for a long time, but then it stunned Angel Haraheliel with its leg and started to get up again. I fired my last bullets into it, and it finally stopped moving." I was praying—ironic, no?—that I was remembering the details right, or at least the details of the version I'd submitted to Heaven's auditors. I had been studying my report and Clarence's for days, like a panicked freshman in finals week. I've got a pretty good memory, but being here in the Anaktoron would be enough to make Einstein put his fingers to his lips and go *bblbblbblbbl*. "Then, when I looked up, Angel Haraheliel was unconscious and Sam—Angel Sammariel—was gone." I was tempted to prattle on, re-emphasizing all the important points, but instead I clamped my mouth shut and waited. Again the awesome, nerve-wracking silence. Moments only, but a moment in Heaven can literally seem like hours.

"Another thing that has been puzzling me, Angel Doloriel," said Anaita in her sweet, childlike voice. "How was it that you were able to defeat a creature of Old Night with nothing more than silver bullets? It seems strange that such a mighty enemy should be dispatched as easily as one of the Adversary's foot soldiers."

Because the silver I put into the monster at the end was more than just any old silver. It was a gift to me from Caz, a tiny silver locket, the only precious object that remained from her life as a human woman. And it was given to me with love, I'm convinced of that. The fact that a monster from the depths of time had died from that fragile little bit of silver but had laughed off all the earlier silver slugs was one of the biggest reasons that I didn't believe what happened between Caz and me had been mere infernal seduction. But I could no more admit that to the ephors than I could claim that God Himself came down in a fiery chariot and crushed the *ghallu* beneath its wheels.

"I still don't know," I said as humbly as I could. "I put quite a few silver bullets in it during the course of perhaps two hours. At the end . . . it seemed to be laboring." Which was a lie. Until I used Caz's locket, the thing had swallowed silver rounds like they were lemon drops. "Perhaps . . . I . . ." If I had been breathing, I would have stopped to take a deep, deep breath, because I had no good answer, and I was just plain scared. "I honestly don't know."

"Don't underestimate an angel of the Lord," said Karael suddenly. He was talking so I could hear him, but he was clearly saying it for the benefit of his fellow ephors. "Angel Doloriel was trained as a member of Counterstrike Unit *Lyrae* to resist the enemies of Heaven, and those angels are as brave and tough a group as we have. I have fought many times beside our Counterstrike Units. If anyone could bring down a creature of such ancient, evil lineage, it would be a CU veteran. Isn't that right, Doloriel?"

I could have kissed him, I swear. I could have wrapped my arms around his fiery, beautiful awesomeness and planted one right on him. "We . . . we do our best, sir. We always do our best."

"Exactly. Doloriel was a Harp." The way Karael said it, it seemed to roll and echo through the great council chamber. "One of those courageous souls who defend the walls of Heaven itself—even if the ones they protect do not always remember. That *means* something."

So was Karael trying to get me off the hook simply because he didn't like to see the angelic equivalent of ex-military being run down by the bureaucrats? Or was there something else going on? Shit, who was I kidding? In Heaven there's *always* something else going on.

"Of course, noble Karael," said Terentia, again speaking so I could hear. "But this angel left the *Lyrae*, did he not?"

I couldn't figure out what was going on, and that scared me all over

again. Why were the top brass arguing in front of me, a mere foot soldier? It didn't make sense.

"Doloriel left Counterstrike because he was gravely wounded in a
battle with Hell's forces." Karael almost sounded defensive.

"And now he serves the will of the Highest as a member of His holy
advocates," said genderless Raziel in a voice like quiet music. "Defending the souls of the worthy from the lies and trickery of Hell."

"Perhaps," Anaita replied. "But it was one of those selfsame advocates who conspired with members of the Opposition to create this
wretched Third Way, causing all the trouble in the first place. And
while there is no doubt that Angel Doloriel has been a brave fighter
and an effective advocate, no one could dispute the fact that he seems
to . . . attract trouble."

"It is true," said Raziel slowly, "that there have been times since I
created the Advocacy when I wonder if we are asking too much of the
Elect, requiring them to take on earthly bodies again, exposing them to
all the temptations and despair that beset the living every day on
Earth."

They fell into silent conversation again, which was just as well because I must have been gaping like someone had broken a bottle over
my head. Raziel created the Advocates? I had never heard that. In fact,
I had never heard anything to suggest our existence came from anything less than a divine order from the Highest Himself. How important *were* these five angels? And why were they spending so much time
with little Bobby Dollar?

Then an idea came to me, stealing over me like a fog, sending chills
up and down my non-corporeal form. Something was going on here
far beyond a fact-finding meeting, or even a meeting about something
as important to these high angels as the renegades of the Third Way.
Sam had told me that he'd been approached by a disguised angel that
called itself Kephas, and everything about Kephas had suggested powers beyond that of Heaven's rank and file, including the God Glove it
had given Sam, a device or power or whatever it was that had allowed
him to do so many unexpected things. Might Kephas, the revolutionary behind the Third Way, be a high angel like this quintet of ephors?
Or, even weirder and more disturbing, was Kephas one of the Furious
Five themselves?

The games they play in Heaven are incredibly subtle, but they're still deadly—no, worse than deadly, because the loser's lot is an eternity bathing in fire. What was I caught up in? And how was I going to avoid becoming a Bobby-colored smear in the grinding gears of heavenly politics?

"Angel Doloriel," said Terentia suddenly, breaking into my thoughts so abruptly that I almost squeaked in terror. I'm glad I didn't, since angels usually don't squeak.

"Yes, Mistress?"

"We must consider all you have told us. We will speak to you again. Be ready for a summons."

And just like that it was all gone, the fiery ephors and the gleaming magnificence of the Anaktoron's council chamber, and I was back in bed in my miserable apartment once more, back in my miserable, shivering human body. It was still dark outside, but I was pretty sure I wasn't going to be able to get back to sleep.

three

coming back

I CAN ONLY look at four walls so long before I start to get a little crazy. It was worse the morning after my inquisition, because almost everything I owned was still in boxes on the floor of my new apartment, and the paltry number of those boxes made me think about how little I had to show for my existence. I suppose one of God's chief servants should have been proud of such a sparse, monkish existence (if a crate of jazz and blues CDs and a couple of boxes of hot rod magazines interspersed with the occasional Playboy and Penthouse counts as "monkish") but it just depressed me. If I'd been a happy little angel doing the work of Heaven it probably wouldn't have been that way, but I'd always felt that somehow there must be something more to my afterlife. Now that I woke up each day with a Caz-shaped hole in me, I knew what was missing but that didn't mean I was ever going to have it.

I'd sworn that I was going to get her back, and I'd really meant it. I still did, but the heat of my anger was less now that several weeks had passed, and I had begun to realize just how unlikely it was that I could make it happen. For one thing, Caz was back in Hell, and nobody just waltzes into Hell any more than they walk into Heaven without a reservation. In fact, you'd have a better chance of rolling a shopping cart into Fort Knox and helping yourself to gold ingots. Both Heaven and Hell are way off the grid, by which I mean almost certainly not on our big old round physical Earth. Even if I managed to sneak in, there would be the little matter of me being an angel. Conspicuous? Yeah, a bit. And last but certainly not least would be the fact that Caz was currently the unwilling property of Eligor the Horseman, Grand Duke of Hades, who'd already demonstrated his intent to torture me for at least an eternity or two, as soon as he cleared a few other matters off his desk. I'm not sure even Karael and an entire heavenly legion could manage to get Caz away from him, so you can imagine the odds against me on my own. In fact, the whole project was really just a complicated, painful way of committing soul-suicide.

But oh my dear Lord, every morning that I woke up, and Caz wasn't with me, I ached. And every night I lay down by myself in that punky little room on Beech Street, and I thought about ways to get her back. But the one thing I could never imagine was an outcome where we were together, happy, and sane.

If I knew Heaven, I wasn't going to hear anything from my inquisitors for a few days: one thing they've got plenty of up there is time. I wouldn't have been surprised to discover they were all still floating around that conference chamber one-upping each other and hadn't even started deliberating my fate. Just about the worst thing to do would have been to sit around my little studio apartment waiting for Heaven to call, even if I wasn't already prone to maudlin Caz-thoughts, so I invented a few pressing errands to give me a reason to get dressed.

I took a cab over to see Orban, the gunsmith. He's the one who built cannons for the Sultan to use at the siege of Constantinople a few hundred years back. Here's how that worked out: Sultan wins, Constantinople falls, Christendom is seriously hacked off with Orban. Because he knows he's never getting into Heaven, he refuses to die and still hasn't done it. That's how he tells it, anyway, and I'm not inclined to argue with him, especially since the stuff he supplies has saved my skin and soul many times.

Anyway, Orban also armors cars, and he still had my custom Matador in storage in his garage. And although I had enough money now to get it out of pawn, I was beginning to think that a gleaming, topaz-colored muscle car might not be the best ride for a man developing such a large collection of enemies. What good was it changing apartments and then parking the Amber Amigo out in front of it? Not that I was going to give that car up—I'd put too much money and sweat and spare time into it—but I was going to have to find something else for day-to-day use. In my business as an advocate angel I drive a lot and at all hours. No way I was going to be sitting at bus stops at three in the morning hoping the Number Eleven crosstown would get me to somebody's bedside in time to be there when they died.

Orban wasn't in the shop when I arrived, but one of his assistants, a bearded guy who looked like he would have felt comfortable with a parrot on his shoulder and his keel being hauled or something, recognized me and opened up the garage, a long building on the next pier over from Orban's gun factory. Most of the vehicles inside had been brought in for some kind of modification, usually shielding, but the owners had either gone broke or had really needed the shielding earlier, and Orban had been stuck with the rides they left behind. He sold a few, especially if the security work had been finished, and kept the rest to cannibalize for spare parts.

The guy with the pirate beard wandered back to whatever instrument of destruction he had been working on, leaving me to walk along the row of grills, footsteps echoing from the stained concrete below my feet to the rounded aluminum roof. Most of the cars were huge, limos and old American luxury sedans, the ones Orban had more trouble selling than the Hummers and pimped-out SUVs today's drug dealers preferred. One of Orban's old classics, a Pontiac Bonneville, had been ripped up like tinfoil by the *ghallu*, so I was in need of a new ride. I spent a few agonizing minutes yearning over a scratched-up but sound 1958 Biscayne that, with a little sanding and a new coat of paint, would have made me a very happy man, but it was just too damn interesting for my purposes. If I wanted interesting, I'd keep driving around in my Matador. Inconspicuous was what I needed, though it went against everything in my character.

Down at the end, looking like the runt of the litter because of its size and pushed-in snout, was a 1969 Nova Super Sport. The paint that remained was a faded coat of candy-apple red, but I could cover that with a less conspicuous color. It was probably a hot little number in its day—the SS's had a standard 350 inch V-8. The frame was basically okay, but it looked like it would be quite at home rusting away on blocks in the front yard of somebody's mobile home. Not bad for my purposes.

I left a note for Orban asking what he wanted for the Super Sport, then walked back from the Salt Piers by way of the freeway overpass, so that I'd worked up a pretty good appetite (and killed an hour or so) by the time I arrived at Oyster Bill's. It was a little weird to think I might never eat there with Sam again, since we'd spent a lot of time there, but I also felt like I was honoring his memory.

The truth was, I didn't know how to think about Sam and what had happened to him. When you know somebody as long as I've known Sam Riley, aka Advocate Angel Sammariel; when you've gotten drunk together, been in firefights together, and watched a few dozen human beings die in each other's company, you kind of figure you've seen everything that other person has to show. So when I found out he'd been working for mystery-angel Kephas and the secret Third Way operation, essentially running a side game right on Heaven's own turf, under my nose and everyone else's . . . well, I still wasn't sure how it all jibed. The last time the two of us had talked, just before he stepped through a shimmering door to somewhere I'd never seen before, he seemed pretty much like the Sam I'd shared all those breakfasts with in this very restaurant, watching the tourists get their money lifted by waterfront locals both legit and otherwise. But all that time, or at least the last couple of years, he'd been hiding the whole Third Way thing from me. It made a guy think, and to be honest, I really wasn't too fond of thinking right at the moment. Still, I missed Sam and his big old country face. I couldn't help wondering if we were going to see each other again and what that would be like.

After lunch I manufactured a few more errands, dropping off a hamper full of laundry at Lavanderia Michoacan and picking up some connectors from Radio Shack so I could finally get my television hooked back up. Then I sloped on home, grabbing a couple of burritos I could microwave when I got hungry. The television thing took longer than it should have—the way the wall jack was laid out I would have had to put my television right in the middle of my bed—so I had to go back to the Shack for another reel of cable. When I got back, *again*, I fixed myself a drink. Okay, maybe two. By the time I finished them the sun had gone down and the television was the only light in the room. I heated a burrito and watched the Giants game (they were playing the Pirates in Pittsburgh) until enough of the vodka buzz wore off that I began to look around at the walls, which seemed closer than they should have. I'd had that feeling a lot, and I don't think it was just because my new apartment was even smaller than the last one. After a while I wanted another drink, but instead of fixing one I got up, put my shoes and coat on, and headed out to the Compasses where at least I'd be drinking with other people—a time-tested excuse for not being an alcoholic. I didn't really want to go there, since I knew all my advocate angel buddies were going to ask me about my hearing with the Ephorate, but the idea of going to some other bar, where I didn't know anyone, was even more depressing. And I was pretty sure that if I didn't get out of the apartment I'd wind up fully dressed and painfully hung over the next morning, lying in front of the television, exposed to horrible people chatting away on some breakfast show, which I'm convinced is one of the torments of Hell. There'd been a few too many mornings like that since I let Eligor take Caz away. So I went to the Compasses.

It's an angel bar—*the* angel bar in downtown San Judas. It's in the old Alhambra Theater building near Beeger Square, a former Masonic meeting hall. The Masons' insignia, the Square and Compasses, still hangs over the door. A lot of the place was recently torn up by a Sumerian demon (it was chasing me, as it happens) but although there were still signs of ongoing construction, the bar was more or less back to normal.

The Compasses was predictably loud, with the usual suspects in residence—the Whole Sick Choir as we sometimes called ourselves. (We'd even put it on softball shirts once, but dropped out of the local league when we found out we were actually expected to show up and play softball.) Chico was behind the bar, looking his usual combination of Mexican biker and aloof Confucian scholar, fiddling with his mustache while deciding which of the guys singing off-key at the bar he was going to cut off first. The serenaders were led by Jimmy the Table, a portly fellow who liked to wear old-fashioned gangster suits and looked like he should be out helping Nathan Detroit find a place to hold his famous floating craps game. He waved to me when I went past, but he didn't stop singing, being well into the middle verses of "Roll Me Over," a song that's always more fun to sing than to listen to. I didn't intend to do either. I had Chico get me a Stoli, and then I crept off to one of the back booths. For about ten minutes nobody noticed me, and I just sat and watched God's warriors at rest and play. Pretty horrifying sight, if I do say so myself, but good for some laughs.

Of course I couldn't stay that lucky very long. Sweetheart, large, bald, and fabulously angelic, spotted me and rolled over to give me a frighteningly detailed account of all the cheap punks and overdressed poseurs in the club he'd visited the previous night, and to quiz me on my latest trip through the Pearly Gates. And of course, a few minutes later Young Elvis showed up, and I had to tell it all over again, or at least the abbreviated and sanitized version I'd cobbled up for public consumption. Most of the Choir didn't even know that Sam was gone. The official word was that he was on some kind of administrative leave, and although the rumors had been flying in the Compasses ever since he disappeared, as far as I knew, nobody but Clarence and me knew what had really happened.

Later in the evening, Monica came in with Teddy Nebraska, an angel I didn't know too well because he worked the other end of town and tended to hang out there, too. Monica was relatively sober, or at least sober enough to remember that I had been kind of a shit to her lately, so after she got the bare bones of what had gone down with me and the bigwig angels she floated off to find more entertaining company. This was an immense relief, even though it left Teddy Nebraska sitting in my booth making awkward chitchat until he thought of an excuse to follow her, or at least to get out of my morose vicinity.

Monica Naber and I have history. She's a wonderful woman (or angel, or angel-woman) but I've hardly dared to talk to her since the thing with Caz started, not because it would be cheating on Monica— we've always been a lot more casual than that—but because she knows me well, and I'm scared to death she'd sort of metaphorically sniff the scent of another woman on me. Normally that wouldn't bother me; many of my other relationships have twined in and out of my weird off-and-on thing with Monica. But if anyone in Heaven found out about Caz there would be nothing left of me but a scorched hole in the sidewalk and the whiff of dispersing ozone.

I decided I'd made a mistake showing up at the Compasses instead of just going to some ordinary bar. My fellow angels wanted to socialize, but what I really wanted to do was sit in stoic, self-pitying silence until I had enough of a buzz on to stagger home. I'd cursed my job for years, being roused at all hours of the day and night and sent skittering across Jude to take up the fight for somebody's immortal soul, but now I was beginning to realize how much I missed it. Being on administrative leave, or whatever bureaucratic limbo I was inhabiting at the moment, was too much like being a prisoner of my own mind. I needed distractions, but not the other-people's-problems kind. I'll be the first to admit that I'm not really that type of guy. I mean, I care about people, really I do, but to be honest I'd rather not have to hear too much about them.

I guess you're beginning to understand why I've never been one of Heaven's model angels.

I had just paid my tab and was heading for the door when Walter Sanders came in. Walter looked like he'd had a couple of drinks or more himself, which wasn't all that common. I'd seen him nurse a single beer through a whole evening while others were downing them in wholesale quantities. He's one of the angels I like, a reserved fellow with a sharp, slightly bittersweet sense of humor. I'd often wondered if he had been English in his pre-angelic life.

He recognized me and stopped in the doorway, swaying almost imperceptibly. "Bobby. Bobby D, I was hoping to find you here. Want to talk to you. Can I buy you a drink?"

"To be honest, I think I've had enough, Walter. I was just on my way out."

"Okay, fine." He shook his head and smiled crookedly. "I think I've probably had enough myself, and I don't really want to talk in here anyway." He looked around. "Too many ears. I'll walk you out to your car. If you don't mind, we can chat for a few minutes in the parking lot."

"I don't have a car," I said. "I'm walking."

"Then I'll walk with you, at least for a block or two." Again the semi-apologetic smile. "The air will do me good."

We made our way out, ignoring Jimmy and the other guys up at the bar who were shocked to see anyone leaving before midnight. A few ordinary humans came out of the pizza place next door just as we passed and there was a little jostling, but they moved along to the parking lot and we turned onto Walnut Street, which was quiet and empty except for a homeless guy sitting huddled against the wall halfway down the block, asleep with his black hoodie pulled down over his head like a monk at prayer.

"So what's up?" I asked.

"I'm just—" He stopped, thought about it for a few steps. "Sorry. I'm not even certain it's anything, and you've probably got enough to worry about, but it just seemed *really strange* . . ." He trailed off again, this time to step over the homeless guy's skinny legs, which stuck half-way out onto the sidewalk. The guy had bare feet, thin and white, and even though it was spring I didn't envy him spending a night on the street without shoes.

I was getting the tiniest bit impatient, wondering if Walter was going to walk all the way home with me before he figured out how to tell me whatever it was he wanted to tell me. "You were saying?"

"Right." He laughed a little. "Okay, I suppose it's best if I just—"

Perhaps because of drink, perhaps because he'd stepped on something, Walter lost his footing for a moment and bumped into me, just enough to throw us both a little off balance, so that we stumbled toward the street side of the sidewalk. He put his hand up on my shoulder to steady himself, and just as he did so he made a strange sound: *tchaaaa*, a huff of air like a cat trying to offload a hairball. And then the stumble became a collapse, and he fell heavily against my legs, almost knocking me off the sidewalk. I spun around to keep my balance, and as I did I found myself staring across Walter Sanders' slumped form at the homeless man, who was standing right behind us, bent in an insect-like crouch with something long, sharp, and gleaming clutched in one hand.

"*It waited and waited,*" the hooded figure said in a strange, creaky little voice, and for just a moment I had a glimpse of the face in the depth of his hood. Then a car came around the corner behind me, and its headlights splashed him. He squirmed away from the glare. An instant later he was sprinting away down Marshall Street, his bare feet slapping the pavement like raindrops on a window. I hesitated only a moment, trying to decide whether to chase him, but the guy was very fast, and within a couple of seconds he was around the corner and gone, headed toward Beeger Square. I dropped to my knees to help Walter stand up, but he was limp and didn't respond when I asked him if he was hurt.

I rolled him over. His shirt and coat were soaked in blood, purple beneath the streetlights, and it was pooling where he had lain, some of it already running over the curb and into the gutter like spilled paint. His face was white, his lips blue. The people in the car pulled to a stop beside us so I begged them to call 911, then I ran back to the Compasses to get help. By the time I got back to Walter the first SJPD squad car had arrived, and the fire department emergency van showed up only a minute or two later from their new station a few blocks away. It didn't make any difference, though. My angel co-worker had already stopped breathing, and although the paramedics did what they could to field-dress him and bundle him quickly into their ambulance and head off toward Sequoia Emergency, lights flashing and siren moaning, it wasn't going to change anything. Walter Sanders, or at least the body he'd been given, was as dead as vaudeville.

But as I stood there letting the shocked questions of the Compasses' regulars wash over me, I was hardly even thinking about Walter. I assumed he'd be back, maybe as soon as tomorrow, decanted into new flesh by the boys upstairs and with a story to tell that would fascinate anyone who hadn't been around tonight. As it happened I was wrong, but I wasn't to know that for a while.

No, the reason I was standing there in the whirling red and blue strobes of the cop cars, waiting as witlessly to be questioned as any normal human victim of a normal human tragedy, was because I had recognized the thing that stabbed Walter, recognized the whispery voice and the momentary glimpse of tiny, misshapen teeth. I knew without having seen it what the wound just under Walter Sanders' ribs was going to look like—a four-pointed star, a puncture made by something more like a bayonet than any normal dagger. But even that wasn't what was bugging the shit out of me. Not only had I seen that creature before, I had been present when it died. Died the real death, the *not-coming-back* kind of death that only an immortal fears. And yet it had come back.

It had come back.

four

cloke and knyfe

"NO OFFENSE, but isn't it a bit early to be drinking?"
I would have laughed if I'd been able to. Instead, I took another sip. "It's a Bloody Mary. There's tomato juice in it. That makes it breakfast."

Clarence looked concerned, which made me want to order a couple more, but to be honest the puddle of red that had collected around the bottom of the glass was making me a little queasy, reminding me unpleasantly of the night before.

"Interesting place." Clarence looked around the joint. His eyes stopped on a man hunched over huevos rancheros and a nearly empty beer. The top of the man's fedora had been cut off, none too neatly. Greasy gray hair stuck up through the hole like an untended garden. "Interesting clientele."

"That's Jupiter," I said. "He's solar powered."

"What?" Clarence blinked and sneaked another glance. "Solar . . . ?"

"That's what he thinks, anyway. He cuts the top off all his hats so the sun can keep him strong." I shrugged. "He's harmless."

The ambience of Oyster Bill's was a bit seedy at the best of times, from the drunks on the sidewalk outside to the streaks of seagull shit on the windows, but particularly so in the morning. That's one reason I don't like mornings—it's life without the grace of shadows, that blessed fuzziness that lets us ignore some of the depressing stuff. But I hadn't slept much, and once the sun snuck through the chink in my curtains and slapped me in the face I was awake for good. At this time of the day Bill's legitimate breakfast crowd had all moved on, so the only people in there were people like me and Jupiter, just looking to get a little buzzed while we ate. And, Lord, did I need to get a little buzzed.

"So you said you wanted to talk."

I had, and with Sam gone my choices were limited. I could have talked to Monica but, as I've said, that's a little dodgy for me right now. I had settled on Clarence the Rookie Angel because I was thinking of tapping him for a favor, and he had connections in the Hall of Records upstairs. But now that I was sitting there peering over my omelette at his alert, scrubbed face, I wasn't so sure. Talking to the kid about anything complicated usually felt like trying to discuss hangovers with a Mormon missionary: What you got was a combination of ignorance and disapproval. Plus, though the kid undoubtedly thought he was doing the right thing, I hadn't forgiven him for working undercover for our bosses to bust my pal Sam. He might have thought he was doing the right thing, and he might be having second thoughts about it now, but I wasn't certain I was ever going to shed that grudge.

He tried again. "Is it about Walter Sanders getting stabbed? Wow, that was crazy! Right in front of the Compasses! I heard you were there."

"Oh, yeah. I was there."

"Scary. But he'll be okay. They'll reprocess him, and he'll be back good as new. You know that as well as anyone, Bobby."

Because it had happened to me. And I also knew that reprocessing wasn't the jaunt in the park he seemed to think it was. "To be honest, Clarence my man, I'm not worrying about Walter. I'm worrying about me."

He frowned at the nickname, which he hated. His true name was Haraheliel, and our bosses had given him the Earth name "Harrison Ely," but Sam had dubbed him Clarence after the movie angel, and now everybody at the Compasses called him that. "I don't understand. Do you think the mugger meant to get you instead?"

"Oh, I can practically guarantee it. See, I recognized him."

"Somebody with a grudge against you?"

"Maybe. But that's not why I think he was after me." I took another drink but the Bloody Mary tasted metallic now, and I put it down and suppressed a sigh. I was going to have to file a report on it anyway, but

I felt a need to share it with someone or something other than the glaring, emotionless light of Heaven. My first choice would have been Sam, but Sam wasn't available to me anymore—and, man, did I miss him.

"Okay," I began, "so this started back in the '70s—"

"Hold on." Clarence gave me that serious junior angel look that always made me want to smack him. "You've only been an angel since the '90s, Bobby. You told me."

"Kid, shut up. Shut up and listen."

It started back in the 1970s. No, I wasn't around then, or if I was, I was still alive and I don't remember. Bodies started turning up in odd places in the Santa Cruz Mountains, the range that separates San Judas from the Pacific Ocean. Usually dumped beside a highway overpass, all of them stabbed repeatedly by a four-edged blade like a bayonet. After the third turned up with the same M.O., someone noticed that all the dumping locations had graffiti on them, and that the same piece of graffiti was always there: a single word, "SMYLE." It was a tag even the gang experts down in LA hadn't seen before, and as a nickname for known criminals it didn't connect with anything in the records. Some reporter remembered his college lit courses and suggested in a column that it might have something to do with Chaucer's description of a murderer as *the smyler with the knyfe beneath his cloke.*" For a few weeks the press was off to the races with that, but even after the murders were solved nobody ever confirmed it had anything to do with old Geoffrey C.

Anyway, the killings kept happening, I think there were six altogether, and after a while the police began to put a few things together. The guy had to have a car, and seemed to find his victims at night. All of them were young people from the coastal towns, and the theory was that he was taking them right off the sidewalks, either by offering them rides or simply forcing them into his vehicle.

Making a long story shorter, the police in Santa Cruz and Monterey and other coast cities began keeping an eye on the local universities and junior colleges, and one night an officer scoped a guy in a battered old VW van acting suspicious, driving back and forth along the road outside Cabrillo College. The driver spooked and ran, the officer called in backup, and it turned into a chase. It didn't last long—you don't outrun a police cruiser in a VW—and the van lost it on a turn and crashed into a streetlight. The driver's side glass was broken and there was no sign of the driver, but the officers smelled gasoline so they approached carefully. Then the van exploded. The huge fireball shook windows for blocks. Burned two of the cops but not critically.

They found the driver's body, or at least they were pretty sure it was the driver's body. It was burned too badly to be certain, and they couldn't get an ID from the dental records, but all the officers on scene swore nobody got out of the van. They also found a weapon in the wreckage, twisted and melted by the heat but pretty obviously the blade that had killed those half-dozen victims; a nasty, handmade thing about eighteen inches long, capable of making a wound that wouldn't close up. In other words, he liked to see people bleed. They found a few things in the ashes that suggested the killer had been living in the van. Apparently he had also been carrying several cans of gasoline in the back and decided to go out that way instead of being taken to jail.

The murders stopped after that. End of story, right?

Twenty-two years later, they started again, here in San Judas. Same M.O., except the guy was burning his victims' bodies this time, but one of the bodies was discovered by a passing motorist who had a fire extinguisher, and when they got the remains to the medical examiner there it was, that four-sided wound. And of course the tags were showing up again too, a little smaller this time and in odd places, hard to see, but the word "SMYLE" was spray-painted somewhere near each body. By the time the fourth victim was found out by the Salt Piers, the police had decided it must be a copycat. The length of time, and the fact that they were so certain the body in the van had been the murderer's, didn't really admit any other possibility.

But they were wrong. It was the same guy. They were right about one thing, though. He was definitely dead.

This was when I was in Counterstrike, the paramilitary unit where I first trained, and word came down to us that our superiors suspected the hairy hand of Hell. If "Smyler" had come back from the dead, then there was only one explanation, and it had horns and carried a pitchfork. That seemed pretty weird from our end, because the murderer's

M.O. was exactly the same as before, students and other young people. See, normally, if the Opposition have an asset like that they put him or her to work doing something more useful than just random killing. Leo, my old top-kicker, said they might be using Smyler to shake people up, improve the climate for Hell's other operations, if you get what I'm saying. Like they taught us in Angel Training, the Opposition thrives in chaos, and it was pretty clear that chaos was what this guy was causing. The newspapers persuaded someone on the force to talk about the "SMYLE" tags and soon it was "Graffiti Murderer Returns!" and "Ghost or Copycat?" and all that bullshit. For months it was like Son of Sam had come to Jude. A couple of cruising dumbasses got shot at by scared college girls carrying their daddies' guns, and half the waterfront tourist business dried up.

I won't bore you with all the details of how we tracked the guy down. Counterstrike Unit *Lyrae*, also known as the Harps, have methods the cops don't even dream of, and that was necessary, because Smyler was no longer a living man. Not that finding him was easy, even for us. Whatever made him into a psychopathic murderer had been refined and polished by Hell, and San Judas was a fuck of a lot bigger and easier to hide in than the little Pacific Coast towns he'd been haunting in the '70s. He actually killed another one after we started looking for him, a paperboy out on his morning rounds, and that burned all of us in the Harps like fire. Also, he was beginning to spread his net wider now, and the papers picked up on it. It was like the whole city was going mental. We had to deal with him quickly. We got a lucky break, a tip from an informant that put us right on his tail.

It turned out the killer wasn't even staying in San Judas itself, but in an abandoned junkyard down in Alviso that had been red-tagged by the EPA for toxins and was awaiting Superfund cleanup. What did Smyler care if the place would have killed anyone else? He was already dead. He wasn't even living in the deserted office; instead, he'd made a burrow for himself in the piles of wrecked autos and discarded appliances, nesting down in the middle like a rat.

The Harps was the first unit to reach him, which was okay with us. Call it the sin of pride, but there wasn't a CU who didn't want to be the ones to get the bastard. Smyler wouldn't come out, even though we had him surrounded. Finally we tossed a couple of incendiaries in after him. That worked. Maybe he didn't want to die the same way twice, I don't know. Anyway, when the flames started, he came out quick enough.

Did I say he was like a rat? More like a spider, at least when he came scuttling out of a hidden hole in the mountain of twisted metal and jumped down before we could even lift our guns and aim, his baggy, hooded black sweatshirt flapping and that ugly, long weapon in his hand. Smyler jumped on an angel named Zoniel so quick that he managed to stab him three times before Sam hit him with the butt of his assault rifle and knocked him off. Zoniel was so badly wounded that he had to get a new body, but Smyler got Reheboth even worse, putting that wicked, four-edged blade right through his eye and into his brain. Reb got another body, too, but he also retired from Counterstrike soon afterward and got a job upstairs. Said it wasn't the getting stabbed so much, but that face-to-face moment with the guy just before the knife went in. Said he'd never seen anyone so happy.

The Highest Himself only knows how many more of us the little shit might have damaged, or how many of us might have gone down from friendly fire, because he was horribly fast and everybody was shooting wildly. But someone got lucky and raked him with an M4 full of silver rounds and took half his leg off. Smyler started trying to crawl away, leaving a trail of blood like a snail's track, and at first I thought I was hearing his death-gasps, but after a moment I realized he was laughing in a terrible, dry, whispering voice. Laughing.

I was close enough to put a dozen bullets into his head, and I was just about to do that when Leo stopped me.

"No," he said. "We're not sending this one back."

I didn't really get what he meant, and I was even more confused when he emptied a clip into Smyler's legs. Blood and bone splinters and ruined flesh flew everywhere, but the horrible thing still wouldn't stop laughing. Leo stepped up, kicked away the long pointy thing lying near the killer's hand, and then put his boot under Smyler's gut and turned him over.

"Good God Almighty," Sam said. I probably said something similar.

We'd both seen a lot of ugly stuff, but Smyler was worse than anything, somehow. He—it—whatever, his skin was gray and pulled tight over his bones like a shriveled corpse, mottled with dark purple-blue patches too regular to be bruises. His jaw stuck out like a piranha's, so that even with his mouth closed you could see his bottom teeth, deformed little things like seed pearls, a perfectly straight line of them. But his eyes were the worst. His eyes were all black, except for a little sliver of bloodshot white at the edges when he looked around, like he was doing now. The rest of the Harps, the ones that weren't tending Reb and Zone, gathered around, and as he looked at us, he opened his mouth and started giggling again. The inside of his mouth . . . well, it looked rotten. That's all I can tell you. Black and gray and oozing and rotten, except for little bright spots of blood.

"Angels," he said in his scratchy voice. "It love you! All for you! All for you!"

Sam was ready to shoot him in the head that second, wipe that horror away in a storm of bullets, but Leo yelled, "No! Stand down, soldier!" Leo waved his phone—they were bigger in those days. "I've called the bagmen."

I'd never heard the expression, and at first I thought he meant the medics. He'd called them too, to treat our wounded, but they weren't the people he was talking about.

"Just keep him here," Leo said. "But don't touch him. We're not sending him back."

"But Leo," Sam said quietly, "the Convention—!"

"I don't give a fuck about the Convention."

And I suddenly understood, or at least some of it. See, the Tartarean Convention says that in conflicts on Earth we can do anything to the demons' physical bodies, just like they can to ours, but when their—or our—bodies die, all bets are off, and everything returns to *status quo ante*. Which means that the souls go back to their respective abodes, Hell or Heaven, and whatever happens next is up to the authorities of those places. Which means you can kill a demon's body and send its soul back to Hell, but you can't do anything to prevent its masters from popping it right back into a new demon body. And as far as I knew then, that wasn't just the Convention's rules, that was the reality—we couldn't do anything to a demon's actual soul any more than they could do anything to ours.

I was about to learn differently.

The bagmen showed up even before the medics did. A sparkling line appeared in the air, just like when we open a Zipper to go Outside and meet the souls of the newly dead. Three guys stepped through. Three angels, I'm assuming, but I couldn't swear to it because they were wearing something like hazmat suits, though not the kind you buy here on Earth. The faces behind those masks were blurs of shifting light. The bagmen didn't say a thing, just looked to Leo. He pointed to Smyler where he lay. The little horror was still wheezing and giggling quietly, but you could tell he was bleeding out. One of the bagmen produced something from out of thin air, or at least that's how it looked, a billowing thing like a parachute made from pulsing light, and then shook it out over the horrible thing on the ground. At first it just lay on him like a sheet, twitching as he moved beneath it, then it began to shrink until Smyler was nothing but a glowing mummy, too tightly wrapped even to struggle.

"Step back, please," one of the bagmen said, then he and his companions produced the strangest guns I'd ever seen, about the size of Mac-11s but with a shiny bell like a trumpet's instead of a barrel. When they pulled the triggers, fire vomited out of the ends of their weapons and engulfed Smyler, flame so white and hot it might have come from the inside of a star. We all moved back rapidly—*way* back—but I still got my eyebrows singed.

In the scant seconds before the bundle on the ground shriveled into smoking ash, I swear I could still hear that awful laugh. Then it was over. The ashes glowed, and a few dark wisps blew up into the air like spiderwebs. The wind carried them away.

The bagmen didn't say anything else, just reopened their sparkling gash in the air and disappeared. Leo took the four-edged blade, maybe as an ugly souvenir, maybe for some other reason I didn't and don't understand. Then we went home.

"I don't get it," said Clarence. He looked like I felt—queasy and depressed. "What . . . did they *do*?"

"To Smyler? I'm not exactly sure. Leo didn't like to talk about it. But as far as I can tell they bagged him in something that rank-and-file angels like you and me don't know about, something that kept his soul from returning to Hell when he died. Then they burned him alive."

"That's horrible!"

"You wouldn't think that if you saw him . . . saw *it*. Whatever he was. But the thing that's bothering me is that I saw him again last night. It was Smyler who stabbed Walter Sanders. Even though I'm pretty sure it was me he wanted."

"But how could it have been? You said this demon's soul was burned. With his body."

"I don't know. But I know one thing, and that's what's got me worried. No ordinary demon in Hell could have brought Smyler back. I mean, Leo said that thing was gone forever, and I could tell he believed it. I think this must be Eligor's work." I paused. Clarence knew about the Grand Duke of Hell and the monstrous *ghallu* he'd sent after me, although he didn't know the truth about Caz, or how personal the quarrel between me and the grand duke had become. "Let's just say Eligor doesn't like me. Not at all. And I'm guessing only somebody as powerful as him could bring that nasty thing back from the dead a second time."

"So, what are you going to do?"

I reached for the rest of my Bloody Mary, distaste overcome by other needs. I drained it and wiped my mouth. "Hell if I know, kid."

five

hog caller

ACTUALLY, I had one idea, but I couldn't do anything about it until midnight. To keep my head straight, I sat up listening to Thelonious Monk and his quartet playing at Carnegie Hall, over and over. It didn't really work, because I kept wondering how perfect music like that could happen in such a fucked-up universe. When the clock finally struck twelve I turned down Coltrane mid-solo and called my favorite hog.

He's only half a hog, really. My friend Fatback (which I never call him to his face) is a were-hog named George Noceda. During the day, man with pig's brain; after the witching hour, pig with man's brain. No, ladies, that doesn't make him just like all us other guys. Not fair.

"Bobby!" His voice was still gruff from the transformation. I should have given him a few more minutes, but I was desperate. "What can I do you for?"

"Information, fast as you can get it for me. It might keep me from being turned into a human kebab."

"So what else is new? One of these days you're going to say, 'Take your time, George. There's no hurry,' and I'll know it's truly the End of Days."

"Don't make jokes, buddy. Not tonight." When stuff starts to slide—and the important stuff in my life was sliding like a jackknifed panel truck—Bobby D's world can turn into a bad horror movie quick, stuff that would make even a were-hog faint. "I need information on a dead guy. Well, a supposedly dead guy." I ran down what I already knew about my latest worry, both the original charmer and Smyler v.2, plus what little I'd been able to see of v.3. "Can you find me some information fast?"

From the snort you might have thought he was changing back to pigbrain again, but actually it's a lot louder and less pleasant when it really happens. "Yeah, sure, Mr. Patience. Just let me get some slops down. I'm starving."

"Doesn't the . . . the other version of you eat?"

"Yeah, but not enough to keep eight hundred pounds of pork happy after I change. But I'll be right on it in half an hour or so, man."

It's always strange to be talking to a pig in the middle of the night, but as swine go, Fatback is definitely one of the best. "Thanks. Call me if you get anything interesting, otherwise just send it all to my phone."

"No problem, Mr. B. If you're trying to find a dead guy, though, maybe you should talk to some other dead people. You know a few, right?"

"Know a few? They're my bread and butter, Georgie. But I've got to get some shut-eye first. I feel like shit."

"Count your blessings, Bobby. That's what I sleep in."

So the next day, when the sun was far enough up the sky that it didn't give me a headache, I went to see the Sollyhulls.

The Sollyhull Sisters are a pair of middle-aged Englishwomen who died in a fire half a century ago—almost certainly one they'd set to get rid of their parents. Because of this, they didn't go to Heaven, of course, but for some reason they haven't gone to Hell, either. Still, the sisters are very nice, if a bit screwloose, so I try not to think too much about the arson part of their bio. I really needed some expert help to find out how Smyler had come back, and the Sollyhulls liked me and were always willing to chat. My world is full of folks like that—inbetweeners who don't quite belong to one side or the other. (My piggy friend Fatback didn't really count that way, because he hated Hell so badly for the were-pig thing that he spent all his time getting up in their shit, research-wise.)

I caught up with the sisters at the latest diner they were haunting. They preferred tearooms, but apparently San Judas was short on good ones. I took a table in the back where it wouldn't be so obvious that I was talking to invisible people—invisible to everyone but me, that is.

As always, I had brought the sisters a gift, so after the two ghost-ladies had finished telling me about the fun they'd had teasing some paranormal investigators who had started hanging around their previous diner, I lifted a small, gift-wrapped box onto the table. "Here, I brought you a little something," I said, and took the lid off the tin.

"What is it?" Doris asked. "Oh, Bobby, you darling—pastilles! Betty, violet pastilles!"

Betty leaned forward for a long sniff. "Ah, lovely. The French kind! Ooh, I loved these! Much better than those Whatsit Brothers ones our gran used to give us."

I let the sisters enjoy the scent for a while. That was about all they could do, but judging by their noises of rapture, that was plenty. Then I asked them if they knew anything about a revenant named Smyler, and told them what I knew of his history—at least, through his first two deaths.

"Don't think so, dear," Betty said after some consideration. "There was a fellow they used to call The Smiler, but that was years ago in England and he was a tall, tall fellow. Lovely teeth, too. Dead since Queen Victoria's day, everyone said, but he had a set of pearlies you could read by on a dark night. Still, he'd done his victims with arsenic, hadn't he?"

"Cyanide, dear."

"Right you are, our Doris. Cyanide. It wouldn't be him, would it?"

I said I didn't think so.

"Then there was Moaning Sally, but she was a girl, wasn't she? She stabbed her lover and some of his family with one of those bayonets. Quite a lot of stabbing, altogether. They said she killed herself in her prison cell, then came back and hung about the street near St. Chad's in Birmingham, but that's all part of that awful ring road now, isn't it, Doris?"

"The Queensway. Dreadful thing."

"So it probably wouldn't be her, not all the way over here in America. Wait, you said it was a fella you were looking for, didn't you?"

I could see they weren't going to be able to help me much with Smyler himself, so I tried a more general question. "But how would something like that happen at all? Have you ever heard of somebody dying once, then coming back, then being exorcised or whatever you'd call it . . . ?"

"Watch your language, dear," said Doris primly. "We've got feelings, you know."

"Well, let's just say 'dispatched' a second time and then coming back *again*. Have you ever heard of anything like that? How could that happen?"

"To be honest, love, I've never heard of anything like it. Have you, Betty?"

"No, dear. And I feel terrible after you bought us these lovely pastilles, and we've had such a nice visit. But no. I'm afraid you'll have to find somebody a bit more qualified to answer that. Have you tried the Broken Boy yet?"

I hadn't, and I didn't really want to, but I was beginning to think I might not have a choice. That's the problem with ghosts. Sometimes they're a lot of help, sometimes worse than useless, but it always takes a long time to find out, because most of them like to talk and they all tend to be a bit loopy.

I thanked the ladies and walked out past other customers and the waitresses, none of whom had come anywhere near me during my entire visit, not even to see if I wanted to order something. Clearly, the Sollyhulls had already begun to freak out the regulars, and I wondered how long it would be until the paranormal fanboys were onto this place as well. I had a worried feeling the sisters might be developing a taste for notoriety.

One of the many problems with visiting the Broken Boy was that, unlike the sisters, he didn't give out information in return for a cheap box of hard candy. In fact, last time I heard, he was charging two thousand dollars a session, and my bank account was pretty much tapped out. Heaven doesn't pay us a whole lot. Then again, we don't have to put anything aside for retirement.

These are the jokes, people. If you came to laugh, you might as well start now.

Anyway, if I wanted to visit the Broken Boy I needed to raise some cash, and I didn't have much in the way of options. I'd been thinking about putting my Matador in long-term storage and trying to scrape up the money somehow to buy that '69 Super Sport from Orban, but since I didn't play the lottery I had trouble imagining a scenario where that could happen without the sudden appearance of Santa Claus.

Now I was beginning to think I might have to sell the Matador out-right. I loved that car and had spent several years finding parts and getting it refurbished, not to mention putting up with endless shit from Sam and Monica and the rest of my friends because of it. It had to be worth at least twenty thousand—there were only a few of them left. Of course, the money might save my immortal soul, which I was also rather fond of. It was a tough call.

I took a walk along the bay to think it over, and by the time I was finished I was at the Salt Piers where Orban has his gun shop and ar-mory complex. I found him in the big garage, smoking his pipe and watching a bunch of his burly, tattooed henchmen use a chain hoist to lower a massive steel plate into an Escalade, presumably to keep the dumbasses who would eventually ride in the back seat from shooting the driver by accident.

Orban cocked a shaggy eyebrow at me. "What do you want, Dol-lar?" he growled in that mouth-full-of-rocks accent he's never shaken in all these years. "You come to pay me finally for warehousing your piece of shit candy car?" Orban's not a big guy, but there's something about him that makes me very glad we get along.

"Let's talk," I said.

Over a glass of the poisonous red wine Orban favors, I made my pitch about the Matador. That bristling brow climbed up again. He knew how I felt about my car. "Tell you what," he said. "I give you ten for it—"

"Ten!" I was so upset I spilled Bull's Blood in my lap. "It's worth twice that! More!"

"Shut up. You don't hear me out. I give you ten for it, I promise not to sell it for three months. You pay me back the ten, you can have it. You can't, I sell it and give you ten more."

In other words, he was going to loan me the money on the Mata-dor for three months, interest free. Which was a pretty damn decent thing for him to do. I didn't say that, of course, because it only would have pissed him off. And I haggled too, because if I hadn't he would have been mortally insulted. Orban wouldn't front me any more money, but he did up the back end two thousand bucks, which confirmed to me that the Matador must be worth about thirty big ones. He's not stupid, even when he's doing somebody a solid. He also threw in a couple of dozen high-velocity silver slugs for my

Belgian FN automatic. If I bumped into Smyler again I wanted to be ready.

I immediately gave him back two thousand of the money for an ugly, unarmored banger, an ancient stock Datsun 510 with so much bondo on the fenders it looked like it had mange. (The Super Sport had a brand new L78 under the hood, so it wound up being a little out of my price range.) Still, the old 510s could be zippy little cars, and Orban said the engine was good. I signed the papers, left the office while he opened his safe, then took the rest of my money in cash. Orban didn't much believe in banks. Eighty benjamins makes too thick a stack to fit in a wallet, not to mention that wallets can be dropped or lifted, so I put the money in my underwear. Yes, I did. Deal with it.

The boxy little car handled surprisingly well. People used to customize the 510s for racing, although nobody'd ever bothered with this one. I stopped to grab some takeout at a burger place in the neighborhood, then I parked the new ride around the corner from my building under a streetlight which had just come on for the evening. I was locking it up when something smashed into me from behind, cracking my head against the doorframe so hard that I saw nothing but flashing sparkles for a few seconds. Then I realized I was lying on my back and something was squatting on my chest.

"Where is feather?" my attacker whispered. "Where? Hided somewhere?" The streetlight was just above us so I couldn't see the face beneath the shadowing hood, but I could smell its breath, smell the rot. I carefully shifted my weight to get some leverage, but then I felt something press against my lower eyelid, sharp and steady as a doctor's needle. "It going to find out. Yes, it will."

six

broken

I KEPT VERY still. A door opened somewhere nearby, and the thing raised its head. The small movement made the blade glint with reflected streetlight, its point only a thin width of skin from my eye and the brain behind it. The door closed again, and the street was silent. I cursed myself for having parked in a residential neighborhood instead of the busier street in front of my building, but I'd thought I was being careful. How had the little bastard spotted me in an unfamiliar car?

"Feather. Tell it."

"What feather?"

The tip of the knife, or whatever it was, pushed down until I felt it pierce the first layer of flesh. I sucked in a breath. "*It* say question. *You* say answer."

"I don't have it with me." Which was mostly a lie—I wouldn't leave a crucial object like that sitting around unprotected—but not completely. The feather was in my jacket pocket, as it always was, but since my buddy Sam had used special angelic powers to hide it there, even I couldn't reach it. See, it wasn't just in the pocket, it was in a version of the pocket that had existed several weeks earlier. Yeah, it's weird, but all you need to remember is: Feather in jacket pocket but not within reach by any normal methods. "The feather's hidden far away," I told the withered horror-monkey on my chest. "I have to get it."

Smyler giggled. It was all I could do not to throw up. Knowing something that should have been dead was perched on top of me was one thing; hearing that papery chuckle again was another altogether. God in His Heaven, I'd seen this thing burn!

"Go? You not go. You tell. Then it find."

It. Smyler called himself "it."

"Why would I tell you the truth? You'll just kill me anyway."

Again the whispery laugh. "Because it see your friends. It see who you like. It very smart."

I wanted to believe that he meant he would just do plain old physical harm to Monica and Clarence and the rest, as he'd done to Walter Sanders. Then again, Walter still hadn't come back. This thing on top of me apparently couldn't be killed—was it possible he also knew how to prevent the rest of us from coming back to life? Not to mention that if he was looking for the feather, he must be working for Eligor, and only the Highest and his closest servants could say what a Duke of Hell might be able to accomplish. I couldn't take that risk.

"All right," I said. "I'll tell if you promise not to hurt anyone else . . ." And as I said it I lifted my left hand in surrender—or at least I wanted it to look that way, because I had a lead cosh zipped into the other sleeve of my jacket. There was no way I would have time to get it out, but during the instant his hidden eyes turned toward my left hand, I swung my other arm up as hard as I could and clubbed Smyler on the side of the skull with the hidden piece of metal.

I'd hoped to smash his head in, or at least knock him cold, but I wasn't that lucky. What I did manage was to snap his head sideways and give myself a moment to kick my way free. Then he was back on me, and we were rolling on the ground. The nasty little fucker still had that long blade, which he was doing his best to stick between my ribs. I managed to get my right arm up and took part of the blow on the hidden cosh, but it was a stab, not a slice, so it bounced off the metal and went all the way through the sleeve of my jacket and raked my belly. It burned like someone had tried to tattoo me with a soldering gun; it was all I could do to roll away and dig in my pocket before the thing came after me again. I couldn't get my gun out in time, so I shot through the pocket, three slugs right into Smyler's middle as he lunged at me, *bang-bang-bang.* If I hadn't been paying more attention to my new ride than my own safety, those slugs would have been silver, but Orban's new rounds were still sitting in my glove compartment, and I was still pushing plain old copper-jacketed hollow-points. Still, Smyler had a physical body, so I knew they would at least knock him down if not completely eviscerate him.

Guess what? Wrong again. The little bastard almost went to his knees, which at least gave me time to roll clear, but the three rounds I put in him didn't do much more than make him stagger. I finally got the gun all the way out of my pocket and tried to put one right in the middle of his hood, but it was like trying to throw tennis balls at a startled cat. He zigzagged as I pulled the trigger, and I don't think I even came close, then he was on me again. I clubbed at him with the gun barrel as that long blade slid past my chest and under my arm, slicing me again, and I realized two things at the same time: The first was that he was only trying to disable me, for now, not kill me—he still wanted to know where the feather was. But if this was Smyler holding back, I was in serious trouble, because he was fast as anything I'd ever faced. My other realization was that the only advantage I had was a little bit of size and the unusual length of his blade, which meant he had to swing his arm way back to be able to drive it home. As the momentum of his next attack brought him toward me, I dodged the thrust, lowered my head so I could smash the top of my skull into his face, then wrapped my arms around him and drove forward.

I didn't do as well at avoiding the thrust as I'd hoped. His blade went through my coat again and took a big chunk of flesh out of my arm, which hurt even more than you're thinking it did. I was bleeding badly now from several wounds and was going to be in a world of pain if I survived, but I was running on pure adrenaline and could only hold on and try to carry him down to the hard pavement.

Smyler seemed to have limbs everywhere. He wrapped his legs around me and squeezed my ribs until I felt one crack, but I had to ignore the pain, because I knew if I let go of one of his arms he was going to poke that nasty long knife thing into the back of my neck and then drag my paralyzed body away somewhere to ask his questions at leisure.

He wiggled his no-knife arm out of my grip and wrapped it around my skull, then squeezed until I thought the blood was going to fountain out of the top of my head. I could hear sirens, and I prayed they were getting louder, but it was hard to tell because my brain was full of thunder and red light. I'd lost my pistol somewhere on the ground but still had the cosh in the forearm of my coat, so I started smashing it against his skinny back as hard as I could, over and over, praying that I could crush one of his vertebrae or at least rupture a kidney.

He laughed. The horrible, pinched face was right beside mine, and if I hadn't been fighting for my very life the stink alone would have made me throw up. As it was, my eyes stung, and not just from sweat. I could feel the sinewy strength in his slender neck and that horrid, jutting jaw trying to close on my ear, my cheek, anything it could tear at, and all I could do was try to keep my head stretched as far away as possible while I crashed the metal bar against his spine.

"It like dancing!" Smyler whispered. "Oh, yes. It dance to glory!"

But now the sirens were too loud to ignore. At least one police car was coming down the street toward us fast, lights glaring and jouncing as the cruiser bounced over speed bumps. I felt my attacker go slack for just a moment, distracted, and I risked loosening my right-arm grip just long enough to swing my weighted sleeve into the back of his skull as hard as I could. I'm stronger than most normal people, and although the hoodie he was wearing muffled the blow a little it would certainly have knocked any ordinary assailant cold if not DOA. My attacker just shook his horrid head as though his ears had popped on an afternoon drive in the mountains, then shoved my skull back against the ground with a nasty, cold hand. I braced for steel in my guts.

"See you, Bobby Bad Angel," Smyler whispered. "Soon!" Then he sprang up and was gone, over somebody's garden hedge and away into the darkness. As I struggled and failed to sit up, I could see the lights of a half dozen open doors, and people standing at their windows looking out. Then the spot from the police cruiser fell on me, filling the world with painful white light, and that was the last thing I remembered.

interlude

I WAS LYING *on my stomach, drifting in and out of sleep. Caz was curled up behind me, spooning me. At first I thought she was just moving randomly against me, but then I realized that she was slowly rubbing her pussy against my tailbone, an almost imperceptible grinding and tightening, slow as the movement of glaciers. I wasn't even sure she was awake.*

I made a joke. I wish now I hadn't. "So, is this a dominance hump? Am I your bitch, now?"

She froze. Seriously, she went rigid, like an animal trying not to be seen. After all we'd just done with each other, I'd somehow caught her by surprise, and it was like a window had opened that looked straight backward, five hundred years into the past, to a shamed little medieval girl, a Catholic nobleman's daughter with feelings she wasn't supposed to have.

"I . . . I didn't . . ."

"Hey," I said. "Hey! It's all right. Actually, it's more than all right. I was just making a stupid joke. You may not have noticed, but I do it a lot."

"I was . . . I was smelling you. It just made me . . . well, you know."

"And what do I smell like? Napalm in the morning? A good little angel?"

"Shut up. You smell like Bobby. I need to remember."

That gave me a moment's pause. I knew why she was worried about remembering, but I didn't really want to think about it. I went back to silliness, hoping to retrieve the moment when we had been alone in the Garden without care or knowledge. "So you're saying it wasn't a dominance thing."

"Don't need to hump you for that, angel boy, it's automatic. I'm a very high-ranking demon, remember."

"Oh, yeah. Like I could forget after you tried to beat the shit out of me earlier this evening."

"See? That was when I established my dominance."

"Dominance, my shiny golden halo. It seems to me that I wound up on top of you, remember?"

"Only because I let you. We females have been using that trick for thousands of years. 'Oh, you big strong man, you've overwhelmed me!' And you always fall for it. Dumb dicks."

"Yeah, well, a wise man once said, 'As the twig is bent, so dumbs the dick.'"

For a moment she just stared at me. "That doesn't many any sense at all."

I considered. "Or maybe it's 'A mighty fortress is our dick.'"

She hit me. Not too hard, though. "No wonder I'm having trouble sleeping. I'm sharing my bed with a dangerous winged idiot."

seven

drummed out

YOU'D THINK getting multiple stab wounds and broken ribs from a twice-dead assassin would be enough fun for one day, but it wasn't over yet.

After my wrestling match with Smyler, I came back to consciousness just long enough to have some momentary sense of my physical body—which felt like a large sack of broken crockery wrapped in scalded nerves—surrounded by harsh white lights and medical machinery, then I was abruptly somewhere else.

That somewhere else, as it turned out, was Heaven, and although being lifted right out of all that pain and suffering into the bodiless exaltation of my celestial form was at least as good as getting a massive shot of Demerol, the relief was undercut a bit by the sight of my boss, Archangel Temuel, and the expression on his not-quite-face.

The farther up the heavenly ladder you are, by the way, the less you look like a regular person. As best I can tell, when I'm in Heaven I look like a shimmery, vaguely blurry version of my earthly self, although it's hard to be certain because reflecting surfaces are oddly scarce upstairs. But Temuel (or "the Mule" as his underlings call him) always looks even blurrier than that, less human. And the higher angels only occasionally look like they really have bodies underneath all that glow. More as if the bodies themselves are just another kind of glow. Hard to put into words, but if you were here you'd agree with me.

"Angel Doloriel," said Temuel. "God loves you. Are you well?"

"Better now, yeah. But somebody did a major number on me, and it's not going to be fun to put that body back on again."

"Of course." Then the Mule went quiet for a long moment. I didn't like the implication that it was no slam-dunk I'd be getting my body back. "We are wanted in the Hall of Judgement," he said at last. "Come."

Which would have sent shivers up my spine if I'd been wearing my regular body, I can promise you. Probably would have hurt like hell with the broken ribs, too. I'd only been in the Hall of Judgement once, and generally the things that happened there fell into the category of Really Fucking Serious.

Temuel reached out toward me and suddenly we were traveling. Or at least, we moved directly from Place A to Place B, which is how you travel through Heaven if you're not interested in meandering around its airy, gleaming streets. The short trip didn't give me any chance to ask questions, which may have been what the Mule wanted. He certainly didn't seem very happy, so I wasn't feeling that way either.

The Hall of Judgement is about ninety times as awesome as you can imagine. The important places of Heaven always seem to have a strangely fascist scope to them, as if the main purpose of their creation was to make individual human souls feel tiny. And you know what? It works. Does it ever.

The Hall is a bit like a human cathedral, but the proportions are so extreme, it's obvious that earthly concerns like gravity, mass, and tensile strength didn't come into the equation; a tower of nearly pure light, with only enough spiderweb-thin structure to let you know you're inside something. At the center of it, surrounded by a space where literally hundreds of thousands could gather even under earthly constraints, stands a massive pillar of liquid crystal—liquid because it's moving, crystal because it's moving so slowly you'd never know it if you didn't know it, if you see what I mean. This diamond waterfall with a zillion internal facets is called the Paslogion, and it's a sort of clock, I think, or at least it represents the same kind of idea. As to how to read it, don't ask me. I don't know if it really even works or if it's just some kind of big decoration like the Eiffel Tower or the Statue of Liberty. I do know it's one of the most awesome things I've ever seen. Just looking at it, you feel that if you *did* understand it, you'd understand pretty much everything about how the entire cosmos works, and that infinity probably sounds like the entire catalogue of J. S. Bach all played at the same time and yet totally in harmony.

All of this grandeur might have been less daunting if something was already going on when we appeared inside the Judgement Hall. But instead the place was empty except for me, Temuel, and the awesome Paslogion.

"And here I leave you." Without any more warning than that, Temuel vanished. I couldn't help wondering why he was in such a hurry to get out of there, and I couldn't come up with any happy answers.

It's hard to think negative thoughts in Heaven. Most of the time I'm there I feel like a baby seal brutally clubbed by joy, but I confess, my thoughts about Temuel going off and leaving me by myself were less than charitable.

What about the consolation of religion for the condemned man, I wondered. *Isn't somebody supposed to at least hold my hand while I wait to be executed?* But if my superiors were finally going to clean up the mess I'd always been, why bother to bring me all the way here and then not even gather an audience? It would be easy enough to switch me off; for Heaven, probably easier than flicking a light switch. Did they just want to remind me how small I was before they stepped on me?

A part of me, of course, was reminding myself over and over and over again that I should never have tried to lie to the higher angels of the Ephorate. *Hubris*, the Greeks called that. "A dumbshit move," might be a more contemporary way of putting it.

Then suddenly I was not alone anymore.

"Angel Doloriel," said the light, in the voice of a sweet child. "God loves you." It took me a moment to recognize the staggeringly beautiful radiance as Anaita, one of the five high angels who'd somehow been appointed to keep me in line, or perhaps to prepare the way for my removal. "I have been sent to deliver the Ephorate's judgement."

I braced myself for whatever was to come.

"But first . . ." she said, and as she hesitated her light dimmed and wavered just the faintest bit, as if she wanted to say something difficult. I've never seen a higher angel show any kind of hesitation before, but I didn't have long to think about it.

"*But first,*" said another voice, "*you realized you had to wait for the rest of the delegation.*"

Karael appeared in a burst of golden gleaming.

And now Anaita's presence definitely guttered. I think I was seeing surprise. That's something else you don't expect to see out of any of the higher angels. "Karael?"

"The Ephorate decided we should deliver the judgement together," he said, becoming a little less of a glow and a bit more of a human shape, or as human as his heavenly form ever got. "But you left before they had completed their deliberations, Anaita."

"I was . . . unaware." She was flabbergasted was what she was, or at least I'm assuming that's how it translated. It was a bit like trying to interpret the body language of a G-type star, but she certainly seemed taken aback. What was going on with these two? Was I witnessing a feud? Or something even stranger? It had certainly seemed like Anaita wanted to tell me something.

"No matter." Karael spread his fire before me. "The Ephorate continues to be troubled by the events that involve you, Angel Doloriel, but of course the Highest wants only justice. Therefore your judgement has been delayed."

I didn't know whether to be outraged or relieved. "What does that mean, exactly?"

"It means that we are still concerned, but that other matters are calling for our attention," said Anaita. She didn't sound happy about it either.

Normally I keep my mouth shut as much as possible when I'm in Heaven, and Heaven's atmosphere of slightly dopey satisfaction makes it easy. But normally, I haven't just been perforated in all kinds of painful places by some kind of zombie hitman and then jerked upstairs to be scolded. "Hey, I'm concerned too. I'm concerned with why it's supposed to be my fault that these things keep happening to me." The best defense and all that. Well, I figured it was worth a try. If they weren't going to terminate my contract, I didn't think I'd push them into it just by mouthing off, and if they *were* . . . well, I'd rather vanish from the universal scheme on my feet instead of my knees.

"Understandable," said Karael. "That is why we have been given this matter for ephoral judgement, Doloriel, to be certain you are treated fairly. I know you want to go back to work."

What I wanted was to be left alone to figure out what crazy shit I was up to my neck in this time, but what I said was, "Yes, of course. That's just what I want."

"But that is just what the Ephorate cannot allow," Anaita informed me, "at least until we have had time to consider all the complications of this case . . . this . . . *situation*." She was definitely putting a spin on it, but was it for my sake or Karael's? "Your work involves you in too many areas we are still investigating, Doloriel."

"So what does that mean, my judgement is 'delayed'? Until when?"

"Until the time arrives," said Karael in his most infuriating, you-don't-need-to-know sort of way. Then his voice hardened. It sounded like a healthy echo of the Almighty Himself. "Until that time, Angel Doloriel, you are relieved of your duties as advocate. You may remain here or on Earth."

I was more than a little shocked, but I knew better than to argue with them. It could have been worse, much worse, and at least this would give me some time to consider my next move. But I had to make a bit of a show. "That's it? Just suspended or whatever? Until some time in the fuzzy future?"

"You're too wrapped up in earthly things, Doloriel," said Anaita. "Time is meaningless outside of mortality."

"Right." I was ready to offer grudging acceptance now. "I suppose—"

"There is no *suppose*," said Karael. "The Ephorate has decided. We will summon you when it is time. Until then, know that God loves you. Farewell."

And just like that it was all gone—Karael, Anaita, the Hall of Judgement, the shimmering complexity of the Paslogion. And yours truly was back in his flawed earthly form, which happened to be lying in a hospital bed with a bad case of Smyler Kicked My Ass.

I had been sentenced to freedom. At least for a while.

eight
old friends

I DIDN'T STAY in the hospital long. Sequoia Medical is short of beds as it is, and since angels heal fast, once they saw how quickly I was getting better they didn't argue much when I checked myself out. I did get a lecture from one nice young doctor about refraining from active sports and strenuous activity for a while. It wasn't me she needed to tell, of course, it was the guy with the piranha mouth and the very, very bad attitude.

The police interviewed me about the attack too, but since they thought I was a private investigator working a major insurance fraud, they didn't kick up too much fuss. Heaven is good with bureaucracy, and I've kept my concealed-carry permit active since my Harps days, so I even got my gun back, which I filled with silver as soon as I could get to the rounds I'd left in the Datsun.

Instead of going back to my apartment (Smyler obviously knew about it, since he'd been waiting for me outside) I disposed of the now-petrified burger and fries I'd been bringing home the night of the last attack, and then drove down the Bayshore.

I parked in Southport and limped out to the ruins of Shoreline Park, because I didn't have any other way of getting hold of Sam and I was getting desperate to talk to him. I had taken a roundabout route to make sure I wasn't followed, and I kept my eyes open as I walked carefully through the filth and wreckage, between walls of corroding tin and broken plywood covered in fading paint. When I reached the Funhouse, I left a message on the mirror that Sam had shown me. I wasn't stupid enough to write anything obvious. It just said, "Where we ate lunch, 7pm." Sam would remember the little Southeast Asian place, I knew, and it would be up to him to get there without being followed. The question was, when, if ever, would he find this note? It looked like I was going to be eating Burmese food for the next few nights, but there are worse things to do, believe me.

I didn't have to explore the menu all that much—Sam strolled through the door of the Star of Rangoon just as I finished ordering, looking very Robert-Mitchum-ish in his wrinkled coat and big, baggy face.

"Did you get me the pancakes?" he asked.

"You want the pancakes, order them yourself, you lazy bastard." It was good to see him. He looked good, too, with a relaxed smile on his wide face.

He shoved into the booth, called the waitress back and ordered for himself, then looked me up and down. "Few new bruises, I see. Did Karael and some of his militant angels work you over?"

"I wish." I told him who had given me all these new cuts, scrapes, and puncture wounds.

"You're shitting me." His ginger ale arrived and Sam drank half of it at a swallow, as if the long trip from Third Wayville had made him thirsty. "Leo bagged and burned that little creep."

It was strange how easily it all came back together, as if Sam and I hadn't been through all that craziness, as if he had never lied to me. There was, however, a little hollow place deep inside me, even if I was ignoring it. "Tell me about it. But it was Smyler. It *is* Smyler, and he's still out to get me. I think Eligor put him on me."

Sam raised an eyebrow, the closest he'll let his good-old-boy persona come to showing actual surprise. "Eligor? Why would he do that? You've still got the magic golden feather, don't you?"

My old chum was the one who had hidden it on me in the first place, trying to protect me from an infernal double-cross. With one thing and another, though, he hadn't bothered to tell me about it until much later, which was one major reason I had almost died about eleventy-thousand times in the previous weeks, in many, many interesting ways.

"Yes, I've got it," I said, "or at least I assume I do, since I can't actually touch it myself. And if Eligor was smart he'd just leave me alone. But I think the whole thing goes a bit deeper than common sense." I took a breath. "I have to tell you something."

And I did. I told him the whole thing about me and the Countess of Cold Hands, the whole bizarre, tabloid-headlines story: *Angel Loves Demon*, or *I Sold Out Heaven for a Roll in Hell's Hay*. Although, the only people actually disadvantaged in any way by our relationship were Caz and myself. Oh, and Eligor, of course. The grand duke definitely counted himself as an injured party.

Sam didn't say anything for a long time after I finished. He signaled for another ginger ale, and the proprietress brought it over with the good grace of a camel trudging through a sandstorm. He took his time pouring and then rolled it around in his mouth like a wine critic about to hold forth on this year's Beaujolais nouveau.

"Well, B," he said. "I have to admit, you have lifted fucked-up to an entirely new level."

I laughed in spite of everything. "I have, haven't I?"

"I've got no problem with you *shtupping* a *dybbuk*, particularly." Sam liked to use Yiddish sometimes. Maybe he thought it made him sound intellectual, maybe he just knew it was funny when an angel who looked so Boston Irish started dropping Brooklyn Jewish. "But you definitely could have picked one who would have been less trouble than Eligor's main squeeze. So what are you going to do?"

And that was the problem: I didn't know. As far as I could tell, Grand Duke Eligor had just decided he didn't want to wait until I made it to Hell the usual way—he was sending me an express invitation. "It's got to be Eligor trying to get me, right? You and I saw the bagmen take Smyler. Leo burned him! How else could he be after me now?"

"Yeah, somebody powerful does seem to have it in for you. What happened to Walter Sanders, by the way?"

"He's still not back yet. No news. Which now that you mention it is pretty strange."

Sam had a last *paratha*, ladling up the curry sauce like a canal dredger, then polished off his ginger ale. "Let's get out of here," he said.

We walked to Peers Park, then settled on a bench. The lights were on and the park was full of parents and kids enjoying the spring evening, which made me feel slightly less vulnerable to being attacked by a twice-dead guy with a bayonet, but Sam himself was on Heaven's Most Wanted List, so I wasn't exactly relaxed.

"Okay, first off," Sam said as we watched a guy trying to get his obviously brain-damaged dog to fetch a tennis ball, "only a butt-hat says, 'my enemies are trying to kill me, so I'd better make it easier for them by going over to their place.' Trying to sneak into Hell is the dumbest thing you've ever thought of in a career of pretty amazingly stupid things, Bobby. You know that, right?"

"I don't know what else I can do, Sam. I can't just leave her there. And it's not like Eligor's willing to leave me alone either. Obviously."

He grunted, the Sam Riley version of a long-suffering sigh. "Knew you'd say that. But how would you get in there? Or get her out of there? Shit, even if a whole pile of miracles sort of happened one on top of the other, and you actually got away with it, where would you hide her from Eligor once she's out?"

"Yeah, I admit there's a ton of questions. I was kind of hoping you might help out with some of them."

He grunted again. It was like sitting next to a hippo wallow. "Man, you're way out of my area of expertise here. But we agree that Bobby Dollar walking into Hell is a stupid idea, don't we? Good. Because you wouldn't last ten seconds."

"What about the bodies you have access to? You Third Way guys?"

"Kephas, whatever he or she might be, only gave me access to a body to help make the whole Magians thing look legitimate." The Magians were the group of renegade angels, like Sam, who had recruited souls for the Third Way—the neither-Heaven-nor-Hell afterlife. "You wouldn't do any better trying to waltz into Hell dressed as the Reverend Mubari than wearing your own ugly mug. This is Hell we're talking about, Bobby, not Disneyland." He gave me a look that should have sent me home crying. "And even if you find a body to wear, how do you get *in*? There are lots of gates, but there are even more guards. Bored, mean guards who used to be murdering psychopaths when they were alive, but haven't even got the threat of Hell hanging over their heads now. Because they're already there, right? And they're in charge!"

"Yeah, yeah, I get it. Don't rub it in, Sam. I'll think of something."

"So many terrible situations have begun with those exact words, B, but I suspect this one will be special even by *your* famously screwed-up standards."

Sammy-boy stood up, gave me the number of a safe phone so I could leave him messages without having to hike all the way out to Crackhouse-by-the-Sea, then took his leave. I sat for a while, thinking as I finished my beer.

Helpwise, I had struck out with both Sam and the Sollyhull Sisters, so if I was really going to try to sneak into Hell, I'd have to find another way. I supposed the Broken Boy might have an answer to that, but the problem was that I already needed to ask him a costly question about Smyler, because I was likely to get stabbed in the eye long before Sam's psychopathic Hell guards would ever get their chance to beat me into jelly, and I couldn't really afford to pay the Boy to answer *two* questions.

Either way, though, it was painfully (and expensively) obvious where I was going next.

nine
ectoplasmic boogaloo

I LIKE TO drive. For one thing, I find it just distracting enough that it leaves my mind free for deep thinking. If you ask me just to sit down and think, all I think about is how I'm tired of sitting down, but behind the wheel of a car I just turn the driving over to the lower functions and let my thoughts loose. Also, with the exception of my bosses trying to get hold of me, or the occasional hellbeast trying to disassemble me, when I'm driving I'm safe from interruptions. I knew my phone wouldn't ring because I was on suspension, and unless Smyler had got hold of something faster than his old VW van, he wasn't going to trouble me on the freeway. So I drove north, thinking.

Sam was right, of course: the whole idea of trying to sneak into Hell was so stupid that nobody in his right mind would even bother with it. There was a reason we'd been fighting these guys for a million years or more, and it wasn't because we didn't like their national anthem. They wanted to destroy us and did their best to accomplish that every damn day. Breaking into the place—well, that would be like a Jew breaking into Buchenwald. You might accomplish it somehow, but what would you do when you got there?

But my alternatives were few. And even if I didn't go, I'd still have to find a way to deal with Smyler, which, despite his comparatively small size and up-close choice of weaponry, had already proved pretty damn difficult. I mean, how do you kill someone who's already died twice?

With cheerful thoughts like these in my head, and the fabulous slide work of Elmore James rasping and clanging from the car's speakers, I drove north through the no-man's-land of smaller communities strung along the peninsula between San Judas and San Francisco, until I reached the industrial ruins at the edge of the Bayview district in South SF. I didn't know exactly where I was going to find the Boy, but I knew he'd be somewhere under concrete in that not very nice part of the world. Bayview was where all the black shipyard workers settled, only to be kept there by economics and prejudice after the dock work dried up. It was a poor community, defined more by what other people thought about it than anything else, a refuge for the old and vulnerable. Which, I suppose, is why the Broken Boy had never left.

I spotted the first piece of telltale graffiti on a concrete stanchion, something that looked like a vertical row of letter "D"s, or an aerial view of a pregnant chorus line:

They weren't Ds, of course, but Bs. Two of them, for the Broken Boy, which meant I was in the right area. It's his obscure way of advertising. He doesn't have many customers, but the ones who need him need him *real* bad, so he hangs out his shingle. I parked my car, locked it, checked to make sure I'd locked it, then set out on foot to see if I could find a greater concentration of BB-tags.

Eventually, somewhere north of Bayview Park, I spotted three of the tags on the same corner under the freeway. More importantly, an African-American kid of about ten or eleven years old was sitting there on a chunk of concrete and rebar, pitching pennies by himself against a pillar. He watched me from the corner of his eye as I approached, plainly trying to decide what kind of threat I was.

"Hey," I said when I was about ten feet away. "I'm looking for the Boy."

The kid gave me a quick *you-ain't-much* look, then went back to flicking pennies against the cement. "So?"

"I've got five bucks if you can take me to him. I'm an old friend of his."

"He don't have no friends that old." Clink.

"Look, you can go ask first if you want. Tell him it's Bobby Dollar. He knows me."

The kid gave me a longer look, then scooped up his pennies and stood, hands thrust deep in the pockets of his hoodie, his shoulders up against the wind. March in San Francisco is kind of like December anywhere else. He just stood there, waiting, until I figured out what was going on. I pulled the five out of my pocket and held it out. When he still didn't come nearer, I set it down on an old plastic paint bucket, put a rock on it to keep it from blowing away, and stepped back. He took it cautiously, watching me the whole time like a cat accepting food from strangers, then turned and disappeared up an incline beside the freeway, leaving me in the cold shadows. I sat on the bucket to wait, but it must have been a slow day at the Broken Boy's office because the kid was back in less than ten minutes.

"C'mon," he said, jerking his head to show me which direction we were going. It was a bit of an obstacle course, uphill through dirt and ancient ice plant spiked with plastic bags and food wrappers, then through a culvert. I had to get down on my knees to get through, and couldn't help but reflect on what a great target for a mugging I was, but there just wasn't any other way to see the Broken Boy. It's not like he has a phone and takes reservations.

I followed the kid through this obstacle course long enough that if I'd been trying to figure out where we were, I probably would have given up. We emerged at last in an even darker, bleaker, and more windswept area beneath another part of the freeway, outside what had once been some kind of maintenance door, its little safety cage still intact, although the light bulb it protected had long since disappeared. It looked rusted shut, but swung open surprisingly easily, revealing a set of steps leading down. The kid produced a flashlight from his hoodie and led me into the depths like a midget Virgil.

The maintenance tunnel was cluttered with old rusted breaker boxes jammed with grubby wires, dumped there when their day had ended. A few more turns and then the kid stepped aside and waved for me to walk past him. As soon as I did, he turned his flashlight off and everything went dark.

"Who goes there?" asked a voice that could not possibly have belonged to anyone past puberty. "Friend or foe?"

"What is this, a road company of Peter Pan? It's me, Bobby Dollar. Tell the Boy I'm here."

One by one lights began to flick on, each one a flashlight held by a kid no older than the one who had led me. It really looked like they were on a camping trip, getting ready to tell ghost stories. There was even a campfire, of a sort—a hibachi in the middle of the room, full of hot coals. The little barbecue was mostly covered with an iron lid, only little bits of red light leaking out to splash the grimy cement walls. One of the junior soldiers went and kicked the lid off, and all of a sudden I could see properly. Not that there was much to be seen, just the half-dozen kids and the damp, ugly nexus of concrete tunnels.

"I hope there's enough ventilation here for that barbecue," I said. "Otherwise you and the Boy are going to wind up dead from carbon monoxide poisoning."

"Don't worry about us." The tallest of the kids stepped forward. He was missing an eye, or so I guessed, because he had a bandana tied over one socket, which made it look more than ever like Captain Hook should be making his appearance soon. "How do we know it's really you?"

"Other than the fact that I found the place? I don't know. Try asking me my mother's maiden name."

One-Eye frowned. "We don't know that."

"Neither do I, so we're even. Look, I brought money, and I'm in a hurry. Can I please see the Boy?"

"Hey," said one of the other kids in a lazy voice I was meant to hear, "if he's got money, why don't we just take it off him?"

"Shut the fuck up," said One-Eye quickly. "You don't know what you're messing with." He turned back to me. "I'll see if he's ready."

Something whispered through the room then, a scratchy little sound that made the hairs on the back of my neck get up and look around. It took me a moment to make out the words: *No, it's all right. Bring him in.* It sounded like a ghost, and not the healthy, lively kind like the Sollyhull Sisters, either.

He was sitting in the corner of a room off the main tunnel. I'd actually gone past his door. The only light was from a dry-cell emergency lantern near him, which cast his distorted shadow high across the walls. He barely filled the wheelchair. He'd lost weight since the last time I'd seen him, and although I was certain only that the Boy was somewhere between nine and fourteen years old, I did know that he shouldn't be getting smaller at his age.

The Broken Boy swung his head to the side so he could see me better. Just the angle at which his neck bent was painful to see. Cross Stephen Hawking with a singed spider and you have some idea. Except for his skin, which is pink and healthy as the hide of a newborn mouse. And his eyes, which are even more alive, alive-oh. "Hi, Bobby. Good to see you." His voice was softer than I remembered, more air, less weight. "Long time."

"Yeah. Well, I've been out of the Harps for a while now, you know."

"That didn't stop you the last time."

Didn't really want to get into that. Tell you another time. "Can you help me out, BB?" I suddenly felt bad. "Are you up to it?"

"Me?" The head lolled, the chest heaved. He was laughing. Quiet as it was in that cement tomb under the freeway, I couldn't actually hear it for a bit. "Never better. Run faster, jump higher. Satisfaction guaranteed." Then those bright eyes fixed on me again. "You don't have to worry about me, Bobby." A sentence that could just as easily have been finished, "because there's nothing you can do." Which was true: the gray areas between my team, the other team, and ordinary human folk are full of people like the Broken Boy, growing and dying like weeds in the cracks of a sidewalk.

"Okay, but I'll have to explain for a bit first . . ."

"Money?"

I dug it out of my pocket, took off the rubber band. "I remember the drill. Nothing bigger than twenties. Your helpers can handle them up to make 'em look less new. They look like they'd be good at it."

For a moment, as I held out the cash, his Tyrannosaurus arms almost seemed to be trying to reach for it out of old reflex, but then he called One-Eye (who was apparently named Tico) to take it from me and put it in the box. Tico swaggered out as if he'd made all that money himself. The Boy watched him go.

"They're good kids," he said from the vast height of the two or three years he had on any of them. "They take care of me." And for just a moment I could hear the child he might have been if his gifts or his past had been different; the lonely, sick kid who wished he could go out and play with the others. Kind of like getting punched in the stomach, that was.

A moment later Tico returned with two of the other kids and began to get the Broken Boy ready. As they strapped him to his apparatus, which was really not much more than a rusty old home fitness gym they must have dismantled up in the real world and put back together down here, I found myself wondering for a moment about where they had all come from, what strange tangle of stories had brought them here together. Boy was the strangest of all, of course, but I knew almost as little about him as I did about any of his pint-sized minions. Even Fatback hadn't been able to track down his real name. By the time any of us heard of him, he was already this tiny, messed-up kid with a very strong gift, selling that gift to support himself and a rotating gang of urchins.

Of course, no gift comes without a price tag, and the one the Boy paid was pretty steep.

First the kids wound his limbs and torso in elastic bandages, the kind weekend athletes use on a sprained ankle, until he looked like a joke hospital patient from a comedy sketch. Next they tied him to the exercise machine with surgical tubing. I was pleased to see they did it gently, with the reverence of priests preparing a holy shrine. They left slack in each connection except for the one around his forehead. The Boy's eyes followed them, showing white at the edges, but I could tell he was calm. After all, he'd been through all of this more than a few times already.

"Hey, Bobby," he said, "Kayshawn, the one who brought you in from the checkpoint?" His voice was so quiet I had to move forward to hear him. "He came to me because he wanted me to teach him how to dance. He heard of me, see, but he thought I was 'Breakin' Boy.'"

"Breakin' Two, Ectoplasmic Boogaloo," I said, apropos of nothing except the vague anxiety I always felt watching the Boy do his thing.

Tico came in from the other room with a can of Sterno burning on an old china plate. "But you don't dance so good, huh, boss?"

"You're tripping," said the Boy. "I dance really, really good. But none of you can see me doing it."

Tico squinted his single eye as he poured something powdery from his fist into the Sterno, then set the plate down on the floor in front of the exercise machine, making the Broken Boy look more than ever like some distorted heathen idol. The can began to spark and smoke a little, then the orange flame began to cool into blue. Tico backed away and crouched against the wall with the others, a rapt little congregation.

"Tell me what you want to know, Bobby," the Boy said. "Then I'll show you my dance."

I'd seen it. It was pretty impressive. Two thousand bucks' worth? That depended on what I walked out of here knowing. So I told him about Smyler and how I'd watched the murderer burned away to carbon in a magical angel net, and how more recently he'd tried several times to stab me.

"Strange one," said the Boy slowly. The flame was entirely blue now, the room cold to the eye as a 1940s gangster film. "Strange . . ." Other than the flicker above the Sterno can, the only movement was the Boy's head as it pulled in short jerks against the tubing that held him, as if his body had decided to escape while his brain was busy talking. "Strange to think . . . who's buying? Who sells . . . ?" He trailed off. His eyes had rolled up beneath his lids. "She makes seashores with a sea shell," he said then, as calmly as discussing the weather, but the way he spoke made him seem very far away. "She masks. No—*he* must . . . ? Mastema? Makers with more of the tiny tiger bright light. Paper white light. White when you . . . while you—"

Then the Broken Boy gasped, and everything between his nose and his shoulders torqued violently to one side, as though struck by some huge, invisible fist. I had seen what happened to him when he plied his talent, but this was something different. For a moment afterward he just hung quivering in his harness of tubes like an exhausted butterfly halfway out of the chrysalis. Tico and one of the others actually scuttled forward, but a quiet yet distinct hiss from the Boy sent them back to their places. The blue flame wavered at their approach and retreat. By the time it had settled, the Boy had found his voice again.

"Sorry, Bobby," he said, each word a dry scrape. "Can't do it for you. Something . . ." He worked for air. "Something won't let me. Something stronger. A *lot* stronger . . . than me."

Which sucked, because it pretty much proved that Eligor or someone else near the top of the food chain was definitely after me. Could it be someone I hadn't suspected? That fat demonic bastard Prince Sitri had certainly enjoyed the opportunity to yank my chain and his rival Eligor's at the same time. But if he was the one who'd sent Smyler after me, this was a lot more complicated than I'd guessed. No, the odds were strong on the grand duke himself, Caz's former boyfriend and current captor. And if the Boy couldn't give me any information about Smyler, that meant the undead little fucker was going to keep coming after me, and I'd have to keep improvising. How many times could I get lucky?

If Smyler was off-limits, then I had to concede that the best defense would be a good offense, as sports journalists like to say.

"You still owe me an answer," I told the Broken Boy.

"Really? After I just got the shit kicked out of me for messing in your business?" He looked like a plucked chicken in a pair of Garanimals jeans and a sweatshirt, but I was out of options. I had to be hard.

"You owe me an answer, kid. I can't afford to pay you two thousand bucks just to admire your decor."

He laughed. A little bubble of spit remained on his lower lip. "You're a nasty man, Bobby." He craned his head to see me better. I moved to make it easier. "What do you want to know?"

I looked around at the bright eyes and dirty faces of the Boy's followers. It was like having an audience of raccoons. "Send your friends away. This one's not for public consumption."

The Boy must have made some gesture, because Tico got up and led the others out. BB had them well trained, I had to admit it. Pretty good for a sixty-pound bundle of rags that couldn't stand by itself. When they were gone, I stepped closer. Even under all this concrete I didn't want to say anything too loudly. I don't know why—I had talked about it in the park with Sam without worrying. But suddenly I felt something heavy on me, the weight of superstition or just the realization of what I was actually intending.

"I need to know how to get into Hell."

ten

a mild, gray man

IT WAS taking the Boy longer than it usually did. Maybe I'd tired him out with the first attempt, maybe it was just a hard thing to discover, but he was laboring like a truck going uphill, and I could tell he still wasn't anywhere near where he needed to be. At first he had simply slipped out of normal conversation like a patient going under anesthetic, flowing seamlessly into what sounded like free-verse nonsense, but that had been the last comfortable thing I'd seen. He very quickly began hitching and writhing within his bonds and now seemed to be deep in some kind of seizure, his wasted limbs rigid, his teeth locked in a skull-like grin, grunts of pain puffing out his cheeks in regular rhythm.

I actually heard the first bone snap, a terrible muffled crack as his contortions put too much stress on his fragile structure. What was worse was that he didn't even scream, as though such a brutal rupture of tissue and bone barely climbed to his attention, but only shut his eyes, slowly, like someone pulling down the shutters in front of a downtown store.

It had been bad the last time I visited him, and it was bad this time but in a wholly different way. I don't know where the Boy goes or what he does—his dance is a complete mystery to me—but I can promise you no explorer of jungles or mountaintops works harder or suffers more. I sat and watched him for what must have been half an hour as he slowly twisted and curled into terrible shapes, the rubber tubes stretching with him so that at times they looked like the external arteries and veins of some completely alien creature. During that time I heard three more bones break. There might have been others I didn't hear. And every moment I watched I felt like a monster.

Like any decent person, when I first met him I had tried to get him off the streets and into some kind of facility, but he wouldn't do it. "I was in one of those places once, and I'm never going back," he had told me. "Never." He told me that if anyone tried to force him, he had just enough control of his arms to be able to jam one of his fists into his mouth and choke himself to death, and that's what he'd do. I believed him.

But of course, nobody could watch what he was doing to himself, or what I was indirectly doing to him, and feel comfortable. Like I said, there are a lot of people that live in the gray areas, the *between* areas. And when you go to those places, it's hard to know what rules apply.

He finally went slack and stayed that way. I went to disconnect him from his apparatus, but he shook his head and whispered something. I couldn't hear him so I bent close. His breath was surprisingly sweet, like cinnamon.

"Get . . . Tico . . ."

I called to Boy's helpers, and they trotted in like a pack of efficient ER nurses, gently untangling the tubes and disconnecting him, pushing up his sleeves and pant legs to reach the knots. As they rubbed life back into his pale pink limbs Tico came forward with a hypodermic, but the Broken Boy waggled his head.

"Bobby . . ." I got down close so he wouldn't have to raise his voice. "They built a gate . . . just for the emperor . . ."

For a moment I thought he was babbling again, but he kept talking and I began to understand. I crouched by him, straining for whispers deep underground, as he told me about the Neronian Bridge.

When Tico had sedated him, the urchins carefully lifted the Boy down from the exercise station and onto a blanket so they could carry him off to his bed. Tico moved up close behind me, letting me know that it was time for me to leave.

The little kid named Kayshawn was back in the main chamber, waiting to guide me out. I looked back as I reached the corridor. Tico was staring at me, arms crossed, frowning past his piratical bandana. "You made him dance twice," he said. "Don't want to see you back for a long time."

I don't particularly like being told off by eleven year olds, but he was right. I shrugged and followed Kayshawn back toward the daylight.

On the way back down the peninsula I was no longer in the mood for anything quite so brisk and bustling as Elmore James, so I put on *Chet In Paris*. Baker's aching blue notes were about right for the mood of someone who'd just spent a lot of money to learn a complicated and extremely painful way to commit suicide. I rolled up the windows and let "Alone Together" fill the car like a remembered perfume.

So was I really going to try to make a trip into Hell? It was worse than suicide, of course, like sending a belly dancer into a Mujahideen rape camp. And even assuming I could get into the place, how could any disguise possibly hold up long enough to get me close to Eligor . . . and Caz? Because from what I knew of Hell, the high rollers lived in ways that even Jude's Young Republicans could never hope to match, each one with his own little fiefdom, fortress, private army. A wig and a fake mustache were hardly going to get me through all that.

As I reached the outskirts of San Judas I realized I hadn't eaten yet. After my long adventure in the Bayview district it was well into the afternoon, and I hadn't had any lunch, or much breakfast for that matter, and for once I had a pocket full of money. I wouldn't get to spend any of it in Hell, and Orban would probably auction off my car anyway, so I took the exit to Redwood Shores and headed for an expensive Japanese place I knew out there, on the water.

By the time I was ready to order I discovered I wasn't as hungry as I'd thought, so I just asked for a basket of mixed tempura to go with my Sapporo. I crunched at it distractedly and let my thoughts flop around as I watched the seagulls dive off the rail outside. I was trying to make things come out in some order other than "you're pretty much screwed," but I couldn't. My options seemed to be exactly two: stay and eventually find myself with a pointy object poking deep into my delicate brain tissues, courtesy of Smyler, or take the fight to Eligor with some farce of trying to sneak my girlfriend out of Hell, like a warped Crosby and Hope movie—*The Road to Inferno*. Either way, I could no longer rely on my bosses to resurrect me if I died in action, me being under suspicion and all.

The restaurant was almost deserted at that time of day, so I took my time eating, and might have had a second beer or two by the time I finally made my way back onto the Bayshore and headed home. It was still light but the sun was showing signs of wanting to get down behind the hills for the night, and downtown Jude was full of the late-afternoon shadows that come so quickly, dropping the temperature in the concrete canyons around Beeger Square ten degrees or so in a matter of minutes.

And, no, when I got to my place I didn't just turn off Chet Baker, leap out of my car, and charge in. I hadn't forgotten what happened the last time. I drove around the block twice with my eyes wide open but saw no sign of anything unusual, just the usual assortment of grocery-haulers and dog-walkers that you'd get pretty much any decent day. Still, I parked across the street from my building and went through the lobby as cautiously as I could manage without looking like a complete idiot. Since Smyler seemed to know where I lived, I would probably have to pack up and move again, which depressed the shit out of me. Little as I owned, I hadn't even unpacked it yet.

The door was locked, which reassured me slightly. As I pushed the door open, I tucked my gun into my waistband so I'd have a hand free in case anything jumped on me. Nothing jumped on me. There was, however, a stranger sitting in the middle of my couch.

My gun was back in my hand so quickly I almost didn't realize I'd pulled it, pointed right at his calm face. It wasn't Smyler, that was the good part, but I couldn't think of anyone or anything else that ought to be in my place when I wasn't there. I'd never seen this stranger before, a middle-aged Semitic-looking guy with a salt and pepper beard and a hairline that inched back almost to the top of his head.

"Who the hell are you?"

He looked at me with mild reproach. "Please don't point that at me. I don't mean you any harm."

"Then what are you doing here? I don't recall inviting you."

He shook his head. "You didn't. But I'm a friend." His hands were folded in his lap. He wore a cheap brown suit and a charcoal gray overcoat, oddly old-fashioned in a San Judas spring. Everything about him seemed tailored toward looking harmless. There are creatures in nature that look like that just so they can get their victims close enough to sink their teeth into them. Some of those creatures even talk as nicely as this guy. I've met them. Until I knew better, this mild, gray man officially scared me, so I kept my gun trained between his mild, gray eyes.

"Then tell me something that will convince me not to put a bunch of silver in you so I can dump you out by the trash cans and settle in to watch *Dancing With The Stars*."

His smile was only slightly more robust than the Broken Boy's. "Let's go for a walk, Bobby." When he saw me hesitate, he slowly lifted those harmless hands. "If I wanted to hurt you, would I wait for you here, then ask you to come outside?"

"You would if you had buddies waiting out there," I said, but he was right, it didn't really make sense. Not that I assumed he was my new BFF or anything.

I got behind him and let him lead me out the door, the barrel of my gun against his spine so that he'd block the view of it from anyone coming toward us. Didn't want to alarm the neighbors any more than necessary after they'd seen me get brutally smacked around on the sidewalk the other night.

As we stepped outside, me swiveling like a turret gunner, keeping an eye out for any accomplices the guy might have brought along, he gave me a look that might have been disappointment mixed with mild amusement. "Do you really not know me, Bobby?"

I stared, but although there was something familiar about his way of talking, maybe even about his slight, small form, I couldn't put my finger on it. For a half-instant I even wondered if he might be my old top-kicker Leo from the Harps, back from the dead, but that wasn't who he reminded me of, and Leo would never have played a little game like this: if he ever came back I'd find him sitting on my chest in the middle of the night demanding to know whether I was planning on sleeping until fucking noon.

My gun hidden away now in my coat pocket (but my finger still on the trigger) I walked with the stranger to Main Street before turning toward Beeger Square. The fountain in the square (mostly known as "Rocket Jude" because the centerpiece is a Bufano statue of our patron saint that's sort of shaped like a missile) is a major hang-out spot, and I knew nobody would give us a second look, but I liked the idea of having people around while I found out what this guy's play was going to be.

We settled onto one of the benches. I left about a foot between us to make it harder for him to grab me. He must have seen this little bit of tradecraft because he shook his head. "Still nothing, Bobby? As much as we talk to each other?"

I stared at him, irritated (and still more than a bit nervous) and then suddenly I knew who he was. It hardly seemed possible. "Temuel? Archangel Temuel?"

"Ssshhh." He actually put his fingers to his lips. "You needn't shout it."

I sat there chewing over what to say next. Stunned is not the word. The higher angels only appear on Earth for important things, and when they do it's like one of the Hollywood elite showing up at your birthday party. Not that Temuel was that glory-hound type. But that was just the problem—he wasn't the type to come to Earth at all, let alone to hang out in my grubby little apartment.

"What are you doing here?" I finally asked. "I mean, is this . . . official business? Like, Heaven-dot-org stuff?"

"What do you think?"

I swallowed. I'm not usually at a loss for words, but I simply didn't know what to say. Did this mean somebody had blown the whistle on me about Caz? Or was it the feather? Was Temuel here to discreetly terminate my employment? My finger tightened a little on the trigger of my automatic, but that was reflex. If my bosses wanted to cross me off the employment roll, a few silver slugs weren't going to help me any. At last, for lack of anything else to offer, I asked, "What do you want?"

"I hear you're interested in going to Hell. I'm willing to help you."

Hearing that was not hugely different than getting slapped across the face. "Huh? What? I mean, *why*?" It's hard to make intelligent conversation when your already feeble grip on How Things Work has just proved a lot more slippery than you ever suspected. "Why would you want to help me do that?"

"Why, so you'll help *me*."

My archangel proceeded to tell me what he wanted and what he'd give me in return. None of it made the least amount of sense, not then; it was all I could do just to listen without shaking him and shouting,

What's going on here? What is my boss doing here on Earth, undercover, tell-
ing me how he's going to help me reach Hell so I can save my demon lover?
(Not that he ever mentioned that part: if he knew about Caz, he was
keeping quiet about it.) But the things he said sounded genuine, as did
what he suggested he could arrange for me. And when he asked me his
return favor, which I had assumed would be something on the lines of
emptying the ocean with a teaspoon, what he wanted was surprisingly
simple. Stupidly simple, even.

"That's all you want? You just want me to find a guy and tell him
that?"

"I want you to find someone in Hell, Bobby. It's not all that easy."

"But still . . ." I shook my head. Questions were good—questions
would keep me alive—but too many questions might lose me this
chance. Yes, of course, every bit of self-preservation in me was screaming "*trap!*" but how could it be? I mean, if the rest of my superiors
knew as much about me as Temuel seemed to, I'd already given them
enough rope to hang me and the entire Mormon Tabernacle Choir, too.
No, the Mule claimed he was doing this alone, and so far that was the
only explanation that made sense.

"Just tell me how you found out," I said. "About Hell, I mean."
Then it came to me. "My phone. Clarence said he tapped it or bugged
it somehow when he was tailing Sam. The bug is still there."

Temuel shook his head, but he didn't outright deny it.

"Tell me you're the only one in Heaven who knows."

"I'm the only one, Bobby. For now. But I can't guarantee you'll get
away with this forever."

We talked for a while longer, and he gave me the rest of the details—
you'll get them too, but not yet—and then he stood, our little chat beside Rocket Jude apparently at an end. I wasn't holding the gun
anymore as we walked back across the broad square, but I wasn't feeling much safer than I had on the way over. I was clearly into something
big and deep, in way past my ability to survive unaided, and the only
person offering me a lifeline was someone who, any time he chose,
could have me busted down to Unidentified Angelic Smear, Second
Class.

Twilight had turned to near dark. Sidewalks were empty now, but
the streets were full of cars, late commuters heading home, everyone
else on their way downtown for movies or dinner. A light, misty rain

swept through, just enough to prickle my jacket with little droplets and make my face damp.

As we neared the end of Main Street an angular shadow suddenly peeled itself from between a pair of dumpsters and stepped out in front of us. It was dark, no streetlights, but I knew exactly who that wiry, crouching frame belonged to.

"It so slick," Smyler said. "It so smart. It wait and wait."

"Shit." I fumbled my gun out of my pocket. Temuel stared at the scrawny apparition. My boss looked frightened, which was not the thing I wanted to see just then. "Stay there," I said to the thing with the long blade, trying to make my voice sound firm and worth obeying. "I don't want to shoot you—I'd rather talk—but I'll blow you into little pieces if you take even one step."

"I can't be here," Temuel said in a breathless rush. "I can't risk . . ."

And then he was gone, just gone, as if he hadn't been standing right beside me. When I turned back a stunned second later, the killer with the underslung jaw and a four-edged knife gripped in its hand was loping toward me, a skinny shadow with the staring, excited eyes of an insane child.

eleven

true names

THIS TIME I had a gun in my hand. This time I was pushing silver. We obviously weren't going to get a chance to discuss Smyler's vendetta or who had put him up to it, so I aimed at his midsection and started pulling the trigger. I put three right through him.

I mean that literally, too: as the gun bucked in my hand, I saw the streetlight at the end of the alley through the big old holes the slugs left, as if the crazy little fucker was made of stars. Then the holes were gone—maybe I just lost the angle—and Smyler suddenly went sideways up the wall, two feet and one hand sticking him there like a fly as he skittered toward me, the long, pointy thing swinging in his free hand, aimed right at my face.

I threw myself down. He just missed me, but his knife tore my collar. Was he trying to kill me or just incapacitate me? And how the hell could three silver slugs zip through him and not even slow him down?

I did my best to turn hitting the ground into rolling myself back upright. It was hard to get a fix on my attacker in the deep shadows of the alley. For a moment I thought he had vanished, then I saw him skittering down the wall toward me like a spider. What the fuck *was* he? Or rather, what had my enemies turned him into? He was just pissing on gravity like it didn't matter, like I was fighting a cage match against M.C. Escher.

I wasn't going to waste any more bullets until I could put one into his head from up close. I still had the cosh in my sleeve, but that hadn't been a huge amount of use the last time, so I grabbed a lid off a nearby garbage can and turned around just as Smyler bounced up onto the wall once more and then dropped on me. I was able to get the lid up, but Smyler's bayonet punched through it like a ballpoint through typing paper and the point ended up an inch from my right eye. I twisted hard on the lid, doing my best to yank the hilt of the four-edged knife out of his hand. I didn't quite manage it, but he had to change his position on top of me to compensate, so I rolled backward and took him with me, holding tight until I heard his head hit the street. I liked that sound. I felt a surge of adrenaline, and for once it didn't just feel like terror.

If it came to endurance, the rubbery bastard was going to outlast me, so I drove into him as hard as I could, like a lineman on a blocking sled, putting the lid right against him and plowing him back onto the concrete as he started to get up. As soon as I felt hard ground stop us I scrambled on top of him and just began hitting him as hard in the face as I could with the can lid. After smacking him with it at least a dozen times I threw the lid to the side, his blade still stuck in it, then kept on with my fist and a chunk of concrete I'd found. I beat my own knuckles bloody, cracking Smyler's head against the pavement again and again, so loud that I could hear it echo in the narrow space. He was scratching at me, but not accomplishing much more. I dropped once on his belly with my knee, then got up and began kicking. I could hear sirens—someone had finally called the police.

At a certain point there's no explaining. I think it was the red mist, like the Vikings used to get. Everything that had happened to me, everything that had seeped in and painfully corroded me, the frustration, the anger, most of all the terror, it all came out. I kicked that horrible little thing until I swear I kicked all its bones to pieces. I kicked his head the same way. I kicked blood into the air. I kicked until the limp thing that had been Smyler just snagged the end of my foot each time like a broken kite. Then I fell back against the alley wall between two garbage cans, gasping and wheezing and trying not to cry. Even after what I'd just done, I felt like the victim of a prison shower rape.

Then the crushed, misshapen head lifted on the broken neck. It contorted, seemed to pull its entire body up toward the disjointed neck, then began to shrug it all back into shape as the bones knitted together and the creature remade itself. It took only seconds to happen, and it shook me so much I could only stare gape-jawed. I couldn't even guess how much power Eligor must be burning to let Smyler do this. Just to get me? Fucking Bobby Dollar, tiny little thorn in the grand duke's very vast side? It was like smuggling in a nuclear weapon to bump off a squealer.

His body almost normal already, my enemy stared at me. The blood-soaked hood still framed it, but the face was healed, the dead gray skin gone tight over the mummy bones. Those ugly little bottom teeth jutted—Smyler was smiling.

"Oh, it *like* this, Bobby Dollar! Said he don't give up. Yes! More! It want your heart." And then he pulled his crazy knife out of the garbage can lid and leaped up onto the wall and stuck there like a lizard basking in a Tijuana courtyard.

I'd lost my gun somewhere in the red rage, but it didn't really matter. I couldn't beat him. As long as Eligor or whoever was pouring this much power into keeping him alive and functioning on Earth, I was going to lose. I had nothing left to fight with but the bloody chunk of concrete in my hand. I backed myself along the wall toward a doorway, where I would have the best chance of defending myself, but the body I was wearing was not going to magically repair puncture wounds in seconds like his did, and he probably wasn't planning to kill me right away in any case. He, or at least his master, wanted to know where the feather was, and I had no doubt he would happily take his time finding out.

The sirens were getting really loud now.

I had lost him again in the shadows, but I spotted movement and realized he had slipped down to the ground where he was harder to see, hidden by the shadow of a dumpster. I braced myself, guessing he wouldn't wait long. I was right.

Smyler came across the alley like a crab, zigzagging sideways at crazy angles. I caught a glint of his sharklike stare, then the longer smear of reflected streetlight that was his blade. I ducked on pure instinct and the bayonet whipped invisibly past my ear. I only knew it was there when it cut my cheek coming back the other direction.

"*Bobby!*" someone said. "*Close your eyes!*"

And I did, a mere moment late, just slow enough that I saw the first burst of fiery light. The rictus mask of Smyler as he loomed over me, his eyes wide but his pupils suddenly no bigger than the heads of ants, was burned onto my retina.

The light burned brighter and brighter even through my closed eyelids, even through the lingering afterimage of Smyler's terrible face, flaring so intensely that my own head seemed to turn all white inside. Smyler shrieked. Despite everything I had done to him, it was the first time I'd heard him in distress. Then the whiteness was too much, and I fell down and pulled the dark around me for a little while.

When I could think again I realized I was crouching on my hands and knees, my forehead against the cold pavement. I struggled upright. Smyler was gone. Temuel, or at least his human form, stood beside me. His hand looked like it was in an ex-ray machine, the skin still glowing so deeply pinkish-orange that I could see the bones beneath the muscle. He offered me his other hand to help me up. It felt pretty normal.

"Where did he go?"

"That thing?" Temuel looked troubled. "It ran away from the light. It's stronger than it looks. You should get away from here. I pointed the police in another direction, but they'll be back."

I should have thanked him, but all I could think of to say was, "Do you know anything about *that thing*, as you call it?"

He gave me a look that said nothing, absolutely nothing. "I can't be here, but I couldn't leave you to be attacked, either." He quickly looked me up and down. "I must go now."

"We still seem to have a lot to talk about."

"Do you know the Museum of Industry?" he asked. Duh. Even tourists knew the place, and I'd been living in Jude for years and years. "Good. Meet me in front of it tomorrow night, by the fountains. Ten o'clock." He hesitated, looking me over. "And take care, Bobby." Then he walked away.

I just watched him go. I was so tired and battered I could barely stand, but I did remember to retrieve my gun. One odd thing had struck me, though, and it was what I kept turning over and over as I limped home. The whole time he'd been here, Temuel had never once called me Doloriel, my true name. My angel name.

With wounds to tend and all this crazy to deal with, I couldn't even take the evening off—not yet. I made it back home with a few rest stops, ignoring the comments of strangers who assumed I was drunk.

It could be that Temuel's disco light show had hurt Smyler bad enough to keep him away a long time. Certainly I'd never heard him react to pain before, and that included the time I saw him burned to charcoal. But I couldn't count on it. The horrible thing had beaten me badly. Only Temuel's interference had saved my life, maybe even my soul. I couldn't gamble that Smyler wouldn't come back.

Once inside my apartment I threw a few nights' worth of toiletries and other emergency supplies into an old suitcase with a missing buckle. I left my real luggage in the tiny hall closet, since I didn't want it to look like I'd moved out if anyone came looking for me, including my own side.

Just to avoid familiar patterns while searching for a place to crash, I headed up the Woodside Highway and then a few miles south before turning east again toward a part of town I hardly ever visited. The Sand Hill corridor was one of the leading indicators of whether San Jude was in boom or bust mode; you could track the square footage costs like a local stock. And because it was ground zero for venture capital money, it was also ground zero for fairly expensive hotels, many with gorgeous views of the hills, which turned dry gold this time of year before the rains brought back the green. I still had Orban's money in my pocket, and if I was going to Hell, I wouldn't be taking any cash with me, so I guessed I might as well spend some on comfort now.

The hotel I chose was a very chic little businessman's special, and since I didn't care about the view I got quite a nice suite for my several hundred dollars. What I really wanted was safety, and I was more likely to get it in a place like this, expenses be hanged. I had stopped at a service station to clean up a bit first, but I'm sure I still looked like someone who'd been mugged. To her credit, though, the young woman behind the counter didn't even bat an eye and actually smiled when she handed me the change from my wad of bills. Inside, I raided the minibar, then took the longest, hottest bath I've ever managed, doing my best to scald away the worst of the aches, along with my compulsive shivering. I steamed long enough to be legally declared chowder, but the tremors wouldn't entirely go away.

At last, I climbed out, wrapped myself in a thick terrycloth robe with the hotel's logo on the pocket, and started another drink. Believe it or not, it was purely for the pain, since it had become obvious to me that I was in one of those dark, miserable moods that even booze wasn't going to change. I know, that sounds unAmerican, but there you go: I know myself, and I know how these bodies I wear tend to work.

I was pretty sure who was behind all this, and it made me feel like I had something jagged lodged between my brain and the frontal bone of my skull. If it had been food in my stomach it would have been something indigestible like gravel or glass, but it was an idea, and that was a thousand times worse.

Eligor. First he had set his horned Sumerian monster to chase me all over creation, long before I had ever touched his ex-girlfriend, just because he thought I had his damned angel feather. Then he had taken Caz away right in front of me, but not before making her tell me she didn't love me. Now he had started all over, siccing his undead psycho-killer Smyler on me like a cat after a rat, so that I had to hide even from my own employers and friends. And *he* had *Caz!* In other words, Eligor owned the game, but he was still going to grind me into the dirt to show me how strong he was and how little I mattered. How could Hell itself be any worse? (Yes, it was a very stupid question, and I was soon going to find out just how stupid, but at the time I was half-lit and hurting.)

If I had been wavering at all, I was now determined. I wasn't going to sit around any more waiting for someone else to try to kill me, or frame me, or anything else. If the grand duke wanted to play for those kinds of stakes, I was going to do my best to take the game right to him.

Exhausted as I was, I couldn't fall asleep for a long time even after I turned the lights out. I lay with my hands behind my head and watched the jittering light from the television make shadows on the ceiling while I thought about how much I hated Eligor the Horseman and how good it would feel to pull his scorched, worthless heart out of his chest and show it to him.

When I did finally sleep I didn't travel anywhere but deeper into that darkness. I woke with the faint taste of blood in my mouth.

twelve

an angel in my ear

WHEN I got up it was past noon, and I could hardly believe any of the previous night had happened. I mean, it just seemed too much like a dream—my boss the archangel telling me he was going to help me get into Hell to save my demon girlfriend. But your pal Bobby Dollar never lets facts or good sense stand in the way of a suicidally foolish course of action, so after I'd caffeinated my body to a functional level, I started thinking through the arrangements I'd have to make if I was actually going to do this thing.

I was on indefinite leave from work and didn't need to let Heaven know where I'd be, so that bit was all right. Besides, I was going to trust Temuel to run that interference for me if necessary, since he knew a lot more about Heaven than I did. I didn't want the folks at the Compasses asking too many questions, though, so I called both Monica and young Clarence to tell them I was going out of town. I hinted I wanted to get lost for a while, just think things through, and that I'd get in touch when I got back.

While I was on the phone with them I had a look through the latest stuff Fatback had sent me, but it was mostly a rehash of what I already knew, the original murders in the 1970s and then Smyler's Greatest Hits tour when he came back and we finally (as I'd thought) finished him. There was nothing about him more recent than a year or so old, and the only new information consisted of a few rumors about his first return culled from various spooky internet backwaters. None of it advanced my knowledge one damn bit about why he was now trying to perforate me or why he wouldn't stay dead.

There wasn't any need to pack to go to Hell, since I wasn't going to be able to carry any actual baggage. Only my soul was going, not my Earth body, though I did have to think of something to do with that body while I wasn't using it. I'd put the first and last down on my current apartment, but the landlord was a nosy older guy, and I could just imagine him letting himself in to "inspect," finding my apparently lifeless corpse, and then calling the police. Even if I got back before somebody decided to cremate my remains, it was still going to be hard to explain. What I needed to do was stash my body where it would be safe until I could get back into it.

Here my options were limited. It wasn't that the body itself needed any care. It was one of Heaven's special production numbers, and would stay alive and motionless and perfectly healthy for as long as I was out of it. Where to leave it, though, was the hard part: I wouldn't know what was happening to it, and I wouldn't be able to return to it suddenly even if I did. I needed a protector—a Renfield, if you know what I mean, somebody to protect my physical shell while I wasn't using it.

At last, and extremely grudgingly, I came up with a name. As with most of the other ideas I'd been having lately, it was so damn awful that I wanted to kick myself all the way around San Judas, but after wrestling with the problem all afternoon it was still the best I could come up with. Which will, unfortunately, give you an idea of the quality of my options.

My candidate picked up the phone and dropped it on the floor twice before he managed to say, "Yo. G-Man here."

I took a deep breath, still wondering if I should just hang up and leave my body in the middle of the road somewhere—surely it would be safer, because if there was a more annoying, less competent person on the round green Earth than Garcia "G-Man" Windhover, I had yet to meet him. I became acquainted with G-Man while trying to figure out how his girlfriend's late grandfather had been involved with Sam's Third Way (although I hadn't known Sam was part of it at the time). Unfortunately, young Garcia had proved harder to get rid of afterward than a tar baby in a Velcro romper. Believe me, he was literally the last person I wanted to involve, but love and desperation often make for strange bedfellows.

"Hey, G-Man," I said. "Bobby Dollar here."

"Bobby! Long time no see, brah! Whassup?" He had fantasies that he was my driver or my operative or something. I'd done my best to convince him otherwise, but it was like talking to a crazy person. What the fuck am I talking about? It *was* talking to a crazy person. But G-Man had access to an otherwise empty house, so pride (and good sense) would have to be swallowed.

I made an arrangement to drop by Posie's grandfather's place that afternoon and ascertained that G-Man would be there and Posie wouldn't, which was good. She wasn't any dumber than her boyfriend (I'm not sure that's scientifically possible) but she wasn't really a good security risk. I was stuck with G-Man already, since Clarence had dragged him along to the Shootout at Shoreline Park, but there was no reason to add more bodies to this clusterfuck.

I made a few more arrangements, then called Sam on the number he'd given me and left a message, explaining what I was doing. It never hurts to have one competent person know what's going on, and I was clearly short-handed in the intelligent accomplices department. It wasn't that I needed Sam to do anything specific, but I was just sunk so deep in lies, complexities, and other people's agendas that I wanted someone who'd be on my side when it all went tits up, as things usually did. Sam might have lied to me about a bunch of things, but as far as I could tell, he was still my friend.

Next I drove down to the Palo Alto district to Edward Walker's big old house, where his granddaughter and her idiot boyfriend were currently camped out. G-Man opened the door, dressed like Hip-Hop's Worst Nightmare. I've got nothing against white kids who want to dress like black kids—street culture is like that, especially appealing to haves who want to look like have-nots—but Garcia Windhover had a really striking absence of good taste. He was draped in oversized chains and necklaces like he'd ordered "Rap Star" from a novelty costume catalog. He wore a black San Judas Cougars minor league baseball cap turned sideways (I'm sure he pretended the "C" was for "Crips") and the waistband of his pants was around his thighs.

I left his fist-bump hanging as I walked into the house. "Is there an upstairs guest room?" I asked him.

"Whoa. You need a secret hideout?"

"Something like that. Is there one here?"

Turned out that G-Man didn't really know much about the house except for the kitchen, the living room (where the television was) and the downstairs room where he and Posie slept. We finally located an upstairs bedroom that suited my purposes, tricked out for guests but clearly not used in a while. I couldn't very well tell G-Man that I needed to leave my regular body here while I visited Hell, so I spun him a ridiculous story about how I was going to be testing a top-secret drug, but that I couldn't do it in the government lab because my employers were afraid there was a spy in the facility. Garcia Windhover flopped back and forth between believing I was a private detective or a government agent, but either way he didn't seem to think this latest thing was beyond belief, which just goes to show you how scary his ignorance was. I mean, if it was you, wouldn't you at least want a better reason why somebody was going to hide in your house while deep in an apparent coma? Of course you would. And that's why you will never be the G-Man.

His only concern seemed to be that his girlfriend might come in and find me there. "I mean, Posie's cool, man, you know she's cool, but she's like a *girl*, you know? I mean, dangerous shit just freaks her right out. If I wasn't here, she might, like, call the police or something."

Which, I had to admit, was a genuine concern. "Don't worry, G-Man," I said, soothing him with his self-selected nickname. "I can be under the bed. We'll just drape a sheet over me to keep off the dust and the spiders, and I'll be good to go."

"Whoa. You're just going to lie under the bed up here for a couple of weeks? Spooky." But that seemed to have addressed his major concern. "I'll make sure nobody bothers you, Bobby man."

"Just make sure that nobody includes you," I said. "Remember, this is a heavy-duty government medical experiment. If you mess with my body, or tell anyone I'm here, you're risking my life and yours . . . as well as the safety of the Free World."

Sorry, but I just couldn't help fucking with him. You'd probably have done it too.

G-Man's eyes lit up. "Aye-aye, dude!" he said, saluting so hard he knocked off his sideways baseball cap.

The Museum of Industry is a big old place in the Belmont neighborhood west of the Camino Real in North Jude. It used to be the Phagan Mansion back in the days when Belmont was on the rural outskirts of

San Judas and people like the Phagans made so much money that they could barely spend it fast enough to keep from drowning in it. A later generation realized the mansion was worth more as a taxable donation, I guess, and gave it to the city.

The museum was made up of what had been the main house, a sprawling three-story structure probably easy to get lost in even when it was a house, and two wings that had been built later. The three parts of the museum were divided into different historical aspects of San Judas and California. One wing focused on the original native inhabitants and the earliest European explorers and settlements; the main house, on the nineteenth and twentieth centuries, when San Judas took off and grew large; then the modern Silicon Valley era in the other wing. It was a popular game among local wags to come up with names for the three sections and their eras—"Ships, Shops, and Chips" was a popular one and, of course, the less politically correct "Injuns, Engines, and Multi-User Dungeons." (The last is a computer game thing, I think, but if you want to know for sure, you'll have to ask someone who's never had sex.)

The fountain in front had actually been salvaged from a derelict, early twentieth-century office building that had stood on another part of the property. When they tore the office building down, some local artist had rescued the maze of copper piping from the fire sprinkler system, then rebuilt part of it in the open space in front of the museum. It was as if the walls of the office building were still there but invisible; the pipes formed empty geometric shapes and drizzled water from sprinkler heads on every level. (It always reminded me of one of those Visible Man models where you can see the circulatory system through the clear plastic skin.)

I was looking up at the fountain when someone approached me from behind. I was a little nervous, what with my run-ins with Smyler lately, and I must have spun around quite quickly. The skinny young African-American kid raised his hands. "Sorry. Didn't mean to startle you. Just wanted to know if you could tell me the time."

I looked at my watch. "Ten o'clock on the dot." But when I looked back at him he was smiling in a sort of odd way. "Something wrong?"

"It's me, Bobby. Temuel."

I rolled my eyes. "You don't get out of Heaven much, do you?"

"Why do you say that?"

"You're having too much fun with disguises."

He looked a little hurt. "I'm being careful. You want me to be careful, don't you? You don't want everyone to know what we're doing, do you?"

Why is almost everybody I know so touchy? "No, no, of course not."

"Good." He looked around. We seemed to be the only people in the vicinity. The Mule reached up and made a Zipper appear in the air. (If I haven't explained recently, these are what we use to step Outside, which means outside of Time itself. That's where we do our job, at least the part where we defend the souls of recently dead customers from the spin-doctoring of Hell.) He stepped into it, then beckoned for me to follow.

Unlike most of what I encounter Outside (because I'm usually at deathbeds or accident scenes) the view inside this Zipper wasn't really any different than the view outside. Temuel and I were still alone, the museum was still closed, and it was still night. The only thing different was that the water from the fountain was frozen, thousands of individual drops arrested in midair. It would have been interesting to look at them up close, but my archangel had other ideas.

He reached up and plucked something out of nowhere. When he held it out to me, it was only a spark of light on his palm.

"This is Lameh," he said. "She's a guardian." That was another kind of angel, the kind that spends a lifetime with a human and records everything he or she does and says and thinks, then advocates like me use the information they've collected to defend the soul at judgement.

"Hello, Lameh," I said.

"She doesn't really talk any more," Temuel said. "Not out loud, anyway. She's very old."

Which was an odd thing to say. I'd never heard anyone mention a guardian angel's age.

"But she's going to help you. She knows a lot, and she's going to share it with you."

"Knows a lot about what?"

"About Hell, of course." Temuel did something, and suddenly the spark was smoldering on the end of his index finger. "You need to know much more than you do, or you're going to be spotted as soon as you get there." His face grew stern. "This isn't a game, Bobby."

"I know, I know!" But I couldn't help wondering why this Lameh had so much information about Hell—not the normal college major for a guardian angel. Before I could think of a discreet way to ask, the archangel leaned forward and put his finger to my ear and something jumped into my head. That's the only way I can describe it. It was just as odd as it sounds. Then Temuel took me by the arm and steered me back out of the Zipper again before closing the fiery, midair hole behind us.

"Now go home, Bobby," my boss said. "Go to sleep and Lameh will do the rest. She'll tell you what you need to know, then take you where you need to be."

I knew the feeling of a guardian passing me information, so I wasn't too upset about having something foreign in my thoughts, but I still had questions for Temuel. He, on the other hand, seemed to be finished with the conversation and was climbing the stairs that led out of the plaza. I called to him but he didn't reply. Halfway up he broke into a trot, then a run, as if he were exactly the twelve-year-old kid he looked to be.

"Call me when you get back!" the archangel shouted as he melted into the shadows of the surrounding buildings.

When I got to the Walker house, I didn't bother to check in with G-Man, but just climbed in through one of the unlocked windows and made my way upstairs. The sheet was still there from earlier in the day, and I took it with me as I slid under the bed, then rolled myself in it so it was under me and over me, covering my face and everything else. It was hard to ignore the fact that it was pretty much exactly like the shrouds people get buried in.

Lameh was in my head, just where Temuel had put her, murmuring words I could barely understand, things that sounded more like incantations than useful facts, and which entered me not like knowledge but like a chemical transfer. I did my best to relax and just let it trickle through me. It wasn't like I could actually understand her anyway. She wasn't telling me the names of things or the chief annual exports of various regions of the underworld. Everything she said was just a feeling I had, as though some benign but strange little animal had made a home deep in my skull and was going about its strange animal business there. But every now and then I could perceive things that hadn't been there before, as if I had fallen asleep in a misty rain and now was feeling the water beginning to pool and run down my skin. I did my best to get comfortable.

At last I slipped into drowsy darkness, and for a little while that hard-to-hear voice accompanied me as I settled down, down. For a time I dreamed I was standing outside a door, knowing that the saddest thing in the world was on one side of it, but I didn't know for certain which side the sadness was on, my side or the one I couldn't see.

At last even the dream was gone, and I was alone with the near-silent whisper, sinking slowly into oblivion.

On my way.

On my way down.

All the way down.

interlude

I WAS ADMIRING *a mole on her back, a smooth brown dot just below her shoulder blade, like a fairy-mound in a snow-covered field.*

"So how did Hell know to put that perfect mole right there on your perfect back to make me fall in love with you?"

She snorted. "Right. Like Hell bothered to plan for you, Dollar. That happens to be my own original mole, direct from the Fifteenth Century."

I bent and bestowed a kiss on the icy skin, then moved up to where the first pale wisps of hair grew on her nape. I spent a little while kissing her neck and ears and savoring the smell of her. I'll never be able to describe it, not in its complex entirety, but I will never forget it even if I somehow beat the odds and survive to become a very, very old angel. Which would be a very long time.

After a while I started back down the other direction, rubbing my face against the smooth, chilly bumps of her spine as I descended, stopping to pay my respects at the fairy-hill mole again, then continuing on down her back to the soft protrusion of her tailbone and the cleft of her buttocks. Some Greek guy, Aristotle or Plato or Onassis or someone, said there were five perfect solids, five absolute geometric shapes. To these I would like to add the shape of Caz's ass, because if you're looking for perfection, well, there it is. I think it's a tribute to my maturity that I'd already pretty much fallen in love with her without ever seeing it in the firm, silken flesh. Once I had . . . well, I don't want to overwhelm everyone with sentiment here.

A little while later:

Her slender back stretched out before me like stone smoothed by ocean waves. The curve of her backside was flattened against my groin. As I entered her, she let out a gasp, and I felt her tighten, then freeze like a terrified animal. I paused.

"Does it hurt?" I asked. I let my hands trail down her skin. "Do you want me to stop?"

"I don't know. Yes. No." She tried to look back at me, but the angle was bad. "It's just . . . it feels so vulnerable. I don't . . ." She trailed off. "I'm sorry, I do need to stop. Can you just hold me?"

"Of course." I withdrew gently, then pulled her with me as I collapsed onto the bed, so that the cold length of her back was against my belly. I wrapped my arms around her and pulled her close. "I didn't really want to have more sex, anyway," I said. "I know people say they like it, but I think the whole fad is kind of overrated." I felt her quivering silently against me. Was she laughing? It hadn't been much of a joke.

When she hadn't stopped a few moments later, I asked, "Caz? Are you crying?"

"No." But I could feel the back of my arm getting damp. I leaned away and tried to turn her face toward me, but she wasn't having it. She wiped angrily at her eyes before she'd let me look at her. "Just fuck off, Dollar. Don't say anything."

"What's wrong? Did I do something?"

"No, you didn't. It's not always about you."

"Then what?"

She blinked, scowled. "I'm just not . . . I don't do tenderness very well." She snuck a look at me before burying her head against my arms again. "Arsehole. Don't make me self-conscious, or I'll go back and get my knife and I will cut off your winkie."

Ah, the romance of threatened castration!

I just held her until she felt better, then we kissed and whispered for a little before dozing again. The Countess of Cold Hands had many wounded places, many broken places, but what was astonishing to me is how much I cared about those hurts, how much I wanted to try to make things better for her. That was by far the scariest thing that had ever happened to me.

Caz was a high-ranking official in Hell, she was my sworn, deadly enemy . . . and she had issues. Any remotely sensible angel, even at that late stage of things, would have got up then and run out the door and never looked back. But, of course, I've never been that kind of angel.

thirteen

gob

SO ONE moment I'm lying under somebody's spare bed like a bargain basement King Tut, the next I'm in deep, deep darkness. And things got even stranger after that, because the darkness was bumpy.

I'm not talking texture here, like undercooked oatmeal, I'm talking about the fact that I could feel myself going *bump, bump, bump* as I went down, as though I were being lowered by very clumsy hands. I was in some kind of closet or tiny room. No, I realized as the entire enclosure lurched around me, throwing me toward one of the walls. No, I was in an *elevator*. I was descending to Hell in an elevator, ratcheting down on a squeaky cable toward the ultimate basement floor. I wondered if other new arrivals got different conveyances. Handbaskets, for instance.

I felt different, I realized, and it wasn't just the sudden absence of Lameh the guardian angel (apparently she herself wasn't accompanying me) or the presence of the ideas she'd whispered into my memory. My whole body felt different in ways I couldn't quite understand, and the feeling was so strange that it took me longer than it should have to realize that I must be in a new body as well, that as part of her duties Lameh had housed my soul in something more suited to travel in Hell. A new body and a few new thoughts, too, but the same old hopeless situation.

I found it all very creepy for those first moments, but as the jolting descent continued, my situation just became boring. Then the very boredom, the length and unrelenting sameness of the journey, became creepy again. If it hadn't been for a few bone-rattling jolts and the very occasional smolder of light through the little window that seemed to be in front of my face, I might have been in some kind of endless video loop, the same meaningless five seconds cycling for eternity. I was fairly certain that Hell's high rollers didn't travel in and out this way, since it seemed to be taking hours.

The long descent gave me time to take a little stock. I lifted up my hands to see if I could get some idea what my Hell-body looked like. They seemed darker than usual and the nails were nearly claws, but otherwise not too freaky. There wasn't enough light to make out any of the rest of me, but I bent what I could bend, felt what I could feel. Mostly it seemed pretty normal, although my skin definitely seemed thicker than before, a bit like the rubbery hide of dolphins and orcas.

At last, the elevator shuddered to a halt with a whine of metal on metal. The door banged open. I half-expected to see Housewares or the Children's Shoes department or something, but instead I stood on one side of a narrow expanse of yellow dust, everything above me and beside me lost in shadow. But it was a big space—that much I could tell. Impossibly big. On the far side of the dust loomed the Neronian Bridge, my first glimpse of that impossible span of stone. The feature-less bridge curved up and across the monstrous abyss until it narrowed into near-invisibility over the pit's dark center, illuminated only by the fiery red glow licking through cracks in the walls.

I had enough light now to look at myself. My hands were roughly human, but my skin color (or *colors*, to be more accurate) wasn't even close; what I could see was ashy gray with stripes of black and orange. At the joints the skin hardened into black plates, and when I twisted my arm or leg I could see bright red flesh appearing or disappearing in the crevices as the plates pulled apart. It was a bit unsettling, to tell the truth, so I stopped doing it. I felt my head, which seemed fairly ordi-nary except that where I normally would have had hair I was feeling something more like bristles or even quills. No horns, then. My feet were flat black and leathery, with only one division, between my big toe and the rest of my foot, like Japanese *tabi* socks. If that was standard issue for demons, I could understand where the idea of hooves had come from. No tail, either, which was a bit of a relief. In fact, everything

I could see except for my color and my toes felt and looked at least human-ish. Could have been a lot worse.

I felt different on the inside as well, but it was impossible to know whether all the new sensations flooding into me were because I was wearing a new body or because I was in Hell. Still, I reminded myself, this body might be strange and the skin tones might be *un peu* poison-dart frog, but what was important was that my new demon shape was like an astronaut's suit; it was going to help keep me safe in this very unhealthy place.

I already told you what happened on the Neronian Bridge. Here's what happened when I stepped off it and into the hot, thick mist at the edge of Hell.

I had been expecting something like the old border crossing into East Berlin or maybe even the Black Gate into Mordor, but instead entering the Bad Place was as easy as stepping out of a taxicab—at least at first.

From what the guardian Lameh had planted in my memory, I knew I must be in the Abaddon levels, somewhere in the upper middle of Hell. But if this was upper middle, I knew for sure I didn't want to visit anything lower, because even before I could see any of it, I could smell it. Abaddon *stank*. I don't mean simple, ordinary foul odors like shit or rotting meat. I mean a combination of every foul smell that biology and geology could create, blended into a heady bouquet that combined not only all that a nose would normally detest, but wafts of things so odd and unexpected—like copper and burning hay, just to throw out a couple of examples—that I simply could not get used to it. I never really did, either. The architects of the underworld were, excuse the pun, fiendishly clever: They knew that a single stench, or even a million unchanging stenches, can become familiar after a while. But small changes can keep anything new, no matter how horrible. As long as I was there, I never learned to ignore the stink.

As I left the bridge behind and walked through the swirl of stinging, acid mist, voices filled the hot, damp near-darkness, some human, some animal, some horribly in-between—shrieks, moans, arguments, even tatters of laughter that sounded as though they had been jerked painfully out of whatever spawned them. The noise of the damned.

Pretty much what you'd expect. The air was horribly hot and slimy, muggy as the worst August day in the New York subway times a thousand. Already I could feel the gears grinding at the interface between what my mind expected my body to do—pump gallons of sweat as quickly as possible—and what the demon body actually did, which was nothing. This was normal, you see, and the body I wore treated it that way. One hundred and forty degrees and drippy as a Florida swamp? No problem.

Lovely day, sir and madam. Expect it might rain diarrhea later so I brought my brolly, eh what? Cheerio!

As I emerged from the mists near the bridge I could see for the first time where I actually was.

According to Lameh's briefing, facts now stuck in my brain like some kind of half-forgotten college survey course, Hell is a monstrous cylinder, wide as a small country and almost infinitely high and low, its countless habitations piled in layers like some impossibly huge core sample, the pith of an entire world. Abaddon, like much of Hell, was a sort of self-contained country made up of several levels, and its cities were built almost entirely from the wreckage of other cities.

"Wreckage" sure seemed to describe what lay before me. Stones and mud had been dragged into new arrangements, the rubble of old towers and walls rebuilt into a thousand new shapes to make an immense insect hive with scarcely two shoulders' width of passageway between the stacked structures, and every bit I could see teemed with hellish life. The variety of body shapes was astonishing. Some of them could hardly be called bodies in a normal sense, being little more than moving piles of goo (often disconcertingly full of eyes); others wore the shapes of beasts or half-beasts, or upsetting reworkings of the basic human form. One of them a short distance away from me, crawling up a muddy facade of linked and interconnected holes over flimsy ladders of wood and mud and twisted rawhide, looked like one of those giant Japanese crabs with incredibly long legs, except each of this creature's legs had a row of human hands growing down its length. The head perched on top of the crab shell was human, too, and looked as if it was whistling a tune.

But now I noticed something even stranger than that. Just a few yards behind me in the mist lay the near end of the Neronian Bridge, a path that led both in and *out* of Hell, but nobody on the Hell side seemed to realize the bridge was there. I watched people walk into the mist and go right past the end of the bridge as if it were invisible. Maybe it was, for them. All those people stumbling around in misery only yards from a way out that they couldn't see. Suddenly, I felt sick. If I had not yet truly realized where I was and how bad it was going to be, I began to grasp it then.

There was no sky, of course. The makers of Hell hadn't needed to bow to physical reality any more than the folk who built Heaven, and the very shape of the place was meant to be a constant reminder of confinement and punishment. Parts of Abaddon, however, did stretch very high above me, especially along the walls where crude materials were scaffolded upward many times the height of a man; but above it all was a great roof of jagged, pitted rock. We looked up at the bottom of the level above us, not at sky.

Weird and new as all this was, I had very little time to drink it in, because as soon as I stepped out of the mist, I was surrounded closely by noise and stink, bumped and jostled by some of the ugliest fuckers you've ever seen.

"Worms!" A froggy-looking guy with no back legs waved a sheaf of blackened, muddy sticks in the air. "Crispy like you like 'em!"

"Gin! Swaller of gin, just a spit." This from a guy who looked as though he'd been sawed apart by a very bad magician and put back together by the magician's amateur-surgeon brother. His off-kilter eyes caught me staring. "You, there. You look like you need one. Guarantee you'll not have a clear thought again 'til last lamp. Only a spit!"

Last lamp. Lameh's inserted memories stirred. There was no daylight or moonlight here, so first lamp was lit to signify morning, a second at midday, then one of those was put out and they went back to a single lamp until day's end. (The fiery cracks in the walls, which provided the only brightness after day's end, were called "afterlights.") And a "spit" was an iron coin. The gin was almost certainly made from something horrible and did not tempt me in the least. Hell is remarkably realistic compared to Heaven, which I guess makes sense—real nakedness, real food, real shit, real money, you name it. The fairy lights and muted, pastels of the Celestial City were looking better and better by comparison, and I'd only been in Hell for a few heartbeats.

The gin peddler shuffled nearer to me, offering me a cup that dangled on a piece of rawhide so long that the cup had been dragging in the dirt. I was feeling pretty thirsty, but even if that filthy thing had been the Holy Grail I wouldn't have lifted it to my mouth—I could smell the ghastly odor of the "gin" past the thousands of other stinks of the place, and no oblivion was worth that. (I really thought that then. I changed my mind later. In fact, by the time I'd been in Hell awhile, I was slurping down whatever I could get, just like back in the real world. If there's ever a place where a person needs a stiff drink occasionally, it's Hell. Hell and parts of Oklahoma.)

But the guy with the booze was interrupted before he could finish his spiel, shoved rudely out of the way by something very large that loomed above me like an arriving bus. The newcomer was female, in an Alice's-Duchess sort of way. In short, she looked like a bitter manatee in a wig.

"Git," she rumbled at the gin peddler. "This fine gennulman don't want your swill. He wants a little of the good times, eh? Eh? Am I right?" She leered as she bounced her breasts in her ragged bodice. They looked like plastic bags of pale gravy and blue spaghetti. "Nothing like what *I'll* give you for a spit, lordship. I'll clean your gulleys and gutters, I will. Blow the ashes right out your chimney!" She hiked up her skirt to show me what was under the dress. If a hairless horse had as many legs as a spider, with a cruel parody of female genitalia at the juncture of each sagging, scarred pair of thighs, then . . . no, you don't really need to know. It was all I could do not to vomit. "Oooh, lovely," she said, reaching for my prick.

I suddenly realized I was naked. I mean, *really* realized. I turned and dove into the crowd, for the moment not caring what other horrors I was rubbing against.

"Asswipe! You won't find any prettier between here and the Uppers," she bawled after me, cantering awkwardly in place as the bodies of her fellow Hell-citizens pressed back around her. "What you think, that you're one of the high boys? Go on and find out what they'd do to you, you stuck up little turdball!"

I had to keep moving, I now understood, because when you stopped, things started to crawl on you. So I pushed on through the crowds, through the filth and the howls and the unending horror-zoo, past things that cringed from me and things that snapped at me, past beggars by the dozens with raised hands like mutant starfish, begging, pleading, weeping tears of blood and other unpleasant liquids. Everybody was scarred. Everybody was crippled, and not in accidental ways—these were *punishments*. It should have become easier to take after a while, the constant flow of maimed creatures, the hopeless and the inhuman, but it didn't, and wouldn't for a long time. I picked up a large rock and carried it in my hand, just to have some kind of a weapon.

Still, as I fought my way through the crowd in search of a way out of this level, or at least a place where the shoving crowds weren't so terrible, I saw that there were things happening here in the labyrinth of Abaddon that had nothing to do with me, or even with punishing people: makeshift shops with actual workers, taverns, houses, and other signs of civilization, however grotesque. I confess I was surprised. People actually lived here in Hell. They sold things, they struggled to be able to eat and sleep safely. But where were the punishments? Not the punishment of simply existing in all this hateful, overwhelming squalor, but the actual punishments?

Then it struck me, and of all the ugly things I had experienced since stepping off the Neronian Bridge, none hit me harder. This horror around me wasn't what Hell was *really* like. Not by a long shot. Lameh had said something about the levels of Abaddon being in the upper parts of Hell, not up where the lords of Hell like Eligor and Prince Sitri made their homes, but not the deeps either. In levels far below us in the great darkness, in the worst of the boiling heat of which this was the merest balmy outskirt, where the souls I had heard on the bridge were made to scream those mind-freezing screams, that was where the *real* Hell lay. Horrible as this place was, an insult to every sense, a horror to every thought—still, by infernal standards I was in the pleasant suburbs. And if I were captured, I would never see anything this charming again.

At that moment I came very, very close to simply giving up.

Lameh's mind-whisperings had helped me with some of the geography of Hell but hadn't given me anything like a detailed idea of how it all fit together, let alone an actual map. In fact, I doubted there could be such a thing, outside of a few broad strokes, because just during the short time I'd been in Abaddon I'd seen a half-dozen passageways made and destroyed. The place grew and changed constantly, like a living organism, a coral reef or something, although the work was done by demons and damned. Between one lamp and the next, a road became two or was filled in; houses were built on top of other houses until they all collapsed, then more were built atop the rubble. Entire neighborhoods caught fire or were shaken down by the intermittent tremors, only to be rebuilt in different form for new inhabitants, often right on the still-screaming bodies of the injured. And they might keep shrieking that way forever, because death can't release you if you're already dead.

I had a couple of places I needed to go, but no idea of how to get to them, except that they were both somewhere above me in the great stack of infernal levels. And if you think it's hard to get directions in a strange city, try Hell. Actually, no, don't bother.

No map, no directions. How was I going to do what I had to do?

As it turned out, Abaddon had an answer for me.

I was standing in a sewage culvert at the outskirts of one of Abaddon's maze of settlements, staring up at a depressingly familiar piece of outer wall when it happened. I was exhausted and frustrated, because I had just realized I'd checked out this area the previous day. In other words, I'd got lost again. It seemed I'd have to hike the whole circumference of the place to find a way out, which might take years just on this level.

Something brushed against me and lingered longer than it should have. I didn't hesitate—I didn't want to be attacked *or* solicited—so I swung my arm hard at whatever was touching me. I heard a grunt and something tumbled to the ground at my feet, felled far more easily than I would have expected.

I looked down and saw a very small shape huddled below me in the churned, excremental mud of the street, a naked creature not much larger than an organ grinder's monkey, hard to separate from the muck underneath. Passersby were stepping on it as often as over it, some of them huge, some of them with hard hooves. I could hear the little thing squeaking, not like something crying but like something desperately trying to catch a breath, so I steeled myself, reached down, and yanked the little bundle up onto its feet. It was only as I turned away again, this small humane act completed, that I saw that the little whatever-it-was held my weapon-stone in his long-fingered hands. The little fucker had picked my pocket, and I didn't even have a pocket.

I snatched back the stone, then pulled the thief into an eddy of the crowd where I could look him over. He had big, round eyes but hardly any nose, his limbs were shrunken and bent with what in the normal world I would have taken for the aftereffects of scurvy, and he was matted all over with pale hair. He was surprisingly strong, though—I had to keep a tight grip on him to keep him from squirming away. The widemouthed, primate face betrayed an intelligence that was enough like my own to make my borrowed heart sink inside my borrowed breast.

"You stole my rock," I said.

He tried to look innocent, but succeeded only in looking more than ever like something that was going to pee on your rug as soon as you turned away. "Nuh," he said. "Didn't. Lemme go. Bilgebark's calling." His voice was high-pitched, like a child's.

"Who's that? Who's Bilgebark?"

His dark eyes went even wider. He was astonished by my ignorance. "The minder, he is, the big hand, big man. Around Squitters Row, anywise. He'll come after, I'm not back to the works by afters." Something about the way he spoke made me even more certain he was a child. His eyes kept darting to either side, and although he'd quit fighting, his muscles were still tense in my grip. If he couldn't convince me to let go of him, this kid was going to do something to get free, probably something violent, but he was going to try to talk his way out first. I liked that. "What's your name?" I asked.

He slitted his eyes as if I'd blazed a flashlight in his face. "Don't got one."

"What do you do? Where do you live? Do you have a family?"

The eyes crept wider still at this, as though he was having trouble keeping command of himself in the face of such bizarre questions. "Don't got one. Live at the works." He licked his lips, then asked nervously, "You Murder?" He saw I didn't understand. "Murder Seck?"

It finally dawned on me that he was talking about the Murderers Sect, armed demon guards who functioned like mercenary soldiers. In the more built-up areas they were pretty much Hell's police.

"No. Not me," I said. "Not Murder Sect, just . . . ordinary."

He tried something new. "Let me loose. Gotcher rock back, yeah? And I bite." He showed me his grin, which was indeed made up of surprisingly clean, even, pointy little teeth, like you might see in a fish or a frog.

But I wasn't letting him off that easily. "I need someone to help me find my way out of here." It was a risk to trust anyone, even a child, but I'd run out of other ideas. "I'm lost."

The little monkey-boy considered. Although I could see he was genuinely thinking about it, I could tell he wasn't ready to give up on just running for it, either.

If you learn to hide your tells better, I decided, *you're going to be good, kid.* But then I thought *Here?* and *Compared to what?* and the whole idea suddenly just made me really sad.

"Three spits," he said at last.

Once he started to bargain I knew I had him. We settled on a deal where I'd feed him while he was with me and give him an iron spit at the end, when I found my way out of this level of Abaddon. I didn't have a spit, of course, but I'd find a way to change that somehow.

"This way," he said, and headed off without looking to see whether I was following.

I stayed alert as the kid began to lead me out of Abaddon, in case he was actually leading me to his big friend Bilgebark, who would then beat me to death and relieve me of my prized rock. That was if you could get beaten to death in Hell, which didn't fit in with what I knew about the place. Of course, children in Hell didn't really make sense, either. I was depressingly sure I had all kinds of disturbing new experiences in front of me.

The kid and I didn't talk any more. He seemed to like it that way. But Monkey-boy kept sneaking glances in my direction as we walked, as if still trying to make up his mind about me. Dogs don't like direct eye contact, and lots of other mammals (including some humans) don't like it either, so I just kept looking forward at where we were going, at the endless passing parade of distorted bodies and unbearably various faces.

"Got one," my companion said at last. He was no longer looking at me, but staring resolutely ahead just like I was.

"One? One what?"

"Name."

I considered this for a moment. "And what is it?"

"Gob."

I nodded. I almost said, "Nice to meet you," out of sheer habit, but realized that probably didn't get said a lot around here. Although the street around us was as disgustingly, stenchfully crowded as before, and just as noisy, there was a different quality now to the silence between the kid and me. Something was settled, at least for the time being.

I had made my first friend in Hell. Sort of.

fourteen

sinners for sale

M Y EYES were burning and I was spitting out foul dust. We had been climbing through termite-nest dwellings on Abaddon's outskirts for a few hours, miles of piled mud, filth, and broken stone, but still hadn't found a way to the next level.

"How far until we get out of here?" I asked.

"Baddon? Dunno." Gob contorted his small face into a mask of thoughtfulness. "Never been to the very uppest of it. Long. Far."

I cursed. Swearing in Hell seemed a bit like coals to Newcastle, but it was an old habit. "And what's beyond?"

"Highwards?"

I decided he meant "upward." "Both ways, if you know."

Gob seemed to have decided I was some variety of harmless crazy. It didn't make for loyalty, but like most children, even immortal ones, he was game to hang around as long as things interested him. "Down below Baddon, that's Airbus. Black all the time. Don't go there."

Erebus. The highest of the Shadow Levels. Lameh had given me enough information to know I definitely wanted to steer clear. Erebus was where the serious mayhem began, the levels of torment and despair. "Above?"

"Above Baddon? Dunno. Think next is Asdull Medders, where the Sinner Market is."

I perked up a little. Archangel Temuel's errand was to someone named Riprash who worked at the Sinners' Market, which meant that

Gob must be talking about Asphodel Meadows (a place which, even though it was in the middle levels of Hell, was probably going to be much grimmer than its charming little name). For the first time I felt a little hope that I might actually accomplish something useful. Caz would almost certainly be with Eligor in the uppermost levels far, far above us, in Hell's equivalent of Park Avenue. But if I found Riprash I could discharge my obligation to my boss and maybe even get some help. "Gob, could you help me find my way to the Sinners' Market?"

The kid looked me up and down. With his straggly hair, scrawny limbs, and massive eyes, he looked like an anorexic PowerPuff Girl. "Maybe. Cost you another spit."

"Sure." Since I didn't have a single spit to give him at the moment, I had no problem promising a bonus.

"Thinking 'bout it," he said as I got wearily to my feet.

He was a hard, cold little thing, my guide. I'd been poking bits of information out of him as we traveled through the narrow, crowded byways of Abaddon. As it turned out, unlike most of Hell's inhabitants, Gob really had been born here. Hell's citizens broke down into three basic types: the Neverborn, who were angels and other high beings condemned here by God; the Damned (which kind of speaks for itself as a category); and the small leftovers called Ballast. Gob was one of these, a child whose mother had been sent to Hell while he was still in her belly. She had, by some unpleasant linkage of their souls, given "birth" to him here, surrounded by screams and horror-mask faces, then later wandered off to explore her own damnation. Ballast—the extra weight in the hold of a ship, something nobody bothers to save when the vessel is sinking. That was Gob. He'd grown up motherless in the anarchy of Abaddon's filth, with no family but the overseer who bossed him and his little fellow thieves and murderers. As I was coming to understand, though, Gob had something the others didn't. Not kindness, or even concern for anyone else—that doesn't really grow in Hell—but I think maybe curiosity.

He was a strange kid, by any standard. Each night, whenever we determined it was night, he made a bed for himself in the same animal way, lying down in dirt or weeds or even prickling nettles, which he scarcely seemed to notice. First he would sniff (he could never explain why, except the spot had to smell "right") then he would lie on his side, knees to his chin, and slide and roll around until he had made a little hollow of whatever was underneath him. Then he'd arrange himself back into the original chin-to-knees position, close his eyes, and fall asleep as quickly as it takes me to say it. Sometimes when Gob slept he made little animal sounds, wordless whimpers and choked squeals that in his dreams or memories might have been full-throated screams. I tried not to imagine what kind of things chased him in his sleep.

When he was awake he was pretty entertaining too, in a sad sort of way. He jumped at any noise as if he had heard a gunshot. When we stopped to rest during daylight hours (if you could dignify the sullen red light with that name) Gob didn't really sit down or relax, but just perched on something or stood and waited impatiently for me to get moving again. He didn't try to convince me not to rest, but he didn't like pausing during the day. Always aware, always shifting his body in small ways to watch his surroundings, constantly ready to run away or fight, he reminded me of some of the things I've seen about African child soldiers, little boys who had gone pretty much from their mother's breasts to committing random homicides.

Hell must be a lot like being born in the middle of a war, I decided: there was no chance for anything better to develop. I could almost imagine Gob as a little machine, a thing that had survived intact this long because it did exactly the right things and would keep doing those things even if it was miraculously transplanted into some other situation, like San Judas. I'd known a lot of street kids, but almost all of them had something that showed they were human, a shallow loyalty to each other if nothing else. Hell must grind that out of everyone, I decided. What relationship could survive being worn away over thousands of years of big and little torments?

Hell is a big cylinder. Imagine somebody dug a hole down into hardened lava, all the way down to where it gets squishy and murderously hot again. Now, remember those cake tins Grandma Flossie used to send you at Christmas with ugly-ass fruitcakes in them, year after year? Take a near infinite number of those tins and stack them in the hole on top of each other, so the bottom is in molten goo and the top of each tin is the bottom of the next. That's pretty much the infernal layout. There are cities on every level but also lots of wilderness roamed by bandits, monsters, and worse stuff. Remember, it's Hell, so they made it big. Even with the more enlightened sentencing laws of the last hundred years or so, it still has to hold billions upon billions.

And I had to get to the top, or near it, to reach Caz. I knew there was a sort of elevator system—they call them "lifters"—that ran right up through the middle of Hell's layers like the string of a necklace, but that was like knowing there's an elevator in Montana when you're on the Oregon coast. The famous rivers of Hell, Styx and Acheron and the others, also provide a way to travel, but first you have to be near a river, which we weren't. So at least while I handled my boss Temuel's errand, I had to make my way up through Hell one slice at a time. Even with Gob's help, it took a couple of days just to find our way to the next level of Abaddon.

To my surprise, Gob decided to stick with me once we reached the next level, a dismal wasteland of stone and mud and smoking sulfur so godawful even the damned avoided the place. There were settlements, of course, but they were like the smallest, poorest, hottest, driest cattle stations in the Australian outback, if someone had pounded on them for a week with a fifty ton hammer made of compacted fly shit.

Don't get me wrong: Abaddon was better than most of Hell, but it was still fucking horrible. I don't know how long we climbed through its levels, from one parched landscape the color of dried shit to another, past ugliness and misery so vast I stopped paying attention, but it must have been at least a week before we found ourselves somewhere different.

Asphodel Meadows was more open than Abaddon, perhaps because the great stone ceiling seemed farther away here, and it was certainly less dry and desolate, but it made up for dry with boiling swamps that could only be crossed by walking on bobbing, leathery leaves, some of which looked (and were, it turned out) more like Venus fly traps than lily pads. We spent days in the weird, twilight swamps, sloshing through mud and kicking our way through thorny vines, dodging murderous flora and fauna and generally besieged by ugly buzzing insects the size of sparrows. To add to the charm, many of the brackish ponds in Asphodel Meadows were surrounded by the bodies of the damned, purple and bloated but still twitching. Poison didn't kill you in Hell, it just made you suffer and suffer and suffer.

What terrible thirst had driven them down to drink from such obviously unsafe waters? I patted the canteen-bag Gob had stolen for us somewhere back in Abaddon, which we had filled the last time at a clean but unpleasant-tasting spring bubbling up at the edge of the Meadows. The bag had clearly been made from the innards of something or someone I didn't want to think about, but right now the water in it was all that kept us from joining those bulging near-cadavers, some of them split and venting gases but still not managing to die. I couldn't exactly feel good looking at these victims of thirst, but I sure could feel grateful I wasn't one of them.

I was afraid I was beginning to understand Hell.

The flat leaves felt as treacherous to walk on as floating plywood, not to mention that plywood doesn't bite, but it kept us out of the frothily poisonous water. The fly traps generally left us alone—we were probably a bit too big to digest—but a few of the bolder ones decided we were worth a try. I pulled Gob out of one of them as it folded on him, just before the pencil-sized spines that served as the thing's teeth sank into his flesh. His leg was all covered with hissing goo. The stuff splashed me as well and it burned like battery acid. When we staggered off the last leaf a few moments later and onto a patch of comparatively dry ground, we immediately threw ourselves down and rolled in the mud like water buffalo, desperate to stop the pain. It took a long time to rub the toxic sap off us, but even so, Gob barely made a sound. That amazed me, since pieces of his skin were coming off his leg in tatters. It was obvious that the crybaby got kicked out of most people down here pretty quickly.

Out of the swamps at last, we climbed talus slopes of spiky, salty crystals and even staggered through a forest of dead trunks in a flurry of caustic snow. Yes, it snows in Hell. All that "until Hell freezes over" stuff is nonsense. It snows in Hell all the time. It just isn't frozen water. I won't spend a lot of time talking about it because it's disgusting, but I traveled through quite a few snowstorms in Hell. Some of them were acid, some were flurries of frozen piss, some of the things that piled up in drifts as we staggered through the gusts weren't even liquids. But all of them stung.

By the time we'd slept three or four more times, the empty spaces of the Asphodel Meadows began to resemble something a little closer to their name: dark, boggy moors covered with pale flowers. Fog crept in as we squelched across them, eventually obscuring the landscape almost completely. In the mist I could see shapes, many of them upright, but if they saw us they never let on. Instead they wandered among the asphodel stalks, plucking the gray blooms and stuffing them in their mouths as tears dribbled down their cheeks. Eventually, I managed to work out from Gob's answers that everybody in Hell ate the asphodel flowers in some form, baked into bread or flat cakes (I'd had a few of these; they were bland, even bitter, but mostly unremarkable) but that those who ate the flowers raw experienced the sins of their lives over and over, like a bad acid trip. Worst of all, though, was that the more they consumed and the more they wallowed in their own terrible mistakes and cruelties, the more of it they wanted. The few asphodel-eaters I saw up close had staring eyes and twitching fingers, like Hieronymus Bosch crackheads.

It was hard to remember that, compared to many, these creatures were among Hell's most fortunate, the few who'd managed to find a place of relative freedom for themselves somewhere between an eternity of slavery in the houses of the demon lords and an eternity in the torture pits.

Eternity? That still stuck in my craw. I knew that some of these people must have been the worst sort of folks when they were alive, murderers, rapists, child molesters. I honestly didn't mind them getting even a few centuries of hellfire, but . . . forever? Even if the damned remembered who they were and what they'd done to get there (unlike me and my angelic friends at the Compasses) how meaningful could any punishment be after a million years? How many of these walking phantoms could even remember what they'd done? And what about the ones like Caz, who had been driven to their crimes by others? She'd killed her husband, sure, but if anyone had deserved to get stabbed into a bloody hash, that guy had.

I couldn't stop thinking about it as we trudged through those misty, treacherous meadows, past rows of nodding, death-pale blossoms, the little damned Ballast-boy following at my heels like a feral dog, perhaps having the most fun he'd ever had in his squalid, miserable (but still nearly endless) life. God knows I tried to stop dwelling on the horror of it, but the unwanted thought kept coming back to me again and again.

Eternity? Really?

We began to see signs of life beside the gloomy, solitary flower-eaters and the endless mist.

The first evidence of civilization was that the faint track Gob had been following finally became something more substantial, a road trod through the swampy grasses and down to the stony soil. We began to see houses, too, although it's ridiculous to use such a word to describe the mean little piles of reeds and stones. Perhaps the inhabitants lived off the flower-eaters somehow, robbed them or sold things to them. Perhaps they harvested flowers and sent them by boat up the crap-colored streams that were beginning to be more common. I didn't know and I didn't care, because now I could see the walls of a city in the distance, which had to be Cocytus Landing, and that was where the hard part of my journey would begin.

All I'd had to do so far was keep myself moving forward and avoid obvious mistakes, but now I would be making contact with this guy Riprash, the demon I was supposed to give Temuel's curious message. I would rather have gone straight for Caz, but I didn't dare leave the Mule's errand for later: I had a feeling that when it was time to leave Hell, I might be leaving in a hurry. So Sinners' Market first, then, if I survived, on to Pandaemonium, the capital of Hell, a mere few hundred levels or so straight up, the demons and freaks getting thicker around me with every step.

It took us half a day to find the ford over one of the Cocytus's last tributaries, a narrow spot where bug-plated demons pulled an ancient barge back and forth on ropes across the steaming river. When I couldn't produce any money for the fare, one of them kindly offered to take Gob instead, but we settled on a small cup of my blood, which they acquired with the quick slash of a dirty blade. My demon-blood looked blacker than human blood, but that might just have been the weird light.

If I'd thought Abaddon was ugly, I was going to have to find a new word for Cocytus Landing, which looked like it had been discarded next to the river by some glacier with a grudge. You've heard of shantytowns, right? Well, Cocytus Landing was pretty much a shanty *city*, as cheaply and dangerously constructed as the meanest hovels of Abaddon but on a much grander scale, a monstrous, multilevel, walled slum centered on its river docks.

The first difference I noticed between this and Abaddon was the industriousness. Not everybody was working, of course, but a major chunk of the populace seemed to be doing *something*, whether hauling spiky logs on creaky wooden carts, or whipping the slaves and other beasts of burden who pulled those carts, or loading and unloading the bizarre ships that bobbed at anchor all along the docks. Visiting Heaven was like a century tripping on E, all laughing and singing and dancing and not caring or even remembering. Hell was gritty and dirty, but things actually worked. The damned made things, struggled for existence, struggled to avoid pain. They ate and shat and fornicated just like people. But they would suffer forever.

As we made our way along the river toward the walls, I watched a stunning variety of ships on their ways in and out of port. Many looked like they'd been turned into boats only as an afterthought, weird arrangements of canvas, wood, and what looked like bones that didn't seem like they could possibly float. It struck me then that I hadn't seen any technology more advanced than you could have found in a European city during the low Middle Ages. All work was done by the brute strength of laborers, occasionally aided by the power of water or fire. I saw water wheels spinning along several of the river's branches, and buildings that might have been mills or foundries looming crookedly beside the wheels. I couldn't help wondering if this technological embargo was a rule of the Highest or some bizarre quality of Hell itself.

At the city gates, we joined the crowd funneling past a couple of dozen squat, muscular demons from the Murderers Sect. These soldiers seemed to be examining the passersby carefully, so I dragged Gob into the shadow of a tall peddler's wagon and we went through the gate that way, out of the driver's sight but picking up bits of spilled rubbish and putting it back on the cart as if it was ours.

The streets of Cocytus Landing were almost as narrow as the most claustrophobic back rows of Abaddon, but many, many times more crowded, and not just with sullen slaves and demon overseers, either. Many of the creatures we saw seemed to live their lives right out in public, eating, drinking, fucking, and fighting, often in the middle of the street, while the rest of the city's inhabitants just swept around whatever was going on, as if the squirming bodies were stones in the middle of a fast-flowing river. As I looked closer I noticed that the folk making themselves so free seemed to be the demonic overseers more than the damned, although it wasn't always easy to tell which was which in that zoo of exotic, disgusting bodies.

We waded on through the ugly crush, past creatures with faces like sad turtles and bewildered insects, creatures with crippled bodies and skin covered with running sores, even a few things that were almost nothing *but* one large running sore. The entire city breathed screams and moans around us like the horns of a bad downtown rush hour. Just as I was convinced I couldn't take another moment of it, I spotted a great pool of torchlight ahead of us that seemed to be the source of the loudest cries, and I guessed that must be our destination, Sinners' Market, the place where slaves were bought and sold.

Just ignore this other shit and find Riprash, I reminded myself, like I was calming a child. *Then you can go after Caz, remember? Just keep taking steps.*

I could almost see her in front of me then, a small, shining thing against all the darkness of this dark place, and for a moment I was calm. I had something to do. All this horror was for a reason. I couldn't afford to forget that.

Weirdly, as I thought of her, a noise rose above the caterwauling crowds, a thin thread of music, slow and mournful. It was a woman's voice, or at least something female, and the wordless melody was so old and simple and arresting that I'm sure it had been sung beside some great river on Earth thousands of years ago and is probably still heard today; some ageless lament of women squatting in the muck beside the Indus or the Nile, washing their clothes. Here, it probably came from some toad-thing who had been in Hell so long she couldn't remember the Euphrates mud between her toes, but somehow she still remembered the tune, and croaked it to herself as she patted together cakes of excrement to dry and burn for fuel.

It gave me chills. It was the most human thing I'd heard either in Hell *or* in Heaven, and for a moment I almost completely forgot where I was. Then somebody got angry and poked out someone's eye right next to me, and the moment was over.

The Sinners' Market is about as nice a place as it sounds. It's largely held under the roofed perimeter of a ruined and ramshackle stone coliseum, although during my visit the huge open area in the middle was being used as well. What was sold in the market was . . . well, sinners, to be used as slaves.

Most of these shackled damned were already slaves, and would go from one kind of specialized slavery to another. But just because these were valuable possessions—many of whom had been trained to do specific jobs or even physically altered so they could do them better—didn't mean they were treated well. I had been seeing how the ordinary folk of Hell treated each other, and it was truly horrifying, but now I was seeing what organized cruelty looked like, and the sheer weight of Hell as an institution suddenly became clear to me. I would see worse things in Hell, and God knows I'd suffer worse things, but nothing ever stepped on my spirit as badly as those first few minutes in the clanking, begging, wailing, and roaring of the Sinners' Market. It was like coming to the end of some very long scientific article and then finding the summary: *The universe is shit.*

We asked around about Riprash, and at last got an answer from a cold, cat-eyed female creature whose slaves all looked like children or other small, innocent things; as I walked past, they set up a pathetic wailing from their cages, pleading, barking, mewing. As the she-demon impatiently told me where to find Riprash, I couldn't help noticing that Gob was keeping his eyes very focused for once, watching me and nothing else. Maybe the bruised and bleeding children in cages hit a little too close to home.

Halfway around the lopsided stadium bowl, we found the large stall the cat-thing had described. A crude sign declared, "Gagsnatch Bros., Dealers in Offal and Slaves." I guessed that the Gagsnatch Brothers must be the single obese body with two arguing heads that were bickering with each other and several other demons at the rear of the stall. I didn't want the owner, though, just his overseer, so I made my way through the crush of stinking bodies, doing my best to ignore what was actually going on as I looked for Temuel's contact. It was kind of like a spy movie but with a lot more human feces.

I found my quarry attended by several smaller demons as he inspected a crew of newly arrived slaves, creatures whose humanity had been so thoroughly tormented out of them that they made no whimper and didn't even look up, but just crouched in the dirt, wheezing. I couldn't help thinking that if the infernal Adversary himself were defeated this afternoon, there would still be work here for a million angels for a million years just to begin to repair the damage. As it was, though, the Highest apparently wasn't feeling too disposed to mercy, or the Adversary was truly beyond forgiveness. Either way, nothing was going to change here until the end of time.

Riprash was a massive ogre twice my size, with huge flat toes and fingers and a face that would have been phenomenally ugly even without the scar, which I'll describe in a second. He was hairless except for bristling brows, with a smashed gourd of a nose and huge blocky teeth that looked like they could crush stone. But the scar was really something else, if "scar" is even the right word: Riprash had a gouge chopped into his head from temple to nose that had obliterated one eye and covered the socket with scar tissue. I say "chopped" because the weapon was still lodged in there—an ax blade, it looked like. I could see the dull chunk of metal resting right in the meat of the ogre's brain, because the hole in his skull had never closed. You get the point. Riprash wasn't pleasant to look at.

I waited until he stopped growling at his underlings. Two of them turned and scurried away, but the third hesitated. It was a hairy little thing like an upright and slightly pear-shaped cat, with an unpleasantly near-human face, and it was looking right at me—really getting an eyeful. Whatever its interest was, I had lots of reasons for not wanting attention, so I glared at the bug-eyed little thing in my best Hellish Nobility Offended kind of way until it got nervous and hurried after the others.

Riprash had noticed me. "What do you want?"

He didn't sound either interested or friendly, but I wasn't going to get uppity with the hired help, especially not help that weighed more than my car back home. Lameh's implanted memories suggested I now looked or smelled (or whatever) like middling Hell nobility, a sort of white-collar demon. That meant I probably outranked this Riprash guy. Yeah, in theory. But he was the strong right hand of an important and rich slave merchant. The stall was one of the biggest at the market, long as a football field and crowded as an Arabian bazaar. He clearly didn't feel any need to kowtow, and I took my cue from that.

"Talk faster," he said. "Busy day."

"If you're Riprash, I need to talk to you."

He gave me a look of calculated irritation, but didn't fold me up like a dirty hankie, which is what he looked like he wanted to do. "So talk."

"I think . . ." Nobody seemed to be paying attention to us, but if my message wasn't as innocuous as it sounded, I wasn't certain I wanted to take the risk of anyone even seeing me deliver it. "I need to speak to you in private."

His thick lip curled. "Piss on you, my lord. If you've got a bribe to offer, talk to my master, not me. I won't cheat on him, not for all the treasure and cooze in Pandaemonium."

"No, no!" I said. "It's not a bribe, it's a message. And not for Gagsnatch. *For you.*" I did everything but waggle my eyebrows like Groucho to help him get the subtext. "I just think it would be safer . . ."

I was interrupted by shouting from behind me, voices raised above even the roar of Gagsnatch Brothers ordinary chorus of bellows and howls. As we turned to look, a scrawny demon dashed toward us from the nearest knot of workers, his batlike ears laid flat against his skull in alarm.

"Boss says look sharp, Master Riprash! Make sure everything's on the up!"

"Why?" Riprash didn't seem to have many other facial expressions besides Annoyed and Dangerous.

"The Commissar's showed up of a sudden. He and his lot are poking their noses in all over. They're going from stall to stall looking for somebody."

"Commissar Niloch?" The ogre clearly wasn't happy to hear it, and now I wasn't happy either. The bat-eared minion skittered away to spread the word to other parts of the large establishment. "What in the name of Astaroth's swinging udders is *he* up to? Old Flaps and Scratches usually doesn't make a show of himself until later in the season when he comes for his tribute."

Now the stir had become more general as a few helmeted Murderers Sect guards came swaggering into the stall at the far end. When I quickly turned away again, Riprash was looking at me. He must have seen the panic in my eyes.

"You don't want to be seen by Murder Sect, do you?" His remaining eye roved from me to little Gob and back again. "Not a friend of the Commissar's, I take it?"

I didn't dare say a word, because almost anything I could say suddenly struck me as potentially the wrong thing. Heavily armed demon soldiers were shouldering into the stall in bunches now. The slavers and even the slaves had fallen silent, nobody wanting to attract attention, and there was no way I could walk out again unnoticed. This wounded giant had my immortal soul in his huge hands, and there was nothing more I could do.

"Over here, then." Riprash folded a giant hand over my shoulder and shoved me into a stumbling trot toward the back of the stall, where all kinds of cages had been dumped. Most were empty, but one was so full of slaves that arms and legs stuck out between every bar, and even the growing sense of terror settling over Gagsnatch's establishment had not stopped their quiet noises of pain. "These need to be washed. Nobody with sense will want to look for you there." The ogre fumbled a huge key out of his ragged garment and threw open the door of the cage, dealt bonebreaking blows to the few prisoners foolish enough to try to leave, then shoved me in. Gob scrambled in on top of me. I say "on top" because there was literally nowhere else to go. The entire cage, not much bigger than an old-fashioned phone booth, was crammed with the hideous, filthy bodies of damned slaves. They were so beaten down I heard only a few snarls of complaint as I pushed as far into the middle as I could get. The two or three prisoners who had been displaced by my entrance were only too happy to move back to the bars and the comparatively fresh air to be found just outside of a slave cage in the middle of Hell.

I got into an awkward crouch so that I had less chance of being crushed and a slightly better angle to see what was going on. Our end of the stall was rapidly filling with demon guards, most of them closer in size to Riprash than to me. The Commissar's soldiers moved with the grace of water buffalos on fire, knocking over everything that wasn't staked into the ground, stepping on everything that was, and yanking on the neck chains of uncaged slaves until I heard vertebrae snap. It was like watching a troop of baboons investigating a structure made of twigs and meat. Yet even these inhuman monstrosities turned up their noses at our cage and did no more than jab with their spears at a few of the more exposed slaves, just for fun.

After awhile the soldier-demons got bored with pulling things apart and began to wander out of the stall. I was beginning to feel I might actually survive the afternoon when a new group stomped into view, looking like nastier and more serious versions of the first thugs, and immediately began throwing slaves and slavemasters alike to the floor of the stall. Then the Commissar walked in.

I swear I felt something like a shock of cold air before I saw him, along with the faint smell of vinegar and something rotting, then the Commissar came into my view and paused before the only employee of Gagsnatch Brothers still standing, namely Riprash.

The newcomer was not one of those demons who waste a lot of energy trying to look like anything human. In fact, at first I could barely tell where Commissar Niloch began and everything else left off, because he was covered with rattling, bone-white tendrils that curled out of his black armor like stray hairs, making him look a little like one of those fancy, frilly seahorses you only see in aquariums. His face was a bit like a seahorse's too, long, angular, and bony, but no seahorse ever had such evil little blood-drop eyes.

"Oh, my good heart, what have we here?" Niloch was almost as tall as Riprash, but despite his armor and helmet, the rattling bone-tendrils made him seem as fragile as the slenderest branching coral. Still, I don't think anyone could have looked at the Commissar's hideous, gleeful face and imagined mere strength would defeat such a creature. "Oh, my charitable works! What is this? A bottom-dweller, a shit-sucker, who does not bow to the Commissar of Wings and Claws, master of all the Meadows and beyond? But why would someone thwart me when all I wish to do is kindness?" He extended an insec-toid arm crusted by a whorl of horns. "Why do you insult me, fellow? Why do you hate your rightful master so?"

Even listening to his lilting voice made my stomach turn over. It was as if someone had taken the skin off your favorite grandfather and made a balloon, then let the air squeak out of it in musical bursts. I would gladly have burrowed down into the dung and stayed there forever to avoid that bony, clicking thing noticing me.

Riprash, I guess, was made of sterner stuff. "I waited until you were close enough to show you proper respect, Commissar." The ogre low-ered his vast body to one knee, but I could tell he didn't like this Niloch much.

"Ah, to be sure, to be sure. And what slave would not risk the anger of the Lord of Wings and Claws to protect his employer's slaves from being disturbed? What is it you attend so closely here?" Niloch's jaw, a hinge of horn at the base of his equine skull, splayed to reveal a row of teeth that seemed too different and too long for even that strange mouth. I guessed it was a smile. "What property of your master's are you so diligently protecting, hmmm?" He took a step forward, his legs creaking and sawing as his tangles of bone rubbed together. "What could be worth keeping even from beloved Niloch? Hmmmm?" Another step forward, until the rattling thing was only a few paces from the cage where I squatted with the other terrified prisoners. Riprash started to get up, but Niloch pointed at him. "Do you object to my inspection? That is a serious matter, slave. Souls have gone into the holes between stars over less." The fluting voice rose. "Would you obstruct Commissar Niloch at his rightful duties?"

For a moment, against all sense, I prayed that Riprash would do something crazy, run, shout, hit the Commissar in his bony face, anything that might cause enough ruckus to allow Gob and me to escape. Then I remembered that we were locked in a cage. Even if they burned the stall to the ground, we weren't going anywhere.

Riprash made a rumbling noise deep in his chest, but didn't say anything. Then his big head dipped. He stayed on one knee. "Course not, Lord Commissar. Our place is yours."

"Ah, lovely." Niloch spat a long thread of something onto the ground. "That's all right then. I'll just come over and have a closer look at these, shall I?" And so he did, stinking of death and vinegar.

interlude

"YOU NEVER told me what you do for entertainment in Hell."
She rolled away and lit a cigarette. "And I doubt I ever will. You don't really care, anyway. You just want to hear all the horrid bits. It's not like that. At least, not always. Not all of it."

"Whoa! Peace, milady Countess. Honestly, I just wanted to know. I'm a curious guy."

She peered over her shoulder at me. I couldn't tell if she was ready to be nice again or not. She was funny that way, I could tell. Under that perfect, ultra-cool surface she was full of broken places. They say that's why cats get abscesses—their skin heals so quickly it often heals right over an infected wound. Caz was a bit feline that way.

Still, she looked so fucking lovely when she stretched to flick her cigarette ash into the ashtray, just looking at her made me want to jump her again. Even an angel needs some recovery time, though, so I just stroked her hip as the sheet slid back, then leaned forward and kissed the cold skin.

"Okay, then I'll ask you," she said. "What do you do for fun in Heaven?"

I laughed, but then I thought about it, and there wasn't really much I could say. Heaven is a lot of things, but "fun" isn't really one of them. "It's hard to explain. It's a very happy place, but not really by choice."

"Enforced happiness?"

"Something like that. Well, no, it's more like how when you live near a really good barbecue place, it makes you hungry all the time, just smelling the meat cooking."

"Wouldn't quite work like that in Hell, Dollar," she said, sending a jet of smoke up to be obliterated by her ceiling fan. "We're fairly used to the smell of burning meat."

Zing. "Okay. But do you get what I'm trying to say? It's not like you turn into some kind of zombie in Heaven, it's just . . . well, being there is very uplifting."

"Boy, does that sound like bullshit, Wings. Uplifting? That's the kind of thing people say about the folk mass down at the local congregational church."

"Look, don't put me in the position of defending Heaven. It's not like I'm their golden boy or anything." I reached over and gently squeezed a pink nipple. She made a little noise. It was very sweet. "I mean, you don't think they'd approve of this do you? Of us?"

Caz smacked my hand away before I could do it again. "Don't change the subject. You asked what I do for fun in Hell. I'm asking you what you do in Heaven."

"Try to leave, most of the time. Quickly as I possibly can."

She gave me a grumpy look. "Come on, sport. I've seen you drink. You've got nothing against a little happy oblivion. What's the difference?"

"Because getting drunk in a bar is my choice. Getting drunk on glory in Heaven when I'm only there because I've been summoned, that's different."

"I don't know," she said, frowning. "I'm finding it a little difficult to feel sorry about someone making you feel happy even when you don't want to. I mean, compared to some of the things I've seen—like, you know, people being eaten from the inside out by sawtoothed worms because they didn't bow fast enough—it doesn't seem so bad." She shook her head. "Shit, I've seen worse things back in medieval Poland. In church on Sunday."

It was, even I had to admit, a no-win argument. Of course I couldn't make her understand what bothered me about Heaven. It was like those things they make fun of on the internet—First World Problems. Except this was an Above The World Problem.

"Look," she said, then reached out and squeezed me in a different place than I'd squeezed her, and a lot harder (but in a very nice way). "I'm making you feel good against your will. Does that mean you're going to complain about me, too? Stand up for your rights? Ooh, you're such a rebel, Bobby!" Then she gently wrapped her lips around my cock, the part of my body least likely to help me concentrate on arguing at times like these. She drew me past her lips and into her mouth. Very, very cold, then very warm.

Normally I don't like it when people make fun of me. I always prefer to be the fun-maker, probably because I'm a complete asshole, but I decided I could let myself be exploited just that once, strictly as a learning experience.

fifteen
riprash

I COULD ONLY watch helplessly as Commissar Niloch approached the cage. His bony spurs stirred and scraped as he walked, like wind shifting dead leaves, and he examined the crush of damned souls with eyes as unfeeling as two shiny red buttons. If I tell you that I could smell him even through the various stenches of being locked in a slave cage in the middle of Hell, you'll have an idea of how pungent his scent was, sweetness and rotten meat combined, like one of those corpse flowers that lure flies to their doom. It was all I could do not to vomit, and I probably gagged a little, which may have been what drew his attention. I was mostly hidden by the slaves splayed against the bars in front of me, but those tiny eyes suddenly fixed on mine, and he moved closer. His smell rolled over me in a nauseating wave, then he opened his weird mouth and things got a lot worse.

The two bits of his lower jaw clashed together like a crab applauding. I hoped it wasn't what he did when he was hungry. He was staring straight at me. My demon heart was going like a jackhammer in my chest.

"Are you interested in purchasing more slaves, Commissar?" Riprash came forward. "I'd be happy to find you some healthy ones. I haven't sorted these yet." Niloch turned and looked at him, saying nothing, but when Riprash spoke again he had a slight tremor in his voice. "Or, if you'd like, I can clean these up so you can inspect them."

The commissar laughed, I guess, although the thin whistling didn't sound much like laughter. "Oh, would you? Perhaps dress them up, too, so they look like little lords and ladies. That would be merry." He turned back to the cage and, just to make sure my heart kept crashing against my ribs, found my eyes again. "But I must say, I've—"

"What's going on here? Oh, Commissar, it's true, you've graced us with a visit!"

"He's expecting something," said another voice almost immediately.

"Shut up or I'll have you removed," said the first voice. "Thank you, Lord Commissar, thank you!"

The tubby, two-headed figure of Gagsnatch, the slave-stall's owner, bustled toward Niloch. One of his heads showed the commissar a wide, ingratiating smile, the other stared with a look of open disinterest. "You do me too much honor!" said Happy Head.

"Any is too much," said the other head, sullen as a teenage boy.

"Ah," said Niloch. "At last you favor me with your attendance, slave trader."

Happy Head immediately screwed his face into a frown of remorse. "I did not know it was you, Commissar! Rest assured that as soon—"

"Shut your mouths," said Niloch, not much louder than a whisper. "Both." Silence followed. "Yes, as it happens, you *can* do something for me. I do have need of more slaves. Send me this crate, just as it is." Niloch turned back, but this time his gaze only touched me briefly, then swept across the other poor schmucks in the cage. "Yes, this should do. Dear me, don't bother to clean them. Waste of sand. They'll serve just fine the way they are." He paused. "Ah, yes. I see my men have finished here, and I have a long way back to my quarters. Draw up the bill and send the slaves to Gravejaw House immediately." The commissar rattled out of my line of sight, back the way he had come.

"Thank you, Commissar!" cried Happy Head. "Your custom is the most generous gift you could give me! You are the best lord in the land!"

"But you said he was the worst," chirped Unhappy Head. "You said he was stupid as a turd and smelled like—"

I had the novel experience of watching someone slap one of his own heads across the mouth hard enough to draw blood. Punishment delivered and Unhappy Head at least temporarily silenced, Gagsnatch hurried after the commissar, spouting words of praise and gratitude.

My heart was finally slowing to a level more like ordinary terror when the door of the slave cage clanked open. "You," Riprash told me. "Out."

The other slaves had no real way to make room for me, so he yanked several of them out, causing at least one or two serious injuries, I'm sure. I fought my way toward the opening, only remembering as I got close to it that Gob was in the cage, too, but when I looked back the little hairy kid was slithering his way after me through the other slaves.

Before I could ask Riprash a single question he picked me up under the arms and carried me like a puppy into the back of the stall, into a little area blocked by a screen made of hide and dropped me there. Gob curled up just behind my legs, watching Riprash with an impressive level of concentration, no doubt fermenting half a dozen plans of escape if things went sour. A survivor, that's what the kid was. That was how I used to think of myself, too, but after meeting Gob I realized now how pathetically easy I'd had it by comparison.

"You lot stay here." Riprash peered at us over the screen, which I couldn't have done standing on a box. In the dark his ruined face looked like it was carved of stone. Ugly stone. "No noise!" Then he went out. After a few comparatively quiet minutes I heard him talking with both of his boss's heads for a while. If Unhappy Head had been cowed by its recent smacking, it had gotten over it; I heard it sniping at almost everything the other head said. At last the three-way palaver ended, and I heard Riprash's heavy tread returning.

"And now I have to find two more slaves, because that's how many Niloch counted and that's how many he'll expect." Again the big hands closed on me and lifted. He set me down and looked me over. I swear, if he had said "Fee Fi Fo Fum," I wouldn't have batted an eye. Instead he pulled over a large stone, which I couldn't have moved with a pickup truck and a tow chain, then sat on it.

"Well?"

I stared at him, my head just about emptied by all the kinds of scared I was. "Well, what?" I said at last.

"You said you had something to tell me. We're alone. I've got the others taking that drift of slaves down to the dock. So tell."

I closed my eyes for a second in a silent prayer of gratitude. Now I only had to hope that Temuel's seemingly innocuous message wasn't some kind of code for "kill the guy who tells you this." I tried to look

Riprash in the eye to show him my sincerity, but I just couldn't do it. All that exposed meat, and the chunk of ax still in there . . .

"I'm not from here," I said, looking attentively at his massive feet. "I'm from . . . somewhere else. Do you know what I mean?"

Riprash made a low noise. "Could be," he said at last. "Could be I don't. Say what you got to say."

"A friend asked me to find you and give you this message. He said, 'You are not forgotten.' That's all. Just that."

Nothing happened, or at least nothing that registered down in the area of Riprash's size sixty-three tootsies. I looked up. Not all at once, but I did it.

He was crying.

I'm not joking. He was. A single glowing tear like a streamlet of lava had made its way down from his good eye across his cheek, and now dangled like maple sap from his chin. "All thanks," he said, almost whispering. He sagged forward like an ancient redwood collapsing, and to my astonishment he landed on his knees, then lifted both massive arms above his head. "All thanks. I am lifted."

You can guess what I made of this, which was nothing useful. Riprash stayed that way for a while as more tears dripped from his face and made bright little splashes on the floor before they cooled and faded. I was beginning to feel less terrified than embarrassed, he was so clearly in the grip of something deep and personal. Since he hadn't smashed me into jelly over the message I'd just delivered, he was still the closest thing Gob and I had to an ally, so I sat tight as it went through him like a storm and made him shake all over. At last it was done. Riprash wiped his good eye with the back of a massive hand then climbed back onto the rock again.

"Ah," he said. "Ah. That was good to hear. All thanks to you—" He paused, his brow fissuring as he realized. "I don't know your name, master."

"It's Snakestaff." This was the first time I'd told my demon cover-name to anyone but Gob, and I was watching to see if it meant anything. I only had Temuel's word (and Lameh's silent memories) that it hadn't been used before. But the ogre didn't seem to find it either surprising or familiar.

"My thanks, then, Snakestaff. May you be lifted."

Which sounded better than most things that had been happening, so I nodded. "Okay, now what?"

He looked at me like a man woken up too quickly. "What? What do you mean?"

"I mean, do you mind if we get on our way? My servant and me? Thanks for hiding me from the commissar, but I have other errands I need to do in Pand—in the Red City, and that's a pretty long walk."

"Other errands?" He looked interested, but not in the cruel, hungry way you usually see demons look interested. "Others like me?"

"No."

"Too bad that you have to go. You should meet some of the other Lifters. Your message will mean a lot to them." His terrifying face grew almost cheerful. "Wait! I am bound to deliver those slaves to the commissar at Gravejaw. If you go with me on the *Bitch* you'll travel much faster, and you can find a lifter when you get there. *That* should speed your journey to the Red City."

All this talk of lifting and lifters and bitches had me boggled, but I was not going to look this particular gift ogre in the mouth. "You mean you'd really help me?"

"I would do any service I could." He spoke with a strange weight to his words. "Can't you guess what your message means to me and mine?"

I couldn't, not really, but clearly it meant a lot, and I was going to do my best to ride that wave all the way to the beach. "Yes, of course."

"I ask only one favor in return."

Shit, I thought, here it comes. Does he want to drink some of my blood, or eat one of my eyes? "And that is . . . ?"

"Tonight you must come with me to fellowship."

Not quite as bad as I'd feared, obviously. "Certainly. But I still don't understand. How will you get me to Gravejaw so much faster than I could walk?"

He laughed. "By boat, of course—my ship, *The Nagging Bitch.* Otherwise it would take you a hundred lanterns or more. But on Cocytus' broad back, we'll be there in nine."

Well, thank you, nasty, foul river, I thought. *I guess you're not all bad.*

Obviously, I still had a lot to learn.

*   *   *

The fellowship meeting, as Riprash called it, took place in a spot so disgusting it's a miracle I remember the actual meeting at all. You've never really been in a sewer until you've been in a sewer in Hell. This one was made of what looked like mud brick, and smelled like . . . well, there just are no words for it. If I hadn't been wearing a demon body, I suspect my sinuses would have committed suicide on first contact with that nose-scorching odor of death and shit and shit and death.

Still, bad smells were nothing compared to being caught by one of the gangs of Murderers Sect guards who patrolled the waterfront, so Riprash's fellowship meetings were always held deep in the tunnels. It was ridiculously crowded with two dozen of us perched on the edge of a drainage culvert, but everybody just squeezed up as close as they could, because even in Hell, even among those being punished for all eternity, nobody wanted to go splashing around in that stuff.

I really did find it kind of touching that all these condemned souls as well as the demons meant to torment them (damned only outnumbered demons in that sewer about three to one) should come together in search of something bigger and better than what they knew. And Riprash himself, as it turned out, impressed me even more.

He was clearly the main dude, at least here in Cocytus Landing, and it showed. When he began to speak, even the poor damned guy covered entirely in shivering porcupine quills did his best to be quiet and listen.

"Once upon a time, back in the World, there was this fellow named Origen." Riprash pronounced it like an Irish name—O'Ridgeon. "And he had a big idea: Nobody has to stay damned forever. Nobody."

A few of what must have been the newer members of the congregation looked startled and whispered to each other.

"That's right." The ogre spoke slowly, as if for children. "Not even the Adversary himself has to remain in Hell for eternity. Even he can lift himself up. Lift himself up! And so can we."

"But what good will it do?" demanded a creature with a head like a skinned donkey. "Those angel bastards will just push us back down anyway. They'll never let us out!"

A few others murmured their agreement, but Riprash was clearly an old pro at this sort of thing, and tonight he had a better than usual answer.

"If you think so," he said, "then you'll be very interested to hear the message this fellow brought to me today." He pointed at me and several of the creatures in the sewer turned to look. "He brought me a message from," he dropped his voice to a near-whisper, but even an ogre whisper was pretty loud, "from that *other place*. The up-high place. Where those angels live who you think only want to push you back down. And what did the message say? What did the message sent all the way down here from the other place say, Master Snakestaff?"

He was clearly waiting for me. "'You are not forgotten,'" I quoted.

"That's right! So think of that. I don't say that all the Halos love us, because they don't. But there are some as know what's done to us wasn't right. And if we keep trying to do it, well, we *can* lift ourselves up, just you wait and see!"

Riprash went on like this for a while more, then asked if any of the fellowship wanted to give testimony. I had thought I would be bored and restless, as I would have been in any religious meeting back on Earth, but instead I was fascinated. The first one to speak was a damned soul that looked more than a bit like a gingerbread man made out of moldy, ancient paper. He explained carefully that when he had lived on Earth he had been a thief in Antioch, and that although he had only stolen food to feed his starving family, he had been put to death by the Roman overlords and condemned to Hell.

"It's good news to hear we might be free again someday," he said in a slow, serious tone. "Good news. And I will do all I can to behave myself and learn the way to do that. Because I want to be free. It wasn't fair, what happened to me. And when I'm free again, I will go find that shit-eating merchant who called the guards on me, and my bitch of a wife who didn't even come to see me executed, and all the bastards who *did* come, and I'll cut them all into pieces." He might have been reading a laundry list. He'd been thinking about it a long time.

"Not sure you really grasp the details of the thing, fellow," said Riprash gently as the gingerbread thief sat down again on the ledge above the stinking flood. "Not about revenge, this. About making ourselves *better* than we were."

"I'll feel better when that stinking merchant is dead," the gingerbread man muttered, but already somebody else had risen to speak. This damned soul was female, although that wasn't clear when she first stood up, because she looked more like a person-shape made of overcooked spaghetti, with eyeballs tucked into the tangle in place of meatballs. For a moment she stood, hesitating, winding her tendrils with equally limp fingers.

"Go on, then, love," said Riprash in an encouraging tone. "It's Deva, isn't it?"

She nodded and seemed to find courage. Several more eyes emerged. "When I was alive . . . well, I was a very bad person. I'm sure I deserve to be here."

"What did you do, dear?" Riprash asked. If you've never seen a ten-foot-tall monster making nice, it's quite an experience.

"I lost my little babies." A few of her eyes retracted into the forest of noodles or whatever they were. "No, that's not right. I didn't so much lose them as . . . I did away with them."

I might have made a noise of surprise, but nobody else did. "Why was that, dear?" Riprash asked.

"I'm not certain now. I was frightened, and they were so sick, and I had no money to feed them. They were always crying, you see, even though they were terribly weak . . ." She trailed off. She was down to only a few eyes still showing. "I tried everything, really I did. I sold myself to men, but I could never make enough, and the woman who watched them for me when I was out, well, she didn't . . . she didn't take very good care . . ." The creature named Deva curled her fingers and tugged at her tendrils so hard I thought she might break them off. "She drank too much toddy, that one, and one day she let my youngest one wander, and my little girl fell from the window down to the court-yard and died. I came home with the smell of a man still on me and found her there on the stones. The bitch taking care of her had not even known she was gone!" The damned woman shook her head, or the lump near the top that I assumed was a head. "I knew then that I would be going to Hell. And the others were still sick, still crying, get-ting thinner and thinner." After a long, long silence that nobody inter-rupted, she said, "So one night, I took them out when everyone else was asleep, took them outside the village and drowned them in the river. It was so sad, because even as I took them down to the bank I was looking for crocodiles. I was going to drown them, but I was still wor-ried that a crocodile might get them!"

She broke down at this point, and it was a while until she could talk again. The strange thing was that the other damned, and even the de-mon members of the congregation, all waited for her to continue. In a place where nobody even bothered to look twice at a badly injured person writing on the ground, or a child being beaten or sexually assaulted, these Hell-creatures were waiting patiently, even kindly, for one of their own to find her way back to herself.

"They stoned me to death, of course," she said finally. "Even the woman who let my littlest one die threw a stone! I have been here a long time. I cannot even guess how many centuries. On and on and on . . . It will sound strange, but even though I am dead, I did not truly know I had been alive until I heard Riprash speak, heard him speaking of how we might someday be lifted. Since I awoke here, I have been like a mole who lives in the ground, go forward, go backward, every day in the dark, and knowing nothing else. My children—I did not think of them. I could not think of them. I could not remember them, because my heart was burned away inside me. But when I heard Riprash talk of the lifting, I could feel myself again. I knew nothing could ever take away my wickedness, that what I had done would be a terrible curse in the mind of God forever . . . but I could hope that someday, perhaps when Heaven and Hell themselves come to an end, I might be forgiven. One day, no matter how dark and dreadful my act, I might see my little ones, my babies, again, so that I can tell them how sorry I am that they were ever born to such a mother—" She bowed her head, and all the tendrils shuddered together. "Ah, God! I am so sorry! So sorry!"

My eyes were dry as I sat in that crowd of damned, doomed folk and listened to her keening apologies to her dead children, but that was only because the demon's body I wore had no tear ducts.

sixteen

a filthy river runs through it

GOB AND I hid out at Gagsnatch's until the second beacon had
been lit, then our new friend Riprash buried us (carefully) under
a load of ship's provisions on a wagon and drove us down to the
docks. My view was entirely of the undersides of coarse sacks full of
dried maggots, but I'm not sure it was any worse than seeing the actual
city of Cocytus Landing, at least judging by the astonishing variety of
unpleasant noises and odors that made their way through the cushion-
ing layers of bagged demon yummies.

Riprash unloaded the provisions himself to make sure we weren't
accidentally beheaded by one of his helpers, then hurried us up the
swaying gangplank.

"You'll stay in my cabin," he said, gesturing proudly around the
low-ceilinged room, which would have been adequate for us if Riprash
never came in. As it was, he took up so much of the space that it felt
like sharing a bathtub with a humpback whale.

When day had passed and only the afterlights burned, the dock-
workers went home. Riprash took us out on deck and showed us
around the ship like a retiree displaying his rhododendrons. The *Bitch*
was halfway between a garbage scow and a Chinese junk, long and
low, with sails that must have looked like bat wings when they un-
furled. It was built with timbers that didn't seem to match, and was so
smeared with tar all over that the ship might have been made from
chewed licorice. But from what I could gather from Riprash's proud

descriptions, despite its age and decrepitude, *The Nagging Bitch* was state of the art when it came to things like shackles, cages, and tools of punishment. I tried to smile and look impressed, but when you're looking at a thing with metal teeth meant for digging into someone's crotch to prevent escape . . . well, like I said, I tried to smile.

Riprash had apparently decided he liked me. He showed this new-found solidarity by clapping me on the back from time to time, hard enough to make my bones creak. He also introduced me to the hellish rum he liked to drink, which tasted like bile and gasoline and packed the clout of pure moonshine. No, I didn't ask how it was made, or from what. Riprash loved to watch me trying to swallow the stuff and re-warded me for the entertainment of seeing me cough, retch, and sput-ter by telling stories late into the night when I would rather have slept.

But the liquor helped, and it wasn't that the stories were bad. In fact, by Hell standards my new, large friend's tales were quite sweet, really, of a simple ogre and his slave ship having interesting adventures around the infernal world. By local standards, Riprash was really an okay guy. Yes, he'd killed a few people—a few hundred, more accurately—during the course of his life, and he had trouble thinking of the damned souls he trafficked in as anything other than mobile meat, but once we got to know him I never felt afraid of him, and there's very few hellfolk I can say that about. Including my girlfriend.

The ship set sail just before the first day-lamp was lit. Riprash let us out on deck once we were underway so we could look around. *The Nagging Bitch* had so many black sails that the masts looked like some kind of vampire nesting trees. Weighted down with a hold full of caged slaves, she wallowed so low that the river was constantly slapping over the gunwales, and the deck was always at least ankle-deep in Cocytus sludge. but I was delighted to breathe the (comparatively) sweeter air outside the cabin.

That first night, as the city fell away behind us and we sailed into the dark, the great black snake of river soon became invisible. With only the distant beacons on the walls of Hell for light, we might have been traveling through a universe of flickering red stars. I felt suddenly lonely, lonelier than I'd ever been, even with Gob beside me, open-eyed and open-mouthed as he journeyed into what must have been a life he'd never dreamed of living. I was desperate for Caz and that unique moment of completeness she'd given me, I was badly in need of friends like Sam and Monica, and I missed my familiar haunts. You've been there, I'm sure, but it feels different in Hell. Chances were very small I'd ever see any of them again. Little Gob was company of a sort, but he wasn't exactly chatty, and since I was planning to ditch him before things got really dangerous, I didn't want to get too close, either.

Riprash thumped toward us and spread his massive arms. "This . . . this is freedom," he said, conveniently ignoring the shrieks of the damned in their cages below. "No master but the winds and the tide. When I felt this, I was first lifted. But I did not even know it then." He laid a huge paw on my shoulder; if he'd pushed down, I'm pretty sure he could have driven me into the deck like a finishing nail. "Perhaps you come to another fellowship with me, Snakestaff? When we reach Gravejaw, maybe?"

I mumbled something noncommittal. I'm not really a joiner, but out of curiosity I asked, "How many are in your fellowship?"

"Ah, it is not as small as it was back in that other day, when your master first spoke to me. More join every day. Still, we are few." He nodded. "But we are lifted, in our thought if not in our bodies."

I never found out where he picked up the Origen stuff, but he had a pretty good understanding. Origenes of Alexandria was a Christian scholar, back in the third century or so, who proposed that if free will and forgiveness were real, even Satan himself had a chance someday to make peace with the Highest and achieve forgiveness. Needless to say, the early church stomped all over this idea, because they thought a Hell that wasn't forever was pretty toothless. Plainly, many of those early Christians had never spent centuries dogpaddling in molten lava, or they would have rethought that concept; even a mere decade of constant, agonizing burns might adjust attitudes, I'd guess.

I was impressed by Riprash's belief, and I speak as a confirmed cynic. Gob was interested too, or at least I guessed that he was, because he listened carefully when the ogre spoke.

"But the lords of Hell . . . they can't like that idea very much," I said at last.

"And they don't, that's a fact."

I couldn't help thinking that my supervisor Temuel was playing a pretty dangerous game, encouraging the rank and file of Hell to start thinking about salvation. Did our superiors have any idea? Because it sounded like just as revolutionary and dangerous a plan as Sam's mystery-angel Kephas had hatched with the Third Way, which I was already trying to wipe off my shoes. Bobby Dollar sneaking off to aid a religious rebellion in Hell wasn't going to make the Ephorate any happier with me. Not that I wasn't already fucked before I got here; I had slept with a high-ranking demon, helped a rogue angel (who happened to be my best friend) escape, bashed another angel over the head while he was pursuing his lawful duties, and then lied to Heaven about all of it.

Slam dunk, I believe our friends in the earthly legal profession would call the case against me.

"Here on the Bitch, we yaw and we pitch,"

Riprash sang in a voice like a slow avalanche.

"And we don't give the bandits no quarter
We're drinking and stinking, but also we're thinking
We might take a ride on your daughter!"

Yeah. Why worry about one more strike against me at this late date? In fact, as long as I was down here in Hell, I decided I should look around for a nice piece of property, because the odds were high I was going to be coming back soon on a more permanent basis.

seventeen
gravejaw house

THE RIVER was as horrible and dangerous as you'd imagine, full of skeletal pirates on leaking rafts and fanged serpentine creatures big as slimy commuter trains. But we were on a large, well-armed boat, and the nightly tales of Sinbad the Split-Skull Sailor almost made up for the stench and the constant terror that something was going to eat us.

Riprash had started out in the service of a demon lord named Crabspatter and worked his way up to a position of responsibility in the guy's personal guard, until Crabspatter was cut to ribbons by another, badder demon in a sea battle at a place Riprash called Sucking Marsh.

"Old Crabby went down to the bottom with a spear through his guts, yes he did," said Riprash in the nostalgic tone of someone talking about a dotty uncle. "He's probably still down there, trying to get out of the mud—he was a mean fucker. That's when I got this." He reached up and touched the huge gash in his head. "And then I woke up, stripped and robbed of everything, chained in a line of captives. The winner kept some of us, sold the rest." He laughed. "Not surprised he didn't keep me. My head didn't stop bleeding for months."

But the slave trader who bought him recognized Riprash's quality, or at least his immense size, and put him to work as an overseer. Freedom is kind of a moot point in Hell, apparently, and Riprash was never granted his, but he worked his way up to positions of greater trust until he was the slave trader's right-hand man. Centuries later, Gagsnatch took over the trader's business (neither a gentle nor a legal transaction, from what I could tell) but he kept Riprash in the same position of trust, and my new chum had worked for Gagsnatch ever since. He gave me a startled look when I asked him how many years ago that had been.

"Years? Words like that don't mean anything much here. Some of the new ones come in and they ask how long this, how long that, but the rest of us find it doesn't do any good to think about it."

It made me wonder how many years Gob had been a child, scuttling through the narrow alleyways of Abaddon. The kid had been born in Hell, but time here didn't seem to mean much, and Gob didn't remember much beyond a few days back, probably because, until he hooked up with me, it had all been pretty much the same.

I was beginning to see that the whole Hell thing, including the timelessness, had been craftily arranged to make the inmates as unhappy as possible. They had to scramble for food and shelter every day, but other than that, things hardly ever changed—or changed just enough to make the repeated doses of punishment more painful. If things are always the same, you get used to them. If they change, if sometimes they get a little better, that makes the return to misery all the more painful. So if any of you plan to open your own Hell, remember this time-tested recipe: Vary the suffering so your victims don't get completely numb. Show them something better from time to time, just to keep them hoping.

I couldn't help wondering whether Riprash's fellowship, the Lifters, might actually be part of the infernal master plan. After all, what better way to insure suffering than to wave a little hope for better days in front of the damned and the doomed? Riprash didn't believe that, though, and I certainly wasn't going to argue. I had come to trust him, and he even seemed to like Gob, in a how-demons-do-it sort of way. Since Gob was always as hungry as a feral cat, he gave the boy little handouts of food and was amused by the kid's elaborate caution whenever we left the confines of the tiny cabin. "Don't you know you're on *my* ship, little bug?" Riprash would bellow. "Nobody even pisses on *The Nagging Bitch* without my say-so!"

I never did find out if Riprash's ship was named after anyone in particular, but Riprash had women (using the term loosely) in every port the slaver traded. Not that I ever encouraged him to share *those* stories. If you ever want to lose your interest in sex, try spending your vacation in Acheron Landing or even Penitentia, the spit of mud, rock, and ramshackle huts where we stopped for supplies on the second day. The dockside hookers looked like extras from *Attack of the Mole Men*, but Riprash assured me that only the best looking ones got to work the incoming vessels.

I won't bore you with a description of the entire trip. From the middle of a river, one Hell city looks pretty much like another—namely horrible. The third day we finally sighted Gravejaw, a sullen knob of black lava rock that stuck out into the black swell of Cocytus like a bunion. A natural bay at its base had made it a port, and the desperate nature of life in Hell had soon turned it into a crawling ant heap of souls and demons. At the top of the great mound of stone, surrounded by walls as high as those of the city itself, stood a castle, a forest of black towers slender and sharp as an eel's teeth. A huge banner flapped on the uppermost spire, a white bird's claw painted on sable ground. It wasn't the tallest thing on Gravejaw, though: at the center of the city a massive column loomed over everything else like a giant central pillar holding up the sky.

"The banner's Niloch's, and that place with the black towers is his," Riprash said. "Don't go near it, that's my advice. I'll tell you how to get across the city from here. See that?" He pointed to the great pillar, which, as we grew closer, I could see was made from some kind of mud brick but loomed higher than any skyscraper. Even now that the second set of beacons had been lit on the walls of Gravejaw—the closest thing to full daylight—it was impossible to see where the great cylinder ended, since it stretched up into the blackness of the monstrous cavern's invisible roof. "You just get there, and the lifter'll take you where you want to go." I could ride it all the way up to Pandaemonium, apparently, many, many levels above us. That part was heartening, but I was still a bit confused by it all.

See, our river trip had taken us up at least a dozen levels, which didn't make any sense at all. I certainly hadn't noticed us sailing uphill, and the Cocytus, black and sticky and noxious as it was, seemed in all other ways to obey the laws of gravity and physics I knew. But this was Hell, after all, and although it was more realistic (for lack of a better word) than Heaven, it wasn't any more real. As an angel I was used to the slippery distances and untellable time of Heaven, so it wasn't much of a stretch to accept that some things in Hell, no matter how illogical, just *were*.

I scrubbed myself with bits of sail-mending canvas to get the worst muck off me, since the river was way too dangerous for swimming. In fact, ordinary souls didn't use water to bathe in Hell: it was too rare. Then Gob and I waited for Riprash to give us the sign that it was safe to disembark. We sat for what seemed like hours, the boy pacing back and forth across the tiny cabin until I wanted to clout him. I was already wondering what I was going to do with Gob. I didn't want to take him with me any farther, because I might have to make a hasty retreat from some very bad place, and it was going to be hard enough to figure out how to smuggle Caz out without adding Gob to the equation. On the other hand, I'd dragged him far away from the places he knew, I didn't have a single iron spit to pay him off with, and leaving him on his own here in Gravejaw might put him in even greater danger.

Then a sudden idea hit me. I left Gob pacing and went to find Riprash. I should have stayed in the cabin like he told me, but I was suddenly fired up with the idea of doing someone a good turn (I am, or used to be, an angel, remember?) and I blundered up the ladder to the main deck.

The first thing I ran into was one of Riprash's minions, the catlike, bug-eyed one who had gaped at me back at the slave stall in Cocytus Landing like I was some long-lost relative. I couldn't imagine any reason why this grubby little thing should be looking at me with such insolent familiarity (you can see that Hell was starting to get to me) so before he could work up his nerve to say something, I demanded to know where Riprash was.

"On the d-d-dock," said Krazy Kat in a high, stuttering voice, "but I th-think, I think . . ."

I probably just looked like his old Uncle Pitchfork or something. Worse, despite Temuel's promises, maybe the little creature had recognized the demon body the archangel and Lameh had given me. Either way, I didn't want that conversation, so I brushed past him. I was a few steps down the gangplank when I realized something about the busy dock looked wrong. Not the weird, insectlike beasts of burden being loaded with cargo, nor the other ghastly, half-naked creatures sweating beneath the whips of the overseers, some of them so deformed it was a wonder they could work at all, let alone carry such huge loads, but something far more disturbing.

Riprash stood on the dock, but he was completely surrounded by armed demon soldiers, a dozen of them or more, all wearing Niloch's white bird claw insignia. What was worse, Niloch himself sat mounted on the back of a tall and only slightly horselike insect creature, and Riprash was talking to him.

Niloch saw me so quickly it seemed like he had been looking for me. For a moment I was convinced Riprash had sold me out, and I cursed myself for ever trusting a demon. After all, that was what had landed me here in Hell in the first place.

"And here he is, dear, dear me! How charming!" His bony tendrils wavering in the sea breeze like the fronds of a sea anemone, Niloch spurred his weird insect-horse toward the base of the gangplank. "Riprash has just told me of your bad fortune, Lord Snakestaff! It is a credit to you that you have climbed so far back after such a nasty little trick."

I was frozen on the top of the gangplank. "Trick. Of course . . ."

Riprash turned and gave me a look of what I assume was mute pleading: It's hard to tell when so much of a person's face has been ruined. "Yes, I told him how you were betrayed and abandoned in the lower levels by your enemies." He turned back to Niloch. "Snakestaff needs only to reach the lifter, Lord Commissar, and then he'll be right as rot."

Niloch let out one of his whistling laughs. "Of course, of course, but first he must come and take his ease with me in Gravejaw House and tell me about all the adventures he has had!" He almost sounded sincere, but even if I'd trusted him I wouldn't have wanted to go anywhere with that fluting, inhuman thing. "Surely you must be longing for a proper meal, Snakestaff, hmmm? Delicacies, yes? And I shall see you have some proper clothes, too. Going naked as the crawling damned will not smooth your passage back to Pandaemonium. They are dreadfully judgemental up at the capital."

"That's very kind," I said, croaking a little in my effort to sound casual. "But there's no need for you to trouble yourself over a creature like me, Lord Commissar." Whatever else Niloch was, he clearly outranked me, so there was no way I could just refuse.

"Nonsense. Where in the Red City do you live?"

"Blister Row. It's near Dis Pater Square." I was glad Lameh had given me a response. I couldn't help wondering if the place actually existed. Perhaps I could use it as a sanctuary when I made it to Pandaemonium. *If* I made it to Pandaemonium.

"A delightful little neighborhood! I'll be pleased to let you repay my own insignificant hospitality when I next journey to the great metropolis. Now come, Snakestaff, brave traveler! You shall enjoy a night with me after so long on shipboard and so many tiresome experiences in the depths."

I only had time for a quick whispered conference with Riprash. I begged him to take care of Gob, and he said he would, at least until he could deliver him back to me, which wasn't really what I'd hoped for. "We'll meet again, Snakestaff," the giant rumbled. "That you can rest yourself on."

I wasn't as confident as Riprash. I said goodbye, keeping it formal because Niloch's beady little scarlet eyes were watching us. "You've been kind to me," I told him quietly. The giant frowned, and I realized it was an unfamiliar term. "You've done me no harm, you've even done me a good turn. I'll remember that."

Then, my heart in my mouth, where it was the only thing keeping my meager yet repulsive breakfast from being forcibly ejected, I followed the rattling commissar across the dock. He directed me to a pallet, already loaded down with the cage of slaves and carried by more slaves who moaned in quiet hopelessness as I added my weight. Then the whole procession followed Niloch up the winding road through the vast slum of Gravejaw, bound for the needle-towered citadel at the top of the hill.

My first impression of Gravejaw House was that I had somehow fallen out of Hell and landed smack dab in the middle of Shoreline Park, the abandoned and thoroughly dilapidated amusement park back home in San Judas. The commissar's fortress, rising like a bizarre tumor from the crest of the hill, looked less like a castle than a pile of giant toy blocks left behind by some bored and colossal infant. It was hard to tell under the red lantern-light of Hell, but the leaning walls and the bottoms of the crooked towers seemed to be painted in broad multicolored stripes and whorls and other odd patterns. The entrance road wound through vast, chaotic gardens, which seemed to consist mostly of partially skeletonized corpses planted waist-deep in dry, stony ground, tangled in vines and prickling thorns so that it was hard to tell where the foliage left off and the muscle fibers and slickly gleaming nerves began. When I saw one of them twitch and its ragged mouth form a soundless cry for help, I was reminded that nothing in Hell really dies.

"Ah," said Niloch, watching my face. "Do you like it? It is so hard in these rustic areas to know what to do with servants when they become too decrepit to work. I could have sold them for scrap, but I wouldn't have got much. This way they continue to serve."

"Wonderful," I said, which was as much as I could manage without throwing up. The worst part was that all the shrub people struggled to turn as we passed, trying to catch the commissar's attention, their mouths gaping and eyes (where eyes still remained) bulging as they struggled to make their ruined bodies plead for them. Not that Niloch would have cared.

"Did you see this one?" he asked. "My old butler." He pointed to a thing I wouldn't have noticed, since it was one of the few ornaments not moving. There was only the barest hint of a face and limbs. "He dropped an entire jeroboam of maiden's tears." The shrub was bent beneath the weight of a stone dish the size of a truck tire. "I told him when he catches enough to make up for what he spilled, I'll put him back to work." The unlikely chance of any maidens happening by and crying into that huge stone bowl, let alone enough of them to fill it, seemed to make Niloch very cheerful. As I went past I saw that I had been wrong, and the shrub *was* moving, trembling so slightly beneath the great weight of stone that there might have been a breeze, but no breeze was blowing.

We reached the front gate, a pair of crude demon-statues with a length of iron grille between them, which swung open at our approach. Beyond it lay a couple dozen yards of curious, bumpy pathway and then the big, black door.

"Are you barefoot?" Niloch asked me. Several of his servants had come spilling out the gate, scurrying out on either side of the path to help the commissar dismount from his strange insectoid horse. "Of course you are, your enemies have taken your clothes. But that is good, good! The house needs to know where you've been so it can prepare the proper hospitality." He pointed one of his strange, bony fingers, and the spiraling horns on his arm rattled a little. "Go on, friend Snake-staff, walk forward. On the path."

I did. It was gray as old meat, and it felt like it as well, spongy and giving beneath my soles. I didn't like it much, but it wasn't the worst feeling in the world, at least not until I was halfway, at which point I felt the bottoms of my feet getting moist. Within a few more steps I was sloshing ankle deep in fluid. The path seemed almost to cling to my feet each time I put them down. The whole thing reminded me of something but I couldn't quite figure out what, until just before I stepped off onto the front porch.

A tongue. I was walking on a huge tongue. I all but leaped from the end in my hurry to get off it. When I turned back I could see the furrow down the middle, the little bumps that had allowed it to taste me, the shine of the saliva that was even now draining back into the coarse pores. It was all I could do to stay upright.

Niloch's slaves had taken off his boots, and as he walked up the path behind me, his cloud of horny extensions shaking gently around him, he muttered little endearments at the thing: "Oh, yes, my hungry beauty. Ah, you like that? Goodness, you do! I trod on that one—it squealed like a puppy. Is it sweet? Yes, between my toes."

I turned away. The toes in question were like armor-plated worms wriggling against the soft, gray flesh of the tongue, and Niloch kept stopping to let the path enjoy them. No sane person should have to see that.

Niloch gestured for me to go inside. It was too late to run, so I stepped forward. The entry hall was a chaos of monstrous angles and pools of shadow. Things scuttled past that I didn't want to look at too closely.

"Why so dark?" Niloch asked, with just a hint of impending may-hem, and several slaves, small creatures like burned apes, leaped forward to begin spinning wheels set into the wall. Translucent spheres mounted on the wall began to glow, driving many of the smallest crawlers back into hiding.

"What do you think?" the commissar asked. Slaves were removing his armor. I turned away, not eager to see more of Niloch's horrible form. "My lanterns are as good as anything in the Red City, you must admit. There is a gas that seeps from beneath this hill that feeds flame. It is why I made my home here. Long after the last lamp is extinguished, lights blaze in Gravejaw House. They can be seen for miles and miles!"

His slaves stepped away. Niloch now wore something like a camel's saddle blanket, a shapeless black thing that could have been a house-dress, covered with splotches that might have been a pattern or just Niloch's breakfast mess, the whole thing stretched over his protrusions like a very ugly parade float waiting to be unveiled.

"Now come, my dearest," he said. "You will dine with me, charm-ing Snakestaff, oh, most certainly. After the poor fare of a slave ship you will be pleased to see what my kitchen can provide!"

I was ushered into a long, low hall. The huge table was solid stone pitted with holes that I only realized later were actually drains. A pair of battered-looking slaves hurried me to my seat, little more than a stone lump beside the table. Niloch had a more elaborate chair, a kind of trestle under a canopy of wrought-iron antlers that duplicated the curls of horn hidden by his caftan. Strange creatures clung to the wall, things like inside-out lizards and globby things as shapeless as amoe-bas. Some were servants, as it turned out, and some were on the dinner menu, but they all came when Niloch called.

With help from his slaves, the commissar clambered up onto the trestle and bestrode it like a saddle, so that he was a good twice my height. He seemed to enjoy that, his sideways jaws positively clacking with good cheer. "Ah, yes," he called, "so good to be home! And now, feed us! Bring us out all the finest delicacies! Your master is back and we have a guest!"

I won't tell you much about the meal. You're welcome. Everything was still alive, and I wouldn't have eaten any of them by choice even if they weren't. As it was, though, I had to smile and pretend to enjoy the feeling of scrabbly little legs in my mouth, or the whimpers of something that didn't enjoy being chewed. Dessert? Dessert was alive too, even after it had been doused in something and lit on fire. Niloch insisted I try it before it stopped shrieking.

The only thing that saved me was the demon body I was wearing, which apparently had literally more stomach for this sort of thing than I did. I managed to get a few things down but knew I would spend the rest of my life, however short, trying to forget this meal.

"Now, my good fellow," Niloch said when the last plate of quiver-ing ruin had been cleared away, "you must tell me of your travels after this unfortunate kidnapping." He gestured for the nearest slave to pour something lumpy as gravy into my cup. "You must have seen some wonderful sights in Abaddon. Did you visit the Fountain of Pus? Travelers come from many levels above and below just to see it! Lovely!"

I did my best to sound like a disgruntled petty noble complaining about his unwanted trip to the depths, of course. Niloch's questions were sympathetic at first, but after a while I began to think he was trying to trip me up, pulling out little inconsistencies and asking me with poison sweetness to explain them.

"You see," he told me after I had finished one long, self-conscious answer, "there are things afoot, my sweet, oh, yes. Apparently an *outsider*," he said the word with a hissing emphasis, "has got into Hell through one of the old, disused gates."

"Outsider? Got in?" I was suddenly finding it hard to talk, despite the absence of small kicking things in my throat for the first time in an hour. "Who . . . ?"

"Who would be so rude as to enter our fair lands without making themselves known—especially if they were sent by You-Know-Who?" He gave me a look. If those little red eyes could have twinkled, they would have, but instead they just sat there like drops of wet paint. "I couldn't say—but I'm sure you can, my dear Snakestaff?" The eyes went opaque. "Can't you? Hmmm?"

"But I told you, I didn't see anything!"

"Oh, come, my squishy, breakable friend. The time for that is over. I am so very certain that you have more to share with me, that I've arranged an appointment for you with my court jester, Greenteeth. He'll jolly it out of you. Come in, Master Greenteeth, I know you're eager!" he called out. "We're ready for you now."

Something waddled in through one of the doorways. It was only about half my height but squat and muscular and slick as an amphibian. I couldn't see any eyes on it, but it had plenty of mossy, sharp teeth. Far more than a reasonable mouthful. When it reached Niloch's side he reached down to pet it with a clawed hand as though it were a beloved pet. Invisible bells jingled faintly when the creature moved. He might have been a jester, but I wasn't laughing.

"You see," the commissar warbled, "I promised to bring back some new toys from the Shrieking Meat Bazaar for little Greenteeth. Oh, and

I did, my sweet lump, I *did*. He'll be aching to try them out, and from the way you have behaved at dinner, I suspect you don't like pain." Niloch raised a hand as I began my desperate protests. "No, no, do not be foolish, darling one. I'm sure you're in a hurry to prove me wrong, but we cannot start tonight when you're weary from your travels. That would dull the piquancy of the thing, would it not? Tired flesh is insensitive flesh." He raised a hand. Instantly, I was surrounded by burned apes. Their rough fingers closed on my arms and lifted me from my stone seat. "We will begin when the morning beacons are lit, or just a little before," Niloch said. "I have not had a conversation orchestrated by my beloved Greenteeth for some time. It will be a joyful day." The commissar patted the thing and it showed its teeth in an even wider grin, until I thought the whole top of its head might fall off and roll away. "Until the morning, then. Take him to his chamber."

I was dragged deep into Gravejaw House, past weeping animals and scarred servants with empty expressions, then shackled to the walls of a bare, dank stone room. The slaves' torches reflected from floor and walls slick with various liquids, only a few of which were obviously blood. Just before my captors left me, I heard something screech in a nearby room, a shrill, ragged sound that wasn't anywhere near human. I was pretty sure it was another guest being softened up for a session with the commissar and his pal Greenteeth.

The door closed. I heard the heavy bolt being thrown. I thrashed in my chains but could barely move them, let alone break them. With the torches gone, darkness filled the room, a blackness close to absolute.

eighteen
a darkness like death

I STRUGGLED, OF course. Shit, yes, I struggled. I heaved at the chains until every nerve and muscle in my body felt like it was going to burst through my skin, but the links were too heavy and thick even for demon-strength. I tried to pull my hands out through the shackles themselves, but although I tugged until my gray flesh tore against the metal cuffs, in the end I just couldn't slip them free. If I could have bitten off my own thumbs to make it work I would have—I was that desperate, because I knew that Niloch and his torturer would have me screaming my real name and mission within an hour after starting on me, and then the pain would *really* begin. But my chains held my hands out at either side of my body, far from my mouth. My legs were free, but my bottom half wasn't going anywhere without the rest of me.

I was slumped in defeat, exhausted and probably bleeding badly when I heard, or perhaps felt, a whisper of sound in the dark cell.

"*. . . And may his every work come undone, and the stink of his shame follow him wherever he goes.*"

"Who's there?" I'll leave out the pathetic quaver in my voice. "Who said that?"

After a moment of charged silence I heard it again, a little louder this time. "You . . . you can hear me?" The voice was female, or seemed to be, but of course you can't trust anything in Hell.

"Who are you?" I asked. "Where are you?" Was it another prisoner in a connecting cell? Or just another torment, although more subtle than most of what Niloch had shown so far?

"Who am I? Now there's a question." I could almost smell her sour amusement. "When I *was*, I was Heartspider, the commissar's favorite." Again the impression of a laugh, bitter and not altogether sane. "But there have been several favorites since me. If you look around, you'll see what's left of them."

"I can't see. It's too dark."

"Not much left of them anyway. Piles of bones in the corner. Picked clean, for the most part. Niloch's sticky little torturer gets what's left, but he's a messy housekeeper."

I didn't want to think about the bones. "But you? Where are you?"

"One of the piles."

It took me a moment, but then I understood. "You're . . . you're dead."

"Nobody dies here, you poor fool. If they ever cleaned up I could at least go on to do my suffering elsewhere, but instead I've been trapped in this place for longer than I can remember."

A ghost. She was a ghost, or at least the closest thing to it I'd encountered in Hell, her body ruined, all but destroyed, but her soul or spirit still haunting the place where she'd been butchered. And the Sollyhull Sisters thought they had it bad because they were stuck with coffee shops!

"Can you help me?" I asked her. "If you do, I'll help you."

"There's nothing I can do for you." A long pause this time. "How? How could you help me?"

"You tell me. If I was free, I could carry your bones away from here. Would that help?"

"It might." For a brief moment I thought I could hear something new in the disembodied voice, but when she spoke it was flat and hopeless again. "But it doesn't matter. I can't bring you the key. I can't command a slave to release you. By my sweet Satan, do you think I'd still be here if I had any power to do anything?" A gust of fury blew through the room, a hatred so intense I could feel it. "I would have made Niloch my own prisoner long ago if I could. I would burn him every day with fire 'til his little red eyes sizzled and popped. I would bind him until his own horns curled back through his flesh. I would tear him and salt him. I would suck his balls out of his vent and chew them like grapes . . ."

My chains rattled as I slumped back against the wall. I shared her hatred; one thing about being trapped in Hell, I was definitely finding it easier to hate. But it did neither of us any good.

Heartspider wore down at last, trailing into whispers. For a long time neither of us spoke. My mind was racing, but like a rat in a maze, each turn led to another dead end.

"The floor," she said suddenly.

I stirred. "What?"

"The floor. I watched you nearly manage to pull your hands out of the shackles. The floor is slippery with blood and fat. Far more than just my own. A dozen or more after me have been dispatched here and the slaves have not washed it down."

"So?"

"Try to get some of it onto your wrists. Maybe then you can slip loose."

I was about to tell her that I could not reach the floor, not nearly, when I realized that I was standing an inch deep in the very muck she was talking about. I lifted my foot as far as I could and heard a dollop of something unpleasant drip from my toes and splatter the floor. I tried again and managed to bend my knee and lift my foot as high as my own waist, but it was still far from my shackles. I twitched, trying to fling the stuff at my wrists, and felt it splash across my chest and shoulder. I tried again. And again.

I don't know how much later it was when the bolt rattled and the door swung inward, but I had been in complete darkness so long that the light of a single torch was blinding. Bells jingled softly. It was Niloch's torturer—sorry, "jester"—Greenteeth. The warty thing lurched closer to examine me, its mouth full of poisonous sharpness like a Viet Cong pit trap. The jester was short, but its stunted arms and legs were heavy as a gorilla's, and though it scarcely topped my waist I had no doubt that Greenteeth outweighed me. I gripped the manacles in my aching hands and wondered when it would notice they weren't around my wrists any longer.

"Ready, you?" it asked in a disturbingly wet voice. I still couldn't make out any eyes, but I could tell it was examining me, especially my bloody arms, pawing at my skin and tasting its cold, knobby fingers. "Trying to get free? Of course, of course, but not too much hurt things.

Will spoil the music of what soon we do." It reached out a hand so it could stroke my chest. Even with all the pain I was already in, the clammy touch of the thing made me shudder and flinch backward. "Oh, no. No fear. Together we will work for goodness. Together we will make something wonderful, quite."

Then Greenteeth finally noticed that I had slipped my cuffs and was only holding them. Still no eyes, but the toothy mouth gaped in surprise. I didn't give the horror time to raise the alarm, but kicked as hard as I could where I thought it might be vulnerable, somewhere between the legs and the chest. It dropped the torch, which guttered but did not go out, and as it stumbled and fell onto its back, wheezing with what I hoped was severe, crippling pain, I jumped onto it with both feet, then proceeded to leap up and down as hard as I could, paying no attention to the sensation of bones cracking beneath my heels because I had no idea how strong the thing might be. When the body got too slippery for me to maintain my balance I stepped down and started kicking, working its head and chest.

"He won't hurt you now," said Heartspider at last. She sounded like she'd enjoyed what had just happened. "Won't hurt anything, not for a long time."

But there was a frenzied anger in me that wouldn't let go, and I kicked the rubbery, broken thing another half dozen times, seeing dim sprays of fluid in the half-light and liking the way they looked. When I stopped I was gasping, and my heart beat like a stamping press set on high, but all I wanted to do was kick the nasty thing some more. Hell was definitely getting to me.

I found the key on its belt, along with a string of little bells and enough sharp objects to get an entire street gang thrown in jail. I wiped scum off the torch until it burned brightly again, and at Heartspider's direction I gathered up her bones, still ribboned with leathery shreds of flesh. I had nothing to carry them in, but I found some rags stiff with old blood and tied them into a hobo's bindle, then slung it over my shoulder. The bones clicked against each other as I made my way out into the dark corridor. I swear, they sounded happy.

Heartspider spoke into my ear, making me jump. "If only we could give Niloch the same, but he is too strong for you."

I had no urge to encounter my host again. "Just tell me where to go. How do I get out?"

"Down. Like most lordlings in Hell, the Commissar of Wings and Claws has many ways in and out of his lair. Down where the boilers are. Down."

I let her guide me downstairs and across several basement floors. Even in the middle of the infernal night, there were sounds coming from behind doors that made me pray—yes, pray—that I never had to see what was on the other side. The place was a maze, and by the time we found our way down to what Heartspider told me was the lowest level, I was certain that Niloch or his slaves must have noticed the mess I'd left behind, especially because most of it had been his beloved jester.

The bottom room was more like the Roman catacombs, endless arches of heavy stone and gigantic pipes that looked like they might have been made of fired clay, lit by the kind of globe lights I had seen in the entry hall. It looked almost ordinary, like the underbelly of a subway station or some other bit of urban architecture, except for the bulging pipes, and the curses written on the wall by slaves or prisoners in their own blood.

"The breath of the underworld," Heartspider said when I asked her what the pipes carried. "It fires the lights and Niloch's machines."

Which must be the volcanic gas he'd bragged about, the endless supply that had helped make the commissar a powerful lord in these central realms of Hell.

I could hear noises drifting down from above now, voices shouting and the slap of feet. I knew I didn't have long, so I let Heartspider guide me through the maze of tunnels and pipes. Unfortunately, she didn't know the bottom level all that well, so I spent as much time retracing my steps as going forward, and each moment I got more nervous. Niloch must be searching the house, and how long before a party would be sent down here? The distances between lights was growing longer; if I hadn't had the torch I would have never found my way.

"There!" Heartspider told me as we rounded a corner. At the end of the passage a ladder of ancient wood led upward into a vertical tunnel. "That passage leads up to the gardens. From there you can find a way off Niloch's land and burn my bones. Then I'll be free to begin again."

Heartspider's words had given me an idea. I searched the floor until I found a piece of loose stone, then stretched up as high as I could and smashed the shining globe at the end of the corridor. I ran back up the passage and quickly smashed a dozen more.

"What are you doing?" Heartspider demanded. "Niloch will be out with his hunting birds in a moment. They'll shred you with their iron beaks. You can't wait. You must get me off his land, or I will never be free!"

I could hear the gas hissing out of the broken lights as I ran back. This wouldn't be the fancy kind of gas that had a smell, but I was pretty sure it could damage me, so I hurried to the ladder and started climbing. At the top I found my way blocked by a rusted iron hatch, but the thing hadn't been all the way closed and I was able to force it open, although not without doing more damage to my already torn and bloodied demon body. When I climbed out into the relative brightness of the lit garden, I pushed the lid down again and sat on it. I could hear excited noises from Gravejaw House a short distance away, so I knew I didn't have long, but despite Heartspider hissing and snarling in my ear, I waited.

"He'll come! He'll find you! His dogs will chew your bones—and mine!"

I ignored her. She raged at me, but I wouldn't move.

"You fool! What are you doing? Do you have any idea . . . ?"

Somewhere just out of my sight I heard the great front doors creak as someone began to draw the bolt, which probably meant Niloch had finished searching the house, or at least had decided it was unlikely I was still inside. Any moment now he would come riding out with slaves and soldiers and his iron-mouthed birds, whatever kind of horror *those* were.

"You traitor! You are dooming yourself, too!"

Even as Heartspider's voice rose to a pitch of despair I felt sure the commissar would be able to hear, I turned and yanked the hatch back open. It screeched as rusty metal rubbed on metal, resisting me, but I only had to get it up just a little way. I pushed the torch through and forced the hatch closed again, then started to run across the stony garden, heading for the shelter of a copse of petrified trees.

The ground shook. For a moment, the grounds in front of me were illuminated by a gust of fiery light as the burning gas forced its way out of the hatch, blowing the metal lid through the air like a communion wafer in a tornado. It almost hit me as it came down, digging deep into the ground, then a roll of thunder shook the ground again, and Gravejaw House vomited fire from half its windows.

Heartspider had been too stunned to speak, but as I crept back toward the hatch she began to beg me not to waste this chance. I'm not even sure she knew that I had caused the explosion. The flames were licking up from the tunnel as though the whole of the catacombs were on fire. The ground boomed and shook beneath me. When I steadied myself again I saw that one of the walls of Gravejaw House was toppling in an avalanche of old stone. I could hear a few screams from the part of the house still standing. Heartspider was right: I really didn't want to hang out there very long.

I took the bundle of her bones from my shoulder and tossed it into the hatch. Heartspider's voice shrieked in my ears. "Traitor! Traitor! I put my curse on—" And then she fell silent as the bones ticked down the hatchway tunnel into the inferno below, and she realized what was happening.

"Ah!" she gasped, like a drowning woman who had finally broken the surface. And then, as baking heat scorched her last remains to ash, she was gone.

"Yes, I did it," I said, although I was talking only to myself now. "After all, a deal is a deal."

As I made my way across the grounds curious bystanders flocked into the gardens and toward the commissar's castle, staring in awe at the pillar of fire currently towering above Gravejaw House, demon spectators mostly. Tellingly, not a single one seemed to be there to help, but stood watching as Niloch's slaves struggled against the hungry blaze. Of the slaves' owner there was no sign, and I wasn't going to wait around to see if the commissar had survived. I sort of doubted you could kill one of Hell's nobles with fire, anyway. The problem was, so many damned and demons were milling around that someone was bound to remember me when Niloch came thundering out after revenge.

One of the spectators, a creature with the discolored head of a pig set on the long body of an NBA shooting guard, followed me as I tried to make my way discreetly through the outskirts of the crowd.

"You there!" he said. "Slave! Stop or I'll have you skinned." My dirty, scorched, bloody nakedness was disguise enough, it seemed, at least with this idiot. But seeing him standing there in his long black robe gave me another idea. "How is our beloved commissar?" he demanded. "Is he safe? You must tell him that his loyal tradesman, Trotter, asked after his health."

I nodded eagerly and beckoned for him to follow me. He fell in behind, perhaps hoping to be led to the commissar himself so he could get in a little timely ass-kissing. When we were out of sight of the rest of the onlookers I hurried through the winding gardens. The skeletonized shrubs were weeping, trying helplessly to shake falling embers off their leaves. When we reached the hatch I did my best to ignore the hot metal against my torn skin as I got close. The flames had retreated, but not far, and the hot air that rushed up from the pipe felt like it blistered my skin.

"See," I said. "See, Master, see!"

Trotter stepped forward, curiosity fighting caution, and stood a little way back from the pipe, craning his piggy head forward on the end of his long neck in an attempt to see. I leaned out over the hatch as if the agonizing heat wasn't hurting me, and beckoned again. "Look!"

When he had leaned far enough, I shoved him down with enough force to crush his windpipe against the rim of the pipe. As he fought for breath, I slammed his head over and over against the edge of the hatch until he stopped struggling, then peeled off his robe with bloody, ragged fingers. Trotter's body was as gray and knobby and unpleasant as I would have expected. I suppose I should have felt sorry for him or bad about myself, since I had just murdered him in cold blood and everything (well, horribly crippled him, since no one died in Hell) but I didn't. I didn't have enough *me* left. All I knew was that I had to get out of Gravejaw and up the great lifter. I no longer had only to reach Pandaemonium and accomplish my business without being caught, although it would be a hundred times harder now that Hell would be looking for an outsider on the loose. No, it was crystal-clear that I had to find Caz and get out of this place of unending horrors before I went truly and finally mad.

nineteen

going down

THE GOOD thing was that I could see the gigantic lifter shaft from pretty much anywhere in the city of Gravejaw. The bad thing was that even after I had scrambled across the endless scorched wasteland of Niloch's gardens and climbed the outer wall, I still had to get across the entire wretched slum to reach it. Apparently the Commissar of Wings and Claws had seen the immense structure as an insult to his own awesomeness, so he had set up housekeeping on the highest piece of land, which happened to be a couple of miles away from the lifter.

Now that his house was going up in flames, the reddish light made it seem like Hell's midday had come early, and I could see a great throng of hellfolk hurrying up the hill toward me from the surrounding city. I was just looking around for something to use as a weapon when the first of them reached me and sprinted past, hurrying toward the disaster. They just kept coming, more and more, shouting, honking, making noises I don't have words for. Some hopped and some flew (although not well enough to write home about) and others teeter-tottered along on mismatched legs, but none of them gave me much more than a glance. The stolen robe helped, and I guess I wasn't burned enough to be worth staring at.

I fought my way against the throng like a queer salmon in spawning season, trying as hard as you'd guess to avoid body contact, but still getting speared, smeared, or dusted every few steps. Very few of the creatures pushing past me seemed upset or frightened by what was happening. In fact, to judge by the hundreds of deformed faces I saw, most seemed downright thrilled, and the rest were at least interested. I don't think the commissar had a lot of fans.

I pushed free of the worst of the mob at last and hurried down to the base of the hill. There were still residents in the narrow streets of Gravejaw, demons and damned who couldn't just drop their business to go watch something fun. Many were blind, and some had sensory organs so alien they might not even have realized what was going on. Others clearly just couldn't move fast enough. I passed a thin man hopping slowly along the road waving his right hand as I passed him. Only when I turned to look back did I realize that he only *had* a right: he had been bisected from head to crotch like a medical cadaver being prepared for one of those see-through views, and was hopping on one foot, trying to balance that thin half body and half head with his single arm. As I looked back, I could see his exposed organs and brain flash wetly as he wobbled.

Creatures like salted slugs, like toads with bone disease, or broken-winged birds, many with heads too big for the bodies or bodies too big for the heads, I hurried past them all, trying not to see too much but still seeing more than I wanted. The lower part of Gravejaw was built on a series of small hills, and following the tiny streets up and down was like being on the world's only human-powered roller coaster. I ran through half the city, it seemed, out of the center and into outer districts where trading and torture went on side by side, as if it were any other night. Even this far away, the ones with eyes must have been able to see the burning castle on the hilltop but none of them seemed to care very much. The only comment I heard was from a mostly skeletal, three-eyed giant with a hammer who was carefully crushing the shinbones of a chained prisoner in front of what must have been a very strange shop: He looked up to the hilltop as I hurried by and said to his companion, who was digging at the same prisoner's eye with a spoon, "It's burning good. Burning *real* good."

His companion looked up for a moment, nodded, then accidentally dropped his spoon into the muck at his feet. He picked it up, carefully licked it clean, and then went back to work.

I passed buildings that looked like factories, the sort of hellish mills that even William Blake probably couldn't have imagined. Some streamed blood-colored sewage, and the doorways were littered with burned and mangled bodies of what were probably accident-prone employees, many of them scraping at the iron factory doors to get back in, despite their horrible wounds. I heard the clang of huge machines and watched smoke and steam belching from furnace chimneys. I couldn't help noticing that things on this level had advanced from the medieval tech of Abaddon to something a bit more eighteenth century, steam and infernal machines dwelling happily alongside plague and utter poverty.

The closer I got to the lifter shaft, the more awesome the structure became. Like a skyscraper, the stone cylinder was nearly as big around as a city block, but that was nothing compared to how high it stretched upward before its length vanished in the upper darkness. I couldn't imagine how something so tall supported its own weight without guy wires or buttresses. It was an engineering feat that would have made any pharaoh proud.

The lifter stood in the middle of a busy town square, an open plaza like the kind you sometimes see around the big cathedrals in Europe. As I approached, more cautiously now, a few people wandered out of the archways at the bottom of the shaft. The crowds in the square here seemed all but oblivious to Niloch's burning citadel, going on with their public business of theft, gambling, fornication, and various other pastimes. I was in an area where someone in a hurry drew no attention at all, except for the usual swarm of pickpockets, rapists, and knife-wielding psychopaths that hang around anywhere people arrive and depart. If I had slowed down I'm sure they would have begun to move in on me, but as it was I must have looked like too much work.

I entered the lifter tower through the nearest arch and saw there were actually several individual lifter cars traveling up and down narrower shafts that ran through the big building like nerves in their sheaths. I stayed back for a bit, watching, but in most ways it looked pretty straightforward, not much different than an elevator bank in a modern office building: One of the lifter doors would open, and those waiting would push their way on while others forced their way out. The passengers looked more prosperous than the wretches lolling outside in the plaza. Many of these travelers were dressed in impressive outfits, and some were so physically imposing that no one else would get into the lifter with them for fear of being smashed or spiked. That made sense, though: the wealthy were more likely to be using the lifters than the pathetic groundlings. I knew from Lameh's implanted memories that Hell's inhabitants were strongly discouraged from going above their designated levels, and who was going to go any farther down voluntarily?

After watching for what felt like ten minutes or so, I waited until the most recent group of passengers had dispersed, then gathered my courage to walk to the nearest lifter door. Another fellow shuffled up beside me, probably the demon equivalent of a Japanese salaryman at the end of a long night's work, and we entered the lifter together.

We were the only passengers, but the interior of the rusty iron box was full of trash and spattered fluids, some still wet. My fellow passenger had a head like a buzzard, but his eyes were multifaceted like a fly's. He was dressed in shabby but fairly clean gray robes that exposed only his clawed feet. He gave me a cold look and an even colder nod, then lifted his hand—instead of being feathered it looked like another bird's foot—and placed it on the wall of the lifter. He mumbled something I couldn't quite hear, but I was already scrambling to imitate him. I put my hand against the gritty iron wall and quietly said, "Pandaemonium." I was half ready to be quizzed about my bona fides, but instead the door slid creakily shut and the lifter started to shudder. The shuddering went on and on for what seemed like a full minute, then at last the lifter groaned, a noise like a giant metal cow giving birth, and to my silent joy and relief the box began to move upward.

Slowly at first, then faster and faster, we rattled up the great pipe. The lifter car, which was built more like a bank safe than a flimsy human elevator, nevertheless shook and screeched so much as it was tugged or pushed upward that at first I was certain we were going to derail, or whatever the hell elevators do when they go wrong. Instead we just kept going faster and faster, so that my ears began popping like popcorn. Then a flat, uncaring voice said, *"Sour Milk Park, Hateful, Lower Childskull,"* and the elevator slowed to a banging halt. The fly-buzzard man waited until the door squeaked open, then stepped out without a backward glance, as if in a hurry to get away from me. Just like folks back home.

I waited as the steam built up again (or whatever), everything hissing and vibrating. The door began to slide closed. It was amazing to consider that after all I'd gone through, I was now only a short elevator ride from my destination. If I had been a regular angel I would have felt confirmed that God really was watching over me after all, and was going to reward me for all my years of good behavior. Of course, if I had been a regular angel I would already have banked a few years of good behavior just in case. Sadly, though, that is one of the many accounts with my name on it that's come up a bit short.

But just before the door finished closing, something dark poked through and stopped it. The appendage gripping the door looked less like a hand and more like something you might find buried in a cat's litter box. The force of the door being restrained seemed to make the whole lifter strain, as if it was determined to break the deadlock or destroy itself trying. The mechanism whined, the shuddering increased. Then the door slid back open.

The thing that stepped in was a bulky man-shape made entirely of mud. It was naked and nearly without features except for a popped bubble of a mouth and a blob of wet clay that I guessed was a nose, mostly because it was somewhere near the two glowing yellow smears it wore for eyes. If I tell you those eyes looked like some kind of irradiated slugs emerging from a scabed, you'll maybe begin to grasp how much I didn't like looking at them. But it wasn't just the eyes. I could *feel* this new thing, feel its age and its inhumanity. I don't know what it was, but it was no ordinary demon.

The passenger-blob stopped inside the door, and its weight actually made the massive car tilt. The shapeless face swiveled toward me for a moment but then slowly kept turning, examining the entire empty lifter, as though I was so insignificant that before it acknowledged me it had to establish what someone *not* being there looked like. Being alone in a confined space with the thing made me feel trapped and queasy. This was no mere infernal salaryman. This was something old and powerful.

The door closed. The thing stretched its flat, muddy paw to the wall. When it spoke its destination, I was so disturbed by the squelchy, inhuman voice that I only registered some moments later that it had said, "Tartarus Station."

Something was seriously wrong. I knew a bit of Hell's geography, both from Lameh and my travels, and I was pretty fucking sure that the direction to Tartarus Station wasn't up, where I was going, but down. *Way* down.

Then the hissing and the trembling crested and the lifter started to drop. I stared in dismay. The mud thing looked back at me, as disinterested as a statue.

"We're . . . going down," I said finally.

The thing gave me as much response as it thought my observation deserved, which was none.

"But I'm going up," I said, trying to keep the panic out of my voice. "That is, I need to go up. To Pandaemonium. It's important." The thing just stared at me with those glowing egg-yolk eyes. "I'm not joking! I need to go to Pandaemonium!"

At last it opened its mouth. The words came out in sticky chunks, like someone digging in a bog with a shovel. "We have taken control of the lifter. We have been given a priority task by the Mastema. Use of the lifter will be returned to you when we have departed."

The Mastema was one of the most powerful tools of the Adversary, a security group of sorts, like the SS were to the Nazis. But I had already guessed that this guy was bad, bad news.

In the silence that followed his proclamation, I heard the announcement voice whispering in my ear as we flashed past Gravejaw again, then Greedy Pile, Cellar of Organs, Cocytus Delta, Brownwater, Toe, and Cocytus Landing. In just a few moments we would be hurtling down through Abaddon where I had first entered Hell. My heart was hammering, but I was so obviously outclassed and outranked by the mud man that I dared not make a fuss. Perhaps once he got out, I could simply make the elevator go back up again.

Did I really think it would be that easy? Well, let's just say I was hoping.

The lifter was dropping faster now, the voice spitting the names of the levels into my ears like a racetrack announcer trying to call a close four-horse finish. *Abaddon Heights. Disease Row. Necro Flats. Acheron Fork. Lower Acheron Fork. Abaddon Waste.* And then we were through the Abaddon levels and still plunging downward. At first I thought it was just fear that was making me feel feverish, but then I realized that the lifter cage was getting hotter and closer by the second. The sweat vaporized from my skin as soon as I squeezed it out. My blood hammered in my ears.

The mud man ignored my gasps, immersed perhaps in thoughts of the horrible place he was going, the horrible things he would be doing, but now he began to *change*. His hide, or whatever it was that had made him look like he was smeared with something sticky, peanut butter or some less pleasant material, was beginning to harden like clay fired in a kiln. As he dried his skin grew smoother, stonier, until he really did begin to look like a statue, a seven foot tall golem, dead but for the smoldering, piss-yellow eyes.

I could barely understand the announcements now, the words running together so that I could snatch only fragments: *"Flensing Scar Tissue Junction Hook Burning Shrike Fistula . . ."* But it wasn't just the heat that made me feel like I was dying now, it was the words turning into pictures in my brain, with no work from my own imagination. Somehow the depth acted on me like increasing pressure, forcing images into my head, endless halls full of screeching voices, reflex cries for help that the screecher knew wasn't coming, chambers as big as grand ballrooms full of stone tables, each table with a ruined but still living body writhing atop it, animals without eyes, rooms full of thunder and blood spray, the pounding of metal against vulnerable flesh, barking dogs, howling wolves, and through it all a sensation of unparalleled misery and hopelessness that squeezed my skull like a monstrous pair of pliers.

"I can't," I gasped.

The clay thing stared at me for a moment, then looked away, as if I were a leaf that had blown across its path.

The pressure grew stronger, but the other passenger had simply become more compact, more shiny, as if it had been glazed and fired in a kiln.

Punishment. Punishment. Punishment. Every name the voice whispered into my head seemed to have that word in it. *Punishment.* We were heading down into the ultimate depths, where the worst work of Hell went on in endless night, pain measured out in just the right size doses to last as long as the universe itself.

Even worse, though, I could feel *something else* now, something that enwrapped and increased the other bad feelings like a crushing, ice-cold fist. I can't explain it—I'll never be able to. Although it came on slowly, when I finally could pick it out from the other kinds of horror, it was the worst thing I've ever felt. Freezing cold, but I'm not talking about temperature, like ice and snow. This was the cold of the absolute dark, the cold in which nothing could live, the point at which even the play of atoms slowed to a stop. Empty. Nothing. The end. But what was most terrifying about it, what blasted even the horrors of all Hell's pain and suffering out of my head, was that this bleak void at the bottom of everything was *alive*. I don't know how I knew, but I did. It was alive, and it thought, and even though it was still tremendously far away, its presence sent my own thoughts shrieking in all directions like chickens trapped in a henhouse by a bloody-mouthed wolf.

I realized that I had fallen on my knees, clutching my head to keep my skull from exploding, retching out what little was in my stomach. Still the pressure and the sense of the thinking, waiting darkness grew worse. I was shrieking, babbling—I might even have screamed that I was an angel, for all I know—but the clay creature sharing the lifter paid no attention. I could feel my eyes forced out of their sockets from within, could feel my guts crushed like I'd been rammed from both sides by garbage trucks, could feel what was left of my sanity pouring out of a me-shaped hole like dirty water down a drain. And then we stopped.

When the shuddering ended, I lay in a limp blob where I was, unable to stand or speak. Something closed on me like a claw in one of those arcade games, lifting me up until I dangled in midair, wheezing and moaning. I could dimly see the stale yellow eyes of the mud man as he looked me over, then the door of the lifter opened and he threw me out like a dirty shirt. A moment later, as I wriggled on the baking stone floor outside the lifter, helpless as a waterlogged earthworm, the lifter door hissed shut. I heard the pressure build again, then it was gone, the cage clanking and groaning as it dropped into the depths.

For the longest time I just lay where I was, boiling inside like an Ebola victim. The physical constitution of my demon body was apparently enough to keep me alive, but not enough to save my mind if I went any deeper. I didn't think I'd last very long even if I didn't—my head was still hammering so hard that I could barely think. I had no idea where I was, but I knew I had to get out, go up, even though moving my fingers was nearly impossible, let alone my entire body.

Up, damn you! I stared at my hand, willing it to extend, to help me lift myself, then I saw the feet of the first thing approaching. They were hooved, but not with anything so simple as cow's or horse's hooves. The great single toe and its nail were metal, dull gray metal. It stopped beside me. I would not have looked up even if I could have.

A moment later something else flapped down and landed. All I could see were legs as thin as a flamingo's but with blue human hands for feet. A third creature joined the first two, thick legs ending in a cylindrical foot, covered in thick hair and gleaming spines.

"Well, look here," said one of them in a voice like a rusty leg trap being pried open. It was pretty clear what they were looking at. "Breakfast is served."

"Let's make it run first," another said in a scratchy mumble. It might have been a parrot with half its beak torn off. "I like them when the blood's really moving. Warm and tender."

"Piss on that," said a third, gruff as Baby Bear on steroids. "I'm hungry. Let's just divide it up now, then you can make your piece run around all you want."

twenty
block

I SWEAR I would have managed to turn myself over eventually, but someone did it for me, scooping me onto my back as easy as a fry cook flipping a burger—not an association I wanted to make, believe me.

I was in a high-roofed chamber, the Punishment Level equivalent of a lifter station, but it was clear this station didn't get many casual travelers. The ceiling looked like it had been liberally splashed with things meant to stay inside of people, which had then dried into stalactites. The cracked rock and dirt of the floor beneath me was splattered with dried black blood and scarred with the countless marks of prisoners and cages being dragged across it. The location was the least of my problems, though. The pressure of these depths was still so strong that it took long moments to lift my head and focus on the creatures surrounding me.

The last one who'd spoken, Baby Bear, looked more like a hairy washing machine than any cousin of Smokey's, his already disturbing body made more so by all the bits of machinery that had been awkwardly attached to him with bloody rivets. The other two, who I'll call Bird and Porcupine, were just as unpleasant in their own way: A cross between a stork and the victim of some terrible Third World, flesh-eating virus, Bird had feathered bat wings, a jaggedly sharp beak, and eyes that were only holes in the bird-shaped, partially exposed skull. Porcupine was even less humanoid, four-footed, with huge flat front claws like a badger and a series of bumps on his back which could have been heads, because they all had eyes.

"I'm . . . suh-suh-suh . . ." I was finding it really hard to talk because of the pressure in my head. Hard to think, too. On the plus side, the feeling hadn't got dramatically worse since I'd been thrown out of the elevator by the mud man, and I was beginning to think the pressure alone might not destroy me, at least not right away. That was the only good news. "I'm somebody . . . important."

Bird clacked her beak as those empty sockets looked me up and down. "Hark at the creature! Of course you're important, little thing. You're our num-nums!"

Porcupine growled and pushed at me with his front head. I couldn't see a mouth, but even through the general stench I could smell his hideous breath. "Too much talking. Eat it. You two take what you want, then it's my turn." He reared up, legs spreading wide like a caterpillar climbing to a new branch, and I finally saw his mouth, which ran down the vertical length of his belly like an unfinished autopsy incision, lined with sharp teeth as if it was an ivory zipper.

I confess that I might have made a noise of dismay. Okay, I sort of squealed like a terrified pig—the unwilling guest at a very ugly luau.

Baby Bear folded one of his claspers around me, crunching muscle and bending bone. I shrieked again and rolled with it, since if I didn't he was going to tear my arm right off. "Stop!" I wailed. "You don't understand! I'm . . . I'm on an important mission. For the Mastema!"

A moment of silence followed this. Well, it would have been silence except a low growl was coming from Porcupine's horrible red, toothy stripe of a mouth right next to my ear.

"Just eat it," Porcupine said. "It's talking shit."

"No, I'm not!" It was so hard to think! "I was . . . attacked. While I was on the Mastema's business. You don't want to have that on *your* heads, too, do you?" I looked back at the more-than-necessary number of eyes regarding me. Baby Bear was drooling what looked like motor oil from a mouth full of crude metal teeth. Bird had tipped her skeletal head sideways as if thinking. "If you get me back on the lifter, I can make my report! You'll all be rewarded."

"Hah." Porcupine dropped back down on all fours and shoved me with its lumpy head. "Now it's really talking shit. Reward? Eating this little piece of gristle is our reward. Enough of this."

"Hold a bit, dearie-dove," said Bird. "Maybe we should take it to the Block. I know you're aching for your nummies, but you shouldn't ever fuss with Mastema business."

Porcupine growled again, and Baby Bear echoed him. "Mastema business," said the furry half-appliance. "Fuck 'em sideways. What have they ever done for us?"

"It's not what they've done for us," said Bird sweetly, still watching me with those empty eye holes. "It's what they might do *to* us. Do you remember what happened in Lesser Organs? When they came for Mudlips?"

Both Porcupine and Baby Bear quickly took a step back, much to my relief.

"Can we eat some of it, at least, before we take it to the Block?" Porcupine whined. "I'm so fucking, scabbing hungry!" I could hear its stomach-incisors clicking together.

"The Block," said Bird firmly. "But don't feel bad, chummy—we still might get to eat it all. Maybe play with it a bit, too."

"We'd better," said Baby Bear.

I could barely walk, but it didn't matter, because Baby Bear dragged me behind him like a toddler's toy. I had no idea what the Block was. All I knew is that the needles on my Going To Get Eaten Now dial had temporarily swung back out of the red. I had a feeling that I might have been able to beat these things or at least escape them if we were someplace else, but here in the crushing depths it was all I could do to stay conscious and even slightly sane. It wasn't just the feeling of pressure that was crippling me; everything I had felt on the way down, especially that singular, fearful . . . *presence* . . . was still in me like an awful sickness, a horror hangover that had me trembling, nauseated, and all but helpless.

The trio of demons dragged me down long corridors echoing with screams and less articulate noises, past room after room, each one a laboratory where new kinds of pain were devised and put to use. I saw prisoners torn, smashed, pulled to pieces, scalded with steam, boiled into nerve-spaghetti and then stretched on hot wires until the nerves vibrated like plucked violin strings in screams I could feel without hearing. On we trudged, through long stretches of flickering darkness, past horror after moaning, gurgling horror, until what little command I had over my thoughts began to slip again. It felt pointless to keep struggling, to try to stay sane. Why fight? Even if I got out of here somehow, Hell was practically endless, and I still had to walk right into my enemy's stronghold and try to steal Caz right from under the grand duke's nose, then escape him and all his power and somehow get back out of Hell again.

The word for that, it seemed pretty clear, was "impossible." I hadn't thought it was a great plan even before I got to Hell, but as my friends often tell me, I have a tendency to be way the fuck too optimistic.

At last, after I had been dragged past too many rooms full of shrieking meat to care anymore, we arrived at a desk in front of a big, black door. The female creature sitting behind the desk had a lovely golden-curled head like a postcard angel, but the rest of her body was a giant centipede's, and she had to coil her segmented body around the arms of the chair to stay seated properly behind the desk. She eyed my captors with suspicion.

"Wha?" The golden centipede girl had the slurred voice of an ancient rummy or a punchdrunk fighter. "Wha you want?"

"We have to see the Block, lovely one," said Bird. "We need to show him."

"Nah gon' habben." I could see now that the reason the receptionist (or whatever she was) talked that way was because she had a mouth full of smaller centipedes. A couple of them fell out onto the desk and then began to climb their way back up her body, heading toward the mouth. "The Block do' wanna be disthurb . . . disturb . . ." She paused to gulp down the ones who'd returned, then lifted a pincered claw to keep the rest from making an escape in the confusion. "Disturbed."

"Oh, he doesn't?" snarled Porcupine, but Bird waved a feathered claw.

"He'll want to see this, sweetling. He truly will."

Golden Girl stared at Bird for a moment, her head so completely human that I couldn't help wondering if she'd looked that way in life, like a goddess of dawn. Then the reception-thing broke the impasse by slithering over the back of the seat and making her way, on all those tiny little legs, along the wall to the door, head waggling like the unstable burden it must have been. She pulled the door open a bit with her front legs and said something through the opening, causing several more little centipedes to tumble out of her mouth to the ground, where they began their long crawl back to, presumably, comfort and safety. Then the ruined goddess swiveled her golden head around to us and said, "It's to go in alone. The rest of you lot stay out here."

Getting up was hard enough. Walking was harder, and I couldn't make it happen right away. Baby Bear finally gave me a shove, and I lurched through the door, catching myself in the doorframe so I didn't go in on my face.

The room was dank and dim, only one tiny oil lamp on the desk for illumination. The thing that sat behind the desk seemed almost human at first glance, eyes, ears, and nose in most of the right places. His facial skin, however, had been peeled down and hung in a fringe around his neck, like a particularly horrible Renaissance ruff. His facial muscles and exposed tissue were white and red, like raw bacon, but his eyes were alert and disturbingly intelligent. He wore the remains of what looked like a fairly modern military uniform. He grinned at me, or at least bared his teeth. Every tooth was black and too big.

"So what are you?" Words like hot fat dripping. "Eat or punish?"

"Neither, great Block, neither!" I had no idea who this wet, red fellow was or what rank he held, but I wasn't in a position to bluster. One look told me that this was the kind of minor functionary who ruled over his personal corner of Hell like a little tin god. "I am a traveler from the upper reaches—Snakestaff of the Liars Sect." The Liars supplied Hell's advocates, my usual opponents in my angelic business. I knew a little about them even before Lameh's briefing, so I'd chosen them as my cover. "I'm on the Mastema's business here in the lower levels, but I was attacked."

"By Polly Parrot and her little crew?" He really thought that was funny. For a moment I had the insane hope he'd choke himself laughing, but then I remembered he was that color of red all the time. "Oh, good. Very good!"

"No, I was attacked by . . . hirelings in the service of my enemies, who were angry that the Mastema favored me with a commission." I was improvising, but considering that my head felt like it was stuck in an industrial paint mixer, and that I'd just vomited out my brain, I thought I was doing pretty well. "My enemies cornered me in the lifter," I went on, "but I was able to escape them here, on this level." I did my best to sound calm and in control. "The ones who sent me will know how I was treated, both there and here." Appeals to altruism weren't likely to be my best approach, so I said, "Of course those who get in my way will be punished, but I promise those who help me will be remembered and rewarded." It was hard to sound authoritative when I could barely stand and felt like a baked turd, but I gave it my best shot.

"Rewarded, rewarded. That has a nice sound." The Block pushed himself back from his desk a little, which was when I noticed that he was tied to his chair with barbed wire; nothing remained below his ribs but a dangling length of nerves and backbone. Something like a large black slug clung to the end of the Block's spine, and pulsed wetly as it sucked at it, like a French gourmet hungry for marrow. Every time it swelled I saw little ripples of pain cross the Block's huge, raw face. It was nice to know he wasn't having a lot of fun either. "Ah, but you see," he said, "I have *already* been rewarded for my loyal service. I have been given the gift of memory, the gift of remembering all the other services I have performed, when I was alive and afterward." The Block smiled again, although now I could see it was a grin of pain as the thing chewed and sucked at his spine. "What greater reward could I wish than the justice of the Highest and the opportunity to serve here?"

He was playing with me. I could feel it. Did he mean to let me go or keep me? Had he decided yet?

I let go of the doorframe, trying to look casual but mostly swaying. "Of course, great Block, you must have all you want. What could give you more pleasure than doing the Adversary's sacred work here? Surely not even being transferred to a position of responsibility on a higher level could tempt a servant as loyal as you." It sounds pretty sharp, but there were a lot of gasps and grunts mixed in as I struggled to stay upright. I was getting used to the insane pressure in my skull, but I sure hadn't learned to enjoy it.

"Oh, it all sounds very important." He gave me another one of those flat black grins as a wave of anguish rippled across his beet-red face. "Very important indeed. I'm sure you know important leaders."

"Niloch, the Commissar of Gravejaw is a personal friend." I hoped Niloch was too busy being a smoldering ash to ever tell this guy the truth. "And I don't want to drop names . . . but there's Eligor the Horseman. The grand duke, you must know him . . . ?"

"Eligor?" His mouth tightened. "I am not fortunate enough to know His Grace, of course. But if he is a friend of yours . . ."

"Yes! Old friend. We're like this." I held up my hand, the two fingers side by side. "Just the other day he told me, 'Snakestaff, when you're back from this errand, you must come and stay with me.'" Which wasn't altogether a lie—I was pretty certain Eligor would be very happy to put me up if he found out I was in town. It was just that the accommodations weren't going to be even as nice as this place was.

"You have convinced me." The Block's face suddenly went darker, as though something was squeezing it in a huge invisible fist. When the spasm had passed, he said, "Come. Give me your hand."

Almost twenty years of Earth life had made me a fool. I stuck out my right, just as if I was about to receive a congratulatory handshake and maybe even a small check. Bobby Dollar, Miss Fucking Congeniality. The Block's thick, all too human hands closed around my wrist and yanked me forward. "There is a toll to pay, of course," he said. Before I could get my balance he shoved my entire hand into his wide, black-toothed mouth, which felt worse than I can describe. Then he bit down.

I may not have been wearing my own body, and the demon body was obviously not remotely human, but I can tell you that it still hurt like an ungodly motherfucker to have my hand chewed off. Before I knew it I was down on my knees, whimpering and gasping as I tried desperately to stanch the blood pumping from the ragged end of my wrist. Block spit the hand back out. It lay for a moment on his desk like a bloated dead spider, then he lifted it and tore off three of the fingers, each making its own dreadful wet snap.

"Polly!" he shouted. The door opened. The bird-thing stood there.

"Yes, great Block?"

He tossed the fingers out to her as if he was throwing scraps to pets. I heard Bird and Porcupine and Baby Bear fighting over them, but I was in so much pain it seemed unreal. The Block raised the rest of the hand to his mouth and began tearing it apart and eating it in great, appreciative bites, the crimson muscles of his cheeks bulging as he smashed the bones between black molars. When he finished, he wiped most of the blood from his mouth and chin with the back of his meaty, hairy hand, then gave a small belch of appreciation.

"They will put you back on the lifter," he said. "Remember that I could have taken more, Snakestaff of the Liars Sect. Tell your masters in the far heights that the Block could have sent nothing back but the head, and they still would have known everything they wished to know." He gripped the edge of his chair with his two strong hands, lifting himself until the barbed wire stopped him. The slug-thing at the end of his ruined spine swung like the clapper of a church bell. I was too busy waiting to die from pain and nausea and fountaining blood to notice very much, but I heard him bellow, "This is my corner of Hell! I rule here! And if the great Black Master himself came to me, I would have my morsel of flesh from him as well. Yes, I would pick my teeth with his tail! Because I am Block the executioner! Block the butcher!"

He was still raving when Baby Bear grabbed me in his heavy claws and dragged me out.

I squeezed the torn end of my arm as tightly as I could while they dragged me back down those scream-echoing corridors, but I was losing blood very fast. I could feel my wrist bone digging into my good hand, but beyond that incredibly strange and painful sensation, I knew the rest of my body was slowly packing up its signaling apparatus and surrendering. As we reached the lifter even the wails of the tormented became muted, and the grotesque faces of Polly Parrot and her gang grew mercifully blurry. I felt a new pain, as though my stump was being sanded with broken glass: Baby Bear was licking the bloody wound. I slipped in and out of consciousness as we waited. It might have been a minute later, it might have been an hour, but the lifter finally arrived, groaning like an overloaded truck bumping down a steep hill. When the door opened, they kicked me a few times, then pitched me inside.

Already blood was pooling underneath me. The vibration of the lifter had almost shaken me senseless, and I seemed to be entering a long, black tunnel, crawling away from light and hope. I slapped my good hand against the wall, and as my other wrist started spurting again I tried to call out my destination. The words came in little wet blobs of sound, like bloody mucus: "The . . . Red . . . City."

The lifter shook even harder, rattling me like a bug in a killing jar. Then the black tunnel of my thoughts collapsed around me.

twenty-one

terminus

"*. . . Fistula, Poor Meat, Heartbreak Soup, and Phlegethon Docks . . .*"

I awoke to the sound of the lifter voice announcing the terrible places we were approaching and passing in quick succession. The pressure in my head was easing, although that was no longer the worst of my problems. As I struggled to make sense of things, the voice announced several more stops along the fiery River Phlegethon, during which time I managed to pull myself into a sitting position with my back against the lifter's shuddering wall. My blood sloshing on the floor looked as though it might reach an inch deep if it ever puddled in one place. I felt like a smashed hourglass.

To my dull surprise, several more passengers had joined me while I was unconscious, an array of mixed sweets that altogether made for quite a diabolical little chocolate-box: beast-things, blob-things, and even a few almost humanoid shapes, mostly better dressed than what I had grown used to seeing. I couldn't look at them long, since my eyes wouldn't focus properly, but these more upper-crusty travelers seemed to have ranged themselves as far away from me along the lifter wall as possible. Under other circumstances I would have found it amusing, citizens of Hell fastidiously trying to avoid a little blood. Of course, not a single passenger offered to help me or even looked at me with anything deeper than casual distaste. As you might guess, Hell is not big on empathy.

When my head stopped spinning so damn fast, I tore a strip from my robe and clumsily tied it around the ragged stump of my wrist to slow the bleeding. If I had been in a human body, perhaps even in one of my enhanced angelic bodies, I would have been long dead, but this demon form was sturdy, at least in terms of blood loss. With the pressure easing, I would actually have felt healthier than I had in hours if I hadn't been so weak and dizzy.

Then again, I had to admit, *maybe I'm just feeling better because I've almost bled out. Maybe this is what it feels like to die in Hell—the nicest thing that happens to you all day.*

I didn't really think I'd be allowed to die, of course. I would either be recycled into some permanent garbage heap of misery or, if I was deemed important enough, get swept up and shuttled off to the infernal body shops for replacement, which would be worse, since they'd probably notice when their meters all read, "ALERT! UNDERCOVER ANGEL! EXTERMINATE! EXTERMINATE!"

The lifter kept banging to a violent halt and then just as violently starting up again as people got on and off, more all the time as we rose higher—Phlegethon Heights, Lower Mandible, Brokebone, Shrill Hollows, and a raft of others I was too fuzzy to understand properly When we started to get to the Lethe levels, starting with the Lower Lethe Basin, I pulled the makeshift bandage tight just a few inches below the wound, preparing to run, or at least crawl, toward safety when I got to my destination.

Upward we shot, through more Lethian stops, then on through a number of the lower suburbs of Pandaemonium. Memories implanted by Lameh told me the Red City itself was stacked many levels deep. The announced stops were all enticing—Ass Crack, Disgust, Filth Lake—but I finally heard the words I'd been waiting for, Styx Loch. See, the waterways of Hell all twine around each other like the strands of a DNA molecule, or at least that's how I picture it in my head. And though the River Styx surrounded and also flowed through the bottom-most levels of Erebus and Tartarus (and for all I know might have lapped gently at the hooves of the Adversary himself down in the ultimate darkness) it also cradled the uppermost levels, and that meant we had almost reached Pandaemonium.

Even through the delirium and weakness, something struck me. An oddity. You'd have expected that if the Adversary and the most important work of the infernal regions were in the deepest pits, that's where those courting power would have built their homes. Instead they were all up here, as far from those terrible depths as possible, as if Hell's most important lords still somehow, at least dimly, hoped one day to climb back toward the light. Maybe Riprash *had* grasped something important.

The announcer voice went silent for long moments, then said in a flat, doom-laden tone, "Terminus."

With a final seizure and a creak like a nail being dragged out of a hardwood coffin, the lifter ground to a halt. Doors hissed open in a puff of steam. The rest of the passengers, now somewhere close to two dozen, all tightly pressed together except in my bloody part of the car, shuffled out. I was terrified the door might close on me and the lifter drag me back down again, so I didn't even try to rise but simply scrambled out on elbows and knees, doing my best to keep my bloody stump from touching anything. The shock was beginning to wear off and the pain was incredible, as if the raw end had been plunged into a bag of salt. Believe me, they may not let you die in Hell, but they're quite happy to let you suffer to the extent of your capacities and beyond.

The Terminus was immense. You could have plugged a couple of Grand Central Stations into just the lifter station, but it was also the hub of a network of pedestrian tunnels, roads, and (as I discovered to my surprise) railways. The trains fanned out from the central terminus, and as I staggered up the stairs I could see some of them waiting on their tracks—long, low things like millipedes, dull black metal with windows so narrow they might have been gun slits and probably were. I had no time to marvel, though, because every second I was staggering lost in Pandaemonium was a second I was vulnerable to being grabbed by one of the roaming bands of thieves and kidnappers or picked up by the Purified, the elite Mastema guardians of Hell and the only creatures who owed allegiance to the Adversary above all his lesser supporters. Still, although the Purified might not dance to the music of Eligor and Prince Sitri and the other bigwigs, they would definitely agree that Bobby Dollar was *persona non grata* in Hell, and my express ride back to the Punishment Levels would have me under torture as quickly as if Grand Duke Eligor personally caught me in his bedroom.

The Purified were uniformed in semi-modern military gear the color of thunderheads, each one wearing a sort of black spiral on the tunic, like the view from on top of a tornado, perhaps an image of the metaphorical Pit we were all in. This somber gray and black motif was made cheerier by splatters of deep crimson, apparently individual to each soldier. In their bulky metal gear and the strange casque helmets that hid their faces, the Purified could have resembled a Victorian writer's idea of astronauts but for their distorted bodies, which had only "big and strong" in common, along with the astounding variety of weapons they carried, including the first guns I'd seen in Hell.

One last dizzy thought as I stumbled across the main concourse through a crush of Red Citizens as thick as anything I'd found in Abaddon: So was this the level of technology in Pandaemonium? Why? Why did this place look like a fairly modern railway station while down in Abaddon even the comparatively well-off were living like medieval peasants?

Stuff like that tends to snag my interest, but I couldn't get distracted. I was woozy, exhausted, and sick, and if I didn't find the way out I'd attract notice from the armored Purified, who seemed to have little else to do but to stare out their eyeslits at everything and everyone that passed. I found a huge stairway that, in my condition, might as well have been Mt. Everest, but it seemed to lead up toward an area of greater light, or perhaps an even bigger concourse, so I tightened the rag around my wrist again and started up.

It took me what felt like half an hour or more to climb those hundreds of steps. I was pushed and bumped the whole way by flocks of grotesque commuters who shoved me whenever I got in their way, but at last I reached another lobby. It was smaller than the great concourse downstairs, but its monstrously tall and narrow windows glowed with bright red light, and I could see a door that looked open to the outside.

As the uncaring, often actively hostile crowd jostled me out of the terminus and into what I realized must be Dis Pater Square, I saw the heart of the great infernal city for the first time. Pandaemonium was built from what looked like only two kinds of stone, great blocks of volcanic black and something more translucent, almost like quartz, that glowed with a fiery scarlet light. The radiance from the great buildings in its center made the whole metropolis seem to burn like a coal. Add the surrounding black city walls and, from a distance, Pandaemonium looked like a pile of embers burning forever in the darkness.

The Red City. It wasn't that different from other Hell cities I'd seen, just bigger and more so. The sky above my head was a tangle: dozens upon dozens of skyscraper towers loomed crookedly against the darkness, linked to each other by an array of fragile bridges, as if someone had stuck a bunch of giant pickup sticks in the ground, point down, and then dumped another pile right on top to let them settle where they would. Just looking up at this helter-skelter made me lightheaded without taking away a single throb from my wounded arm.

Suddenly I realized I was no longer standing but lying on the ground in front of the Terminus. I had fallen but didn't know when or how long I'd been sprawled there. I climbed back onto my feet and staggered forward again, but the exhausting climb from the lifter had almost ruined me. I had to find safety, but where? I dimly recalled Lameh mentioning a Red City safe house where Snakestaff could hide in an emergency, but my blood-starved brain couldn't summon it up. If only Lameh were still in my demon-head like she'd been in my Bobby-head . . . but I'd left her behind along with my world, hope, and sanity.

Where should I go? I was a sick animal, and I needed to get to ground and lick my wounds, but there were more than a few problems to solve first.

Problem number one: I was in Hell. I had no money, and there was literally no such thing as a free ride here. Even if I could remember where the safe house was, I had no idea how far away it was, though it was likely to be outside the center of the city, and I was so weak I'd barely made it out of the station. I stared blearily at vehicles speeding past me along the narrow streets, the cars of the wealthy, exhaust-belching, low, and slick as snakes. I saw fancy coaches, some drawn by huge rhinolike creatures and others towed by strings of shrieking, beakless birds. I saw jitneys pedaled by near-skeletons and big cargo wagons pulled by headless slaves, but I didn't see a single thing that was going to carry me without charge, and I was pretty certain that if I didn't rest I wouldn't last much longer without fainting again.

I spotted a food-peddler's rickety wagon on the far side of the street, loaded with steaming vats. The owner had a jackal's face and the legs of an anorexic spider, but he seemed the least likely candidate to turn me over to the Purified. All I could think of was climbing into his cart to hide and sleep while he was looking the other way. Everything was darkening in front of my eyes, and a very enticing heaviness was sweeping over me. Bleeding out, it's called, and the idea of "out" was definitely there: I could feel myself diminishing, like something swirled away down a drain. I took a step into the road—no curbs in Hell—and found it was difficult but not impossible to walk. My vision had lost focus, but I could dimly see the shape of the wagon, so I took another step and another. Then something hit me.

I can't really tell you much about what it was, or at least I couldn't at the time, just something big and loud that was suddenly on top of me. Then I was rolling, or flying, spinning across one of the main streets of Pandaemonium, and it was black and white and red all over, just like in the old joke. Rolling, bumping, then another, smaller impact. A feeling like the entire stony sky of Hell had fallen on me, then blackness rushed in.

The last thing I heard, as though spoken into a tin can down the longest, shakiest string any child had ever strung from a tree house, was a surprisingly sweet, feminine voice exclaim, "Oh! The poor, pretty creature!"

Then it all went away.

interlude

*C*AZ WAS *asleep. I was lying beside her, too buzzed to do anything except think, think, think. God knows, I should have been sleeping too, after the day I'd just had—ambushed while trying to auction off something I didn't actually have, shot at, chased by an ancient supernatural monster, several minutes under extremely cold water breathing through a tube, then a couple of hours of vigorous sex with a she-demon. I should have slept for a hundred years like Sleeping Beauty. Instead, Not-Sleeping Bobby lay in Caz's curtained bed with his hands laced behind his head, watching the translucent fabric sway gently in the air-conditioning. The curtains were red, bright yellow, and several shades of earth tones. It seemed odd to me that she would choose such flamelike colors, but the entire apartment was like that, a cross between a grand opera about the Middle East and a Dutch prostitute's red-light flat.*

I was thinking, but not about anything important. I couldn't afford to think about anything important, because at that moment I couldn't do anything about anything. I could have closed my eyes and tried to force myself to sleep, but that never works with me. So instead I just lay there, listening to Caz's quiet breathing and fantasizing about an impossible day when we could be together like this without threatening the entire balance of Creation. But any attempt to imagine a future for us quickly fell apart. Even assuming we weren't vaporized for our crimes by her bosses or mine, where would we live? What would we do?

Before that night, I would have immediately recognized the stupidity of even thinking about an angel like me living a normal, human life. I would have shaken my head, laughed ruefully, then gone out with Sam for a couple of drinks to soak the ashes of the extinguished dream and render it harmless forever. But I wasn't sure that was going to work this time. I wasn't sure if I wanted it to work.

But what was my alternative? This one night, as Caz kept saying, and then nothing? Only memories? I'd been born into my angelic existence without any real memories at all, so I couldn't imagine what it would be like to have memories that were better than the rest of your life could ever be. How could someone live like that? How could someone keep any kind of faith that the universe made sense?

Then again, whatever made me think the universe should make sense? I worked for God Almighty Himself, the Highest, and I was just as confused as every other thinking creature.

Was this really the end? Would I never see this beautiful woman, demon, whatever she was, after tonight? Or, even worse, would I see her again but be unable to do anything except watch her walk past, she condemned to her business, me to mine?

I felt so cold at that sudden vision, so empty, that for a moment I thought my soul might actually be dying.

As though she sensed it, Caz opened her eyes and looked at me. She didn't say anything, just spread her arms as if welcoming me back from a long, hazardous trip. I moved in close until I felt the cool length of her against me from chest to shins, the chill pressure of her cold little feet and her cold little breasts.

We held each other in silence, because there really wasn't anything left to say.

twenty-two
sweet lady zinc

"YOU DEAR man," she said. "You must tell me who did this to you. There was blood everywhere!"

My eyes, which had been sending me nothing useful for some time, just a vague sensation of light and shadow, the kind of thing even a snail can accomplish, finally began to focus on the moving shape. Considering all I had seen and been through, the object slowly coming into view was strangely human. And not just human but quite lovely—a woman in the glowing prime of adult life, with dark, curly hair that turned into a spreading cloud down her shoulders where it had worked loose from her hairpins. Her face was heart-shaped, her cheeks plump and pretty, and even in my pathetic state I couldn't help but notice that she had some serious décolletage (an old-time word for cleavage) going on. Her bright eyes took in my own wandering gaze, and she colored a little with a flush that not only touched her pale cheeks but her breastbone as well, like a dusting of rouge from an invisible brush.

"Who?" I said, then, "What . . . ?" My brain was, I swear to you, prickling like a limb that had fallen asleep. I figured it could be my thinking tissues regenerating after all that oxygen starvation, but it was also possible I'd been so damaged that I was going to be permanently fucked in the head.

"You are safe. I am Lady Zinc, but you may call me Vera."

I suddenly remembered why I had been losing consciousness before

I was struck and darted a look at my injured right arm. The hand was still missing, of course, but it had been carefully bandaged, and the blood had been scrubbed away. What was weird, though, is that I could feel my hand at the end of my arm as though it were still there; I chalked it up to "phantom limb" or whatever they call that syndrome. I was even dressed in clean clothes, some kind of old-fashioned nightshirt of flimsy material, the kind of thing the Sheriff of Nottingham might have worn to a slumber party.

"How did I get here?" I managed all five words without coughing, but it felt as though I hadn't spoken for years. My head was a little better, though. Either I was learning to ignore the prickling in my brain, or it was going away.

"You ran into the street in front of my car, dear man. I thought I'd ruined you, but you've cleaned up very nicely." The dark-haired woman smiled. This couldn't be happening, I thought. Not in Hell. Nobody did anything for free in Hell. Still, I was definitely one of those beggars who couldn't afford to be choosers, so I did my best to smile back and look properly grateful.

"Thank you, Lady Zinc."

"Oh, Vera, please. After all, you're a guest now!" She laughed and stood up. "Which means I really should know your name. Do you mind telling me?"

For just about a half second I couldn't remember—not my Hell-name, not my real name, as though I had just dropped out of the sky into this crazy dream without bothering to bring along any baggage. How much blood had I lost? How close had I been? Then both of the names came to me. I gave her the right one. "Snakestaff of the Liars Sect, my lady. And I'm in your debt."

She laughed again with what sounded like genuine pleasure. "No, no, I am in yours. It was a filthy morning, and it's been a miserable, pointless week. You have cheered me up hugely."

It was the first time I'd ever heard anyone in Hell use a term like "week," and I wondered if that was just Vera's way or something peculiar to Pandaemonium. "Where am I?"

"My house in the Trembling Heights. Now rest. We will have plenty of time to talk as you recuperate. If you need anything, ring the bell for Belle."

It took me a moment to realize the second bell was a name. I was distracted, because Vera had been sitting at the foot of my bed but now stood, and I could see her whole. There was a lot to see. She was curvy but slender-waisted, with a graceful neck, and although she wore a long dress that covered her legs I suspected they were nice, too. Yes, even nearly dead guys notice things like that, even when they're angels in demonic bodies. It had nothing to do with Caz, and it didn't really have anything to do with sex, since I felt so weak I couldn't have put up a convincing tussle with a ball of yarn. That's just the way the male eyes and brain are hooked up. Go sue the Highest if you don't like it.

Lady Zinc went out. I spent a moment surveying the room, which looked like Old Hollywood's idea of the Middle Ages, including stone walls and a high window with no curtains, but I was too exhausted by the short conversation to even think about getting up and finding out whether the door was locked from the outside—whether I was a prisoner—because at that moment, I couldn't have cared less. Some of the higher demons liked to play-act, I knew. Maybe this was all some elaborate game. It couldn't be real, could it? I couldn't actually be safe, at least for a while? Could I?

Safe or not, I was still exhausted by what I'd just been through. I sank back into the richness of a bed and the fuzziness of my wits and let sleep take me.

I woke up to find a very different woman in the room, this one tall and heavyset. I groggily remembered that dark-haired Vera had mentioned someone named Belle, and this woman did seem to be dressed in the plain style of a servant. Unlike her mistress, though, Belle was visibly demonic, with rough gray skin and spurs of horn or bone jutting through the hide at her shoulders, elbows, and other visible joints. I'd seen lots worse. I rasped out a request for water and she brought me a cup; when I had finished, she refilled it for me and set it on the stand beside the bed. She looked stronger than me, especially the weakened version of me lying in the bed, but she seemed kind enough, showing me a sort of smile and squeezing my hand when I handed the cup back to her.

"Don't worry, sir. You will be well soon," she assured me as she went out.

The prickling was definitely almost gone. I felt less dizzy than before, as though I had slept for some time. I wondered how long I'd been out. I literally had no idea if I had been in Lady Zinc's house for hours or days, and I couldn't see a clock. You'd think, considering how much of a curse of modern civilization clocks are, that Hell would be full of them, but no. In fact, they don't have calendars either, although they kept dates and even seasons of a sort. I guess when you've been condemned to infinite punishment you don't want to dwell on how slowly time is passing. Not to mention that if it was anything like Heaven, time *didn't pass*, at least not in any normal way.

As my wits came back, I also realized that I couldn't trust any of this apparent kindness. Even if it wasn't some trick, even if Vera herself was the Riprash of her upper-class demon set, that didn't mean everybody she knew wouldn't happily eat me or turn me in. I had to be careful.

I staggered toward the window, which to my happiness didn't look barred or defended in any unusual way, as if I truly was a houseguest. I was hoping a view of the outside might give me an idea of what time of the infernal day it was, which would be a start at orienting myself. It seemed to me that I had been in Hell for months, and although I didn't have a formal deadline on leaving again, I knew if I didn't find the Countess of Cold Hands and get out soon I'd never get out at all. The crushing weight of the place, the sheer, dull horror of it was wearing me away. Only the memory of Caz was keeping me moving, the knowledge that if I didn't do anything, her lot was going to be the same as all these others: eternal misery. In fact, I had probably made it worse for her, and not just by exposing her to my sparkling, charming self. I doubted Eligor was going to let her get back to the real world ever again, so even that small solace was denied her.

No, I couldn't worry about that now, I told myself: it was too far away, too unlikely. One thing at a time.

I reached the window by standing on a heavy chair made of some kind of animal bones. But even when I got to the windowsill I still couldn't tell anything about the time. We seemed to be at the bottom of one of the soaring towers, a few hundred feet beneath the tangled forest of spires and connecting bridges I'd seen when I came out of the Terminus. One of the city's massive black walls loomed nearby, effectively cutting off my view of anything but the giant stones themselves, as though a starless night had been tipped on its side and shoved up next to the window. The light that painted the courtyard in red could have been anything, a day beacon, a dangerous fire nearby, or even just the glow of one of the open lava pits that pocked Pandaemonium like titanic gopher holes.

As I shakily climbed down from the window, awkward with only one hand and my whole right arm still throbbing with pain, I noticed something lying on top of a broad chest at the foot of the bed. Face-down in the middle of a gentleman's grooming assortment, tweezers and brushes and such, lay a heavy hand mirror. I hadn't seen my own face since I'd been in Hell. I'd grown quite familiar with my gray-and-black skin, patterned like some creature of the African Veldt, even fond of it (because it was tough as buffalo hide) but my features were still a mystery to me, except that they felt human to the touch. Hell was very short of reflecting surfaces; almost no clear standing water, of course, and most metal too defaced by rust and corrosion to show a reflection. I lifted the mirror with a mixture of unease and curiosity.

I got a shock, too, I can tell you.

It wasn't that the face didn't match the skin, because it did. The dark gray and light gray had the same streaky pattern, and black stripes rose from my jaw on either side of my mouth, over my eyes, and up into curls that looked a little like Maori tattoos across my forehead. The mouth was fanged, but I knew that already, and even the eyes were pretty much par for the course: a pale, goatish orange with vertical slits like a cat's. But the astonishing part was that it was *my* face under it all; Bobby Dollar, immediately recognizable, like a hastily painted stolen car. No shit. The demon-body amounted to no more than camouflage, and I had real doubts that it would fool anyone who had met up with my earthly self—a group that included Grand Duke Eligor, the monster I was planning to rob.

Panic swept over me. I had been walking around in more or less my own face the whole time I'd been here. How could that be? Had Lameh failed me? Or had Temuel betrayed me somehow? But why would he go to such elaborate lengths when all he needed to do was report me as AWOL and let his superiors do the rest? The Ephorate investigating my buddy Sam's Third Way movement had seemed to be only a moment's irritation away from condemning me anyway.

I'd been walking around Hell wearing a huge "KILL ME" sign for weeks without knowing it.

I tried to calm myself. Perhaps it wasn't anything to do with Temuel betraying me, but some effect of the body transfer. After all, I'd never heard of any angel using a demon body before. Back on Earth, my bodies always looked kind of similar. Maybe this was the same process at work. But did that mean that our souls had built-in facial features? That seemed crazy to me.

The door opened, startling me so that I dropped the heavy mirror. I tried to grab at it with the hand I no longer had, but only kept it from breaking by flinging out my (bare) foot and letting the mirror fall on that instead.

"What are you doing, my lord?" said Belle. "You will hurt yourself!" The servant hurried to me, picking up the mirror as though it were light as a playing card, then used her other strong hand to guide me back toward the bed. "Too soon! Too soon to be getting up!" She shook her head like a mother gorilla with a wayward youngster and gave me a gentle push that almost flung me across the mattress and off the other side. "Back you go. My lady will be angry with me if you harm yourself. Do you want me to lose my position?"

I assured her that I didn't, and in truth it was rather nice to settle back into the sheets, but I still couldn't figure out what was happening. Why was Lady Zinc treating me so kindly? I was at best a very minor member of the demonic nobility. My hostess, by comparison, clearly had an awfully nice thing going here. Did she want something from me?

And now I had to worry about my treacherous face, too. Worrying is hard work, though, and my body was still very weak. Sleep soon chased my thoughts away.

I woke to find Vera and her servant tenderly changing my bandages. The wrist had almost completely healed, the ragged marks of Block's teeth now covered with new, pink skin, but what was astonishing was that my wrist seemed to be growing new bone already. I don't know what they put in these Hell-bodies but they heal faster than the ones Heaven provides, and at that moment I wasn't complaining. The worst of the pain was gone, nothing left but a mild throb, and although my brain still prickled when I first woke up, I had a sense of physical well-being I hadn't felt since beginning my infernal adventure.

"You are doing so well!" Vera said when she saw I was watching. She got up quickly, as though sitting on the bed of a man awake was different than sitting on the bed of a slumbering invalid. "I think you are ready to go outside. Would you like that?"

No shit. I was feeling surprisingly well, and although the timer in the back of my thoughts was still ticking, I nodded. A chance to reconnoiter could only do me good.

"Wonderful," she said, and the look of pleasure on her pretty face was girlish. Why was this woman in Hell? Did I even want to know? "Then we shall go out tonight. Francis and Elizabeth are having a party, two of my very closest friends, and you shall be my escort, handsome Snakestaff."

I suffered getting dolled-up by the two women with as much good grace as I could muster, since no matter what secret worries I might have, Vera had done me nothing but good so far. Eventually they rigged me up in what they thought of as suitable clothes, including a tie and what seemed a distinctly Victorian-looking long coat. A pretty damn fancy outfit. Once I was dressed and seated, Vera herself very tenderly tied the tie, a narrow affair more like a ribbon than anything I was used to. I thought it made me look a bit like a posh Old West gunfighter (with a skin condition and yellow eyes). "It's the climate, of course," she told me, breathing on my ear. "Too hot for an ordinary tie."

"Do I have to wear one?" I've never liked the things.

Vera gave me a look of undisguised horror. "Do you think I could take you to meet my dearest friends without you being properly dressed?"

While I waited for her to finish her own preparations, I sat stiffly in a chair and watched brawny Belle tidy my room. "She likes you," the big woman said with a distinct twinkle in her eye. She pushed heavy furniture around as if the pieces were made of balsa, then swept beneath them. "She thinks you're handsome."

I did my best to smile, but felt a little as if I was betraying Caz—not that I'd done anything or planned to, but this sudden emergence into a life of parties and fancy dress didn't seem exactly in line with my mission, either. Still, it made a welcome change.

I just need to get the lay of the land, I told myself. *I'm a spy, after all—an enemy agent. Nobody blames a spy for trying to blend in.*

We were driven in a chauffeured car—Vera called it "the motor"—which was my first chance to see the vehicle that had run over me in front of the Terminus. It was long and low, but the front grille was armored like a train's cowcatcher, so it was something of a miracle (if those were available here) that I'd survived the collision. The chauffeur was a thickset, nondescript man named Henri, silent as he opened the door for me and ushered me into the luxurious interior. He had a distinct, sickly odor to him, like formaldehyde. Also, I had stopped noticing the deformities in even the most ordinary looking citizens, but I couldn't help noticing that Henri's wide-set eyes were filmed over with milky cataracts. Not the most inspiring thing to see on your driver. Still, we zipped across town quickly and without incident. I was getting my first proper look at the Red City, and although we seemed to be traveling mostly through the richer neighborhoods, where wide streets were hemmed in by the tall walls of rich tower houses, there was still plenty of horror on display, a carnival sideshow of freaks and monsters staggering along the muddy streets. When we slowed at intersections clogged by heavy traffic—there are, of course, no traffic lights or stop signs in Hell—some of these street-folk looked as though they were considering approaching the car, perhaps to beg, perhaps with something more sinister in mind, but none of them ever did. A couple of times I actually saw someone pull a companion back, as if warning them that we were a bad target for whatever they planned.

"Sometimes when the fires are hot, the streets are simply unbearable," said Vera, almost dreamily. "We are lucky, darling man, that the weather is mild tonight."

"Mild" meant the heat and stench were manageable, but only because I was wearing a body made for Hell. Pandaemonium's air felt so thick that I wanted to wave my arms as I walked to cut a path through it, and I never completely learned to ignore the acid stink. It was like standing over a boiling pot of urine.

Things were a little better once we were inside Vera's friends' house, a magnificent, shambling series of castle towers connected by horizontal branches like a coral formation. The angular rooms had been decorated in extreme rococo, gold leaf everywhere, fabulous wealth on display in every corner, but just in case I was tempted to forget where I was, the sculpture and paintings all portrayed brutal suffering, contorted figures and famous scenes of terror, including a detailed series of engravings of Joan of Arc being burned at the stake, which showed her body being eaten by flames even as she prayed and wept.

Other than the creepy taste in art, I couldn't immediately spot any-thing hellish about Vera's friend Elizabeth, another pretty young bru-nette, slenderer than my savior, who wore her hair piled high above her pale forehead. Her husband (or boyfriend—it wasn't quite clear) Francis, did show signs of his citizenship: his bearded face and all vis-ible skin were covered with bumps and pustules. It didn't seem to matter to Elizabeth, who referred to him several times as "my great love" and "my only man." They both wore Renaissance fashions that made my Victorian gear look quite modern, and their guests were dressed in clothes from at least a dozen eras, including styles I had never seen. If it hadn't been for the obvious physical deformities of many of the guests, the whole thing would have looked like any old costume party. It was hard to reconcile the ungodly misery I knew lay all around us, and especially underneath us, with this cheerful happy hour gathering. In fact, for these rich demons it seemed more like an entire happy eternity of partying while the damned slaved for them. I should have been outraged, but I confess I was too worn out for out-rage, and it was nice not to be running for my life.

What can one angel do, anyway? I thought. *It's been like this for thou-sands upon thousands of years. Blame God, not me.*

One of the most disturbing guests was a man named Al, who had the look of a months-buried corpse, his eyes sunken and filmy, nose black with rot, and his suit covered in grave mold. Despite the unfes-tive appearance, he seemed quite at home, and at one point he leaned over to me and said in a confidential whisper, "You've fallen in with the best, lad. Couldn't have struck better. Our sweet Lady Zinc is a wonderful woman."

I smiled and nodded, but Al didn't just look like a corpse, he smelled like one too, so I moved on.

I took a drink from a servant. It wasn't all that much better than Riprash's demon rum, but the glass was clean, and I could feel my demon body repairing the damage to my throat and stomach after each sip. The guests talked about many things, and as I moved restlessly from room to room I listened in on dozens of conversations, but I didn't hear a single one mention anything about the past or their lives on Earth. Instead the talk was the sort of things rich people chatted about everywhere—the problem of finding good servants, gossip about their social set, and discussions of the best places to go on holiday. It was like hanging around with a bunch of rich fascists; after a while, I just stopped listening to the cruelty underneath the words and let it all wash over me. I did begin to feel a bit better about my chances of passing undetected, since they seemed like a pretty incurious lot. Nobody asked me a single question about my background or seemed to need any more information than that I was "Vera's guest." I was one of the crowd now, it seemed. The in crowd.

I found Vera and Elizabeth again in the main parlor, a candlelit room whose high ceilings were decorated with golden cobwebs. As we chatted, a young man who had been introduced to me earlier as "Fritz," a handsome fellow in a military uniform, hurried up to us. Other than a ridiculously puffed-up chest under his military tunic, he was perhaps the most ordinary looking person in the room, at least by earthly standards, but there were a surprising number of demons there who looked nearly as human.

"Elizabeth!" he squealed to our hostess, "you'll never guess who's arrived!"

"Fritzi, my chicken, do you have to be so common?" Vera asked. "We're gossiping."

"Then I have something you'll really like to gossip about," he said, grinning. "The president himself is here."

I turned, half-expecting to see Richard Nixon with a party box of wine coolers or something, but the figure coming through the door with a small entourage of lesser demons was unfamiliar to me, or so I thought, a tall, spare figure in a black tailcoat whose elongated face and sharp, curved nose made him look like a humanoid crow. Then I realized who he was. Even worse, he had actually met me in my Bobby Dollar body and might recognize me.

"Caym, the Grand President of the Council of Hell," a servant announced loudly. This was the bastard who had run interference for Eligor at the big Heaven/Hell conference in San Jude, just before the grand duke tried to roast me like a marshmallow.

I couldn't do anything but watch as that infernal raven, black eyes bright as blobs of oil, came toward us. Worst of all, he was looking right at me and beginning to smile.

I didn't think it was a very nice smile at all.

twenty-three
a long night at the opera

CAYM APPROACHED with a grin on his beaked face like the cat that ate the canary—except in his case it would have been the canary who ate the cat. My heart was pounding, and if hell-creature bodies could sweat I would have been dripping like a melting popsicle. I had only a couple of seconds to decide whether to run or stand my ground. If the grand president and his entourage hadn't been between me and the front door I probably would have bolted, but I had already discovered that the rest of the sprawling house was a maze that I couldn't navigate even with a compass, so I took a deep breath and waited.

Caym took his eyes off me long enough to bend his long, skinny body and kiss Elizabeth's hands, then he did the same for Vera.

"It's so kind of you to grace us with your presence, your Honor," Elizabeth said. She sounded like she meant it, breathless and pleased.

"It's always a pleasure to visit your splendid residence, Countess," he said, which was the first time I'd heard any of the guests give Elizabeth that title, and it reminded me of Caz, my own Countess, captive somewhere in this mad city. "And Lady Zinc, what a sublime thrill it is to see you again as well."

Vera colored quite charmingly. She seemed more impressed by the president even than Elizabeth had been. "I'm flattered you remember me, my lord."

"Caym, please. These are my leisure hours." And then he straightened and turned to me, his wet, bright eyes flicking up and down as if I were a tasty bit of roadkill he was examining from a convenient height. "And you must be Vera's guest. Snakestaff, is it not? When last we met she could speak of nothing else."

"Oh! You have such a good memory, Grand President!" She turned to me. "It was the night we found you in the road."

"Knocked him down is what you told me." The grand president made a merry, flirtatious face, particularly horrible on his bony, exaggerated features, like some kind of exotic tribal mask. "And please, Lady Zinc, I do not wish to keep correcting you, but you must call me Caym."

As Vera made fluttering little sounds of agreement, the president turned back to me. I was just beginning to relax. Apparently he had been looking at me only because Vera had mentioned me.

"But now that I see you up close, sir," he said, "I find that there is something familiar about you." He might as well have reached into my chest and squeezed my heart. "Is it possible we have met before?"

"Ah! Ah, I mean, no, no—I don't think so." I felt as if everyone within twenty yards was staring at me. "I come to the Red City so seldom. The most of my business is . . . is in Perdition Valley, several levels down."

"A lovely little province," said Caym in a pleasant tone that suggested he'd never heard of the place. "Well, there are several of your guests that I would like to greet, Countess, including your husband who I see over there plotting some mischief with that old villain Pope Sergius, so I hope you will forgive me if I drag myself away from your far more charming company. This may be my evening for recreation, but I still cannot ignore my duties." As Elizabeth and Vera gushed, the crowlike figure turned away, then stopped and turned back. "You know, Countess, I am sponsoring an evening at the Dionysus two nights from now, that grand bit of Monteverdi we all love. It should be quite an event—Himself is going to take the leading role in the opera, of course." You could practically hear the capital "H."

Himself? For a moment I had an absurd vision of Satan all decked out in a Valkyrie outfit, singing an aria. That seemed unlikely, but both Elizabeth and Vera gave out muffled shrieks of glee, as though Caym had said something deliciously naughty. "Is he really?" Vera asked. "What fun!"

"Yes, and I would be honored if you ladies would be my guests. And bring your gentlemen, of course." He sketched a little bow toward me. "I humbly suspect the evening's entertainment will be the talk of the Red City."

On the way home Vera was as happy as a teenager who'd just found out she was going to be on some MTV reality show, bubbling about what an honor it was that Caym should remember her, and how astonishing it was that the grand president had asked us to be his theater guests.

"What did he mean, 'Himself'? Who's going to be playing the lead?"

"Never mind." She was being coquettish. "You'll see. It will be delicious. But let's talk about you, you lovely, darling man. You impressed the president so! He's not like us, of course. Most of the old ones don't have our . . . urges. But he clearly thought a great deal of you. Wondering if you'd met! But you haven't ever met him before, have you, darling? You'd tell me if you truly knew him, wouldn't you? A president!"

By the way, there's not just one president at a time in Hell like in the U.S. It's merely a title, but it's a pretty oomphy one. I've only heard of about three or four other demons, all original Fallen, who have that in their resume, so in a way it's actually a lot more exclusive than being the guy in the White House.

Anyway, Vera was in a very cheerful mood. Once I'd gotten undressed for bed and had donned that Dickensian nightdress, she came into my room, still dressed in her party finery, and insisted on going over all the exciting events of the night, the people she'd seen and the astonishing things she'd heard. Of course, Caym's invitation was the crown jewel and thus required lots of consideration. She sat on the bed beside me, her on top of the covers, me under them. The servant Belle was in the room too, waiting to help her mistress get ready for bed. As Vera talked and gently stroked my hair I felt a strong fondness for her, the last thing I had expected to feel for anyone or anything here. It was sexy, too, in a weird way, the old-fashioned clothes and the old-fashioned manners. Vera was pretty as a porcelain doll, girlish in her enthusiasms, and like Caz, could have passed for human (and a very attractive human at that) anywhere on Earth. She seemed to like me very much, and I couldn't ignore that either. Just the feeling of her fingers trailing through my hair made me sleepy and content, comfortable in a way I rarely felt on Earth or even in Heaven. But there was nothing more in it for me than that, I swear. I admired her, I was grateful to her, and I couldn't help but acknowledge that she was very, very attractive, but I already had one demon-girlfriend, and look where that had gotten me. More than that, Caz had grown so big inside of me since our first night together that there truly wasn't much room for anyone else.

But Vera had been good to me. I reached up to squeeze her hand. For a moment I thought I felt something strange when I touched her, something hard and sharp, and we both jumped a little, but by the time we had recovered, laughing, I realized that it must have been the tips of her fingernails, which she kept long and perfectly trimmed and polished.

"Oh, but here I have gone on and on!" she said. "You must be exhausted, my dear. Belle, come and help me out of these clothes. I shall not bathe tonight; I am too tired and too excited. I think I shall just crawl into bed naked."

She and the tall servant went out, leaving me alone to think about that interesting image, but I was suddenly so exhausted that I fell asleep within moments after the door closed behind them.

The strange days of my official citizenship in the Red City slipped by. Snakestaff might be an unimportant minor demon of the Liars Sect, a sort of small town lawyer compared to the sharpies I had faced as Doloriel, Heavenly Advocate, but now, Snakestaff and I had been whirled into the heart of society, or at least the damned version of the idle rich.

It wasn't easy to make sense of the way Hell worked, because everything here seemed as bizarre and chaotic as Heaven was ordered and seemingly unchanging. It was clear to me at least that Vera was not exactly at the heart of things. Her friends Elizabeth and Francis were much bigger players than she was, but she was an enthusiastic participant, an infernal social butterfly with a love for the trappings and protocols of her lost earthly life. She took me to various gatherings, and although I met some truly hideous people (and I'm using the term "people" very loosely here) I met others who, except for their appearance, wouldn't have been out of place at any smart gathering. Many of the damned and demonic were funny, colorful, even charming (in a don't-turn-your-back-on-them sort of way).

I was often referred to as "Vera's new man," although nothing definitively romantic had passed between us. Sometimes I was "Vera's discovery," as though my clodhopping, lower-level ways revealed Lady Zinc's cleverness, or at least her open-mindedness. A few in her social set were openly hostile to me, mostly the kind of young (or young-appearing) males who probably would have liked to be in my place, but that was just another interesting facet of what was a truly rich and complex society. In fact, I was beginning to find myself almost comfortable in Hell, which terrifies me now and should have terrified me then, but a weird kind of contentment had gripped me. There were times, especially as Vera sat on my bed at night stroking my hair and murmuring to me, that I could scarcely remember the earlier part of my journey, let alone my angel life on Earth.

Only thoughts of Caz kept me grounded at all. Every time I found myself relaxing into the comfortable companionship of those I knew must be murderers and thieves of the worst kind, I remembered her pale face and a chill of guilt brought me back to myself, at least for a moment. Eligor was out there—I heard him mentioned occasionally in breathless tones, as if he was a rock star who lived nearby—which meant Caz had to be out there too, somewhere, even though I would probably never meet her by accident in a city this big. But there were other times when I could hardly feel her at all, could hardly feel anything except the warm contentment of being safe and being admired. Things were looking up, after all. My hand was growing back; new finger bones had sprouted, growing out of my wrist stump like early cornstalks. But mostly I just liked being safe. I had been hunted and haunted for a long time now, and not just in Hell.

The night of the opera came. After I got dressed in my Prince Albert finery I waited a long time for Vera who, unsurprisingly, wanted her appearance to be perfect. She settled at last on a sumptuous red velvet dress with a low neckline that showed off her full, almost exuberant figure. After I had complimented her as extravagantly as I knew how (I still wasn't quite comfortable with what felt to me like intentionally old-fashioned ways of talking and acting) Henri brought the car and we were off to the theater.

Pandaemonium no longer seemed like it had when I first arrived, bleeding and near death. It was still dark and grotesque, but now it seemed more like one of those foreign cities you encounter in spy stories, like Cold War Berlin or Bogart's Casablanca, full of terrible danger, yes, but also full of excitement and possibility. Did that mean I could overlook the monsters in the streets just because I traveled in safety? Overlook the terrible suffering, worse than you could find in the most desperate third-world capital?

Yes, to an extent. I was already beginning to feel like I'd do anything to avoid the horror of being cast out to wander Hell again without allies or protection, forget my principles if I had to, forget my angelic training, forget almost everything. It sneaks up on you that way. But I still couldn't forget Caz, no matter what else happened. I'm not exaggerating when I say that she was the only thing that kept me from tumbling into the abyss.

I'd guessed that the Dionysus Theater would be like La Scala or something, one of those fancy opera places, a big classical building with columns, meant to proclaim, "Hey, we got culture!" but I was reckoning without Hell's sense of humor. The theater was a few blocks off Dis Pater Square, tucked in at the end of a wide street full of strange, misshapen buildings, not the high towers of the wealthy but the hive-like habitations that the rest of Pandaemonium's residents fought to get into, with their bottom floors given over to small shops and other businesses. But the joke, I realized when I saw the electrical sign with its vertical letters glowing through the permanent dusk, was that the Dionysus was a dark-mirror copy of the Apollo Theater in Harlem, a place I'd actually been once—the closest your friend Bobby Dollar had ever come to a religious pilgrimage.

Cars and carriages and even more bizarre forms of transportation crowded the street as the high and mighty arrived, along with interested spectators and crowds of beggars who were one tossed bone away from turning into a snarling wolfpack. The Dionysus had a large troop of brawny house soldiers armed with what looked like most of the history of warfare, from clubs to steam-driven Gatling guns, and since most of the really well-to-do traveled with their own household guards as well, even the most dangerous and desperate of the onlookers kept a respectful distance. But it was a reminder that, like any place that specialized in the snatch-and-grab style of wealth acquisition, the only real security was what you could buy.

As we waited to go in, I asked Vera again who the "Himself" was who was performing. It wasn't advertised out front, only the name of the opera, *The Coronation of Poppaea*. I'd never heard of it. Then again, I've never been big on classical music or opera, at least compared to what jazz and blues do for me.

As much as I was getting used to Hell, I still had a gut-clenching moment when I saw that the interior was built in the style of one of those old Parisian catacombs, made literally out of bones and skulls, although here they had been crafted into far more than simple walls and doorways. The arched ceiling was paneled with scenes of nature that incorporated the bones of all manner of animals, frisking sheep and placid cows, and of course the human skeletons that watched over them. It might have been the flickering torchlight that made these skeletons seem to move slightly, as though alive but under a spell. Yeah, it might just have been torchlight, but I don't think so. The immense candelabra, the balconies, the very pillars that supported the building were also made from human and semi-human skulls and bones, many brightly painted in red or gold or white, giving the theater the look and feel of a truly disturbing circus tent.

Grand President Caym waved to us from his private box above; a little flourish of his long fingers that made him look more than ever like some immense bird shaking out its feathers. Vera was thrilled to be singled out in public by the great fellow himself. I tried to smile.

The curtain rose and the opera began. I couldn't make a lot of sense of it, but it seemed to be about ancient Rome. The first bit was singing gods and goddesses, but the music was something even older than the kind of opera I was used to hearing on television and radio, something from the Renaissance or even earlier, I guessed. For a moment I found myself wondering if Caz would have regarded it as too modern, since she had told me the Renaissance was after her time. The thought made me sad. It was easier to send it away, like an extra being directed offstage and out of sight behind one of the immense brocade curtains.

Not wanting to think about Caz, and not even certain why, I pulled myself back to the opera and the mystery of the "Himself" that Caym had referred to. None of the performers seemed unusual, all clearly talented, none of them recognizable. As I did my best to listen to the lyrics, I came to realize that the opera was about the Roman Emperor Nero, the very same Nero whose crumbling bridge I had crossed to get into Hell. The irony of it amused me. I wondered how many other people in this charnel house of an opera palace even knew that the Neronian Bridge existed?

Then the singer portraying the emperor made his entrance, and for the first time I sensed something odd going on. It wasn't anything about the performer, at least, not to look at. He wasn't particularly handsome, a bit thick-faced, with a sagging, wrinkled neck, and his legs were a bit skinny for the toga he was wearing, but I sure didn't recognize him. Others did, however, and he was greeted with applause and, to my surprise, a few catcalls and some laughter. Also, unlike the other singers, he did not look particularly comfortable on stage, which made him an odd choice to play the monarch. I supposed he had a fabulous voice to make up for it, because everyone else in the cast seemed world-class. I was mildly startled when he got ready to sing, because his throat swelled like the bulging neck-sac of a bullfrog, though even that didn't seem unusual: a lot of the other cast members and most of the audience bore some physical sign of what they were. But when he finally began his aria, the emperor's voice was a distinct disappointment, more than a bit rough and not very strong. Some in the audience actually laughed, which made him falter, and the jeers grew louder as he doggedly pursued the song, his throat sac distending and shrinking like the bellows on an accordion, his face growing more fearful by the moment as the crowd shouted at him.

He finished and someone else began singing, but the spell of attention had been broken and many in the audience were talking or laughing out loud. I couldn't figure it out at all, but as I wondered why such a poor singer should be trotted out in front of the nobility of Hell that way, I was distracted by a late entrance in the upper boxes. A hush fell over the crowd and some poor soprano's aria was suddenly less important than everybody turning around to see who was being seated in President Caym's box.

The late arrival didn't look the same as the last time I'd seen him, but I still knew him instantly. He was dressed in a beautifully-cut white dress uniform, the kind of thing you'd expect to see at a royal funeral in some old newsreel, except that the white fabric was so artfully splattered with arterial splashes of scarlet that I had no doubt it had been designed that way. The only question was whether it was real blood or just dye. I thought I could guess.

Grand Duke Eligor looked less human than he did on Earth, but for the moment he also looked less demonic than the monstrous form that had overtaken him as he dangled me by my neck a couple of feet above his office carpet back in San Judas. His blond hair was shaved very close to his head, and his facial features were bonier and older than on his Kenneth Vald persona. Less like a California billionaire and more like the fascist dictator of some imaginary Northern European country, a creature of hard angles and fierce, unyielding principles. But it was definitely him, Eligor the Horseman, my least favorite demon. My hackles went up. I was relieved I was in shadows, that my treacherous, underwhelming disguise wasn't visible to him, even from this distance.

Only as I (and most of the other patrons) sat staring at Eligor settling into his seat did I have a moment of wondering where Caz was. That only lasted a moment, because once the grand duke had seated himself, one of the guards at the back of his box opened the door, letting in a gleam of pure white gold.

That was Caz, of course.

twenty-four

fickle

M Y HEART felt as though it had stopped, literally stopped, and would not start again. Caz's face was rigid, blank as a mask. She wore a long red dress whose spatters and splashes of white made her a mirror of her master, an even clearer mark of Eligor's ownership than the guard who seated her next to the grand duke and then stood behind her chair like a jailer.

Oh, God, my heart. Everything came back in a moment, our desperate nights together, the months of longing since, and it was all I could do not to climb out of my seat and run toward her. The crowd, many of them still whispering, had turned back to the action as the emperor stepped up to sing again, but I couldn't look away. I can only imagine what my face must have looked like. Finally, Vera's elbow applied briskly and with obvious anger to my ribs brought my attention back to the stage, but I could think of nothing else for a long time. I snuck a few glances at Caz, but she was never looking at me or anyone else in the audience, not even looking at the performers. Instead she sat like a frightened schoolgirl, eyes downcast. Eligor ignored her, watching the action below through a pair of opera glasses.

The snickering and jeering resumed as the singer with the bulging throat laboriously climbed the mountain of his aria, looking more than ever like someone who desperately wanted to be somewhere else. The catcalls got louder; then, as he strained for and badly missed a high note, something came hurtling out of the lower galleries and past his head. He did his best to dodge it and suffered only an unpleasant stain on his tunic as the clot of mud or excrement bounced off him.

For a moment, as I watched what looked like a small riot beginning in the seats below us, I almost forgot Caz, so tantalizingly close. I assumed that whoever had tried to assault the performer was being caught and hustled out, but it quickly became clear that the ruckus was more general. Something like anarchy broke out on the floor of the Dionysus Theater, and before a few more bars of the aria had wavered by, a heavier projectile hit the emperor right in the gut, knocking him to his knees. Something else struck his head. Blood coursed down the side of his face and onto his white imperial tunic. For a moment he cowered as more missiles hit him, arms wrapped around his head for protection. The jeering grew louder and a whole cloud of rocks and rotten food and less pleasant things arced out of the crowd, seeking out the cringing singer as though he were the condemned at a public stoning.

The music played on but the singer was on his hands and knees now, bloody and weeping. The crowd shrieked at him, an animal sound that seemed to grow louder by the second. Then they quickly, if not uniformly fell silent, and all eyes turned again to the grand president's box. Caym was standing at the rail, and the contortion of his crowlike face showed he was furious, but instead of berating the unruly crowd, he leaned out and pointed a long, clawlike finger at the performer.

"Get up, you tub of mischief! Who do you think you are? You have been brought here to sing, and sing you will!"

The actor looked up, his face bloody, his throat sac deflated and hanging over his chest like a dirty bib. "Please, Grand President, please . . . I cannot!" A rock hit him in the shoulder and he almost fell. "It hurts! It hurts me so!"

"Shut your mouth, you pathetic ingrate. You wanted to sing, and sing you shall. And what better role for you than your own wretched life?"

For an instant even Caz and my hated enemy Eligor fell out of my thoughts as I finally realized what was going on. This was Nero himself! The emperor who had tried to cheat Hell, singing the story of his own wretched life for the amusement of Hell's high rollers.

Like I've said before, nobody can carry a grudge like a demon.

Order was restored, but it only got worse for Nero from there. Time and again he would begin to sing and be pelted by garbage and shit or knocked down by stones, some of them big as a baby's head. I distinctly heard one of them break his arm, but Caym wouldn't let him stop, although it was harder and harder to distinguish his singing from shrieks of pain and terror. I kept sneaking looks at Caz. Her face showed no emotion whatsoever, but Eligor was clearly enjoying the spectacle, laughing and whispering with Caym. At last, nearing what seemed to be the middle of the opera, a thunderous barrage of larger missiles, great jagged things that might have been broken paving stones, crushed Nero to the stage, and though he struggled to get up it was hopeless. At this point things went completely mad. Members of the audience leaped up on stage and began to kick him and beat him with the largest pieces of stone. Nero offered no resistance—it all had the feeling of a ritual enacted many times. Even with the musicians still playing gamely along, it sounded like someone jumping up and down on a barrel of eggs.

As Nero was reduced to a bloody wet tatter I looked up to see Eligor saying goodbye to Caym. Caz was already gone.

"That was his best performance yet," a man said in a loud, braying voice behind me. "Folded him up before they even got to the part about Seneca."

In other words, this happened all the time. Two thousand years Nero had been in Hell, and they still humiliated him in public on a regular basis, not to mention tormenting and destroying his body over and over again. What would they do to me if they found out? After all, Emperor Nero had been on *their* side.

On the way home Vera was quieter than usual, and although she stroked my hair as she liked to do while we sped through the red-flickering streets of Pandaemonium, she did it roughly, distracted perhaps by what she had seen, so that again and again she pricked me with her fingernails. As for me, I should have been as excited and terrified by seeing Caz as I had been during those first moments after she entered the theater, but instead I was suddenly exhausted. Too much for one day. I was finding it hard to keep my eyes open as the roar of the steam boiler and the red strobe of the city lights dragged me down into a half-sleep. For a moment I imagined myself on that stage, broken and bleeding, laughed at by Hell's leading citizens, but even that horrific image couldn't keep me from being pulled down, down, down.

"Tighter," I heard Vera saying to someone, as if down a pipe or from a long distance. I was groggy, I realized, but understanding didn't improve anything. Groggy and weak. Why was she talking? Why wouldn't she let me sleep? "No, tighter," she said.

"I can't, my lady," said a deep female voice—Belle. "It doesn't fit right, even with his hand growing back. The strap won't stay."

"Then tie it. Use a piece of cord."

Belle was apparently helping her mistress put on her nightclothes, but why were they doing it in my room? Or was I in Vera's room? And why were they talking about my hand? Wherever it was, I couldn't be lying in a very comfortable position, because my joints were aching.

I tried to open my eyes, but that wasn't as easy as it sounds. Even my lids felt weighed down, like someone had set Charon's heavy coins on them. But I had already made that journey, hadn't I? I had already crossed the River of Death because I was in Hell. Could you cross twice? I was confused, my thoughts thick like syrup.

At last I got my eyes open, something that took actual hard effort. I was in my own room, all right, and Vera and Belle were indeed struggling with cords and straps, but it had nothing to do with Lady Zinc's nightware because Vera was still dressed for the opera. The cord in question was being tied around my wounded arm, which apparently had kept coming out of its restraining strap. My other arm with the whole hand hadn't been a problem for them—it was bound securely to the headboard of the bed.

As Belle pulled on the cord knotted around my arm just below the elbow, I realized for the first time what was going on, although for a moment I didn't quite grasp the why of it. Had I fallen out of bed? Injured myself? Why was I being restrained? But then the first cold gust of reality blew through me and some of the grogginess receded.

"You may go now, Belle," said Vera when both of my arms were pulled out straight on either side. My ankles had been bound as well, and I was helpless as any sacrificial victim. "I have things to say to Lord Snakestaff that require privacy."

"As you say, Mistress." But Belle clearly didn't want to go, and she paused in the doorway, filling it with her huge frame, to look at her handiwork: me, trussed like a turkey about to go in the oven.

Vera was pacing back and forth beside the bed, the color in her cheeks darker and deeper than I had ever seen.

"Ingratitude." Her voice had changed. All the charm and life had gone out of it, and although it's hard to believe, I promise you that her cold tones frightened me in a way that even the straps hadn't. "Ingratitude and fickleness. Again. All of you! I thought you were different, Snakestaff! Oh, I had such hopes for you!"

"I don't know what you're talking about." It was hard to make words properly. I felt drugged or drunk.

"All men are *liars*." The hatred was so strong in her voice I couldn't believe it was the same woman. "Whores! You call *us* whores! But you are the ones without shame! I saw her! I saw you staring at that filthy, white-haired slut of Eligor's! Why do you like her? Why do you like her?" She came to my side and grabbed my hair so hard some of it came out, shaking my head until I thought she'd snap my neck. She was stronger than I'd ever guessed. "I gave you everything! I gave you my love! I would have given you more than that! I would have made you one of my immortals! But now you'll rot in the dung heaps of Gehenna. Pig!"

Even as Vera was shouting at me, tears of anger running down her red cheeks, she clambered onto the wide bed beside me. Helpless, I could only turn my face away, certain that she was going to hit or scratch me, but instead her fingers plucked frenziedly at the strings of her bodice as if it were too tight and she couldn't breathe. She put a knee squarely on my belly and then pulled down the front of her opera dress, spilling her breasts. She was beautiful and, perversely, never more so than at that moment, her chest heaving, dark hair swinging as she straddled me. I braced myself again to be hit, but instead she bent and fumbled with my trousers. I yanked at my restraints but couldn't pull either my arms or legs free, and although I did my best to buck her off me it was like wrestling with some great, wild cat. She flattened herself between my legs as she pulled down my clothes, then she sat up straight, my legs locked between hers. She reached down and grabbed my cock and squeezed it until I shouted in pain.

"Miserable thing. Man!" The eyes staring into mine now were terrifying. I'd known—I'd kept reminding myself—that Vera was in Hell for a reason, but meeting Caz had changed me. Why had I been so willing to believe Vera was only another lost soul, that the kindness she had shown me was real? It was like I hadn't been myself.

But what I'd thought of her didn't matter now. What mattered was what she truly was—a raging mad thing. And I was her prisoner.

Even as Vera cursed me she rubbed herself all over me, tore open my shirt and dragged her heavy breasts across my skin, across my face, for a moment even pushing one swollen nipple into my mouth like a grieving, hysterical mother trying to suckle a dead child. It was all I could do not to bite down, but she hadn't hurt me badly yet, and for the moment I was in her power, the good arm and the bad one both immobilized. My only hope was to let her work out her anger and hope that afterward she would listen to me. But what could I tell her? I didn't love her, of course, and even if I hadn't discovered this truth about her I still wouldn't have been able to give her what she wanted. Whatever was in me that could love belonged to Caz, and seeing her at the theater had rung me like a bell, so that even as I struggled to keep Vera's nails from my eyes I was still vibrating with that powerful, astounding need for the Countess of Cold Hands.

Weeping now, Vera climbed down and grabbed my balls. I tensed, terrified that I would find out what it was to lose something even more important than my hand, but she seemed intent on pursuing her parody of passionate affection. She began to stroke, lick, and squeeze me, holding my cock against her face, muttering both endearments and the ugliest kind of threats. It wasn't what you'd call a romantic situation unless you come from the outermost rooms of bondage and degradation, and I've seen too much ugliness in my years on Earth to enjoy that. Not to mention my well-known aversion to pain. But Vera was determined. She tugged and squeezed, she kissed me all over, she even put a finger up inside me, nudging until I hardened against my will. Then Vera slid up my body and sat on my chest, naked from the waist up, her hair now completely down and wild on her shoulders, her pale breasts, flushed unevenly, swinging above me like church bells.

"I would have waited," she panted, still holding me by the root, still squeezing me with her hand to keep the blood in me, to keep me rigid. Her eyes were fixed on mine. They had changed again, her stare wide-eyed and full of something that looked like desperate affection. "I could have waited until the time was right, darling. It has been a long time, but I have gone a long time before. I wanted it to be perfect!"

She was squeezing my cock so hard I could barely speak. "It doesn't have to be . . ."

Then her eyes went empty again, as if a switch had been thrown. "You could have been one of my immortals, Snakestaff. You would have been treasured forever. Instead you are just another . . . miserable, fickle, lying man. But you'll never go to your white-haired whore. You belong to me. I found you, and you're mine!"

Her knees against my armpits, Vera began to fumble at her long skirts, pulling them upward with a loud rustling of crinoline, exposing the layers of snowy white petticoats. I could feel a heat against my belly from between her legs, but no matter how I squirmed and fought I couldn't roll her off me. She was lost in some kind of frenzy of anger and misery, something primitive and not very human. She rose into a half crouch and pulled the rest of her petticoats out of the way.

Between her legs, a horror.

Purple and dark blue and angry red, it was a bulging, quivering thing like a jellyfish, its ropy strands of translucent flesh dangling on my belly and thighs. A prickling where they touched me became a stinging, then a scalding fire. I screamed. Vera squatted above me and reached down to put her hands flat on my chest, and just before her fingers touched me I finally saw the translucent, flexible spines, like the bristles on a toothbrush, growing out from beneath Lady Zinc's fingernails and into my flesh. She had been poisoning me. All that time petting me, stroking my hair, she'd been pumping her toxins into me, some stay-happy fluid to keep me stupid and cheerful. But those toxins had been mild. What she gave me now definitely wasn't.

The acid burn in my groin suddenly went nova, filling me up like flaming brandy in all my veins. I could feel my flesh swelling everywhere. Blood pounded in my brain, and I could hardly see, but her eyes held me. Vera's mad eyes.

The thing between her legs made a wet noise, a ghastly squelch like nothing I'd ever heard, and then it opened. Beyond the ragged, mouth-like frill, the edges were lined with tiny needle teeth, hundreds of them, gaping from the slippery, shining purple and pink.

I'm sure I tried to scream again, because she pulled one of her hands away from my chest—the finger-tendrils came loose with a string of sucking pops like ivy being yanked from a wall—then used it to cover my mouth as she lowered herself onto me. My heart wanted to jump out of my chest, but my groin pushed up toward her, offering itself, riding the tide of my own infected, blazing blood.

Then she eased herself down, and I felt those tiny, impossible teeth, and I screamed again from behind her hand, screamed and screamed and screamed without stopping. Her face sagged down toward me, mouth open in a kind of ecstasy, then some kind of membranes slid down from her eyelids, turning her eyes milky-white.

She rode me without stopping, the obscenity between her legs chewing at me, milking me, until I burst and filled her. Lady Zinc collapsed on top of me, and my mind finally escaped into blessed darkness.

twenty-five

the other white meat

"YOU'RE AN ingrate," Belle said, and hit me again, a close-fisted shot to the mouth that made my teeth feel like the beads on an abacus. Vera's servant had very large hands, and she was also pretty damned strong. "She gave you her love. She made you special!"

Boom! Pow! I could almost see the cartoon violence captions appear in the air over my head as she hit me again and again. The big bitch didn't seem to mind at all that I was tied up and helpless. She didn't even seem all that mad at me. She was just enjoying thumping the shit out of me.

I didn't say anything, since I'd discovered there was even less point arguing with the servant than with her mistress. I stayed loose and tried to go with the beating, but there was a part of me that was definitely having a few fantasies about what I'd do if I ever caught this large, nasty piece of work when I was free to fight back.

Several days had passed since the opera and so had the pretense that I was anything but a prisoner. Each night, and sometimes during the day, Vera took me. I've never thought rape was anything pleasant, but I had never understood it the way I did now. Helpless, raging, burning with shame, all of these things I now grasped in an extremely intimate way. I even understood the deepest fear now, the feeling that my life was not my own, that whatever happened to me would be beyond my control. There were times when I wept, and not just from the pain of being used, but I always waited until I was alone. That was all I had left.

Belle hit me one last time, a backhand blow that thumped my skull against the headboard of the bed. It had become a ritual: she cleaned the room, although nowhere near as carefully as before, she emptied my chamber pot, and then she beat the crap out of me. She was built like a heavyweight boxer, our Belle, like one of the old ones, long arms and big torso. I was guessing that in life she must have gone about two-fifteen, two-twenty, almost linebacker size, but here, with the sharp spikes of bone growing from her joints, I'd guess she was a good twenty or thirty pounds more. Bigger than me, in other words, and with all the strength that a demonic body can give you.

"You should kiss her hand and thank her that she's kept you," Belle said from the doorway. "I would have pulled your head off and thrown you on the midden. I know how to treat your type."

"I'll bet you do." My head was still ringing and it would have been smarter to keep my mouth shut, but I didn't really care. Even being destroyed would be better than this, and it would certainly be less humiliating. "I'll bet the boys loved you, with that pretty face and figure."

She smirked. "You think I couldn't get a man? They came and knocked at my door. They brought me money!" She jutted her heavy jaw. "I had as many as Vera. I just wasn't so sentimental. No 'immortals' for me. No, I would have put you in the fire and watched you sizzle, little fella."

She really was a charmer. I'd like to say that she was bad cop to her mistress's good cop, but given a choice between the two I'd rather have just been beaten instead of raped, even if my rapist was crying as often as she was cursing me. Man, was I ever being reminded not to trust anyone in Hell. Vera's joy-juice had lulled me, but my brain had still worked fairly well, so I couldn't dodge the blame. I'd grown careless, and now I was paying for it. And paying for it and paying for it.

Most nights, Vera wouldn't even look at me after she'd finished: when her spasm was over she would crawl off me and rearrange her clothing into respectability. Tonight, as if in parody of one of those old movies where the couples sleep in separate beds, she was dressed in an extremely modest nightdress that she smoothed over her long legs, hiding the alien horror between her thighs. She was Mina Harker as well as Dracula, the Victorian maiden and the beast of darkness rolled into one.

"Vera. Vera, talk to me." It was hard to speak in a normal voice after the pain I'd just suffered, but I was fighting for my life. "Why does it have to be this way? Because I looked at a woman at the opera? I thought I knew her, that's all. It was nothing to do with you."

"Nothing to do with me." Her voice was heavy, the words bleak. She was always like this after her attacks on me. "That is just the problem. I wanted you only to care about me. I wanted you only to see *me*."

I tried to get her to talk, to explain, anything that would keep the lines of communication open. Already she was losing interest in me, I could tell. The worst of her anger, her almost operatic feeling of betrayal, was beginning to cool, but I didn't fool myself that when she was done with me she'd just let me go.

"Listen, we could try again!"

She didn't even bother to reply, just shook her head and slid off the bed, then walked out of the room, bare feet whispering on the stone floor. Belle, who always stood guard now during Vera's frenzies, gave me a look of contempt.

"She'll be done with you soon. Maybe she'll give you to me. I'll break your neck like a chicken's and then you'll be no trouble to anyone."

I didn't say anything, but I wondered what this breaking of my neck would mean in a place like this. It probably wouldn't kill me, since as far as I knew you couldn't die in Hell, but it would make things pretty unpleasant, especially if it was combined with being thrown on a garbage heap somewhere or burned, as the two women had both threatened to do. Not to mention when my soul arrived at the depot for re-bodying, and Hell's authorities realized it was the kind that usually sported a halo. Lameh's implanted briefing made it clear that mere destruction of my demon body would not free me from these horrors. Unless I left Hell under my own power, by the route Temuel and the guardian angel had given me, I was going to stay there forever.

When the door shut behind big Belle, I went back to work on my strap. What she and her mistress hadn't realized was that not only was my hand growing back, but I now had movement in the regenerating fingers. The thick gray skin of my demon body might have been striped like a gazelle's, but my hands were weaponized, with curved black nails sharp and heavy as parrots' beaks on the good hand. The claws were much less impressive on the hand that was growing back, but if I twisted it until it hurt so badly it felt like Block was biting it off all over again, I could just touch the strap around that arm with my index fingernail.

It was a start. I decided that if I sawed away for a long stretch, ignoring the pain (and good lord, was it painful) I might be able to fray the edge of the strap that held my wounded arm to the headboard of the bed. The leather was thick, and after an hour or so my claw was too dull to do any more work, but I found out that if I performed another agonizing stretch in a different direction, I could rub the claw against the metal bedpost and eventually put enough of an edge on it to get back to work.

Needless to say, this was slow, achingly miserable work, and the chances I would survive long enough to get all the way through the strap were minimal, but I didn't have a better plan. Lady Zinc and her servant were both crazy. Nobody was going to rescue me, and I was getting weaker by the hour. It was ironic, really: Vera had saved me when I was bleeding to death and nursed me back to health, but now she was taking something at least as vital from me, even if I wasn't quite sure what it was. It wasn't just my precious bodily fluids, it seemed to be my very essence, and there was less of it each time she drained me.

Big Belle had just finished tightening the straps on my good arm one night—I was so weak they didn't even bother to tie my ankles anymore—when I gasped out a question: Why did she and Vera hate men so much?

Vera had taken so much out of me that Belle had hardly bothered to slap me around, and now she looked at me with genuine amusement. "Hate men? That just shows you know nothing. For me, men have never been worth hating. A means to an end, that's all. All my husbands, my boyfriends, my lodgers, they brought me money. I didn't need them alive to spend it with me—in fact, I didn't want to argue about how to spend it—so I did away with them. But if it had been women I could have lured, women who had the money, well, so it would have been. I certainly killed a few. But my lady, she is very different. She *loves*. She loves so much that she is helpless against it."

"It's a pretty goddamn funny way to show it."

Belle shook her head, her big jaw jutting with irritation. "It's a perfect way to show it. She's like a butterfly. She lives for love, and she dies for love."

"She's not the one dying."

Belle grunted, then reached out and gave me a lazy slap that loosened a few of my teeth. "You understand nothing. Do you know why she is called Lady Zinc?"

My ears were still ringing from the blow. It was all I could do to shake my head.

"Back in the old life, in Bucharest, she was a wealthy woman. She took many lovers. Nobody ever saw those lovers again. She made only one mistake—letting a local banker into her bed. When he vanished his wife made a stink. The police came, and when they searched Vera's house they found nearly three dozen zinc coffins in her cellar, each with a window over the corpse's face, all those zinc boxes arranged like a group of admirers at a party. There was even a chair so Vera could sit and speak to them, look at them, all her beloved, unfaithful lovers. She couldn't bear to lose them to other women, so when she saw their interest beginning to die, she poisoned them, and they died, too. Too much love, you see? Too much love. It was quite beautiful." Belle put her great, callused hand on my face and shoved me against the headboard so my brain rattled in my skull. "She offered you a love like that, and you spat in her face. You will not be one of her immortals, like those men were."

And that was what I was left with, as I struggled through another desperate, painful night trying to scrape through the heavy leather strap on my wrist. Zinc coffins. Thirty or more. That was the measure of Vera's love. I was only the latest, and I wasn't even going to have the distinction of earning one of those gray metal boxes.

I lost track of how many nights Vera came to me, how many nights she drained me. It was just as well I was tied to the bed, because my groin itched and stung so horribly, I'd have scratched myself to ribbons trying to relieve it. There wasn't much left of me now—I had been sucked nearly dry. I didn't even dream of Caz any more, but floated between two kinds of being half-asleep, with brief interludes of searing pain and then the wretchedness that followed, and bouts of weakness that lasted longer each time, broken by desperate sawing at the thick leather strap. Soon Vera would feast on me one last time, take the rest of me, and that would be it. Belle had already told me that I was going into the furnace when I was through, that she didn't want anything left for her mistress to become sentimental about.

I no longer dreamed of Caz, but I did dream a little, the kind of sickly fantasies you have when you're in the grip of a fever, complicated but basically meaningless. That was why it took me quite a while on this night to realize that I was actually awake, and something really was kneeling beside me on the bed, resting a splayed hand on my chest.

I was so weak that for a long moment I just stared at it, blinking against the light of the single small candle that lit the room. In one sense I had never truly examined the face that now swung down close to my own, staring at me with an intensity that seemed as hungry as Vera's; in another sense, I knew it better than I knew mine, that dead gray expanse of shrunken flesh, the jutting lower jaw, the tiny teeth like pieces of gravel, the glittering little shark's eyes. Smyler.

"It look for you." The voice was a scratchy whisper. "It look for you so long, Bobby Bad Angel. Now it *find* you."

The scrawny thing climbed onto my torso and then began to poke solemnly at the skin of my face with the depressingly familiar four-sided blade, each little stab as painful as a botched injection. The murdering creature looked different somehow, his skin darker, body thinner, the ropy musculature more exaggerated than before.

"What . . . what do you want?" I shifted my weight, trying to get into a position where I could throw all my force against the frayed strap. I didn't think I had done enough damage to break it yet, but it wasn't like I had a lot of choices. My movement irritated Smyler. He pushed his blade against my upper eyelid. I went very still. A drop of blood caught in my lashes and began to leak into my eye, but I didn't dare blink.

"What do you want?" I must have sounded terrified, because I was. I had already been down to my very last reserves of belief—of faith, if you will—and now things had become dramatically worse.

"What it want?" Smyler gave a little chortle, as crisply dry as the shake of a rattlesnake's tail, *t-t-t-t-t-t*. "It want the feather. Come a long way for the feather. Tell where it is, or it will have the wicked angel's eye in its pocket and the wicked, bad angel's heart in its lunch box." Suddenly the deformed mouth spread in what must have been a grin. "Bad angel is sweetest meat. Bad angel always taste *so good*."

twenty-six
immortalized

EVEN WHEN free and carrying a gun, I had barely survived my encounters with this murderous little bastard, but this time I was tied to a bed after being drained by Lady Zinc for many days. I couldn't really think of anything to do but stall.

"Why do you want the feather?" I asked, knowing damn well he wanted it for his master, Eligor. "I mean, I don't have it here. I couldn't give it to you even if I wanted to. I'd have to get back to Earth. You know what I mean, right? The real world?"

Smyler only poked the blade a little harder into my eyelid. I swear I felt it touch the surface of my cornea. Not good.

"Feather," he said. "Give it."

"I don't have it!" I wondered if he was too stupid or broken to understand, and as my already shaky faith in a negotiated solution began to dwindle, I slowly drew my legs up a little closer to my body. "I can get it for you, though, but you have to get me out of here—"

He leaned in even closer. His breath . . . I won't even try to tell you. Vermin. Disease. Open grave pits. "Want feather," it whispered. "*Now.*"

I jammed my feet against Smyler's skinny chest and shoved as hard as I could, with particular care to aim him toward the dresser stacked with glassware and other breakables. He weighed practically nothing, as light as a nine-year-old child, and I was able to get enough strength into my surprise shove to send him flying like a badly made kite. He crashed into the dresser and took at least half the objects off the top, a cascade of breakage like Hummel Armageddon. I put my full weight against the strap I had been working on for days and yanked down as hard as I could. I felt it give a little as the remaining leather stretched, but it held. It also hurt like eleven bitches on a bitch-boat.

Smyler still had his long knife in hand as he popped up like a jack-in-the-box. His smile was horrible, but he wasn't smiling now. His shriveled face was a perfect blank, the expression now as dead as everything else about it. In the middle of my panic I realized that in all the years of horror movies only Boris Karloff had ever got it right, that slack, weirdly sullen look of the animated corpse. Then Smyler came over the footboard of the bed like a wolf spider out of its hole, and it was all I could do to take the first nasty thrust with my calf. Hurt like a screaming motherfucker, and that's all I have to say about that.

My enemy was so expressionless that I began to wonder if I hadn't kicked him right out of his wits, such as they were. He seemed to be completely uninterested now in anything but trying to stab me, the blade snapping out like a snake's tongue. I blocked every thrust with my legs or body, but sometimes I had to take it in something meaty to protect my more valuable stuff. The knife kept darting here and there, and I was still tied to the bed. The whole thing was just shitty, and I knew I couldn't survive the attack for more than a few more moments.

"Stop! I'll give you the feather!" I gasped, but Smyler seemed to have forgotten about his original purpose. His attack became less frenzied but more considered. He was moving around now to keep the bedpost between my feet and his midsection.

The light changed suddenly, the shadows all jumping to one side as though something had startled them. A cluster of little flames appeared in the doorway, a candelabrum, and beside it the startled face of Belle. "What's going on here?"

I was a little crazed at this point, as you can imagine, but I also thought my best chance would be to set Belle or her mistress on the freak that was trying so sincerely to stick holes in me right this minute, so I yelled, "That's her! Kill her, just like I told you! You can free me later!" (I have no idea if this fooled anybody, or did anything at all except make me look like an idiot, but I'm going to guess it was what saved me.)

Belle slammed the heavy candelabrum down on Smyler's arm, making him drop his blade, then she shoved the candles into his face and burned his cheek, which made him hiss and strike at her. Staggered, she dropped the candleholder on the floor. The candles bounced out, but enough remained burning to make long, extremely grotesque shadows from the two struggling monsters, the small, skinny one biting and scratching at the big one like an angry ferret.

I got my legs under me and pulled against my right arm strap as hard as I could, shouting in agony despite myself. It felt like I was going to tear my entire arm out of the shoulder socket. I had frayed the strap just enough, because it finally tore, and I was swinging only by the other arm, the good arm with the uncut leather cuff. This was another kind of miserable, but I had work to do, so I started gnawing at it with my sharp demon-teeth. The sounds from the floor were becoming more animal by the moment. I couldn't tell who was winning, and to be honest, I wasn't rooting for either of them.

It was hard work, but I finally chewed through the thick restraint. The first seconds of freedom were glorious, but lowering my arms after a week or two of being tied in crucifixion position was kind of like being stabbed in both armpits at the same time. Still, I'd become pretty used to pain at that point. I sort of fell off the bed, grabbed my pants, and ran.

The fact that Vera hadn't shown up to see what all the fuss was about told me that she was either in another part of the house or, if I was lucky, out altogether. Still, even if Vera really was gone, Belle and Smyler also had to maim each other badly, because there wasn't a snowball's chance that I could beat either one in my current condition.

Belle's long, thick leg lashed at me like a grumpy anaconda, but she was still tangled with Smyler, and I jumped over her and into the hallway. Vera's bedroom was only a few doors down. If milady was out of hearing range then the room should be empty, and I needed some things from there.

Vera had been careful, in her weird, old-fashioned flirtation with me, to let me see her boudoir several times, either inviting me in for morning tea—she received me in a high-necked dressing gown—or "accidentally" leaving the door open long enough for me to notice the undergarments artistically draped here and there. Because of that, I had no problem finding her room and also had a fairly good idea of where she might keep her jewelry and perhaps some cash. On my way to the suspect dresser, I paused to lift the poker from its spot beside the fireplace. (Yes, they have fireplaces in Hell. In fact, some parts of Pandaemonium are hot enough to use fireplaces as air conditioning.) The poker had a good heft to it; I was pleased to finally have something I could protect myself with, but I also kept my eyes open for more conventional weapons. I knew I could have found some sharp stuff in the kitchen, but I didn't want to cross the house—there were exits closer to where I was.

I found a few dozen copper handfuls (that's what they're called, "handfuls") hidden in a jewelry box with Vera's rings and necklaces. As I stuffed my pockets, I noticed a strange shadow at the back of the room. One of Vera's pictures, a fruit tree whose limbs swarmed with birds, looked as though it was thicker on one side. No, I saw as I stepped closer, the painting itself concealed a door that hadn't quite shut all the way.

I froze. Did that mean Vera was here? But why the secret door? Was it an escape tunnel? Had she heard the shouting and decided discretion was better than valor?

I opened the door and discovered a passage, walled with brick, that stretched ahead and down, vanishing around a corner. A lit torch hung in a bracket. Someone was almost certainly down there. But just as I was turning away, I heard the Smyler-Belle donnybrook crash out of my bedroom and into the hall behind me, thumps and gasps and the wet *slish* of knife in flesh. No matter which one of them survived, my route to the rest of the house was blocked. I had nowhere to go but down.

I held the poker in front of me like a rapier as I crept forward into the tunnel, since it was going to be a lot easier in that low, narrow passage for me to stab than to swing. The brick walkway curved then curved again, always sloping down, so that within just a few moments I knew I must be lower than the house itself. Soon I could hear voices, or perhaps one voice thickened and complicated by echoes. I took a few more steps, then saw there was more light ahead of me, so I made my way as quietly as I could down the passage, staying close to the wall and stopping at every bend to peer ahead, until suddenly the corridor widened dramatically.

I was in a subbasement, I guess, but that doesn't do it justice. It was a *cave*, was what it was, a cave underneath Vera's house, complete with stalactites and stalagmites, all pointing in the proper directions. As I moved out of the light of one torch and through a darker area toward the next torch, I suddenly heard Vera's voice clearly. I couldn't make out all the words—something about "disappointed," and "you certainly know"—but it was obvious she was talking to someone. That worried me. I had no urge to fight with Vera, who was quite a package by herself, and if she had allies I definitely wanted to avoid a confrontation. I thought about just turning and heading back, but by now either Belle or, more likely, Smyler had finished up with the other and would come looking for me.

I did my best silent slink. It was more than a cave, I could now see, it was some kind of warehouse or distillery or both. On all sides of me, barely visible in the dim light, stood dozens upon dozens of thick glass vessels, each about the size of a restaurant soup kettle, stacked in rows on shelves that reached to the low ceiling. It looked like Vera was running some kind of medical supply warehouse down there.

"I do not blame you, of course," I heard her say. "I don't blame you at all. Every one of you has earned his place here. Every one . . ."

As I tiptoed forward, trying to find a vantage point through the crowded shelves so I could see who Vera was talking to, I caught an odd flash in one of the jars and let my gaze drift back to it.

Something looked back at me. A head. A bodiless head.

No, I realized as I bent down, it wasn't completely bodiless, because it looked like many of the pieces that would constitute a body were bobbing in the jar with it, only none of them were connected to each other. I looked at the other jars and saw forearms with hands attached, the fingers splayed against the glass like gray-green starfish. I saw feet, and faces that had been removed from the skull and now looked more like masks, and of course penises—quite a few of those, too (although no more than one per container). And in every jar, as if it were the sun around which those nasty pale planets revolved, floated a head.

Revolted, I let my eyes slide back down the row, then up to the rows above, and then ahead to those that still lay before me, shelved on either side of the central passage. I knew I must be looking at Vera's Immortals, all the lovers she had honored, the men who had treated her as she expected to be treated.

Fat lot of good it did them, I thought.

Then the nearest bodiless head winked at me and grinned.

Generally I try not to squawk like a frightened child when in surveillance situations, but it was too late to take it back now. Not only had I alerted Vera but I had probably been loud enough to let Smyler know where I was, too. In fact, I had probably let the people down in the Abaddon levels know where I was. Even the heads around me were beginning to wake up, rolling their eyes to see who had sent little-girl-scream waves through their formaldehyde.

No use pretending or skulking now. I stepped out into the center of the walkway and went forward. Vera stood at the center of the cavern room in the midst of rows of sturdy, ugly shelves, each nearly full of glass jars, each glass jar with its own set of hands and hearts and balls and staring eyes.

I underestimated Vera. I had expected her to be surprised to see me, or at least to weep and shriek at me before she attacked. Instead she came after me immediately and without a word, arms spread wide. She swung her hands toward me as if trying to claw my eyes; I wondered why, because she was too far away for that to make any sense. Then about three thousandths of a second later those horrible little fingernail-filaments of hers snapped past me like taser wires, just missing my face.

Her toxin-tubes obviously weren't just for close-up work.

So, I had a fireplace poker; she had, whipping from the fingers of either hand, six-foot jellyfish tendrils that could poison me. Vera lashed out again. I threw myself down as her stingers swept a jar off the shelf behind me. It crashed to the floor, belching broken glass and foul liquids, ejecting body parts in all directions. I had to jump over the corpse-hands, which immediately began crawling toward Vera. She snapped out both her arms at once. I dove under the nearly invisible strands and rolled, then jabbed with the poker when I was close enough, ramming it into her gut as hard as I could. It doubled her over but that seemed to be all: I was still staring at her when she yanked her hands back and tried to catch me in the trailing strands again. One of them got me, wrapping around my neck like a thread of burning napalm. As it tightened on my throat I could feel the ability to think running out of me like sand, the pain getting stronger, darker, like a powerful electric charge, no, like an entire eel, wrapped around my neck and squeezing the life out of me.

The surge of agony lessened. From the corner of my eye I saw Vera kicking at something. One of the hands from the broken jar was clinging to her ankle. She finally managed to shake it loose and turned her attention back to me, but by then I had my idea.

I grabbed the stinger around my neck with my hand. It was like holding a white hot wire, but as I said, by this point I could *do* pain. I yanked at it hard, then braced myself and kept pulling, even though it felt like I was cutting my own head off with a power saw, until the tendril finally snapped. Vera let out a screech of rage, but she sure didn't sound injured. Those translucent folds snapped over her eyes as she hissed in fury and heaved her filaments at me again. I ducked, then smashed the closest jar with the iron poker, then smashed another. As she pulled back her tendrils I struck out around me as widely as I could, knocking one jar into another, sweeping the unbroken ones as well as the shards off the shelves. Glass was everywhere, and the stinking clouds of the preserving liquid all but blinded me.

But there were body parts all over too, and like a school of slow, slow fish they were making their way through the glass and spilled liquids toward Vera.

Now I pushed over whole rows of jars, trying to fill the floor with broken glass and free as many of Vera's immortals as possible. As they piled around her, different parts from dozens of different bodies built bridges with each other, clinging, climbing. Hands worked together to lift a head up to other hands. Many-headed, many limbed piles of dripping meat built themselves up from the sloshing floor like volcanoes being born. The composite creatures quickly surrounded Vera, and despite the love she had lavished on them and the kindnesses she had shown them, none of her immortals seemed willing to miss out on this reunion.

She had forgotten about me and was trying to fight her way free, but the coral reef of fingers and feet and kidneys and faces had already risen to her waist. Hands climbed her body like crabs—many already clung to her dark, loosened hair. She shrieked and tried to knock them away, but more flung themselves onto her and then made chains so that other hands could cross, until Vera swayed at the center of a crowd of these teetering, squirming piles, white-faced and astounded, still screaming but almost without sound now because she had shrieked herself hoarse. Hands scuttled closer and pulled themselves to her so that the heads could kiss her. As the body-meat piles grew higher, the heads ran their tongues over her, tongues that sometimes came loose and dropped to the floor like overfilled leeches.

Much as I hated the bitch, I didn't stay to watch. The moment I could see a clear space, I stumbled past the bizarre reunion, ran, heart ratcheting, until I found the stairs at the far side of the cellar, then climbed for what seemed like days upon lightless days. Vera's hoarse shrieks followed me for a long part of that journey, until I finally found myself in a regular part of the tunnels near the Terminus. From there I was able to make my way upward, to stand free at last beneath Hell's vaulted, claustrophobic night sky.

I could never have guessed how glad I would be to see that terrible blank firmament again.

twenty-seven

chancery

ONE GOOD thing about Hell is that there's never any problem getting rid of stolen goods, no matter how late it is. I'd had a lot of time to think between visits from Vera and her vampire groin, and I'd come up with a few ideas of what to do next if I ever got the chance. Now I had it.

Vera's fancy neighborhood was on the edge of Sulfur Lagoon, a prestige location close to, among other things, the Night Market, a vast array of stalls and tents and shacks made of various awful things where you could buy or sell pretty much anything. Limping and bloody (two things that fortunately don't attract much notice in Hell) I made my way to the market and asked around until I found the bazaar of a fellow named Saad Babrak who looked like a hairless tarantula from his neck downward and had a reputation as a discreet disperser of goods. In other words, a fence.

I could only hope Vera's jewelry was good quality. I hung onto one necklace of lumpy, lagoon-grown pearls (I'll explain why later) but dumped all the rest of the stuff on Saad's counter and let him piss all over me in the guise of "bargaining." I didn't want to give in too easily because he'd remember that, but I also didn't want to be there so long that Smyler or some other survivor from Vera's house found me. At last I got a price I could live with, spent a little on the spot purchasing some of Saad's other goods, including some clean clothes which I didn't put on right away and a long, sharp, well-made knife with a backward-curving guard; the kind of thing I wanted to have in my hand the next time I wound up fighting for my life.

I'd made two gold weights, three copper handfuls, and a couple of iron spits in change from the stolen stuff, plus the coins I'd already taken from Vera's jewelry box, so I was pretty much wealthy, at least for a while. Jewelry dumped and pockets jingling with money, I picked the inn with the least horrifying reputation I could find, a place called the Black Ostrich, that overlooked the stinking backwater where the Styx bellied out into Sulfur Lagoon. I probably looked pretty beat up already, so as I paid I showed the innkeeper my knife, informed him I wouldn't be sleeping during my stay so there was no point trying to rob and murder me, and suggested strongly that he and the rest of his employees would be happiest if they avoided my room entirely. Then I dragged myself upstairs and went to work.

One of the things I'd bought from Saad's bazaar was a jug of firewater. Yes, that's what it's called, and it's not the Dodge City kind. It's made from the waters of the burning river Phlegethon, it's uglier in the mouth than Riprash's rum, and you don't need to drink much before you want to go out and beat some people to bloody pulp. I drank a bit more carefully than that, just enough to kill the worst of the pain from my long captivity and dull what I was about to do to myself.

I'd bought one more thing from Saad's place, a cracked hunk of mirror glass: very few people in Hell want to own mirrors, for some reason, and there certainly wasn't going to be one in a cheap hostel like the Black Ostrich. Now that I could see myself, I went to work, slicing lines in the skin of my face and liberally dousing them with firewater, pausing every few minutes to stick my bloody face into the filthy mattress and scream, because it hurt really fucking bad, let me tell you.

Once I'd cut myself along the brow line, forehead, cheeks, nose, and jaw, I dabbed away the slow-moving blood, then sliced the cord on Vera's pearl necklace and began tucking the individual pearls into my bleeding weals. I'd seen a ritual like it on a National Geographic TV show; young guys in Africa or New Guinea or somewhere stuffing their sliced skin with stones and ashes to make impressive scars. I didn't care about impressive, I just wanted to change the look of my face. I had almost vomited out my own heart when Caym the President seemed to recognize me. Ultimately I might wind up trying to fool Eligor himself, but as I had discovered to my surprise and shock, whatever process Temuel had used to get me into this body had left me looking a lot more like my Bobby Dollar self than I could risk. So, self-mutilation.

I kept drinking little nips of the firewater, and that blotted out the worst of the agony, but there was so much blood that I quickly soaked the few rags I'd lifted at the bazaar. No point in putting on my new, clean clothes until the bleeding stopped, so I dabbed my wounds one last agonizing time with Phlegethon-liquor, then laid myself down to sleep through the worst of the pain.

I dreamed of Caz, of course, of our last night together in Eligor's hotel before he blew the fucking thing to kingdom come, but in my dream we couldn't make love because bits of me kept falling off and crawling around on a floor slippery with blood. At one point I roused myself from the mattress long enough to douse myself in the burning liquid again, then did my best to fall back asleep, but I could actually feel the skin knitting together over my new scars—a disturbing, tingling sensation like ants dancing in little white-hot metal shoes. After awhile I just gave up and lay with gritted teeth, waiting for the pain to subside enough for sleep to come.

It took more than a few hours. I was beginning to feel right at home in Hell now—angry, miserable, hurting, you name it. Cheated, too. Like everyone else here, I was having trouble understanding what I had done to be suffering this way.

Now that I was comparatively safe I gave the scars a full day to heal, going out to the Night Market only long enough to grab something disgusting to eat before slinking back to my room at the Ostrich. When the pain of my self-surgery had dwindled to a dull ache, I got out the broken mirror and examined my handiwork. It was a strange look: my bumpy new brow and the lumpy lines along my cheekbones and jaw made me look like some kind of desert lizard. I used a little carbon from the candlewick so my eyes would seem more deep-sunk beneath the knobby shelf I'd created. It made me even uglier, but that was fine. There's no right or wrong in Hell as far as how people look, and my only goal was to look less like Bobby Dollar, Enemy of the State.

I lay down again to think, because I had a lot to think about. How had Smyler found me? Had Eligor brought him back here from the real world like recalling an employee from a field office? It was the only thing that made sense. But if the grand duke could find me to set Smyler on me, why hadn't he done it sooner? Why hadn't Eligor sent the Murderers Sect instead? And why hadn't any of my enemies showed up here at my new hiding place?

Commissar Niloch and others had mentioned someone the authorities were hunting, an intruder, and I'd assumed that was me. But what if it was Smyler all along? What if he'd somehow followed me into Hell and only caught up to me when I was stuck at Vera's house?

That was about all the thought I could give it, since there wasn't much point in trying to figure things out from so little information. I was here for Caz, that was what mattered, and I had a lot to do, some of which was going to be downright terrifying. Putting it off would only make things worse. Only the Highest knew how long I'd already been in this horrible place, but it felt like half a year or more. For all I knew, there was already a heavenly APB out for me. In many, many ways, I was running out of time.

The Ministry of Justice, also known as the Chancery, was in the deepest, most overbuilt section of the Red City, a crooked maze of close-leaning towers and guarded doorways behind Dis Pater Square. I had been praying I wouldn't have to see Chancellor Urgulap again, the hideous giant-beetle-thing that had interviewed me back on Earth about the death of Prosecutor Grasswax. Luckily, as a member of the minor gentry Snakestaff of the Liars Sect was far too unimportant to get a meeting with the chancellor, and was instead fobbed off on a (literally) very sharp young woman, who seemed to be made entirely out of scissor parts. Urgulap was present only in a portrait that hung on the wall, watching over the dark office, his shell buffed to a gleam and his inhuman face frozen in a glower of determined leadership.

"We cannot give you that information, Lord Snakestaff," the Scissor Sister told me. "The chancellor has not completed his investigation, which he will present to the Senate and Council soon."

"That's okay," I said, trying to imagine how reckless a guy would have to be to go to bed with a woman whose thighs were sharpened blades. "I just need to do something with this thing." I tried to hand her a piece of vellum, but only managed to knock several of the files off her desk. She gave me a look of shiny distaste, then her metal surfaces rasped as she bent to pick them up. When finished, she examined the writing on the piece of stretched, smoothed skin. "What is this? Some sort of debt?"

"That's right," I said. "Grasswax owed me almost two weights. Gambling debts." (The real Grasswax had indeed liked a wager, and lost pretty frequently from what I'd heard. But not only hadn't he lost to me, I didn't even know what contests or games he liked.) "So, could I get, I don't know, paid out of his estate? When the investigation's over?"

"Doesn't your sect allow you to pursue these matters out of Grass-wax's redenture?"

I did my best to look embarrassed, which wasn't that hard since I had no idea what a redenture even was. "Yeah. They sort of . . . kicked me out. I'm not in the Liars Sect any more." I shrugged. "I caught on with the Thieves."

She rubbed one of her blades down her nose, which was also a blade. *Skrrkkkkkkk.* "All right," she said at last. "Fine. Leave this with me, and I'll put it into the files. With an explanation." She frowned, which looked pretty odd, I can tell you. "But don't expect too much."

I stood. "Why would I? This is Hell."

Outside, I stepped into the dark space of a tower doorway to make certain I'd grabbed the right thing while Scissor Sister was picking up the stuff I knocked over. I took a quick look at the out-basket files I'd stolen, a few pieces of vellum with official Chancery letterhead. More important, though, was the other thing I'd lifted, a wooden stamp that looked like it might have come right off Ebenezer Scrooge's desk, except instead of "Scrooge & Marley" it said "Ministry of Justice."

Perfect.

I didn't sleep very well that night, and it wasn't just because of the intermittent shrieks of agony from the promenade along Sulfur Lagoon. They weren't really any worse than the stink of the lagoon itself, and both were easier to ignore than the weird buzzing, gagging sex two or three somethings were having in the room above mine.

I was finally ready, after all this time, to do what I had come to Hell to do, or at least to begin doing it. If you know me at all by now, you know that I'm not so stupid as to do the same stupid thing every time—I prefer to alternate my stupidities. I had been discreetly check-ing into Eligor's setup (loyalty is almost nonexistent in Hell, and bribery is one of the favorite pastimes). I wasn't going to just charge into his fortress of a house. I knew I couldn't just saunter in and liberate Caz. I wasn't even going to make a plan until I knew more. That was why I had been sitting up all evening making fake Ministry of Justice documents for myself, until I had come up with something that satisfied my intention to walk in and out of Eligor's stronghold with my skin on and my vital organs still in their original places.

When I'd tackled Eligor in his earthly stronghold at Five Page Mill back in San Judas, I hadn't known who and what I was dealing with. I did now. I was pretty sure I'd only get one shot to get her away from him, and I'd have to be very lucky to get even that. I needed a real plan, but first I needed to see his castle, called Flesh Horse, up close.

Just getting near it was difficult, because although the top levels had the same kind of connective branches leading horizontally to other great mansions, they were all closely guarded. Like the Infernal Cabinet House and most other important buildings in Pandaemonium, the base of Flesh Horse sat in a wide park, walled off from its neighbors. The grounds were tangled with blood-colored trees and aggressively guarded by legions of what looked like albino scorpions with wolves' heads. They didn't worry me too much, because I was intending to walk right in through the front door, at least this first time.

Flesh Horse was many acres wide at its base and stretched up so far into the smoky sky that even with the red day lamps burning in the walls I couldn't see its top. The great, stony castle didn't actually look like a horse, or like flesh, but it didn't look like a nice place, either. Still, Caz was in there somewhere, and I desperately needed to get her back. It felt like doing that was the only thing that might keep me sane.

So I spent several days on my due diligence and lots of money on bribes, gathering information and prepping myself. I had a special set of clothes made by a tailor at the Night Market, and paid another visit to Saad the pink tarantula to pick up a few additional necessities. My scars were all but healed now, the bumpiness of my face still just as ugly but a lot less recent-looking.

The night before I started my mission, I drank myself to near-unconsciousness with Phlegethon firewater because I was too tightly wound to sleep otherwise. In the near darkness Hell calls morning, I took one last swallow to burn out the hangover and the musty taste in my mouth, then carefully dressed and prepared myself before walking out into the Red City, whistling the theme to *The Good, The Bad, and The Ugly*.

Okay, I wasn't doing that last part. I admit that I *was* wishing Clint Eastwood could have been there too, but it was only yours truly.

twenty-eight
the drowned girl

HERE'S A tip. If you're a Mormon missionary or a door-to-door salesman, don't waste your time and outer skin visiting Flesh Horse. My forged documents got me more attention than I would have liked, but they also got me inside the tower and into an appointment with Eligor's Chief of Security. The grand duke's previous head of security, my old friend Howlingfell, had been eaten by a large supernatural monstrosity that was supposed to eat me instead—something I can honestly say I enjoyed a great deal. The new chief, a hideous thing named Snaghorn, resembled a bloody, skinned grizzly bear with snail-stalks for eyes. He'd never seen me before, which doesn't mean he heartily invited me in, of course: Snaghorn spent a good fifteen minutes just sniffing me. I'm sure he was just doing his job, but he seemed to do it for a very long time. A very, *very* long time. But at last Snaghorn seemed satisfied. Instead of biting any parts off me, he touched a curving black claw to my forehead. It felt like I'd been branded, and in a way, I had: he'd given me his mark, which meant limited permission to move through the lower levels of the house. Not by myself, of course, and not freely. I had an appointment with someone Snaghorn curtly referred to as "the drowned girl."

Fun, fun, fun, any way you sliced it. It's a wonder more people don't make Hell a holiday destination.

Considering we were in a building that looked from the outside like some kind of giant tubeworm had excreted it, and from the inside like a bad acid trip version of a Renaissance tower, the drowned girl's office was surprisingly ordinary. She sat at an ancient wooden desk, the old-fashioned kind called a "secretary," with lots of pigeonholes to stash things and a large framed mirror sitting front and central in the middle of the desk surface. The windows of the quiet, dark room looked out over a backwater of the Phlegethon called the Bay of Tophet. The whole expanse of river seethed, flames floating on the black boil and sending curls of steam into the red-lit air; the view out the window seemed like a piece of theatrical scenery. The drowned girl herself looked pretty much the way you'd guess. Although swollen in places, she was still slender, the effect heightened by the lank, dripping hair that hung down to the shoulders of her wet, vaguely medieval-looking dress. Her skin was exactly the kind of blue-white ghastly and puffy-at-the-edges you'd expect. Her pale, bleached-out eyes watched me intelligently (if a bit resentfully), but every now and then they just rolled up behind her lids and stayed that way for a while, which left me staring at a very realistic corpse in an office chair.

"I am Marmora." She sounded like she still had some water in her lungs. "And you are apparently Pseudolus of Prespa," she continued, reading the sheet of vellum I'd handed her. (I'd decided "Snakestaff" had pissed off too many people for me to walk into Eligor's and use that name again.) "What is your business with the Grand Duke Eligor?"

Cutting off the duke's Grand Nuts, I wanted to say, or anything similar that would express my feelings about the huge amount of bullshit I owed him for, not least of which was stealing back the girlfriend I'd stolen from him. "It's regarding another member of my sect, the late Prosecutor Grasswax," is what I said instead. "The Liars Sect has sent me here." They hadn't, of course, but that was what my forged documents showed. "I just want to ask him a few questions about Grasswax."

"That will not happen." Her sour smile was made a little creepier by the stream of liquid that dribbled from her lower lip. "His Grand Ducal Highness is far too busy to see someone like you."

"I understand." I hadn't expected to get an audience, and in fact I didn't want one, I just wanted a chance to get in and explore. "Who else could I talk to?"

"Nobody." She pushed the vellum back to me, her fingers so soft, damp, and swollen that they left little shreds of skin on the document. "Grasswax was never in the grand duke's employ."

"But he came here often. And I've been told he performed some, well, informal tasks for Grand Duke Eligor—"

"That doesn't matter. His Grand Ducal Highness will not see you, and nobody else here can tell you anything about our master's . . . informal arrangements. I suggest you take your inquiries elsewhere." She stared at me for a long moment, a strangely intimate moment, although it was hard to look back into those cloudy, ruined eyes. "I would prefer not to have to call Snaghorn and his guards to show you out, but I will if I must." She said it almost as if she truly meant it, which was kind of her, but it was still bad news. I'd hoped to get farther and stay longer, maybe even work up an idea of where Caz was being held.

I stood there clutching my forged documents, wondering what to do next. All I'd come up with was either asking for a public restroom or faking a seizure when I heard a harshly musical tone like a long icicle cracking. Marmora turned her bleary stare to the mirror on the desk. "Yes, Countess?"

Needless to say, I was suddenly pulled as tight as a guitar string. I stepped back from the desk and wandered a short distance away, as though respectfully giving Marmora her privacy, but I was really just trying to find an angle where I could see the front of the mirror.

It was *her* in the glass, her amazing face, right there in front of me. I couldn't hear anything she was saying, although the drowned girl obviously could, but that didn't matter. It was her, Caz, and after all this time she was actually within reach. All I'd have to do would be to interrupt Marmora, and I would be speaking directly to the woman I loved. I wasn't going to do anything that stupid, of course, but I wanted to, I really did. There she was, the same beautiful, terrifying vision I'd first met when she appeared at the Edward Walker death scene, blood-red eyes and all. But Caz looked pale and tired now, oh so tired, and even from where I stood, I could see how much effort it was taking her to carry on this domestic conversation with Marmora. God, I wanted her. I wanted nothing but to sneak away from the drowned girl and try to find her, but I knew that would be suicide of an extremely certain kind.

"Yes, Countess, of course I'll arrange that," Marmora said. "When would you like to go? First night of the Wolf? I'll arrange it. How big is that party?" I watched Caz speaking and wondered where in this vast tower complex she was right now. It was agonizing. Could I just sneak out and find her? Take her with me *right now*? Was I making things too difficult?

"Do you want to be on the Leopold Square side of the Circus?" Marmora asked. There was an odd tone to her voice, as if she was dealing with Caz in the hell-minion version of arm's-length. Did she dislike the Countess of Cold Hands, or was something more complicated going on? And why should I care anyway? "Right, then, the Leopold Square end," the drowned girl said. "Very good, my lady."

Caz's face vanished from the mirror. I thanked the drowned girl for helping me. Marmora gave me a strange look that reminded me "thank you" was not commonly heard in Hell.

"You should leave these matters alone and go back to the lower levels, Lord Pseudolus," she said as I walked out. "You will be a mouse to the cats of Pandaemonium."

I think she was being nice.

As soon as the dripping secretary had said "Circus," I was pretty certain I knew where Caz would be going on the first night of the Festival of the Wolf, only a couple of hellish days away. Wolf was the closest thing to a holiday they had in Hell, a great orgy of public bloodletting and even worse-than-usual behavior. The Circus had to be the Circus of Commodus, Pandaemonium's version of Madison Square Garden or Wembley Stadium. It might be my only chance to talk to Caz outside of Flesh Horse, which might mean it was also my last chance to carry her off. (Yes, even at this late date I confess I was still considering the thing in romantic terms like that, despite the fact that Caz was at least as strong as me and knew Hell a lot better than I ever would. Or at least a lot better than I hoped I ever would.) So, I now needed to change tactics. *Just slip out the back, Jack. Make a new plan, Stan.*

I remember stuff like that at the weirdest times.

Dis Pater Square is the biggest public space in Pandaemonium, the heart of Hell's capital city. But just as the center of Paris starts at Notre Dame and stretches along the Champs Élysées to the Arc de Triomphe, so the center of Hell stretched all the way along the Via Dolorosa, the wide, grim avenue where triumphant demon-generals marched. The Circus, otherwise known as the Amphitheater of Commodus, was at the end of the Via Dolorosa, next to Leopold Square. Commodus was one of the worst of the Roman emperors, a murderous psychopath in the vein of Caligula and Nero, but unlike Nero, Commodus had never tried to cheat Hell. In fact, Commodus had a major landmark in Hell named after him instead of a forgotten bridge, so my guess was that Eligor and Caym and the boys weren't making Emperor Commodus sing opera in front of heckling crowds, either.

It cost two spits to travel by ferry across the steaming expanse of the Bay of Tophet, but it was much faster than walking, and I didn't want to jam myself into one of the lurching, packed trains. I reached the landing at Leopold Square before the second beacon had even been lit, leaving me the infernal afternoon to reconnoiter. The amphitheater was closed, but a bribe to a guard—who looked like someone had tried to make walrus jerky and failed—got me inside, then a wearying hike up stony steps got me to the top to look around.

Commodus' amphitheater looked a lot like the famous colosseum in Rome, except longer and about five times bigger. I'm pretty sure you could pack a few hundred thousand people into it, or what passed for people down here. A track extended around the entire length, but there was a separate space at the middle, clearly meant for something like gladiator fights. The sands of the track and the arena were rusty with dried blood.

Down in the lower part of the stands near the center of the amphitheater, a large section was sheltered by roofs of stretched skin, like giant albino pterodactyl wings. Since there was no sun in Hell, I was pretty certain the roof was for privacy for Hell's most important, and perhaps to protect them from the missiles and saliva of the braver or at least crazier of the less fortunate above and behind them.

I wandered around long enough to get a feeling for the Circus, paying close attention to exits, hiding places, and good and bad spots for making a desperate last stand. Then I sloped back to my room at the Ostrich to rest and think. Neither of those came easy. Every time I started to get a little focus, I would see Caz's wan face again in that mirror and my thoughts would be scattered like bowling pins. I had never dreamed it was possible to want something or someone so much, and the fact that I had almost no chance of getting her just made me more obsessive. I fell asleep and dreamed of her, of course. In the dream she kept telling me to forget her, to turn away and go back, but even in my dream I couldn't give her up, and so I followed her into endless shadow.

What went on at the Amphitheater of Commodus on the first day of Wolf? Well, it was pretty much exactly what you'd expect during a holiday in Hell in front of a quarter of a million gathered demons and damned souls, and all of it was ugly, ugly, ugly.

The holiday festivities began with the ritual slaughter and dismemberment of dozens of types of animals and damned souls, the kind of fun that would have been familiar at a real Roman colosseum, except neither the animals nor the damned could die. That didn't stop horrendous, bloody things from happening, and in many ways it was worse to see creatures suffering that badly and knowing that even death wouldn't end their pain. Then the races began, leading up to the big one, the Lykaion Rally, which drew most of the betting action. The track around the outside length of the amphitheater had been turned into an obstacle course with every manner of hard, hot, and sharp object you can imagine, then a gang of a hundred or so naked sinners were set loose at the same time to make their way once around the track, probably about two or three miles long. They had to make this circuit past the "ordinary" obstacles—pits of flaming oil, forests of barbed wire, and what looked like minefields—but also dozens and dozens of armed demons and ferocious beasts.

Other than the very strong possibility that this was a race nobody was going to win, the first thing I noticed was how battered all the runners-slash-victims looked, many as stooped and crooked as Richard the Third, some with limbs clearly different lengths or with huge unhealed wounds, clumsily stitched. When the race began, and the first of them lost limbs to the traps and wild beasts and the armed demons, the reasons became clear: Since they couldn't die, when they became immobilized, they were dragged off the track along with whatever limbs and other body parts happened to be lying round. If the parts were theirs, so much the better, but they were crudely attached regardless, and then the damned's literally hellish ability to heal reconnected those limbs, no matter whose they had been.

Anyway, the race was as ghastly as you'd guess, and the crowd loved it. The fans were particularly thrilled when the temporary leader ran onto the tusks of a skeletal mastodon and was flung to the sand, stamped into something that looked like a strawberry fruit roll-up, and then hoisted on the skeletal trunk and waved like a battle flag by the triumphant beast.

I took advantage of this excitement to make my way down from the cheap seats toward the winglike awnings that marked where the nobles (including Caz, I hoped) were sitting. I bought a sack of some horrible stuff from a vendor—I think they were paper cones full of bubbling, salted slugs—just to look like I had a reason to be there, then casually made my way down the stairs to the aisle behind the covered section.

My heart started to beat very quickly when I saw a flash of silvery-golden hair in the midst of all that shadow. It was Caz, but she was sitting next to Grand Duke Eligor, and much as I wanted to run up behind him and give him the old Welcome-to-the-Theater-Mister-Lincoln, I didn't have a single weapon that would do more than annoy him, not to mention all his guards and ugly, powerful friends.

Two of the race's leaders were now tearing each other's faces off with their bare fingers, something that had the folks in the enclosure whooping and calling for more firewater, but I couldn't look away from Caz. She leaned slightly toward her captor and said something. He gave her a quick, contemptuous look, then nodded at someone. Two big, gray-skinned fellows got up to escort her. I recognized them—oh, yes, I most certainly did. It was my old pals Candy and Cinnamon, her former bodyguards, but now just her guards, I felt pretty sure.

I watched that beautiful, somber face go past me, only yards away, her bearing slow and dignified, the two guards so close that they were nearly pinning her elbows. She climbed up the stairs toward the top of the amphitheater and for long moments I couldn't understand what she was doing. But when she got to the top, Caz merely stopped along the wall and turned her back on the amphitheater, staring out across Pandaemonium as though pretending she was somewhere else. The air must have stunk just as badly up there as it did anywhere else in the city, but I guessed she still preferred it to the air next to Eligor.

Candy and Cinnamon stared at her in irritation for a moment, then moved a short distance away so they could watch the action below, but they were still keeping a close eye on her. She was definitely a prisoner, and probably had been the whole time I was back in the safe and comfortable real world, trying to decide whether I should come after her. I wasn't liking myself much just then.

I moved farther along, then climbed up an aisle so I was also in the topmost tier, although with hundreds of people between us. Then, when one of the racers below fell into a pool of flaming oil but continued his race as a shrieking torch—which the audience just *loved*—I snuck a quick glance over the edge of the amphitheater.

I was in luck. There were harnesses for banners or perhaps some kind of windbreak along the outside, and a stone track where workers could stand below the outside rim, putting these harnesses up or down. I waited until the burning runner was being extinguished by a laughing giant with a club, which brought a large part of the audience to its feet, yelping in glee, then I slipped over the rim of the amphitheater and onto the ledge. It turned out to be a great deal narrower and less sturdy than it had looked.

I made my way along the stone track by sheer strength of fingers and toes until I had reached the approximate spot where Caz had been standing, her guards hopefully still another ten or fifteen yards farther away, then pulled myself up carefully. I had to take my feet off the ledge and use finger-holds, and it was a long way down. Still, when I popped my head up, there she was, her white-gold hair shining red, reflecting the light of the wall beacons.

I slipped back down again, out of sight. "Caz!" I said as loudly as I dared. "Countess!"

Nothing came back to me. I raised myself to the top again, hanging by my aching fingers. "Countess! Caz!" I hissed.

She turned, looked quickly in my direction, than looked away again just as fast. Candy and Cinnamon were still talking to each other, not even watching her. "Whoever you are," she said with quiet urgency, "go away. You can't imagine how bad . . ."

"Oh, yes, I can," I said. I edged a little closer so I could keep my voice low. My fingers were really beginning to hurt. "Because I've been through it. He already sent that thing with the horns after me, remember?"

I saw her face swivel toward me again, sudden and pale as the moon appearing from behind trees, but only for an instant. "Go away," she said, or at least I thought so. I could barely hear her over the crowd.

"Have you forgotten me already, Caz?" I was desperate to get back onto the ledge because my fingers felt like they were caught in a giant mousetrap, but it was *her*, it was her and she was talking to me. "Your locket saved me. I never got to tell you. It saved me."

She went still as stone. For long moments I thought something had happened to her, that her soul had flown right out of her body. When she did speak, she still kept her face turned away.

"I don't know who you are, but if you say another word I'll call the guards, and then Grand Duke Eligor will peel your skin off and carve your bones into toothpicks. Do you understand? *Leave me alone.*" She started back down the stairs. Clearly irritated to have to move again, Candy and Cinnamon fell in behind her, a wall of nasty gray muscle. I could only hang helplessly against the amphitheater stones like a dying lizard as she left.

twenty-nine
breath of heaven

CAZ WALKING away like that—well, it felt like a tornado had touched down in the middle of my chest, torn up and destroyed everything inside me, and then suddenly moved on. I could hear the damned and their jailers all around me, screaming with glee at the spectacle below, but all that horror was suddenly just noise. I was so shocked I could hardly think.

At last, my survival instincts kicked in. Obviously I couldn't just cling to the facade of the colosseum all day, so I worked my way back to where I'd been and crawled over the rim and into the Circus. The customers below me didn't notice because they were busy bellowing their pleasure as the last two crippled, bleeding almost-men confronted each other on the sand below, each with a long dagger in his teeth, neither able to crawl the rest of the distance to victory without disposing of his rival. The spectators were also throwing rocks and other heavy things down at the two struggling figures, either trying to help the one they'd bet on or just wanting to see a little more suffering.

I slumped down on a bench and let the hot stink of the place wash over me. I was beginning to feel like I belonged there, just another self-pitying loser in the Big Basement. I'd blown it, and I didn't even know how. My only chance to see Caz alone, and she'd turned her back on me. She'd even promised Eligor would destroy me if I didn't leave her alone—I mean, talk about rubbing my nose in it . . . !

It hit me then, the obvious thing I'd missed. After I thought about it for a few seconds, I rose and made my way back up to the top row. Down below, one of the contestants had managed to slit the other's throat, and was crawling away as his victim writhed on a spreading expanse of red sand. I could feel the excitement of the spectators rise even higher. They were like sharks—if there was blood, they were interested.

I sat down a couple of feet from where Caz had stood. "Go away," she'd said at least twice, but she never moved closer to her guards, several yards away, and she'd barely looked up. Why would she keep her back to a potential problem? Why wouldn't she at least raise her voice to get the guards' attention? Because she knew it was me, and she knew I was quite capable of doing something this stupid. Maybe she was trying to protect me from my own eagerness. Had I really expected her to have a joyous reunion with me out here in front of all of Hell, with Eligor only a few dozen rows down? Caz was too smart for that.

While pretending to watch the last Lykaion survivor crawling toward the finish, I looked around carefully in case she had dropped a note or a key, anything to tell me what we should do next, but saw only the usual filth. I even got down on my hands and knees where she'd been and searched in every crack of the ancient stone, but there was nothing to find, nothing hidden or discarded.

Despair washed over me again. For a moment, I'd been so certain that she'd been telling me to be more careful, that she needed more privacy, or time, or something, but now I began to think I'd been right in the first place: She'd either forgotten me or didn't want to see me. After all I'd been through to get here, I was fucked, and there just wasn't any other way to spin it.

Then I spotted it. It wasn't easy, because it was almost the same color as the stone—a long thread only a little brighter than the great blocks of lava in the wall—snagged on an edge about waist-high. I reached out and lifted it gently with my finger. It was very fine thread, something that would have been expensive even on Earth, I guessed, but much more so here in Hell. It was almost the same length on either side of the snag, as though someone had held it by each end and draped it carefully in place. But if Caz had done it, what did it mean?

Of course Caz had done it. This was the woman who had managed to steal Eligor's angel feather, and to sleight-of-hand her locket into my coat right under the Grand Duke of Hell's pointy nose. She'd left the thread for me. She wanted me to use it to find her. I refused to believe anything else.

Another roar came from below. The seemingly defeated contestant with the slashed throat had caught his rival from behind, sunk his teeth into the poor bastard's leg, and ripped out his hamstring; he might have lost the race but he was going to make certain his rival didn't win either. The spectators, like most Hell-dwellers, were big fans of fucking up the other guy's chances. They responded with cheers of approval as the two bloody bodies wriggled more and more slowly before coming to a halt at last, only a few yards from the finish. A squadron of large Murderers Sect demons with no-shit pitchforks was marching toward them, and I doubted either of the contestants was being retired to stud.

I didn't bother to watch the very end. I was already on my way down the stairs, headed for the Night Market.

Saad the fence lifted the cracked lens he wore on a cord around his neck and squinted an eye. He held the thread up to get as much light on it as possible and examined it from several different angles, his pink spider legs tilting it up and down. Then he dropped it back into my hand.

"One handful," he said. "Take it or leave it."

"I don't want to sell it, I want to know what it is—where it's from!"

Saad licked his cracked lips with a tongue like a black garter snake. "I know. Cost you one handful to find out." He gave me a harshly amused look. "You don't think I tell you for free, do you? Hah! I don't shit on someone for free."

I still had quite a bit of Vera's money, so the cost itself wasn't an issue, but I didn't want anyone around here to know I was comparatively wealthy, so I haggled and fought with Saad until he was waggling most of his arms in fury, and I got it down to four spit. Trust me, in Hell, fighting for every penny is just common sense, like hanging your food so the bears don't come into your camp at night. Actually, it's almost exactly like that, except bears are easier to negotiate with than whoever's after your money in Hell.

My iron spits finally in Saad's cash box, he directed me to a silk merchant named Han Fei out at the far end of the Night Market. I learned a few interesting things from that unpleasant gentleman, who imported the incredibly expensive silk from down on the Phlegethon levels. It was so expensive because it was actually made from the silk of real silkworms, or at least the kind of silkworms that could grow in Hell, apparently. I found out later that what they called "silkworms" in Hell was very much the same as what they called "slaves," "prisoners," and "the usual suspects"—the shiny threads were derived somehow from the torture of prisoners who had apparently been reborn in Hell as something that could be farmed for thread to keep the most wealthy of the hell-lords beautifully clothed.

I watched Han Fei eat a nine-course meal as he lectured me about infernal silk and the infernal economy. By the time he finished his dessert of honeyed eyes, I was exhausted. Most of the night was gone, and although I now had a list of a half-dozen or more places that traded in these most expensive fabrics, I knew it was too late to start working through them. I trudged back to the inn by the lagoon, to my small but still sweaty and uncomfortable bed, and did my best to sleep.

I guess it was irony, but for once I didn't dream of Caz at all.

Within an hour of setting out the next day, soon after the first beacon had been lit, I eliminated half the places Han Fei had mentioned. They were all huge establishments, warehouses, really, dealing not just in silk but in exotic skins and all manner of other objects which would eventually wind up clothing the leading lights of Hell. It was pretty clear that if Caz had wanted to send me to one of these warehouses, she hadn't given me enough information to take the next step. Like most places in Hell, the cloth merchants kept their records in their heads, and nobody was going to tell a stranger all the places they sold their fabrics, not even for a bribe.

I had a little more luck in one of the smaller shops, where a bedraggled old woman-thing with a face like a bunch of parsnips stapled together and fingers like dead twigs told me my sample was "the real thing," the dye being something that nobody used anymore except for Chateau Machecoul, one of the most exclusive clothing stores in Pandaemonium. She told me this for free, which made me suspicious, but she also took a look at my clothes and declared I'd never be allowed in looking like such a gross peasant, which made me feel a little better. If someone isn't saying something unpleasant to you in Hell, you should be checking to see if they've stuck a knife in your back.

I asked her to recommend a few things for me that might make a visit to Machecoul more successful. The prospect of extorting some money from me brightened her up considerably, and she spent the good part of an hour rigging me an outfit that wouldn't have drawn attention in a community theater production of *The Pirates of Penzance*. She assured me that I looked like a leader of Pandaemoniac fashion, and as I examined my reflection in a polished sheet of metal I could almost agree. Yet another reason for me to get out of Hell as quickly as possible.

I knew better than just to walk up to a place like Chateau Machecoul. In Hell, going anywhere on your own little hooves is like announcing that you're poor as dirt and eligible to be eaten by anything higher up the food chain, so I hired a cab, a sort of huffing steam crab on huge spiked wheels, and had it drop me off on the corner of Torquemada Street and Ranavalona Avenue in the Tumbrel District, a wealthy neighborhood where the mistresses and catamites of powerful demons did their shopping. I could believe that, since most of the demons and damned I saw there were either ridiculously beautiful in some very extreme ways, or deformed in some specifically sexual manner.

As I watched Hell's beautiful people go past in ones, twos, and threes, I suddenly wondered whether Caz's oh-so-attractive appearance wasn't her own choice but rather something Eligor had insisted on. Certainly there was a fad among some of Hell's highest to look very human. I'd seen it in Vera's crowd, and I was seeing it even more clearly here, as Pandaemonium's best and brightest window-shopped and held little tête-à-têtes at the equivalent of chic little restaurants. I say "equivalent" because, believe me, even a starving beggar on Earth wouldn't want to eat the swill they served in those places. Doesn't matter how rich you are, you can't make anything taste good in Hell because *nothing tastes good in Hell*. It's that simple. It may look like fine wine and nouvelle cuisine, but it tastes like vinegar and ashes. The only things that didn't actively taste foul were the ever-present asphodel flowers, the food of the dead, and they were as bland as poi.

Chateau Machecoul looked no different from the outside than the small, expensive shops on either side of it, a jewelers and some kind of gentleman's clothiers that seemed to specialize in sharp and pointy outfits that would have made any activity more intimate than waving across a room painful or actively dangerous. The ancient, mud brick buildings were decorated with awnings, window boxes, and swags of lights—electric, of course, because in Pandaemonium, electricity was a sign of wealth. I'm sure generating it involved some kind of hideous torture.

The door of the shop was locked. I rapped on it, and a moment later it swung open, but there was no one on the other side.

Fabric was everywhere inside the shop, hanging in huge sheets like a thousand overlapping tapestries and rolled in bolts in the wall alcoves, an almost claustrophobic array of different kinds of cloth. Headless dressmaker's dummies—at least that's what I hoped they were—stood all around me, but I didn't see any customers, dressmakers, or salesdemons.

"Is anyone here?" I walked deeper into the store, my hand straying toward the pocket where I kept my Night Market knife. It was beginning to smell more like a trap by the second, like one of those Mafia things where the guy looks up from his cannelloni and realizes all the other customers have walked out. When a hand lightly touched me on my shoulder I turned around with the knife out, ready to cut the shit out of whoever had snuck up on me. Except, of course, I couldn't. Because it was her.

She wasn't as certain, of course—I didn't look quite the same as the last time she'd seen me on Earth—but her eyes stayed on mine and she didn't flinch. "Bobby . . . ?"

I could hardly speak. "Caz."

"You idiot!" And then she hit me. Right across the chops. Knocked me spinning, too. Every time I saw that woman I wound up getting the crap punched out of me. Believe me, that's not my idea of a perfect relationship.

"Ow! What the hell are you doing?" I said, pinching my nose shut to keep the blood off of my new clothes, but a moment later she was pressed against me and soon I was smearing my blood on both of us. Everything felt unreal. After so long . . . !

"Why are you always hitting me?" I murmured, my lips pressed so hard against hers that it probably sounded like Pig Latin.

"You shouldn't have come! You shouldn't!" She pulled her face back. Tears had started down her cheeks and frozen solid, little sparkling bits of white like irregular sequins. "You'll get yourself killed, Bobby. You can't do anything for me, so go home before he catches you." But no matter what she might have been saying, she was holding on tightly. I already had her bodice open and had yanked it down so that I could reach her nipples, which stuck out like little pointing fingers. If I could have got both of them in my mouth at the same time I would have, but I had to take turns.

"No," she moaned, but she was yanking up my shirt even as I suckled at her, grabbing the skin of my back as though she would somehow pull me into her, through her, like a doorway, and although she was still angry with me, still crying in frustration and fear, she never once pushed me away. Her hunger was as great as mine. As for me, seeing my strange, gray demon hands on her white skin suddenly made me feel as though I was staining her somehow, as though my foreign body was some kind of violation, an unfaithfulness, but Caz didn't seem to care. After a few heartbeats I didn't either. This was the body my soul was wearing, after all, and my soul didn't care about anything except Casimira, Countess of Cold Hands. This *was* my real body now, and after the moment of strangeness had passed, it had never felt more that way.

We fell to the carpeted floor, scattering clothing, half dressed as we wrestled, our only goal to obliterate ourselves in each other. For that moment, everything I'd been through, everything that still stood before me—treachery, torment, death—they all fell away. I didn't even stop to consider that making love in one of Hell's most famous boutiques wasn't exactly discreet, because at that moment nothing existed but the two of us, separated for so long but never truly apart, still burning for each other. It doesn't make sense in Hell or on Earth, but if you've been there, you know. We were making a cathedral of sweat and skin and stifled cries in the worst place that ever was, and nobody was in it but us.

We gave up on the clothes at some point, having removed enough of them that I could climb on top of her and sink myself to the root. My demon body, I was discovering, reacted pretty much like my earthly one. I guess the scientists are right: most of sex is in the mind.

Caz gasped and stiffened, her nails driving into my thickened hide like the tips of knives, ten stabs at once, but it only made me crazier, more animal. I rubbed my face against hers, taking in her smells in insane gulps even as she wrapped her thighs around me, urging me past the chilly bite of her petals to her deep inner heat. She groaned. So did I. We were pushing against each other so violently, striving for some impossible completeness of connection, that we kept bumping into things on the floor, legs of tables, dressmaker's dummies, knocking things over until we must have looked a lot like those two damned souls in the Lykaion race, trying to destroy each other in the bloody sand of the Circus Commodus.

At last I paused, panting, dripping sweat and blood, still too exalted and too stupefied to come. Caz pushed me onto my back and then slid her body over me, pushing her pussy in my face as she licked me and smacked at me with her clawed fingers, then she climbed back onto my cock to ride me as though I were a dying horse, pulling everything out of me she could. When my orgasm finally burst out of me it felt like a heart attack. I shouted and pulled her against me as tightly as I could, and this seemed to squeeze her into climax as well. She clenched my ribs between her knees and rode harder and harder until her ragged breathing rose to a sustained growl of desperate and only coincidentally pleasurable release, then she rolled off me and lay like a dead thing. I didn't say anything. I couldn't. I could barely breathe, but what air I could draw in smelled like Caz. She might be a woman who had been damned since before Columbus sailed, but she was the woman I had crossed Hell to find: to me, it was the true breath of Heaven.

At last her own panting slowed, calmed. She reached out a hand, nudged my arm with it. For a moment I didn't know what to do, then I realized she wanted me to hold it.

We lay there, both of us still breathing very hard, hand in hand in a pile of Hell's finest couture.

"Well," she said at last. "We're *really* fucked this time, Dollar. I hope you're happy."

"Strangely, yes," I said. Of course we would both suffer terribly when we were caught. Dying would be the luckiest possible outcome, but neither of us were that lucky. "Yes, I am."

thirty
a different universe

SHE GOT up. I hated that. I hated anything that wasn't the two of us lying close and connected, preferably forever.

"Don't." I reached out a hand, barely touched the back of her cold thigh as she moved past me. "Stay with me."

"I need to get out to some of the stores and look like I'm spending money, since I'm supposed to be shopping today, and I'm due back soon. And I need to let Poitou have his shop back. He only let me borrow it as a favor." She smiled, but it wasn't a nice one. "He thinks he's doing it for Eligor, of course."

The grand duke's name was like a bucket full of cold water. I sat up. "Don't. Don't go back. That's why I'm here, to take you away."

"Let go of me, Bobby. This was already an incredibly stupid thing for me to do. You'll just make things worse."

"Worse? How could they be *worse* Caz? We're in *Hell!* You live here, and I've spent better times in DMV offices—not counting what just happened, of course."

She shook her head and kept gathering up her clothes. "Enough. My keepers are going to be after me any moment."

"Keepers? You mean your former bodyguards, Crunchy and Yum-yum? I can take them. I can take them both."

"Candy and Cinnamon. No, you can't. Not here. Not in that body." She was moving faster now, spinning out of my orbit, probably forever. "They'd tear your arms off like pulling the wings off a fly." She nodded toward my partially regenerated hand. "Looks like you're already having a hard time hanging onto body parts."

I stood up. "Don't, Caz. As long as I've known you, you've been telling me, 'No, no, no! Don't do it! Leave me alone! I don't love you!' But I'm not buying it. You just put yourself in terrible danger for me. You said it yourself, your big gray guidance counselors might come bashing through the door any second . . ."

"Not in here. They don't know about this place. I've borrowed it before."

"It doesn't matter!" But a steam-jet of jealousy turned my insides scalding hot. Who had she brought here? I suppose I should have applauded her cuckolding Eligor any way and any time possible, but my feelings were a bit more complicated than that. "Just listen to me. I came here for you, and I'm not leaving without you."

She was trying to ignore me but not doing a very good job. I wasn't going to make it easier for her, so I got up and followed. When she sat down to pull on her shoes, I crouched beside her.

"I'm not going away, Caz. I've been missing you so badly for weeks—months! Can't sleep, can't do anything but think about you. I'm not leaving without you."

"Months?" Her laugh was harsh, startled. "Do you know how long it's been down here? More like years. Don't tell me about missing someone. I was an idiot to let myself care. And now I'm paying for it. Just go away, Bobby. Let me heal."

Years? Had it really been so long for her? "I can't, Caz. I'm sorry. I shouldn't have let myself care, either—but I did. And now I can't stop."

She stared at me for a long, quiet moment, eyes narrowed so that her irises were only blood-red stripes. "You're a fool. *I'm* a fool! It's going to end badly," she said at last.

"What doesn't?"

Tears suddenly welled in her eyes and spilled over. They slowed as they ran down, freezing on her cold cheek. I reached out and touched one, watched it flutter to the floor, a lost snowflake in Hell.

"Where?"

"Where what?" But she wasn't pulling away now. She held her bag and her wrap in front of her chest, as if they were all she had left to protect herself.

"Where do I see you again? When?" The sight of the pale, vulnerable skin on her neck made me so hot for her that I began to drag my own clothes back on in self-defense. I didn't want to get her caught, no matter how powerful my need for her. I also wasn't ready to take her away yet. I still had a few things to prepare, and I hadn't expected to find her so quickly.

She was so beautiful I kept getting distracted from my clothes. I crawled toward her and ran my hands up the insides of her legs, lifting her skirt as I went, rolling it back until it lay in an untidy pile across her belly. I bit her gently on the flesh of her thigh, just above the femoral artery. She was cold and hot, both at the same time. She pushed my head in irritation as if I were an overly familiar dog, but she didn't push very hard. I nibbled further up her leg until I could barely hear her because her thighs were pressing against my ears.

"Stop it! You're like a teenage boy." She made a little moaning noise of indecision, then finally shoved me away me more firmly. When she could manage it, she stood and shook down her skirt. "Tonight, at last lantern. Dis Pater Square, in front of the old temple. I'll send someone for you."

"Temple?"

"Just look. You'll know when you see it." She let me kiss her, sinking right into me for a moment, so that I almost thought she'd fainted. I think it was the first time I'd felt her without any of her armor, although it didn't last long. I could sense her toughening up again in my arms. "I have to go," she said, pulling away.

"You love me, don't you?"

"I . . . care about you. I don't love anything." She shook her head. "That's not my word."

"It's mine. It's the same thing."

"It's an entirely different *universe*, Bobby," she said. "Lock the door when you go." Then she hurried out.

It took everything I had not to follow. Instead, I waited a decent length of time, tidied things up a little, then made my way out of Chateau Machecoul to the crowded streets. They looked different now, but it was hard to put my finger on why. More familiar, perhaps. The Halloween parade of hideous shapes and faces was never quite as bad in the expensive parts of the Red City, anyway, but it was still horrifying. If you dropped an ordinary human being into the midst of what I was seeing, they would have made a pants-wetting conversion on the spot to the most puritanical religious sect they could find. But to me, still floating on the high of having been with Caz, it looked endurable. It looked . . . ordinary. I really was beginning to get used to the place.

It was worse than when I quit smoking. Just knowing I was going to see Caz again in a short time made waiting for that time to pass the most painful, frustrating thing imaginable. It wasn't just that I was going to see her and be with her, it also meant I could finally take her away. But it had to happen soon. After all, I had other problems besides Caz. I didn't have any idea how long I had been in Hell by Earth reckoning, and there hadn't been much I could do about it anyway, but if I was away too long I was going to have serious trouble with my job. But I was almost done. Now that I'd found her, all I had to do was steal her from one of the biggest, meanest bastards in the universe and then sneak her out of Hell. It was impossible, I knew, but just being near her again had reminded me that I really had no choice.

According to Lameh's implanted memories, to escape I would have to get us both back to the place I'd come in—the Neronian Bridge, many levels below Pandaemonium, on the outskirts of one of the deep Abaddon layers. But whether it was entirely rational or not, I no longer wanted to go anywhere near the lifters. It wasn't just that my experiences had been so horrible, although that was very much in the picture, but because they were so easy to police, with only one outlet at each level. I was pretty sure it was no accident that Hell had been set up like some kind of ideal fascist state.

But if I didn't use the lifters, I needed to make some other arrangements, and that's why I headed to the shipyards down by the Stygian docks.

Some of the biggest ships had smokestacks, and some of the most modern looking, most expensive vessels looked like they might have even more sophisticated forms of locomotion hidden beneath their dark-gleaming decks. But even here in the great harbor of the Red City, most ships had masts, and it looked like an endless thicket of black trees, the swells swaying the trunks of these tree-ships like a strong breeze.

The noise of the place grew louder as I made my way to the docks, until I could scarcely hear myself think above the pounding of mallets and the groaning of saws, not to mention the usual whip cracks and screams. Demons and damned in harness swarmed the hulls of the sailing ships or scuttled like crabs over the rough metal of the armored steamers, scraping away the worst of Hell's noxious marine life from the previous voyage, blood-red barnacles as big as traffic cones and disk-shaped creatures that humped away from the sailors who were trying to catch them like manta rays skimming the bottom of a muddy river.

As I stood wondering how to find a ship that could carry me to the lower levels, I realized someone was watching me. I didn't even see who it was at first—it was just a troubling sensation that made my neck tingle. But then I turned and saw a weird little fellow staring right at me from a dozen yards away, across the busy wharf. A somehow familiar little fellow like a pudgy, upright cat, with buggy eyes and a too-human face.

I thought he might run when I took a step toward him, but instead he only stood, goggling at me like someone who didn't even realize he was staring. By the time I'd reached him, I'd remembered.

"I kn-kn-know you," the little creature said.

"The slave market. You work with Riprash."

"Y-Yes," he piped, "I d-do. But there's something . . ." He scowled, his little face wrinkling like a dried apple doll. "I know *y-y-you* . . ."

"Shut up. Is Riprash *here*? In Pandaemonium?"

"Of c-course." Krazy Kat was still staring. It was beginning to bug me. "K-Kraken Dock."

I was stunned. Good luck, for once? "Can you lead me to him?"

He shook his head, the faraway look replaced by a sudden fear. "Can't. Already late. He wants his supper fetched." He backed away from me, then turned and tottered off at speed, like a raccoon forced to run on its hind legs. "Kraken Dock!" he called back over his shoulder.

Kraken Dock was one of the farthest down the main pier. I hurried past all manner of disturbing cargoes being unloaded from an equally strange assortment of ships, from great, flat-drafted swamp wanderers to deep-hulled slavers. I saw more than a few slender trading sloops from the distant lower levels, too, but most of the craft had the look of Chinese junks, built more for reliability than for speed. When I remembered some of the hideous things I had seen coiling in the depths of Cocytus during my journey with Riprash, I completely sympathized.

The Nagging Bitch lay at anchor, her hull shiny with black pitch, her sails furled but ready. Grim as she was, I was so thrilled to see her again that I almost ran up the gangplank, but I had been in Hell long enough to know better. I couldn't even guess what eyes might be on me in Hell's greatest harbor, so I took my time, mounting to the deck with the weary slouch of someone with nothing to look forward to but more slavery. I was challenged by some of the sailors hauling supplies on board, but before I had any serious problems with them Riprash appeared at the top of the aft stairs, the huge wound in his skull glinting in the lantern light.

"Snakestaff!" he rumbled.

I held my finger to my lips. "Pseudolus."

For a moment he just stared, but then he nodded. "Soo-doh-luss." I suppose you don't survive on the rivers of Hell for as many centuries as Riprash without being fairly swift on the uptake. He beckoned me toward his cabin. It still smelled like a giant sweat sock, but felt pleasant and familiar compared to most of the places I'd been.

Gob was crouching on the floor. He looked up when I came in with the same expression you see on dogs who get kicked more often than not. If I'd expected him to run and hug me, or even just to grunt, I would have been disappointed, though I could tell he recognized me. Folks just don't hug in Hell, unless they're rich and pretending they're actually people. Still, I was definitely glad to see him. He looked a little fatter and healthier, I thought.

"I owe you something," I said to the boy and crouched beside him. I took his hand and put two iron spits into his palm. "That's what I owe you." Then I shook out another handful and a half's worth of iron. "And that's because you spent so much time helping me."

Gob looked at the money, his apelike little face deadly serious.

Riprash laughed. "He's trying to think where he'll hide it from me."

I frowned at the ogre. "You steal his money?"

Riprash laughed even harder. "You're joking! I wouldn't take a quarter-spit off the little hairwad. But he doesn't trust me. Likely he doesn't trust you, neither."

I remembered how long it had taken before the boy would let himself sleep while I was awake. "It's likely you're right."

To my relief, Riprash said he was heading out the next night and would be happy to take me, which meant that if I could somehow convince Caz to come with me, I wouldn't have to keep her hidden from Eligor very long. The grand duke was a rich, powerful figure, and I felt pretty sure he'd send everything at his disposal after us.

Riprash seemed pleased by the prospect of my company on his voyage back to the slave market at Cocytus Landing, but just to help him keep his priorities straight I gave him a copper-handful coin, worth six spit, and told him I'd give him two more like it once we'd lifted anchor.

His chuckle was pitched so low it made my teeth hurt. "Pay me when we get to Cocytus Landing. You never know what might happen before then, and I like to earn what I make." He looked a little surprised when I stood up. "Where are you going?"

"Believe it or not, I have a date."

Gob barely seemed to notice that I was leaving. He was still looking suspiciously from the iron segments in his hand to Riprash, then back to the money.

Somehow, when getting dressed to go out means hiding your knife and various other small weapons, not to mention covering important bits of you with strategically thicker clothing, it undercuts the romance a bit. I hasten to say that even though Caz had a bad habit of belting me across the face from time to time, she wasn't the reason I was dressed-to-protect. Any errand in Hell, including a walk down to the corner grocery, was likely to turn into a major bloodstorm. Wander out of the house without any means of defense and you might as well stuff your pockets with money and consumer goods and go out fishing with Somali pirates. In fact, I'd have liked to wear armor, but I didn't know what the rules were for my sect, and the last thing I wanted was to be picked up for some bullshit dress code violation.

I made my way back across the center of the city to Dis Pater Square, where I was supposed to find what Caz had called "the temple." I wasn't sure what that was, and it didn't seem like it would be easy to find: Beeger Square back home was a pretty big place, but you could have dropped about ten of them into Dis Pater and still had lots of ugly space left over. Also, Dis Pater wasn't kept anywhere near as tidy as Beeger Square. Hell has no building codes and pretty dubious physics, so if there was such a thing as an old temple, it might easily be obscured underneath squatter camps and impromptu markets. Dis Pater was the center of Pandaemonium. Like big cities back on Earth, it drew refugees from all over, but didn't have enough places to put them all.

I walked past some of the most bizarre gypsy-type camps you can imagine, including tents aerated by eye, nose, and mouth-holes still visible in the stretched skin. Others had been cobbled together from the shells of giant infernal bugs. On one side of the square a massive flock of winged demons perched like the pigeons of Venice on the facade of an abandoned palace, fanning themselves with their wings. Dozens of other creatures squatted in the shadows beneath them, perhaps enjoying the breeze from the winged ones' flapping squabbles, but more likely feeding off the garbage or even the guano they dropped.

I found Caz's temple at last, a structure that would have been small and unprepossessing if not for its aura of immense age. The blocks were so crude that only time had brought any smoothness to them, but you could still see where they seemed to have been torn loose from the mother stone. I climbed the steps to the open doorway, which gaped like an idiot mouth, and peered inside. Nothing seemed to prevent me from walking into the shadowed interior, but it would have taken a lot more than the threat of mere physical pain to get me to do so. The ancient temple was dark, hot, and airless, of course, and quiet but for the buzzing of an unusual amount of flies. It seemed deserted, but something about the place was so creepy that I still think about it today, even after all the other things that have happened to me.

When I turned away from the door, I saw a robed, hooded woman standing at the foot of the temple stairs. For a brief, happy moment I thought it was Caz, but as I started down she beckoned for me to follow her, and one glimpse of her bloodless, water-swollen hand told me who it was. Marmora, the drowned girl, led me out of the square and down a series of narrowing back streets. We walked blocks and blocks, but she never stopped dripping and left wet footsteps everywhere.

We went on for what felt like the good part of an hour, the last half of it uphill through a series of increasingly overgrown, silent streets. It was still evening in the Red City, but this neighborhood was in an angle of the Lamian Hills where the beacons didn't reach, so shadowed that it might have been full night. It was a lonely, silent place that kept me on my guard. I didn't see the little cable car station until we were right on top of it.

I say cable car, but I think back on Earth they're called "aerial tramways"—at least the ones in America. We have them in the wine country north of San Judas, and there used to be a cool one on Mount Tamalpais near San Francisco that went down in the '98 quake. If you still don't know what I mean, it's the kind of cable car that hangs way up in the air. I've never loved the things, but compared to what I was looking at now, the earthly ones were safe as a kid's tricycle. These cables led up at a truly impossible angle, and the machinery, un-manned, looked incredibly old and unsafe. Nevertheless, there it was with its huge gears and huge cable, and there was the car, a rusted box with the rotted remains of what had perhaps once been some nice fit-tings.

When Marmora reached the steps she lowered her hood, showing me her lank hair and poached-egg eyes. "The Countess is at the top," she said in her quiet, slightly soggy voice. I couldn't guess what she was thinking. "She's expecting you, Lord Pseudolus." She turned and walked away down the winding path.

I stared at the clanking, groaning machine, which reminded me far more than I liked of the lifter. At least this time I wasn't bleeding to death.

I stepped up into the small tram and found what looked like the brake. I disengaged it and, after a moment of rattling indecision, the car began to lurch upward along the swaying cable.

Just get through this bit, I told myself, *and Caz is waiting. Then it's all good.*

I was extremely wrong, of course. As usual.

thirty-one
snips and snails

I WAS ABOUT halfway up the slope, the black and tangled vegetation of the valley falling away beneath me, when I saw Eligor's car parked in a cleared space below me. It looked like a cross between a steam-powered Duesenberg and a Humvee, except it was covered with ornate lanterns and the bumpers were studded with long spikes. It was also heavily armored and probably full of weapons. Leaning against the car were two big demon dudes, their bald, gray heads perched on grotesquely muscled bodies—Candy and Cinnamon, the Countess's former bodyguards, keeping an eye on their boss's property.

So, the sugar and spice boys were here. The good thing, though, was that I saw no sign of Caz herself in the crude clearing that served as a parking lot, and no obvious way to get the grand duke 's car farther up the mountainside, so it suggested they were going to wait there for her. I ducked back into the rusty gondola in case one of them decided to look up.

The sudden thought of having Caz alone was enough to make me almost breathless, but the cable car still crept slowly as a caterpillar, leaving me with nothing to do but look at the scenery, which by Hell's standards was pretty interesting. I could see now that Pandaemonium was actually built on a series of hills, with the great black city walls around the outside. I was traveling up the tallest hill, Mount Diabolus, which showed bones of black obsidian and a variety of plants and trees growing on it, mostly in shades of red, black, and gray. (One thing I had begun to understand is that absence of color itself could be a punishment, and I was certainly getting tired of those colors. No wonder the infernal gentry liked to dress up.)

But it was only as the tram car shuddered its way into the uppermost reaches of the peak that I saw the true glory of the place, such as it was. Nestled between the peak I was ascending and the dark jut of the nearest of its neighbors was a saddle in the hills, and in it, surrounded by wiry trees and black grasses, was a lake, flat and shiny as an irregular mirror.

The tram ground to a halt in the rotting remains of the hilltop station. I got out.

"I almost didn't believe yesterday had really happened," she said.

Caz stood at the edge of a path between the dark trees. I hurried toward her, but although she let me take her in my arms and kiss her, after a moment she wriggled free and not too gently.

"What's wrong?"

"Walk with me," she said in a flat voice. I took her chilly hand as we stepped under the trees, which looked like the scorched remains of a pine forest. It was clear, however, that underneath the black char, beneath the gray soil, the trees were still quite alive.

We walked down the slope, the lake always before us, gleaming in these last hours of the second beacon like a red gem. I wondered how dark it got up here when only the afterlights burned. Caz broke our silence to point out a winged, long-beaked creature sitting on one of the black branches. "They call it a shrike here," she said, "but it's not really a bird. Not the kind with feathers. If you look close, you can see that it's more like an insect." She shook her head. "They call it 'shrike' because it impales its kills on tree branches, just like the bird. The difference is, the birds do that to eat, but these creatures do it to lure a mate."

"Are you telling me that I should be building a wall of corpses if I really want to impress you?"

"Not funny, Bobby. I'm trying to make a point. Evolution works differently here." I raised an eyebrow. She scowled. "What? Are you surprised that I know about evolution? I might have grown up in the Middle Ages, but I've seen a lot since then, and read a lot too. I actually met Darwin once, you know." She let go of my hand and waved her fingers in dismissal. "No, forget it. Another time. I'm trying to make a point."

"And what point is that?"

"We'll never work, Bobby. We're too different. I'm like one of those shrike-insect-things. I was only alive for a few years on Earth. *This* place made me what I am, Bobby. No matter what I feel about you, and no matter what you . . ." She shook her head, unable for a moment to speak, but she kept walking. "No matter what else is between us, we just don't have a future."

I considered this for a second or two before sharing my thoughts. "Bullshit."

"It's not. You can't just make it all go away by disagreeing—"

"I didn't say everything you said was bullshit, Caz, just your conclusion. How do you know? Look, you pointed out that this place *evolves*. But here's the interesting bit—Heaven doesn't, at least as far as I've been able to tell. Nothing ever changes there, and that's the way they seem to like it. But here? Everything's changing all the time. It's like . . . some kind of crazy experiment or something."

"And do you know why?" she demanded. We were nearing the edge of the trees now, the lake stretched just beyond like a mirror set down by a titan hand. Caz grabbed both my arms. I'd almost forgotten how strong she was. "Because it's *worse* that way! That's how everything works here. It's about punishment. It's about suffering."

"So? I already figured that out. What does that have to do with us? It's not like I fell for you because I thought you'd be a load of laughs."

At another point in our relationship she might have at least looked amused, but now she was too tired, too sad. "Don't, Bobby. Don't make fun. What this is all about is goodbye."

It was the one thing I hadn't expected to hear, at least not quite so baldly, and it took me off-guard. I walked a few yards ahead, stepping out of the trees to stand on the lakeshore. Parts of the black surface steamed, while other parts were lively with the movement of slippery shapes just below the surface, rolling up into the air only long enough to make the waters splash and ripple. I had no idea what they were; something that could have happily eaten a plesiosaur, judging by what I could see, slippery bodies big around as redwood trees. I stayed several yards from the water's edge.

"Goodbye?" I said at last. "Look, it took me a long time to get here. Do you really think I'm just going to turn around after all this and go back without you?"

"Yes." She had stopped a little behind me. The dusty gray soil had already made a mess of her white stockings where they showed beneath the hem of her old-fashioned dress. Dinosaurs and pinafores. Hell was the craziest place. "Yes, Bobby, that's what I think. That's why we're here. Love me one more time—leave me one more memory—then go away. I'll never be happy in your world. Not in either of them."

"Are you trying to tell me you're happy *here*?"

"Of course not. I'm trying to save your soul, you fool, something you never seem to think about. So just go."

Now I was really angry. Now I was the one grabbing her, clumsy because of my still-regenerating hand. I wasn't planning to let go. "No, Caz! And it's not just because I went through all this bullshit to find you. I'm not that shallow. No, we belong together, and just because you're . . . too frightened to believe it doesn't mean I'm going to let you talk me into giving up."

She was crying a little, the tears becoming spots of frost almost as quickly as they leaked from her eyes. "Stop it, Bobby! Stop it! It's . . . cruel." She slumped so suddenly, so bonelessly, that for a moment I thought something bad had happened, but she was just overcome with exhaustion and emotion. "Don't you understand? Don't you know what you and your so-called love are doing to me?"

"What I'm doing to you? I'm not holding you prisoner—that's your arch-shitheel of an ex, sweetie."

"Do you think I care about Eligor? Do you think I even care about what he does to me? I just told you how Hell works. Why don't you get it? I finally learned to live with the pain, or at least how to exist with it, but ever since I heard your voice at the Circus . . ." She choked a little as she fought for composure. "Since that moment, I have *truly* been in Hell. Because you brought it all back. Not just yourself but *everything*. What we had, what we pretended we had, even what we could have had if the entire universe had been different. Yes, I thought about it too. For a couple of seconds I almost let myself feel it. But it was always a lie, Bobby."

"I'm not just Bobby," I said quietly. "I'm an angel, Caz. I'm Doloriel, too."

"Yes. And you always think the glass is half full. But even if that were true, the glass is half full of poison." She extended her other pale hand toward me. It trembled. "Just love me, Bobby. One more time.

Then go back to your angel games and your pretend-people friends. Let me grow some scar tissue, because that's all I'm going to have."

"No." I had been waiting ever since we'd parted in the dress shop to make love with her again, but I was too angry, too hurt. "No, I'm not doing it. I'm not saying goodbye and neither are you, and I'm not having one last isn't-this-sad pity fuck, either. I'm coming back for you tomorrow, Caz, and I'm taking you away. If you can get out on your own you can meet me in front of that old temple in Dis Pater Square where I met your soggy friend today. If not, I'm coming right into Eligor's place to get you, and I don't care how many of his guards I have to cut into little pieces to do it. Got it? Tomorrow, just after the last beacon goes out." Then I turned and walked away along the edge of the lake.

"Bobby, no! That's just crazy!"

I heard her but I kept going.

"Bobby! You can't go down that way! Take the tram!"

But I was too angry. If I didn't burn off some of the rage coursing like napalm through my veins, I was going to strangle something. Not that random strangling was such a no-no in Hell, but it might attract more attention than I wanted. Still ignoring Caz's calls, I reached the nearest end of the lake and headed off the path, down the slope through the black trees. My brain felt like a wasp's nest that someone had kicked.

I had made it perhaps a mile downhill, dusty gray dirt filling my lungs with grit, thorny branches scratching my exposed skin, when the worst of my anger began to wear off. In fact, I was just beginning to wonder if I had been a little hasty (or, God forbid, overly dramatic) when I stumbled out into a clearing and realized I was face-to-face with Caz's two bodyguards, still waiting by the parked Hell limo. They stared at me for a second, not so much recognizing me as recognizing that I probably didn't belong there. I had just realized the same thing when one of the two ugly bastards shouted, "Oy! You!" I turned and ran back into the trees, cursing myself for the self-absorbed idiot that everyone always says I am. Everyone is right, of course, but shut up.

Now it was a race. They weren't coming after me as hard as they would have if they had recognized me, but names aside, Candy and Cinnamon were strictly the snips and snails and severed puppy-dog tails sort of guys—military-grade weapons in hypermuscled, vaguely human forms. They didn't have to go around trees the way I did, just through them. The sound of shattering trunks and exploding branches followed me down the hillside like artillery fire.

Judging by the noises, I seemed to have pulled ahead of at least one of them, but his ugly brother was right behind me. I followed the tramway cables as best I could, half the time sliding down the slope on my ass because the loose black soil was treacherous under my feet. The much heavier Sweetness Twins didn't seem to have the same problem: When I looked back, the nearest of the two was only about ten yards behind me. He was holding something in his hand that looked like a short whip made of loops of glowing barbed wire, and I decided that I really, *really* didn't want to find out what that would feel like. Sadly, it didn't look like I was going to have much choice. A couple of dozen yards in front of me the slope fell away sharply, the tram cables swaying in midair above a drop of at least a few hundred feet. I had to slow to a stop.

I was pretty sure the one thundering down behind me was Cinnamon, although there wasn't a huge amount of difference between the kinds of ugly the two of them wore, but even in demonic form Caz's driver retained a sort of mustached look, a greater thickness to his leathery upper lip. I was tempted to remind him of my many humorous comments about his porn career in the hopes of making him angry and reckless, but I figured since we were both wearing different bodies and he hadn't recognized my new one, that would definitely count as asking for trouble. Instead I took a few steps back up the slope toward him and lowered myself into a kind of wrestler's crouch, my arms spread wide.

"Hold up, you," he growled at me, slowing down a little as he saw me ready to fight back. He lifted the glowing, rattling wire whip. "Tell me what you were doing . . ."

If I was any normal idiot he would have caught me off-guard, because halfway through that sentence he suddenly swung his flail, with every clear intention of swiping my head right off my neck. Luckily for me, I already knew that neither of us meant the other well. I ducked the weapon and then scooped a handful of black dust from the slope into his eyes.

He screamed in fury, but he wasn't anywhere near as angry as I wanted him to be, because instead of charging down the slope in an insane rage, he groped toward me with small steps, sweeping with the glowing flail, angling himself so that I would find it hard to get back up the slope past him while he was momentarily blinded. I've faced off against more good fighters over the years than I ever wanted to, and Cinnamon was definitely one of them.

However, he was a fighter, and I wasn't, which was my only advantage. I'm just a survivor. I kept throwing things at him, making enough fuss and ruckus to keep him staggering downhill toward me, wiping at his streaming eyes while also trying to keep me in front of him. Another few steps and I stumbled and fell back, ending up in a crouch. I tried to look exhausted, which wasn't hard since I was. Cinnamon could see just enough of me to know that he had me, so he hurried to reach me before I could get up again. And that was the mistake I'd been hoping for.

Just before he got to me, I jumped as high as I could. The Highest was with me, or at least not actively trying to kill me at the moment, and the tips of my fingers just curled over the tramway cable. I pulled my legs up as Cinnamon lunged at the place where I'd just been, then as soon as he had tottered past I twisted around and shoved him in the back of the shoulders as hard as I could with both feet, sending him stumbling down slope. I wasn't strong enough to hurt him much, and he would have recovered his balance within a few more steps—he was massive, at least twice my size—but he didn't have a few more steps. I had lured him far enough back that we were at the edge of the drop-off, a near-vertical, and by the time he tried to put his second foot down there was nothing beneath him. Even in Hell they don't tread water in midair like they do in the cartoons. He dropped out of sight like a big bag of rocks. Unluckily for me, when he threw his hands up in astonishment at the complete lack of anything solid beneath his feet, the wire flail brushed me before it disappeared with Cinnamon into the emptiness below.

It wasn't like electricity, and it wasn't like fire, but whatever was in that flail combined many of the least pleasant parts of both. I don't even remember letting go of the tram cable, and if I'd been a little closer to the edge I would have gone over right behind the big gray guy, but I dropped to the ground so limply that instead of rolling I lay at the edge of the hill like a half-filled sandbag.

I was wondering idly how I kept winding up in situations like this when the streaky reddish light of Hell's late afternoon was blocked by another large, dark silhouette.

"You little smear of shit," said Cinnamon's buddy, Candy. He leaned forward, and I felt his knee come down on my chest like someone had parked a truck on me. He shoved something like an oversized flintlock pistol at my face, a huge thing of cast-iron, brass, and wood. I had no idea what level of pit technology it represented, but I was pretty certain it would blow my head off. Candy's finger was so huge I was astonished he hadn't already pulled the trigger by accident. He was breathing hard, and what little I could see of his big, ugly face looked pretty unhappy. "You messed up my partner," he growled. I could swear his knee was touching the ground, even through my chest. "Oh, yeah. You're going to be screaming for *years*."

thirty-two
lifted

IN MORE normal circumstances I might have tried to talk my way out of it, not that Candy was going to let me walk away, of course. It was far too late for that. But I would have tried to bullshit him long enough to get some distance between us, then done my best to outrun him. For some reason, though, I had been getting angrier and angrier for most of the last hour. Perhaps getting dumped had something to do with it. Also, I'd just kicked Candy's partner over a cliff, which meant he probably wasn't going to listen to me very carefully. So instead of trying to find a less violent way to deal with an elephantine knee in my chest and a gun in my face, I ducked under the gun barrel and yanked the long, curved knife I'd bought at the Night Market out of my boot. I did my best to hamstring him as I pulled it forward, but didn't spend too long worrying about whether I'd succeeded or not, because the main thing I wanted to do was drive it into his groin, which I did about a quarter second later. Candy screamed and fell across me, fountaining blood, but I was already rolling; I managed to kick my way out from under him, but not before getting covered in sticky red stuff. If he'd sunk his thick fingers into me with his weight on top of me, I'd still be there.

To his credit, when he realized how badly I'd cut him and that I'd slipped out of his grasp, the big fellow didn't spend a lot of time cursing or shouting in frustration, just levered himself up off the ground and came after me, lumbering like a lame elephant. I was already scrambling sideways, trying to find a less dramatic way down the slope than Cinnamon had taken, but couldn't see one. Candy still had his gun, and he squeezed off a shot so loud that my ears popped. If he'd hit me, my head would have popped, too. As it was, a tree about two feet from my head exploded into flying, flaming shreds of wood.

I had literally no idea whether his gun was a single-shot or some kind of repeater, and I didn't know how to find out without letting him fire at me again. Candy's gray, heavy-boned face, never pretty at the best of times, was now a mask of snarling mouth and smeared blood. He was bleeding heavily from the crotch, but from the way he smashed his way through everything I tried to put between us, he wasn't going to bleed out until he'd had time to unwind my guts like a tangled yo-yo. As I ran along the edge of the cliff, I scooped up a jagged rock the size of a cantaloupe.

The next time he staggered and slowed for a second, I was ready for him. I didn't bother to wind up, I just set my feet and pegged it at him hard, like I was making the turn on a double play. I actually have a pretty good throwing arm, and I've often wondered whether that and my inexplicable love of baseball are traces of my unknown past, but at that particular moment all I was thinking about was trying to heave a large stone through Candy's even larger skull. It hit him in the forehead with a godawful loud *thud*, hard enough that I saw the bones of his skull crunch inward beneath the skin like somebody had dropped a hard-boiled egg on a tile floor. He let go of his gun and fell to his knees, blood now gushing out of him top and bottom as he raised shaking hands to his face.

I could have just kept running—he was going to be in no shape to follow me for at least a few minutes, no matter how fast he healed. I could also have picked up his gun and given him a few rounds in the head or chest, enough to keep him down so long that I could have walked the rest of the way to the bottom in peace, stopping to pick flowers along the way (if any flowers grew on that miserable shitpile of a mountain). But as I said, I was in a crazy, violently angry mood, so instead of doing any of those things, I ran back to him and began to stab him over and over in the neck, face, and chest with that big old demon-sticker. He roared—actually, it sounded more like gargling, which I guess in a way it was—and did his best to get his hands on me, but I kept dancing back out of reach after each stab. When he eventually *did* get his big hands on me I'd already made a tattered, red, and soggy mess out of his upper body, and because I was behind him all he managed to do was pull me toward him. I jumped up onto his back, wrapped my legs around his neck (which was at least as thick as my waist) and started sawing away at his throat.

It was horrible. I barely remember most of the end, to be honest with you. Every now and then above Candy's rasping bellows I heard my own voice, and I was making the same kind of incoherent noises, just in a higher register. I wasn't thinking of those good times when I'd threatened to shoot his dick off, and he'd promised to smash me like an insect on a car grill. I didn't even realize until it was too late that for long moments he hadn't been pulling at me with his hands but had been trying to signal his surrender. By that time he had tipped forward until he was on his knees and elbows, and the ground all around him was a churn of mud and pooling scarlet.

"*Stop.*" It was the only word from him I'd understood, and it was the quietest by far, a mere gurgle, but it came just as I was sawing through the last of his neck. I yanked his head free, and held it up in front of me. It was so heavy I could barely manage, but I saw his filming eyes go wide with surprise, then saw his mouth move, silently this time, forming the word, "You . . . ?" and then I threw his head as far as I could. It bounced heavily down the slope a couple of times, then rolled over into the void and was gone.

I fell down right on top of Candy's headless body, my insane rage suddenly gone.

When my brain finally rebooted itself, I sat up and looked around. The light hadn't changed much, so the last day lamp was still burning. It was never easy to guess how much time had passed in Hell, but other than the corpse of Caz's bodyguard (made considerably handsomer by the removal of its head) I was still alone. I was very grateful for that, believe me, and not just for the obvious reasons. I'd lost control so completely that I would actually have been ashamed—yes, even in Hell—for anyone to have seen me, especially Caz.

I was completely soaked in blood. I did my best to clean the knife, then slipped it back into my boot. I knew that Candy and Cinnamon's car had been just a few hundred feet above me, but I didn't want to risk going back to steal it, which would force Caz to walk all the way back to Flesh Horse by herself through some of the worst parts of the Red

City. I didn't want to put her in that kind of danger. This led to another Bobby Dollar Special Moment: I was actually leaving her the car so she could get home faster and report the disappearance of her bodyguards sooner. And she'd have to, of course. You didn't just go out for the afternoon, misplace about a half ton's worth of demon-gorillas, and then not mention it to their employer.

I probably should have tried to find Caz then and take her with me, but I didn't know how long I could hide her from an angry grand duke and his soldiers. Riprash wasn't leaving until the next day, and the last thing I wanted was to have them start checking the ports. If she went home now, Eligor would be alerted to what happened to her bodyguards, but I hoped Caz herself wouldn't be suspected of anything. Of course, it was going to be more difficult now for her to get out to meet me at the temple. (And yes, I know she'd never even hinted she would, but I needed to believe it just to keep myself going.) I had my own bad decisions to blame for that.

My personal situation was a bit more difficult. Even if I could wash off everything that had leaked, dribbled, and spurted out of the beheaded bodyguard, I was sure I was covered with bleeding wounds of my own. I really didn't want to go back to the Ostrich looking like that and hope nobody noticed. Hellfolk might not care much about stuff like that as a general rule, but they'd sell you out in a hot second if there was a chance of profit.

I was lucky that I hadn't left anything I really needed there, because the more I thought about it, the less I wanted to go near the place. I was exhausted, shaking, and looked like I'd fought a cage match with a pride of lions. I needed to go somewhere safe, if only to rest. That really only left me one option.

Before I reached Riprash's ship, I took a few moments to slip into the oily black shallows of the Styx and wash off as much of Candy's blood as I could, then I climbed quickly back onto the dock just ahead of a flotilla of large, corpse-white eels who had come wriggling toward the smell of diced bodyguard.

The one thing I couldn't fix was how I felt on the inside, which was *pretty fucking awful.* I'd never experienced anything like the killing frenzy that overcame me, not even in the worst moments with the Harps, on the most violent and terrifying of missions. And I had to admit something to myself that I'd been ignoring a long time: Hell wasn't just getting to me; it had already *gotten* to me.

The realization made me cold all over. By the time I stumbled into Riprash's loading operation, I was shivering like someone in the final stages of malaria.

The ogre didn't bother to ask me what had happened. As soon as he saw my bloody, dripping clothes, he just threw me over his shoulder and carried me up the gangplank to his cabin. He and Gob washed out the worst of my wounds, then bandaged me with comparatively soft cloth and gave me water to drink. I had just enough strength to marvel at how much like actual life it was living in Hell. I could bleed here. I could go mad here.

I could also sleep here. I fell into feverish dark.

When I woke up I was alone. I got to my feet, shaky as a junkie just gone through withdrawal, and climbed to *Nagging Bitch*'s top deck. It was dark except for the distant red glow of the afterlights. Riprash was just sending home the last of his stevedores.

"Good you're up," he rumbled, " 'cause the boy and I are going out, and I was about to wake you up to tell you. Didn't want you fretting when you woke up and found us gone."

"Gone?" I wasn't crazy with anger any more, but I still had a healthy dose of Hell-induced paranoia. "Gone where?"

Riprash looked around carefully then leaned toward me. "Fellowship meeting," he said quietly. "It's our last night in port, so I'd feel bad if I missed it."

I'd already attended one of Riprash's meetings, and as interesting (and even touching) as it had been, I didn't need to go to another. Still, I would be waiting by myself on the ship, perhaps for hours, knowing all the time that Eligor's household must be looking hard for whoever had killed the two bodyguards. I hoped if they had a way to slip them into new bodies, it would at least take a while, because I was pretty sure that Candy had recognized me at the end. No, the more I considered it, the less I wanted to stay anywhere alone.

"I'll go with you."

Riprash, like most religious folk, was pleased. "Good. Good! I'll tell Gob. He'll be right pleased. He's really taken to the Lifters, you know."

Gee, the kid felt drawn to a credo that said there might be something more to his life than an eternity of pain, hopelessness, and utter misery? I couldn't imagine why.

The meeting was in one of the huge warehouses that fronted on one of the main Stygian channels. The floor of the warehouse was stacked full of sacks and earthenware jars, but the upper levels were less crowded, and on the highest floor there was a room that suited the Lifters' purpose. It was empty but for black straw on the floor, and had a big window that opened onto the roof. Remember, kids, if you're going to start a heretical sect, always make sure you have at least two available exits.

At least three or four dozen of the damned were waiting there, and the way they perked up at Riprash's arrival told me he was just as important to this little coven of malcontents as he had been to his Lifters group back in Cocytus Landing.

"Here, let me tell you about a fellow I heard of," Riprash began when the crowd had quieted a little. "I said, listen up, you scum!"

Shushing by ten-foot-tall monstrosity is actually pretty effective. In the new silence, I could hear the faint sounds of work gangs shouting a short distance down the dock, and the screams of the whipped slaves whose hard labor drove the crane that lifted and lowered the cargo. Even after weeks in Hell, it didn't make for a soothing background.

"There was this fella," Riprash began. "I got no idea whether he's here with us or in the Other Place, but when he was alive, he had a big idea. His name was Origen and he lived in Alexandria—"

"I lived in Alexandria," said one of the larger, louder audience members. "I never knew anybody went by that."

Riprash shook his big head. "Enough with your yapping, Poilos. You said that about Alexander the Great, too. 'How could he be so great if I never heard of him?' Just keep your mouth shut for a change, and you might learn something." He scowled, something that would have stopped the heart of most living humans. Poilos didn't curl up and die, but he did stop talking. "Good," said Riprash. "Now let me get on with it . . ."

Having heard the talk about Origen and his ideas before, I admit I phased out a little. I was still wrestling with Temuel's connection to these poor damned bastards. It wasn't like Riprash was starting an open rebellion or anything—rather the contrary, as far as I could tell. Instead of urging his infernal fellows to rise up and overthrow their post-angelic overlords he asked them to imagine a better day that might come at some unimaginably far date in the future. How could that be useful to Heaven?

A sudden idea occurred to me. Maybe it wasn't. Maybe this had nothing to do with some larger plan, nothing to do with the war between Us and Them, between the Highest and the Adversary. Maybe this was just something that Temuel really believed in. Maybe he actually thought that nobody, not the damned, not even their cursed jailers, was beyond redemption.

That sort of took my breath away. I was suddenly filled with a sense of how big and tragic Hell really was. God, if He was as responsible as my superiors claimed, had built a huge machine to concentrate suffering and institutionalize His punishment. The quid pro quo, as far as I'd ever been able to tell, was, "If you do wrong, even if it is only once for a brief moment, you will be tortured for it forever and ever, amen." Period. No appeal, no parole. But old Origen of Alexandria hadn't believed that, and maybe Temuel didn't either. Could that make any difference in the larger scheme of things?

It could if these damned souls believed it. It would give them something they had never otherwise had—hope. So was my archangel really trying to bring comfort to the most afflicted of all? Or was it, as I had first assumed, just a cynical way to make trouble for the Adversary?

After all the time I'd spent here in the Pit, and despite everyone who had been trying to destroy me, I was having more trouble than ever with the whole idea of Hell. It's hard to think of the enemy the same way when you've seen them at home, met the wife and kids, etc. And I was definitely far into the "etc." phase, considering that I thought of a female demon as my girlfriend, even if she said she didn't want to be. Was there still a chance Caz was going to show up tomorrow night? And even if she did, how was I going to get her safely onto Riprash's ship?

All of those unanswered questions made me restless, so I got up to walk around. That didn't last long, since the room was full of hideous hell-creatures annoyed with me for creaking the floor while they were trying to listen to Riprash, so I wandered out into the open corridor that crossed the upper level. Most of the storage rooms were empty and their doors were open. For a moment I thought I saw a disturbingly familiar shape, gray and hunched, in one of the doorways. After a moment's stunned surprise, I pulled my knife out of my belt and cautiously approached the door. When I stepped through, the room was empty of even the piles of black straw that I expected, and the window at the far end was open, the shutter still propped up.

Could it really have been Smyler? But if it had been, why would he run? Was he afraid of all of the others in the nearby room? Somehow that didn't seem quite what I expected of him. Maybe he was just waiting for a better opportunity to get me alone.

Rattled, I hurried back to the greater security of Riprash's Lifter meeting, but I had barely slipped back inside when I was startled by a crash and harsh voices from downstairs. I wasn't the only one: eyes widened in the near darkness all around the room, then a second later our quiet gathering of damned turned into a cockroach party suddenly exposed to light, malformed shapes scuttling in all directions as the first of the Murderers Sect guards burst through the door with whips and torches and nets.

Had Smyler been spying on us for the authorities? It didn't really make sense, but it was hard to believe his being here was a coincidence, either.

I struggled through the chaos looking for Riprash, but the ogre appeared as if from nowhere, picked me up by the back of my neck like a stray puppy, and carried me toward the window. He held Gob in his other massive hand, and before I could even make sense of his plan, Riprash had leaned so far out of the window that the boy and I were dangling in midair, nothing beneath us until the hard stone cobbles nearly a hundred feet below. I didn't have much time to think, however, because a moment later I felt a massive yank and Gob and I were flying through the air with everything spinning around us like the view in a kaleidoscope. It took me a panicked half-second or more before we crashed and rolled and slid to a halt, and I realized that Riprash hadn't flung us down, but all the way up onto the roof of the warehouse. After that, I was too busy to think about anything much, trying to find my weapons and dodge the shrieking Lifters who had found their way to the roof.

I quickly got separated from Gob in the mad skirmish. It was no longer just the other Lifters on the tiled roof now—the Murderers Sect bullies had arrived, climbing up after us, and they were wading into the nearest of the squealing heretics, dealing out what looked like serious pain, tearing flesh from backs with their bladed whips, crushing limbs and skulls with heavy maces. Those they had beaten down were hauled away in nets, trussed, and left at the corner of the roof while the guards concentrated on those of us who were still free.

As I staggered toward the edge of the roof, waving my boot knife and trying to put as much space between the guards and myself as possible, I heard a scraping, rasping crash and then thunder from just below us. I looked over the edge and saw that Riprash had taken the easiest way out of the room downstairs, smashing his way through the constricting windowframe, taking a lot of the surrounding wall with him as he jumped to the distant ground. He had apparently landed safely and now stood in the middle of a pile of debris and shattered paving, looking up.

"Jump down!" the ogre bellowed when he saw me. "I'll catch you! Don't be afraid!" He held out his massive paws. I hesitated, not because I didn't trust him, but because I still didn't know where Gob was, and I couldn't just leave the kid behind. He never would have been in Pandaemonium if it hadn't been for me.

I saw him at last, struggling like a wet cat in the arms of a guard. Gob's captor had leathery skin and lips that stuck out in bony, beaklike plates, as if to demonstrate how a real life mutant ninja turtle would be anything but cute. Gamely as he was fighting, Gob clearly didn't stand a chance; his assailant had already all but immobilized him and was only a moment from getting him into the net with a bunch of others.

I dove on the guard from behind, jabbing my blade deep into where his kidneys should be. I was slowed down by the chain-mail stuff he was wearing, but the demon-cutter was a big knife, and I slammed it into his back with both hands. He made a surprised, croaking noise and let Gob drop. I didn't bother trying to retrieve the knife, but snatched the kid up and dodged through the chaos of guards and Lifters on my way to the edge of the roof. Down below, Riprash was fighting with three guards, but he was winning, and when I screamed his name he looked up, then made quick work of his enemies, literally knocking the head off one of them with his fist.

I threw Gob down to him. I had a second or two to watch the boy tumble into Riprash's massive hands, then I was snatched back from the edge of the roof by a couple of Murderer Sectarians. Two or three more joined them, fell on me like thick men on a rugby ball, and that was about it. The last I remembered was someone beating the thoughts out of my skull with some kind of club. It was the worst drum solo ever, and for me, that's saying something, but fortunately I didn't have to experience it for long.

thirty-three
the conference room

I WAS AWAKE for some time before I opened my eyes, but my senses kept telling me I was in a meeting room in some Holiday Inn or a Hilton business hotel when I knew I was actually in Hell. Still, I could definitely smell coffee and glazed donuts and the scent of room freshener purchasable in bulk quantities. I was just trying to make sense of it when someone spoke.

"My, my, Advocate Doloriel, you are a persistent little beast, aren't you?"

My heart didn't just sink, it crawled into the darkest, deepest corner of my chest and refused to come out ever again. My eyes popped open, too, even though I immediately wished they hadn't, so I could have pretended a little longer the whole thing was a clubbing-induced dream.

Grand Duke Eligor stood over me in full hellish nobility drag, seven feet tall, in Renaissance-ish robes of flowing black, with a high collar that came up right under his chin. The only odd detail was that, except for the inhuman smolder of his eyes, he was wearing his Kenneth Vald, human billionaire face instead of one of his really scary ones. Not that I wasn't scared.

I did my best anyway. "Nice outfit, Ellie. Remind me again what the safe word was."

He didn't say anything. The room looked exactly like it smelled, with Vald/Eligor standing at the other side of a perfectly ordinary conference table in a perfectly normal hotel conference room (at least it would have been in Visalia or Bakersfield or San Leandro). There was even a box of donuts and a coffee service, with artificial sweeteners and powdered creamer. The only thing missing from this vision of Rotarian perfection was a window with venetian blinds open to a view of the freeway or a business park next door. But this room had no windows.

Eligor folded himself gracefully into a chair just across from me. I didn't seem to be restrained in any way, but I wasn't quite ready to test that—not yet, since it was almost certainly what he'd expect me to do. I had no leverage at all except possibly to do something unexpected, and I probably wouldn't get a second chance, so I was going to wait until I actually thought of something worth trying. In the meantime, I knew Eligor the Horseman well enough from our previous encounters to know he didn't mind talking.

"So that was all some trap of yours?"

The grand duke smiled a little. "What, that little holy-roller meeting you were attending? Do you really think I would set some elaborate trap for you? The Countess was right—you *do* have an exaggerated sense of your own importance. No, nobody even knew you were here, little angel, although you were trying very hard to get noticed. Honestly, you came to my own house, Dollar. I thought Heaven didn't allow suicide."

"And I thought Hell would knock the pussy out of someone after a few million years, but clearly I was wrong. You saying you didn't come after me?"

He shook his head as if it almost wasn't worth answering. "We've been looking for 'Pseudolus' ever since you made your little visit to Flesh Horse. Did you think we wouldn't check with the Liars Sect to see if you were legitimate? Then, when somebody took out his bad temper on Candy and Cinnamon—well, as you can guess, we were getting *very* interested. When the Pandaemonium City Guards picked you up with those Lifter idiots, one of my informants recognized you as the one we were looking for . . . so here you are." He shook his head. "You've all but ruined the Countess's bodyguards. Was that really necessary? First you kill my assistant back in San Judas, now you come all the way to my place here and do in a couple of harmless wage-slaves. You have something against working folk?"

"Enough of your bullshit," I said. "Let's cut to the hugs and learning so we can finish this. You want the feather. That's why you sent Smyler after me. Our business with the Countess aside, I had to do something, since it was obvious after that you weren't going to leave me alone. And you knew I'd made it into Hell because Smyler followed me here, so don't pretend you're surprised to see me."

He looked at me for a long moment, his face as blank as a weathered statue of some ancient king. "Yes, Smyler," he said. "Of course."

"You don't need to play games, big man. You hold all the cards. Do what you're going to do. I'm not giving you the feather, and I'm not going to tell you where it is. You'll just kill me anyway, so why should I make it easy on you?"

He smiled, his lips curling slowly back, an unhurried predator with a staked-down meal. For the first time, I could see that he was probably as old as the planet, if not older. "Very good. The hero speech. But I think you're supposed to say that *after* I've tried to soften you up a little. Has more resonance that way."

"Go ahead," I said. "Take your best shot. What are you going to do with this—" I gestured to the conference table and the bad oil paintings, "—make me sit through a sales pitch for a time-share condo?"

"Oh, you don't approve of the decor?" Eligor looked around. "I requested it just for you. I thought it would make a small-timer like you feel at home. We can do something else if you'd rather—"

And just that suddenly the room was gone, and I was falling through whistling blackness, grabbing at nothing, helpless.

"How about this?"

Watery light all around me, dirty glass, stainless steel tables striped with old blood, ancient linoleum brown with the dried scum of countless vile fluids. Hanging above the operating table on which I was strapped was a gallery of machines that would have made Torquemada flinch: drills and bone saws and claspers and graspers whose purposes I couldn't even grasp, but whose rusted, stained surfaces spoke volumes.

"Or if you're more of a traditionalist," said Eligor's voice, "we could try this."

The light dimmed. Now there was only a single torch, just bright enough to reveal that the ancient stone floor around me boiled with crawling things. The walls, too, were alive with moving, clicking shapes. I gasped and jerked, but I couldn't get up, let alone away.

"How about Surrealism? You like all that 20th century stuff, don't you?"

I was stretched in a dozen directions, my eyes impossibly far apart, binocular vision in two separate directions. A vast mouth had replaced the pale ceiling above my head, lips as big as the front end of a car that giggled and made kissing noises and murmured things I couldn't quite hear while a fine mist of saliva fell down onto my face. Spiders with the heads of birds and birds with the heads of medieval harlequins hopped and fluttered all around me. The lips made a choking noise, then rounded into an "o" and something gray and ropy and as big as a gorilla began to climb down from between the teeth, eyes floating around in its body like bubbles in a bag of liquid.

"Or maybe you're beginning to appreciate the original theme," Eligor said, and suddenly the hotel conference room snapped back into being around me. "You see, it doesn't really matter. You're not in a place, Doloriel—you're in *my* place. And you will tell me where the feather is. It's only a matter of time, and we've got . . . forever."

Great roiling, billows of crematory flame leaped from the walls, red and yellow and orange, the same hideous orange as Eligor's eyes. I couldn't see Eligor anymore, though. I couldn't see anything but the flames.

I felt my skin charring. I felt it dry and then crack, then burn away. I felt my nerves become blackened wires, my muscle tissues shrivel and catch fire, my very bones burst into flames. I felt just what you would feel as you burn to death, a level of shrilling pain in every fiber that cannot even be described, agony beyond anything I could have imagined. And I kept feeling it. It went on. It went on, and on, and on.

I don't know when it stopped. Hours later. Days later, maybe. I was somewhere else by then. I was *someone* else. The person who had been burned that way, that Bobby, that Angel Doloriel, was gone now beyond retrieval. That person could never exist again. And the thing that remained behind would never stop screaming, I felt sure. Never stop burning.

Eligor carefully picked out a donut. "The last powdered sugar," he explained. "So, where's my feather?"

It took a while to form words, although from what I could see of my trembling hands I was whole and unburnt again, as though I hadn't just experienced a lifetime's worth of scorching, unholy agony. "Fuck . . . you."

"Right, then!" he said and saluted me with his *World's Greatest Boss* mug as the flames blazed up once more.

He had lots of other ways to hurt me when he got bored with hellfire, some of them quite inventive. I had to watch Caz tortured and raped by Eligor himself and various demons, or at least something that looked like her. Then later I had to watch another version of Caz participating happily, even enthusiastically, in all the same activities, even as my own nerves were stretched and burned and scraped and tormented. Eligor liked to cover all the bases.

I talked, of course. Fuck, yes I did. I told him everything I knew about the feather and everything else. Pain hurts. Pain in Hell hurts even more. And this was personal pain that Eligor *wanted* me to feel, and he made sure I got every last drop. I don't think it had as much to do with Caz as it did with me being an annoyance. The fact that unimportant me had managed to waste so much of his precious, infinite time. You'd think he'd have thanked me for the diversion. But no.

It didn't seem to matter that I was vomiting out every secret I had, though. Eligor went right on hurting me. After the flames I found myself in a place bright and white as an industrial clean room, where men with faces featureless as thumbprints pounded on me with iron hammers, smashing every bone in my body, flattening me like a cutlet. Each blow forced more screams out of my mouth, which changed shape with each strike, so that it was almost impossible to form words. But still they kept hitting me, and I kept screaming out what I knew.

Dark, oily liquid. Writhing things sinking their teeth into my flesh and wrapping around me like sex-crazed eels to pull me down. I managed to kick free just before I drowned and made it back to the surface, gasping out foul, poisoned air and taking in lungfuls of something not much better, only to be yanked down into the darkness again. And again. And . . . you've got it by now, right?

Packs of rotting skeletons trying to eat my face as I struggled to escape over mounds of garbage. This was less fun than it sounds.

My skin trying to tear itself loose from my body. Exactly as fun as it sounds.

A chamber full of stinging ants and biting flies the size of pigeons. Me with no arms or legs.

An all-black room, where nothing happened except an excruciating pain blooming right in the middle of my skull, like an insane sea urchin with thumbtack spines trying to shove its way out through one of my eye sockets. It got worse and worse until I finally tore my own head off my neck, at which point my head grew back and the process started over.

And every now and then, just to remind me why I was literally suffering the tortures of the damned, I would be back in the original conference room with Eligor. He would ask me a few more questions, or the same questions again. Sometimes he just looked at me and laughed, then I went back into the acid bath or dangled on the electric fence again. A couple of times he was reading emails on his cellphone and didn't even look up. Once I saw Caz, standing straight and silent as Eligor held her with one hand around her neck, like a chicken going to the chopping block. Her eyes were wet and her lashes frosty with crystallizing tears, but she didn't move, didn't speak.

Back to the crematory flames again, but this time all my friends from the Compasses were there with me—Monica, Sweetheart, Walter Sanders, all of them shrieking as they burned, begging me to help them.

The next time I came back to the conference room, Lady Zinc was waiting for me, eyes bright with madness. While Eligor watched and drank his coffee Vera raped me again, just as she had before. Then she took me in ways she hadn't been able to do before. It all hurt worse than you can imagine—merciful God, a lot worse.

Vera disappeared after a few thousand hours.

"Little man," said the grand duke, grinning. "You've had a busy day."

He sent me to a room whose floor was wire mesh painted with acid. The flesh kept melting off my bones and dripping through, and as determinedly as I crawled, the door remained just as far away.

An endless desert of broken glass and salt.

A dim forest full of predatory birds with teeth. They laughed like demented children.

More fire. Needles. Filth. Innocents suffering. Over and over and over.

Over and over.

As kind of a break between bouts of indescribable agony, Eligor would pause the torture ride to explain how things in the universe *really* worked. Kind of like those old educational fillers they used to run between the Saturday morning kids' cartoons.

The first time, he appeared as I was screaming helplessly and said, "You know, you've got it all wrong."

I didn't answer, being too busy spitting out blood and bile.

"You see, Heaven has you suckered. They're not against what we do—they ordered us to do it. We're the official alternative. We're as much a part of God's system as the guards who work in a prison."

I spat again, and mustered a single, "Bite me."

"No, really. You might as well hold a grudge against the factory that makes judges' gavels. We're doing our job, same as you."

Another time he popped in to say, "Actually, I lied when I told you we're doing Heaven's work. Because there's really no such thing as Heaven."

I wasn't going to respond this time. Something had pulled my tongue out a few hours earlier and hadn't bothered to reattach it yet.

"It's kind of like a science fiction story, really," the grand duke explained. "Hell, Heaven—it's all nonsense. Earth was conquered a long time ago by invaders from space, but humans don't realize it yet. The aliens lifted all this stuff right out of our subconscious to keep us docile, toeing the line and behaving like a good little captive populace. Do you see how it all makes sense now?"

Later on, when I had my tongue back, Eligor had a new explanation. "Actually, it wasn't aliens. I lied about that. It was humans from the future, when they mastered time-travel. They realized that the kindest gift they could give their benighted ancestors was to create the kind of universe the primitives already believed in. So they did. All this stuff, me, you, the Highest, everything, was invented by mankind's own descendants. Kind of like being humored by your grandchildren, huh? 'Yes, Grandpa, that's right, a loving God watches over you and punishes all the wicked people. Now finish your nap.'"

The grand duke seemed to love doing this, and kept reappearing with some new explanation of how the universe was ordered, many of them possibilities I had considered myself. Maybe one of them was true. Maybe more than one. Maybe none. I'm pretty sure that he was just shitting on everything that might explain things, everything that might mean anything at all, so that I was left with the belief that nothing made sense.

A bit like modern political advertising, when you think about it.

Anyway, even Eligor got tired of that game after what seemed a few centuries, and left me to the serious physical torture, which went on and on despite the fact that I had no secrets left. Or perhaps *because* of that. It's hard to know with Hell. You can't even be sure about death and taxes there. The only certain things are pain and sorrow and then more pain.

"So, Doloriel." Eligor put down his cup and sat up straight in his conference chair, as if the flames and poison and murder had just been the preliminary handshakes and bows, and now the business meeting could begin. "Tell me where the feather is now."

It felt like it took me about an hour to find the strength to talk. "I . . . *told* . . . you. I told you everything."

"No, as a matter of fact, you didn't. You told me it was in your jacket pocket, hidden by some angel trickery, with your body in a house in San Judas. My people went over every inch of the place. Your body isn't there."

Even out where I was, on the far side of a million years of torment, this scared me, not because I cared about my Earth body at this point, or even G-Man and his girlfriend Posie, who were living in the house, but because all I wanted to do now was die the real and final death, and I knew Eligor wouldn't kill me until he had the feather back. "It's . . . gone?"

"In fact, now that I think of it, the whole thing's a bit convenient. You had the feather all along and didn't know it? And it was your buddy Sammariel who caught Grasswax trying to plant it on you? Cute, since your friend's hiding out in that discount version of Heaven the Third Way dreamers created. And to make it even more suspicious, we both know who Sammariel takes his orders *from*."

I was having trouble keeping up and not just because of the pain. Eligor was wrong, I hadn't tried to hold anything back. If the feather was gone, if my body had disappeared, I was just as surprised as anyone. "Sam takes orders from . . . ? You mean Kephas?"

"Yes, 'Kephas,' or whatever name you want to use. The architect of this whole fiasco."

The mysterious higher angel had recruited Sam to the Third Way, and had given him the tools to make it happen, including the thing Sam called "the God Glove," which he had used to hide Eligor's marker for his deal with Kephas, namely Kephas' own angelic wing-feather. Hid it on *me*, as it turned out, although I hadn't known it at the time. It was what got me onto Eligor's radar in the first place. I really wished I had never seen or heard of the thing.

Bam! Eligor hit the table and made his cup jump, sloshing coffee across the imitation wood grain Formica just as if it were real coffee in a real room in a real place. "I want it. And you're going to fetch it back for me."

"Yeah, right. If it's gone, I don't know where it is, either. Get thee behind me, Shit Hat."

I didn't really feel him hit me, it happened so quickly. I just suddenly realized I was on the other side of the room, lying in a heap on the patterned carpet with my vision blurred and my head clanging like a church bell. Eligor stood over me, twenty feet from where he had just been sitting. "Watch your mouth. You wouldn't be the first dead angel I've made." He leaned in closer. His Vald disguise seemed perfect from a distance, just like a human body and face, but from inches away I could see the fires beneath the skin leaking through his pores. "However, I'm a pragmatist, so I'll make you an offer, Little Wing. You may live to fight another day for the glory of your bullshit Holy City in the Sky."

I didn't dare breathe, let alone speak, because I was still nearly paralyzed by how hard he'd hit me, and even after all the shit I'd just been through, I was terrified he'd hit me again. It felt like he'd shattered every bone in my body, and I was quite ready to roll on my back and show him my belly. What had made me think I could mess around with something like Eligor and survive? Nobody that stupid deserved to live.

The grand duke was suddenly back in his chair. A moment later, with no conscious understanding of how it happened, I was sitting in the chair across from him once more, trembling like a whipped puppy.

"Here's the deal," he said. "I want that feather. It should never have left my possession. It's my insurance policy for Kephas keeping faith. I don't trust anyone, but I trust ambitious angels least of all, and Kephas is nothing if not ambitious. So you're going to go back and get it, then give it to me. If you don't . . ." he lifted his hand and suddenly Caz was there beside him. This time she had a blindfold over her eyes and a gag in her mouth, her hands bound behind her back. "If you don't, I'll give her everything I've just given you, and a lot more."

I had no power, no leverage, nothing. I was completely outgunned, outsmarted, and outclassed. I didn't have any choice at all.

"No," I said. "No deal."

"WHAT?" Eligor's cry of fury was so loud it toppled me onto my back. "Do you want to see her burn right now? Burn until there's nothing left? RIGHT NOW, YOU LITTLE INSECT?"

"Don't do that, please." Eligor was so much more powerful than me, than pretty much anything I knew, that it was exactly like having fallen into the lion's enclosure at a zoo. The only thing I could do was move very, very slowly and hope that he didn't destroy Caz out of sheer irritation. "It would be a mistake."

"You have a couple of seconds to explain before I render you into individual atoms, each one extremely pain sensitive." Eligor's face was shifting now, as though I'd made him so angry he was having trouble looking even remotely human. I saw a hint of goat horn, a glimpse of suppurating skin, a glint of shiny metal skull, flashes that came and went all in a moment.

"Look, I'll give you the damn feather—I don't want it. I only came here because you sent Smyler after me, looking for it. But you have to let us both go. Me and the Countess."

"Both?" Eligor was pushing his anger down now, but I could tell he wasn't enjoying himself. "Why should I do that?"

"Because otherwise I'll just keep saying no. Then you can torture me forever, or kill me when you get bored. You can torture and kill Caz, too. I could never stop you, and the only thing I have that you want is the feather. So let me go and let her go or forget it."

He raised an eyebrow. He had regained his composure, was handsome and incredibly successful Kenneth Vald once more. "I'll say this for you, Doloriel. You've got balls like grapefruits." He moved his finger and Caz was gone so quick I didn't even have a chance to look at her face again, in case it was the last time I saw it. Then he flicked his finger at me and the conference room, the donuts, the spilled coffee, everything around me disappeared, and I was alone with my pain and the horror of my recent memories in yet another version of the conference room, this time floating in an endless space as empty and gray as the evening fog coming through the Golden Gate back home.

Emptiness is another form of torment. Loneliness, too, especially when they both go on forever and ever, and ever.

thirty-four

thing

I DON'T KNOW how long I hung/lay/floated there in the gray nothing. Forgive the confusion of verbs, but I honestly couldn't tell you what I was doing. I was in my hell-body, the Snakestaff body striped like one of the antelopes of the African veldt, naked and helpless. I wasn't wearing restraints, but that didn't make any difference, because I couldn't move anything but my head and neck.

Obviously, that was better than being actively tortured, but only for the first thousand or so hours, after which I began to go a little crazy. I know, I know, you're saying, "Hey, he's already said he was tortured for hundreds of years or something, and now this." You're right, time does pass in Hell, even if it passes differently than in the real world, and the subjective time I'd experienced would have made at least a bunch of years of earth-time, but the key word here is "subjective"—as long as I was Eligor's prisoner, I was out of normal time altogether. He could make it feel like whatever he wanted. It was entirely possible, perhaps even likely, that this was still the same morning of the day I entered his hospitable clutches.

Still, for the first time since I heard the grand duke's voice and knew he'd caught me, I felt something a bit like hope. Not much, but he'd offered me a deal. It might be just another trick, but the mere fact that he'd taken a break from flaying my skin and boiling my nerves like vermicelli suggested he wasn't sure what to do with me. Paradoxically, my threat to let him torture me to death was keeping me alive, at least for the moment.

I wasn't bluffing, either. I had realized, somewhere in the worst of it, that my situation was truly hopeless. Eligor was just too strong. I couldn't escape him, I couldn't fight. The only thing I could do, I realized in that cauldron of pain, was suffer. But I could keep on doing it if I had to. Yes, I would beg for mercy. Yes, I would tell him anything, say anything. But as long as I kept refusing to actually *do* what he wanted me to do, he could only subject me to more torture. He could torment and kill Caz in front of me, but he could do that to her whether I helped him or not. The only way I could do anything for her was by refusing to do what he wanted and forcing him to bargain.

So I hung, or floated, or lay there suspended in nothingness, forever or even longer, trying to build up my strength for when the hurting would start again. And I knew it would start, because I would have to prove to Eligor that I wasn't bluffing. I would have to make him give up on pain.

It started again. I won't bother to describe it. After a few millennia, even Eligor seemed to get bored and left me to the eager attention of something named Doctor Teddy, which looked like a plush bear toy but had the stunted fingers of a human child and the eyes and whisky breath of a terminal alcoholic.

Doctor Teddy made Niloch's torturer look like the weekend amateur he'd been. Not only did he give me everything all over again, Doctor Teddy also had a few cute ideas of his own, but even my furry new friend seemed to run out of ideas after a while, and at last I was sent back to the gray place again, weeping and trying to remember my name, even though I knew that if I remembered that I would also remember why I was here and what was happening to me. They'd done something strange to me so I couldn't sleep, and although I could tell time was passing by the slow easing of my suffering, there was nothing else to make the hours and days pass in that dreadful, empty, uncolored place.

When things finally changed, I was at first aware only that something was in the gray with me, and that whatever it was wasn't quite in or out. The best way I can explain it is like being underwater, somewhere there's more shadow than light and distance distorts things and plays tricks. For long moments what I was looking at was only a slantingly vertical shape, wildly distorted as though coming at me from a dimension I couldn't entirely see, and then it stood over me, gray corpse face and pinhole eyes, that weird underslung jaw hanging open like a fish's as it stared at me. The rest of it was gray, too, gray dead skin stretched over bone. Smyler hadn't gotten any prettier since our last encounter.

I didn't even care much anymore, to be honest, but I still flinched a little at the sight. "What do you want, Handsome?" I said when I found my voice. "Getting impatient? I'm sure you'll get to play with me when your master's done."

Smyler leaned in so close I could see the lines on his skin clearly for the first time ever in the flat, medical light of the gray, and I realized that they were not just random wrinkles or even a tattoo but something much more intricate, much more strange. The murderer was covered in writing—trails of tiny letters laboriously cut into the skin with something very sharp, thousands of characters in some illegible text that covered every exposed inch of his skin. I looked down to the grayish hand pointing the four-bladed knife at my face and saw that the skin on his gnarled fingers was decorated too. His other hand was hidden behind his back, but I would have bet it was the same, covered in little scars as numerous as crawling ants.

"Why did you do . . . what was reason?" Smyler still ran his words together in the same slow but breathless way, monotonous as a bored priest reciting a too-familiar catechism. "Why you not run?"

"I don't know what you mean. Look, if you're going to stab me or something, just do it. It'll give me something new to think about."

"No." He leaned even closer, until the leathery flesh of his face was almost touching mine, and I could see his eyes moving wetly in the deep holes. His voice was strained, even desperate. "*Tell it*. Tell it why."

"Tell what?" I could smell the faint odor of his decay even in this gray nowhere, the musty, nauseating sweetness of something that had spent a long time dead and undiscovered.

"Tell it why you go back. Why you help little thing. Why no run, save you."

It took me a while. In my defense, may I remind the jury about the thousands of hours of sadistic torment I'd undergone. Anyway, at last the astonishing truth dawned: this horrible creature wanted to know why I'd gone back to save Gob. He had watched the whole thing, it seemed, not just Riprash's meeting but what happened afterward.

"Why did I go back? Because it was my fault the kid was there in the first place." It had suddenly occurred to me that maybe Stabby McMurder-Mummy was now searching for Gob too, so I tried to make the kid seem less important. "I forced him to come with me in the first place. He didn't want to leave Abaddon. I was just trying to help him . . ."

"*No!*" It was the first time I had ever heard anything like anger out of Smyler. Ordinarily he was as weirdly cheerful as one of those old grandpas who don't speak any English that you see sitting in the back of Chinese grocery stores watching the news in Mandarin. "No," he said a little more calmly. "You no help. Angel help. You devil. Keefs tell me. Devil in angel clothes."

"Keefs . . . ?" It sounded weirdly familiar. Again, it took me longer than it should have. "Wait a minute—*Kephas?*" Sam's mysterious bene-factor. The angel who had made the deal with Eligor and used the golden feather as a marker. "*You* know Kephas?"

"Keefs . . . *Kephas* so beautiful. Beautiful like clouds and silver." And suddenly the thing smiled, a full display of those ugly little bottom teeth as well as the few nubs in its upper gums. "Kephas tell it, do my words, and it will be an angel too."

"What will be an angel? What is 'it'?"

Smyler pointed the knife at his own chest. "It. It will be an angel if it do everything right. Kephas says it will."

Oh my sweet God, I realized. *He thinks he'll get to be an angel by killing me.*

"I *am* an angel," I said, slowly and carefully. "I'm Doloriel, Advocate Angel of the Third House. Are you saying that Kephas told you I was . . . some kind of devil? It wasn't Eligor who sent you after me?"

Smyler tipped his head to one side like a puzzled dog. For the first time I realized that he was as naked as I was, but whatever external features he'd once had, like genitalia, were gone, just more ruined, dead flesh. "Eligor?"

"The big old demon who owns this place. The one whose prisoner I am. You weren't working for him, but for an *angel?*"

"It loves angels." The corpse-puppet head bobbed up and down. "It will be angel when it's done."

I don't like these "everything you know is wrong" moments when they happen to me in the course of absolutely ordinary life, but I like them even less when I'm a prisoner in Hell, taking a little break between bouts of indescribable punishment. What was going on here? This monstrous thing, this gibbering killer, didn't belong to Eligor and maybe never had? Now that I thought about it, the grand duke's reaction when I mentioned Smyler's name had been a bit strange, a bit . . . noncommittal. But why would Kephas employ such a creature? Wasn't Kephas hiding his or her identity from the rest of Heaven precisely because Kephas thought the Highest was too rough on the souls of the dead? How did that gibe with sending a serial murderer after a perfectly blameless angel? Who was the real villain here, Eligor, Grand Duke of Hell, or Kephas, supposed heavenly idealist? Neither of them? Both of them?

"How did you meet Kephas?" I asked.

Smyler stared hard at me, perhaps sensing some of the unhappiness behind my words. "Kephas came. Kephas spoke. Showed it Heaven. Showed it the light. Told it Papa Man and Mama were wrong. It wasn't bad, it was made for . . . something else."

"Papa Man? Mama?" Smyler had been alive once, so of course he must have had a family, or at least a mother, but it had been a long time since I had thought of him as anything other than a force of supernatural evil. "Were those your parents?"

"It was their cross to bear. Mama always said. It was borned because Papa Man had the sin of pride. Because he tried to make a baby at her when she was blessed by God to stay a version."

"A . . . virgin?"

"Yes. Version. But Papa Man put the dirty in her. He made it inside her, and when it came out she saw it was ugly bad. That was what she said, what Mama said." Smyler was getting worked up again, his voice getting monotonous and rushed as though the words were carried along on a river of feelings too fast and deep to be reached or even looked at closely. "Dirty thing, dirty thing, and Papa Man left it behind like dirt on the floor. Like mud on her dress. Can't beat the dirty out of it, that's what Mama said. Can't make it die because God has reason for it. God wants it in the world, no matter how ugly bad. No matter how ugly bad and mean and wrong . . ."

I almost wish I'd never asked. It had been unpleasant enough just knowing it was out there and wanted to find me, this vile thing, this monster that had killed so many innocent people. Knowing how it had become such a monster was worse. Much worse.

It told me its story in bits and pieces, in strands that at first seemed to have no connection but later proved to be bits of a larger web. In some ways the tale was depressingly familiar, the dreadful story of so many sociopaths and religious psychopaths, a child treated like an animal or worse, the name of God used as the excuse for torture, an existence with no safe place, no kindness, no love. It was almost like Smyler's vicious, dreadful parents had done their best to make something even more terrible than themselves, and they succeeded.

But every time he had killed, at least during his mortal life, Smyler had thought he was sending something beautiful to Heaven, a gift for the angels. Even the name he had given himself, the name he had left at the scene of so many brutal crimes, was not meant to evoke Chaucer's "smyler with a knyfe," but because when she had finished beating him, or puncturing him with sharp things, or burning his fingers or toes or face with a hot iron, Mama would always tell him, "Stop crying. You'd better smile. Remember, God loves you."

And that was how he thought of himself, how he still thought of himself, no matter how deep the blood and madness. He was God's smiling little soldier.

The story trailed off at last in confusion, because Smyler himself still didn't know what to make of me. His tunnel-vision idea of the world, the same crazy focus that had set him to murder and driven him to follow me all the way to Hell, was not able to easily absorb new information, and the new idea that I *wasn't* some kind of demon pretending to be an angel had left him baffled and uncertain of what to do next.

"It has to think. It has to pray. God will tell it what to do." Smyler revealed the hand that he had kept hidden since he entered the gray space. It looked no different from the other, until first his fingertips began to glow, then the fingers themselves, then his palm too, until I could see his bones through the skin as though they were made of blazing phosphorus. His hand was so bright it was hard to look directly at it.

"What . . . ?" I blinked. If I could have raised my hands in front of my eyes I would have, but I was still helpless below the neck. "What are you doing?"

"Hand of Glory. Kephas gave it the Hand. To do God's work." Smyler swiped the glow at the gray nothing that surrounded us. The nothingness tore, leaving a ragged, smoldering edge and more nothingness beyond. Then Smyler climbed through the hole.

"Wait!" I cried. "Don't go! Don't leave me . . . !"

But it was no use. He was gone. The gleaming wound healed over in an instant and vanished. The gray was empty once more and I was alone.

thirty-five
hounds

WHEN THE gray finally dissolved, I found myself back in the conference room. There weren't any donuts this time, just the moldy ruin of the box in the middle of the table where it might have sat for years. The coffeepot lay on its side, shrouded in cobwebs and covered with a thick film of dust. The table and carpet were filthy with dust, too. It was a bluff, I felt sure. Well, fairly sure.

Eligor had changed his outfit. Instead of his Count Richelieu drag, he'd opted for something a bit more like a male Victoria's Secret model, if you can imagine such a thing: blue jeans, bare chest and bare feet, and beautiful, spreading white wings.

"I was an angel once, remember," he said when he saw my expression. He was still wearing the Vald face. "And a bit higher up the ladder than you are."

"Yeah, but I heard you got downsized."

For a moment I saw a little of the white-hot anger beneath his achingly handsome, golden-haired disguise; a ripple through his entire being as though a stone had dropped into a pond. "I *fell*."

He's not hurting you at the moment, Bobby, I reminded myself. *So why don't you shut the fuck up and stop making him angry?*

I stayed silent while he stared at me. He stared for a long time, as though I'd grown several new and interesting features since our last meeting. At last he extended his hand and an instant later Doctor

Teddy was standing beside him, no taller than Eligor's waist and cute as a wind-up abortion doll.

"I have a proposition for you, Doloriel," said the grand duke.

"I'm listening."

Eligor sat down in midair. "Here's the problem, troublesome angel. You make me uneasy. Not because you're as smart as you think you are, but rather the reverse. You're so stupid that I don't trust you at all." He frowned as he considered. A lot of Renaissance painters, and not just the gay ones, would have burst into tears at the sight of such beauty. "You might think you've successfully hidden the feather from me and everyone else, but I can't trust your idea of successful. Knowing that you're all that stands between me and an *infernalis curia* makes me . . . well, if I was a delicate little thing like you, I'd say 'nervous.'"

He wasn't hurting me, but he wore a very strange expression, so I swallowed my natural tendency to crack wise at the dumbest possible time. "So?"

"So I'm going to offer you a bargain. I'm going to let you go back to Earth and get the feather. If you turn it over to me, you stay free. I have no reason to go after you once I've got it back, anyway."

I couldn't believe it. Could this really be happening, or was it just a trick? Eligor was actually bargaining?

I did my best to stay calm. "No. I take the Countess with me. If we both get back safe, I'll give you the feather."

He laughed. It was nearly a pleasant sound, which just goes to show you how powerful he really was. "You're joking, of course. I could just erase you both right here and right now, then take a chance that wherever you've hidden the feather, it'll stay there."

"Then why don't you?"

Again the long, considering look. It was only when he was doing such small, human things that I could really see how inhuman he was, because there wasn't the faintest glimmer of emotion on that perfect face. It was like trying to stare down a marble Michelangelo. "All right, angel. My last offer. I will let you go. You will return to Earth and retrieve the feather. Then you will trade it to me for the Countess, if that is really what you want most from me." A sly smile. "I would have chosen a better harvest of the riches of Hell if I were you, but we won't belabor it. In return for the feather, I will give you the whore and promise you both immunity."

"Don't call her that."

The smile widened. "Believe me, compared to what I could accurately call her, that is a compliment that would make a maiden blush with pleasure. But never mind. That is my offer, my only offer. Give me your answer *now*."

I was desperately trying to see the trick. I knew there had to be one. "How do I know you'll keep your promise?"

"Little angel, the entirety of what you call reality only exists because of the promises of things like me. I cannot break my word any more than you could dismantle the sun or turn time backward. Also, you have no choice."

"And if I get the feather and give it to you, you'll let the Countess of Cold Hands go free? Casimira? You'll release her and bring her to me and we'll swap? Right? Then you'll leave us alone? No revenge?"

"Exactly."

"Say it. I want to hear you say it."

He shook his golden head. "My, you are demanding for someone in your situation. Very well. I, Eligor the Horseman, master of Flesh Horse and Grand Duke of Hell, promise that if you return the angelic feather you've hidden to me, I will exchange this she-devil you call Casimira, Countess of Cold Hands for it." He gestured lazily and suddenly Caz stood beside him, bound in chains and still gagged. Her eyes widened when she saw me, and she shook her head violently. I knew she was trying to tell me Eligor couldn't be trusted.

Like I didn't know that. But no matter how cool I was playing it, I also knew I had no other choice. "All right. I'll make your deal. And then you'll leave us both alone? Wherever we are? Forever?"

Eligor nodded. "Once I have the feather, I will leave you two alone forever, wherever you are, as long as you keep silent about what you know. But if you try to sell me out later in any way, our bargain ends, and I'll do things to you that will make your time in the conference room seem like the games at a children's party. Agreed?"

I took a breath, looked at Caz, who was still struggling. What choice did I have? "Okay. I agree. Now, take those chains off her, will you? If you hurt her, you'll never get what you want from me. Never. I'll just call Heaven and hand it over."

A moment later Caz was gone. "She is free, but of course she is still in my . . . care. She'll stay that way until I hear that you have the feather, and you're ready to give it to me."

I felt like Sky Masterson, putting my entire bankroll and my immortal soul on a single roll of the dice, but like I said, what other choice did I have? "Am I free to go, then?" I asked.

Eligor nodded slowly. "Almost. But if I were you, I wouldn't hurry off until you've heard what else I have to say. You see, somehow my old friend Prince Sitri discovered that you were my guest. You remember Sitri, of course."

I remembered the monstrous creature very well. "Oh, yeah. He's a charmer."

"He's a jealous, interfering fat turd," said Eligor with just a trace of rancor. "He's informed the Senate that the prisoner I borrowed from Murderers Sect's custody is, in fact, an angel—a heavenly spy."

"What?"

"Because of that, a bit of . . . controversy has erupted. And because I have supposedly corrupted the guards of the Murderers Sect, Sitri and the others have sent the Maslema's Purified to my house. They answer only to the Adversary, so bribery is not going to work this time."

"Sent? You mean they're on their way?"

The grand duke looked bored. "I would guess they're probably already outside, being stalled by my household staff. But that won't work for long."

"So you had no choice. No wonder you made a deal with me! If you didn't, they were going to take me anyway!"

Eligor shook his head. "No. I would never turn you over to the Senate alive. But if I give them your remains, there's still the chance that someone will find that feather. I don't want it . . . hanging over my head, if you see what I mean." He fluttered his pure white wings. "Thus, our little bargain."

"But how am I supposed to get out of Hell?"

"Not my concern. You found your way in, you can find your way back out, little angel."

"But you said that if they catch me, they'll make me tell them where the feather is, tell them what you did, everything . . . !"

"Ah." He nodded. "Yes, there is one more arrangement to be made." He pointed and the teddy bear monster was suddenly dressed in hospital scrubs. "Did you bring along our little friend, Doctor Teddy?"

"Of course, Master," said the toy bear in his gruff little voice. He produced a sphere about the size of a golf ball from the pocket of his smock and held it out in a furry paw. The thing was partially transparent, like a cloudy bubble, and I could see something sliding wetly inside it, something with very little room to move.

Eligor took it from him and held it out for me to see. It had too many teeth and too many scrabbling legs, and its eyes watched me through the filmy sphere as if it were already thinking about drilling into me and laying eggs or something. "Do you recognize it, Doloriel? You've seen more than a few."

I leaned away from the hideous thing. "What are you talking about?"

"It's an intracubus, our version of one of your guardian angels. These are assigned to every human born, to keep track of all the things they do that will eventually bring them to us here. On Earth, intracubi are insubstantial, but here they're quite real, quite . . . physical. In fact, to implant this one, Doctor Teddy's going to have to do a little surgery on you."

"Surgery . . . ?"

Eligor smiled and gestured. The hotel conference room disappeared, instantly replaced by the chamber with the rusted, stained table and cutting tools. A moment later, without anyone touching me, I found myself facedown on the table and unable to move. I felt little Torture Me Elmo climb up onto my back, then move forward until he straddled my neck. Worst of all, I could feel that he had a little furry erection.

"It has to go in at the base of the skull," the grand duke said. "That way, if you talk to anyone in Hell, I'll know about it, and if the Mastema catches you—well, our little intracubus will just eat his way out and we won't have to worry about your saying something you shouldn't." He chuckled. "But if you *do* somehow make your way out of Hell and back to Earth, Mister Dollar, the intracubus will disappear with the demon-body you're wearing now. And I'll be waiting to hear from you. You know my office number. Call me when you have the feather, and we'll arrange our little swap."

Then Eligor was gone. I could feel his absence like a flame suddenly extinguished. It was just me, the thing in the sphere, and the furry monstrosity who promptly began to gouge a hole in the back of my head with what felt like a rusty screwdriver. Anaesthetic? In Hell?

I had really hoped I was done screaming for the day.

You would have thought that after all the terrible things that had happened to me lately, after all the attacks, torments, violations I'd suffered, this would have been just the latest and the least, a small price to pay for escaping alive or, at least, being given the chance to escape. You'd have thought that, but you'd have been wrong. The hideous sensation of having my skull gouged open paled into absolute insignificance next to the thing that Doctor Teddy pushed into me until it nestled against the meat of my brain. It felt like a hermit crab made of razor blades forced into far, far too small a shell—a shell that just happened to be attached to my neck. Then those legs and teeth closed on my nerve stem, anchoring the thing, and worse by far than the pain was the feeling of its connecting itself to me in a thousand horribly intimate ways. I've talked with spirits and demons and guardian angels, and I've met things that would make a Green Beret wet himself and never even notice, but I swear I've never felt anything as disgusting as having that thing get comfortable inside my head.

When the toy doctor was finished with the skull-rape, he took a few brisk moments to close me back up, sewing the wound with what felt like baling wire, then Doctor Teddy and the conference room suddenly swirled and evaporated, as though a drain had opened up and let it all flow away.

I found myself standing outside on the grounds of Flesh Horse, hidden in an ocean of shadow. The great tower loomed so that it blocked even the light from the highest beacons. Still, enough light filtered down to the great house's main entrance to let me see the host assembled at Eligor's gate. Any one of the huge, fierce, mounted Purifier soldiers could probably have crushed me by himself, and there were dozens of them, armed to the teeth with strange guns, long spears, and axes with oversized, jagged blades. Their horses were carcasses, skin tattered to reveal yellow bones and drying organs. But what really made me uneasy were the tracking beasts that slavered and pulled impatiently at their harnesses. They were smaller than the horses, although not by much, but so strong and so eager to be after their prey (me, remember?) that several times they yanked bulky handlers off their feet and had to be dragged back by many hands pulling together, as though they were drifting four-legged zeppelins.

In the middle of one such struggle, one of the animals lifted its malformed head and howled, a noise that turned my bones to water. The others chimed in, until the grounds beneath Flesh Horse rang with their chilling cries. I'd heard of hellhounds, but this was the first time I'd ever seen them in their native element, and suddenly I felt more sorry for Robert Johnson than I ever had. As I stood there, my heart beating so hard I could barely stand, I heard the old bluesman's mournful, doomed voice singing for me and me alone.

And the days keeps on worryin' me
There's a hellhound on my trail

As if sensing the hopelessness of my thoughts, the intracubus tugged at the strings of my mind like an impatient driver racing the accelerator, making everything that was in me turn cold. I reached up and touched the back of my head where the unspeakably nasty thing had been inserted. Doctor Teddy's stitches felt big as shoelaces, crudely knotted, and the incision was still oozing. A little bit of Eligor was going with me, whether I liked it or not.

Bad as it all was, I didn't really have any options left. It was time for me to run for my life and my eternal soul.

thirty-six
the deeps

ELL'S DARK hours were coming on, which helped a little. I was naked and bruised, bleeding in a few places, but most of the horrible things that Eligor had done to me hadn't left marks. Nakedness was less common in Pandaemonium than in other parts of the inferno, but it certainly wasn't unheard of.

As I scuttled through the shadowed places, across cinders and broken stone, I prayed that Riprash hadn't already sailed back to Cocytus Landing. For all I knew, I could have been Eligor's prisoner for months or even years, and although I doubted that, some time had definitely passed: the hand that Block had bitten off was now mostly regrown. The gray skin was too smooth, and puckered like burn scars, but the fingers all worked, and I could touch them with the thumb, which meant I could hold things in it. Weapons, was what I was thinking about, of course. Angel bodies are ambidextrous and, apparently, so are demon bodies; I hadn't suffered too badly by being one-handed, but when it comes to fighting, two hands are definitely better than one.

Even as I made my way down through the outskirts of Sulfur Lagoon, not too far from where I had been entertained so interestingly by Vera, I heard the alarm being raised around the city, the shriek of sirens and the howl of my animal pursuers, the last thankfully still distant. That was little old me everyone was being warned about. Luckily, most of Pandaemonium's citizens would be locking themselves behind doors, since nobody would want to come into contact with the hellhounds, which weren't always real selective about what they caught and ate. "I didn't do anything!" is not an excuse that went very far with either the hounds or their masters. A massive sign hung above the Via Dolorosa at the entrance to the city, where most municipalities had things like "Welcome to Sheboygan!" Pandaemonium's said "Nobody's Innocent" in ten-foot flaming red letters.

I was in such a hurry to get to Riprash that I was careless entering the Stygian docks and was stopped by a guard. I had to beat the creature senseless, and when I dragged him into the light I saw he was just a ragged old thing, batlike and frail. I didn't know if he'd raised some kind of silent alarm, though, so I couldn't waste a lot of time feeling sorry for him. I shoved him into a dark corner behind a huge coil of rope. I still didn't know what to think about average folks in Hell. Some of them had probably done such horrible things that if I knew the truth I'd want to burn them to ashes on the spot. Others might have been driven to their crimes by circumstance, like Caz, or might have done so many comparatively good things since their crimes, like Riprash, that it seemed petty to keep punishing them. On the other hand, this was Hell—how much sympathy could I afford to waste on its common folk, especially when nearly all of them would be delighted to see me captured and tortured again?

I made my way to Kraken Dock without running into any more port employees. To my immense joy, I could see *The Nagging Bitch* bobbing in its slip. I had a bit of a disagreement with the sailor guarding the gangplank, a scaly fellow with webbed fingers and toes, well-designed for a mariner's life. But I kept my temper, nobody got stabbed, and eventually Riprash himself appeared. When he saw it was me, the ogre hustled me aboard and into his cabin. Gob was sleeping in a corner, curled on a pile of hides like a pet.

Riprash insisted on doctoring me on the spot, dousing my wounds in stinging brine and then covering them with hot tar, a cure that seemed worse than the injuries. Still, I was profoundly grateful just to be in a situation where someone would even think of trying to give me some comfort.

Gob woke up during the doctoring and watched the process with interest. One or two of Riprash's crew wandered by as well to see who was, as one put it, "Yawping like a pig with the wrong side of its neck cut."

I warned Riprash that I was currently Hell's Most Wanted, so he ordered his men to pull up the gangplank and prepare to leave port.

"Might get the Harbor Guard when we reach the outer breakwater," my favorite ogre told me. "Don't want a fight, but if we get one, you'll need something." He frowned at me. "Wouldn't hurt to put some clothes on you, too. Styx gets colder as we get out in the center of the channel."

I was nearly dead on my feet, but I did my best to remain upright while Riprash dug through what he had. None of his own clothes would fit, of course—I might as well have tried to wear an old Sears family camping tent—but he found a few of his boss Gagsnatch's things in a sea chest. The shirts all had two neck-holes, of course, to go with Gagsnatch's redundancy in the head department, but with a flick of his dirty fingernail Riprash turned two holes into one large one, and the pants, though baggy, were a better fit than anything of Riprash's would have been.

None of this helped with the ache in my skull from Doctor Teddy's brutal surgery, or the knowledge that some kind of crab monster was crouched at the end of my brainstem, ready to execute me, but I couldn't afford to be picky. I was out of Eligor's clutches except for that, and it beat the shit out of being flame broiled, I can tell you.

"Now, weapons," Riprash rumbled. "Hmmm. Stab-stab or boom-boom? Maybe both." He lifted out another, much heavier chest like it was a shoebox, and after rattling his way through a pile of his own weapons he pulled out a knife that looked like a slim lady's dirk in his massive hands but which would serve me well as a sword. I slid it through my belt, feeling like a Halloween pirate, but Riprash wasn't done yet. At the bottom of the chest he found what he'd been looking for, a brace of pistols wrapped in waterproof canvas. Not the flintlocks I had seen several times in Hell, but something a bit more modern, closer to the cap-and-ball Colt revolvers that had solved the most crucial disagreements of the American West. They were made of rough, black iron, and the grips and other trim were yellowed bone, minutely carved.

"Fellow traded those to me for passage. More or less." Riprash laughed.

I had been helpless and tormented a long time, so I liked the idea being able to shoot at things that wanted to hurt me. I slipped the guns into my belt on either side, butts forward, then took turns drawing them cross-handed, individually and together, Billy the Kid style. My regenerating hand ached after only a few tries, but the guns were well-balanced. I planned to fire them later on to see how accurately they were sighted.

"You said, 'more or less'?" I asked as I practiced.

"He stowed away in Foul Bitters. Wanted to get to Pandaemonium. I told him I'd take the pistols as payment. He said no and pulled one of them on me." Riprash shook his huge head, the wet wound in his skull looking as fresh as if it had just happened. "So I threw him overboard in the Hungry Rock Straits and kept his guns. But I can't even get a finger into the trigger guard, so you might as well use 'em."

"I guess the original owner won't mind."

"When we go through the Straits you can ask him." Riprash laughed. "But you'll have to shout. I hung an anchor on his belt, so he's probably still on the bottom."

When Riprash left to see to his duties, I stretched out on the floor of the cabin. Gob watched me silently as I pillowed my head on a set of oilskins.

I fell asleep almost immediately, a deep unconsciousness that would have been dreamless but for the nagging sensation that I was sharing my skull with something far more unpleasant than just my own brain. Which, of course, I was.

I woke to a quiet ship, at least by hellish standards, and for a little while I just lay on the floor of Riprash's cabin and enjoyed the sensation of not being actively tortured. I probably should have been up on deck keeping watch for dog-paddling hellhounds, but it was my first chance to think without agonizing pain in a long time, and I had a lot to think about, especially the possibility that Smyler hadn't been working for Eligor after all, but for Kephas—an angel, Sam's benefactor, and the other half of the grand duke's little agreement. It made sense in a way, since Heaven had been the last party in possession of Smyler (or at least his ashes) after we captured him and the Bagmen finished with him. But why would Kephas send a psychotic murder machine after St. Jude's favorite angel, namely me? I knew Heaven's politics were less squeaky clean than they looked, but that still seemed a bit extreme.

I puzzled over it for a long time, but I was clearly missing some pieces, not least of which was: Who the hell was Kephas? And how did trying to get me stuck with nasty, pointy things gibe with that mysterious angel's supposed improving-the-lot-of-human-souls agenda?

Frustrated, I heaved myself up and stumbled out to the deck. *The Nagging Bitch* was in the deep center of the river, and Pandaemonium had shrunk to a distant glow behind us. The Styx was almost beautiful, black and shiny, the waves sprinkled with coppery reflections from the far-off afterlights, the waters undisturbed but for the occasional rolling, cylindrical length of some terrifying river serpent breaching the surface. We had the current and seemed to be making good speed. New mysteries aside, I felt almost hopeful for the first time in longer than I could remember. All I had to do was make it out of Hell and recover the feather, then Eligor would exchange Caz for it. After that—well, if there ever *was* an "after that," I'd worry about it then. How I was going to get on with dating a known demoness was a problem of success. I'd deal with it when I had to.

Over what must have been the next couple of days, we raced along the pitchy Styx, past countless disgusting harbors. Riprash wasn't worried about hiding me from the crew now, since nobody was going ashore, and soon I was spending hours at the ship's rail watching the coastal towns of Hell slide by.

"Y'see, I been thinking about all this," Riprash explained to me one night. "It comes to me that maybe it's time I should be doing something else."

I was a bit surprised. "Something else? Like what?"

"Bringing the Lifters' Word to more than just the few," Riprash said, looking as philosophical as a monstrous giant with a split skull is able to look. "Ever since you brought me that word from you-know-where. I only half-believed Donkeysmile told me a real story until now, y'see, so I never really got up off my haunches to do what I know is right."

I shook my head in confusion. Riprash explained that a long time before, when he first worked for Gagsnatch, a demon named Donkeysmile had been thrown from another ship, and Riprash rescued him. He found the newcomer to be surprisingly intelligent, good company on the long voyage. Eventually, the newcomer had confessed that he came from somewhere else—in other words, outside of Hell—and passed along the gospel of the Lifters to Riprash. Riprash had been alive so long that he had become, as he put it, "a mite philosophical in my age," and what the stranger said touched a chord inside him.

I was darkly amused by "Donkeysmile." If that was what Temuel had chosen to call himself in Hell, then "the Mule," our nickname for him at the Compasses, had been pretty much right on the money after all. But what had Archangel Temuel been doing in Hell in the first place? Another question that led me nowhere useful.

"But these days, since you came and gave me his words," Riprash continued, "I'm thinking that there's more for me to do than just to live on like nothing's changed. I'm wondering if you coming with Donkey-smile's message, if that's like a sign, d'you see? A sign for me that it's time to do different. To take the Lifters' message all round, to those who've never heard it."

If Riprash really planned on becoming a missionary in this, the least missionary-friendly place I could imagine, I was glad he and I were going to be parting company pretty soon, probably as soon as we reached Cocytus Landing. I felt bad that I had dropped little Gob in all this, but I told myself the life he'd had in the filth of Abaddon wouldn't be anything he'd miss much.

I also kept running into Riprash's strange little employee, the one I had privately named Krazy Kat. He was some kind of bookkeeper, which brought him frequently into Riprash's presence, and yet every time he saw me he goggled like he had the first time, although he always stopped when he saw that I'd noticed. It was beginning to annoy me and, to be honest, to worry me a little. I asked Riprash where the little catlike fellow had come from.

"Wart? I don't think he'd been with me for a season before you showed up. He just walked up to Gagsnatch one day, said he'd heard we needed a body could do sums. As it happened, we did, and he's been with us since. Quiet, and he does seem a bit fixed on you, but other than that I've had no trouble from him. I'll make him come and tell what's what."

"I'm not sure—" I began, but Riprash had already sent Gob to fetch him.

"Now," said Riprash when Gob had returned with the little accountant-creature, "why do you want to be plaguing Snakestaff here with your nonsense, Wart?"

The little fellow looked up in abject terror. He gave a single squeak but otherwise couldn't summon any useful noises. Out of pity, I convinced Riprash to let me take over the interrogation.

"You're not in trouble," I said as reassuringly as I could. "It's just that I want to know why you're always looking at me the way you do."

Now he wouldn't look at me at all. "Don't know."

"Well, think about it. Nobody's going to hurt you."

"Lest he tells a lie," growled Riprash, " 'Cause then I'll have his head right off and eat it," which probably wasn't as helpful as the ogre had intended it to be. A good length of time passed before Wart could be roused from his faint, and then it still took a while before his teeth stopped chattering so he could speak.

"Don't know," he told me in a tinny little murmur. "Just . . . something about you. Your face. Not those things," he said, pointing at the bumps I'd added after Vera's house to disguise myself. "Saw it first time. Feels like . . . I know you. Seen you, anyway."

But no matter what else I asked him, he couldn't clear up the mystery. Like a lot of the residents of Hell, little Wart didn't really remember much about the previous week, let alone the details of his earlier life in Hell. I examined the little demon carefully. He was unexceptional in appearance, at least by hellish standards, somewhere between an alley cat dipped in motor oil and a very ugly lawn gnome, but now that I was really looking hard, there was something about him I couldn't quite put my finger on, but which nevertheless plucked at my memory. Had I seen him in one of my earliest moments in Hell? If so, his features were so ordinary by local standards I couldn't believe I'd spent more than a moment looking at him. And if my memory was that good, I should have been out of Hell and cleaning up on Jeopardy.

"Right, Wart, you can go," Riprash told him at last. "If you think of anything, come tell me, but not in front of anyone but these two," he said, indicating Gob and me. "Too many ears."

Wart nodded slowly. "Too many ears," he said, but the phrase seemed to have caught his attention and he repeated it as if hearing it for the first time. *"Too many ears . . ."*

The little creature turned to gape at me. I think it came to him just as it came to me.

"*Walter . . . ?*" I said. "Walter Sanders? Is that you? What are you doing *here*?"

And it *was* him, I could see it now through all that weird—Walter

Sanders, my angel buddy from back at the Compasses, stabbed by Smyler and missing ever since. Was I hallucinating? Had I been in Hell so long my mind was crumbling? But the little bookkeeper wore an expression that must have been a mirror of mine—the slow dawning, the unlikely facts caught in the bottleneck of logic and unable to slide past.

"Yes," he said, his words barely audible. "Yes! Walter Sanders. No. Vatriel. That's my *real* name." He looked around the cabin, then looked over Riprash, Gob, and me, blinking as he did so like a slow loris caught in a flashlight beam. "What am I doing here?"

"You don't know?" Fat lot of good any of this was going to do me. Just more mysteries on top of the ones I already had and didn't want. "You don't remember?"

He was shaking his shaggy head when a crewman rapped on the cabin door, urging Riprash to come to the quarterdeck.

Walter and I were no closer to solving what had happened to him between his being stabbed by Smyler and taking a job with Gagsnatch's Quality Slaves when Riprash shoved open the cabin door. "Trouble," the ogre said. "Come up." I'd scarcely ever seen him look worried, but now he really did, the great shelf of his brow frowning until his eyes were almost invisible.

Gob and I and Wart aka Vatriel aka Walter followed him up onto the deck. The shape on the horizon was so small and its lights so faint that it took me a long moment to realize it was a ship.

"What's the ensign?" Riprash asked Gob. "Use those young eyes."

Gob climbed up so he could lean out over the rail, then spent a half minute squinting into the foggy darkness. "Bird's foot," he said as he scrambled back down to the ogre's side.

"Feared that," said Riprash. "That's the sign of the Commissar of Wings and Claws. It's Niloch's ship, *The Headless Widow*."

I was frightened but didn't want to show it. "Charming name."

"Whole thing is *Raping the Headless Widow*, but that's too long for most folks, 'cause they don't want to talk about that ship much anyway. She runs on steam, she's got something like twenty guns to our eight—and only two of ours work—and she'll catch us by tomorrow or the next day, certain."

I could see Niloch's ship a little better now, a dark shadow hunkered low in the Stygian waters, its lanterns peering at us like eyes in the fog.

I had hoped I'd burned the ugly, rattling bastard to ashes when I blew up his Gravejaw House, but hellish nobility are extremely hard to kill. And as I think I've mentioned, they're also very serious about holding grudges. Apparently, the commissar had managed to get himself appointed to head up the Bobby Hunt. "Can we fight them?"

"If by fight you mean get cut to pieces, burned, and sunk, then yes, we'll put up a fine fight. Ah, well. I always suspected I'd wind up at the bottom of the Styx someday."

As if to underscore this cheery thought, the wind changed direction and our sails sagged. As I stared out across the dark expanse of river I could hear the hungry rumble of the *Headless Widow*'s engines.

thirty-seven

walking on water

HERE'S A little rule about warfare at sea: *Avoid it.*
Here's a corollary pertaining to warfare against a ship full of
angry demons, on a mythical river inhabited by monsters, and with no
better hope, even if you win, than fighting your way across the rest of
Hell afterward on the off chance that you might find your way out
again, at which point your angry angelic bosses or any number of other
interested parties will get on with the job of ripping your soul out of
your body and sending it right back to Hell again: *Avoid that even more
strenuously.*

But there I was, standing at the *Bitch*'s rail, watching just such a
demonic ship bearing down on us, as it had been doing for hours.

In ordinary circumstances we'd have been all right, because we had
the current with us and our ship was small and fast. Slavers had to be,
not because slavery was illegal in Hell (not bloody likely) but because
slaves were valuable cargo that other ships were only too happy to
steal. But according to Riprash, Niloch's ship was powered by four
huge steam engines, so even if we could get through Styx Lock ahead
of them, they would gain on us even faster when we reached the
thicker, more resistant waters of the Phlegethon.

If we ran all night, Riprash said, risking going onto a rock and only-
the-Highest-knew what else, and we managed to stay ahead of Niloch,
we'd probably reach the lock in the earliest hours of the morning. But
after that, it would be only a matter of time before he overtook us. Rip-

rash and his crew were busy keeping us alive until then, coaxing every bit of speed out of the old slaver's tub, but I had nothing to do but walk back and forth on the deck nursing a growing sense of disaster.

In less fucked-up circumstances it would have been interesting to watch the crew working together to keep the *Bitch* running ahead of our enemies. Many of them had the apelike look of Gob, which stood them in good stead as they swung through the shrouds even more nimbly than the most experienced human sailors. Others less suited for climbing looked as though they'd be most useful when it came time to fight, especially a pair of brothers named Retch and Rawny, who had razor-sharp talons on hands and feet and were covered all over with spiny plates. Still, if the enemy caught us, even those two were going to find it hard to do much more than outlive us by a few moments. *The Headless Widow* was closer now, and even in the dim red light reflected from Hell's awesome ceiling, the only glow on this stretch of the oily river, it was plain that their ship was far larger than ours and their crew far more numerous.

It was my fault that Niloch was bearing down on the *Bitch*, my fault that when he caught up, he'd sink Riprash's ship and take the survivors into slavery. It was up to me to help save them, or all this hopefulness about redemption was just noise.

Then, as I paced, I suddenly remembered what Riprash had said about throwing the owner of the pistols I was wearing overboard, and that gave me an idea—a crazy, hopeless one, but I wasn't in a position to be picky—so I went to ask Walter about supplies we might have on board. I found my former co-worker standing at the starboard rail watching the *Widow's* lights slowly grow closer.

"Riprash says Niloch's the worst kind of demon," said Walter quietly.

"There's a kind that's worse than the others?"

"He said Niloch's the sort who wants to make a name for himself, but he's basically mediocre. Mediocre—that's my word, not Riprash's. He said, 'useless.' He says it's the ambitious, stupid ones who make the most trouble."

"Not just here, either," I said, thinking of Kephas. "Still can't remember anything about what happened?"

Walker shrugged. He didn't meet my eye. "Sorry. I do know you, though, Bobby. It took me awhile, but I remember you now. I think you treated me square."

"We were friends," I told him. "That's how I always saw it. Do you remember anything else? The Compasses?"

He rubbed his wrinkled little face. "Not really. I mean, I know it was a place and that I used to go there. I sort of remember it was a place where people laughed and . . . sang?"

"Not so much singing as putting money in the jukebox and shouting along," I said. "But, yeah. More or less."

"I think . . . I think I remember Heaven, too." He spoke slowly, as if wanting to be certain of what he said. "At least, that's what it seems like. Beautiful, bright light. Someone talking to me. A sweet, sweet voice."

"Yeah, that sounds like Heaven. But you can't remember anything else?"

"No." He was frustrated, almost tearful. "No, but it's important. I know it's important."

I felt like his pain was my fault, too, but it had to be better for him to know he didn't belong in Hell, didn't it? It wouldn't have been kind to leave him in ignorance. That's what I tell myself, anyway. "Well, if you think of anything, let me know. Because something is definitely weird. You were attacked by the guy they sent after me, then . . . you just never came back. I expected they'd put you in a new body . . ." I broke off, having noticed something happening on the horizon, where *The Headless Widow* had grown taller as it approached, so that it now looked almost like Gravejaw House itself had taken to the river. "Is Niloch's ship . . . on fire?" I stared, positive that I was seeing things. Certainly it was too convenient otherwise, for our enemy simply to catch fire. "Riprash!" I shouted. "Come here!"

When the ogre arrived, the cloud of smoke and fire around the *Widow* had spread out a good way on either side, and I truly began to believe that fate might have saved me from an extremely unpleasant end to my infernal vacation. "It's fire, right? It's burning?"

Riprash didn't look like someone ready to celebrate. "It's fire, right enough. But it's not their boat burning. Fact, whatever it is, it's coming toward us."

"What? Is it a gun? Did they fire something at us?"

I never got an answer, at least not from Riprash, because the dark cloud full of fire was growing so fast that I couldn't see Niloch's ship any more. A moment later something shot over our heads, flaming like a tracer bullet. It hit the deck, bounced once in a shower of sparks, then smacked into the far gunwale. A nearby sailor threw a bucket of black Styx water on it.

"What is it?" asked Walter, but a moment later a dozen more whipped past us and we could see that they were birds, gray and plump and fast, and every single one of them on fire.

A couple struck the mizzen sail and started the fabric smoldering. A pair of simian deckhands scrambled up the lines to put it out, but even as they climbed several more birds struck the mizzen and the topsail. Another winged blaze came hurtling over the water toward us, bobbing crazily, and smacked right into Gob, catching in his hair and setting it alight. Riprash roared and grabbed the boy, then leaned out over the rail, stretching his huge arm to dunk the boy in the river and extinguish the flames.

"Niloch's doing! He's the Commissar of Wings and Claws," Riprash shouted as he dropped soaking Gob to the deck. More birds flew past as if shot out of a gun, trailing flames, trying to fly even as their wings burned away. "Man the buckets, every helljack of you!" he bellowed. "They're trying to set the sails alight, and if the sails burn, they'll catch us before the next glass. Pass those buckets! Keep the water coming!"

I joined the madness, taking my place in a line, passing sloshing pails of stinking Styx water from the bilge up to the masts. The best climbers were kept busy putting out the fires wherever the hell-pigeons struck, but even so, the mizzen sail was gone and the topsail almost entirely aflame, and only heroic work by the crew kept it from spreading to the other sails.

The flock finally thinned, but without the topsail we were losing ground even more swiftly. I squatted down on the deck beside Walter and struggled to catch my breath before the next wave of flaming birds.

Something pale flew past me, rattling. Another pale shape struck the mainmast behind us and fell to the deck, thrashing and snapping. It was a flying fish, or at least part of one—an almost fleshless skeleton. But the fact that it was mostly bones and empty eye sockets didn't keep it from trying to sink its teeth into everything it could reach before it died. Several more flew past, then suddenly a whole flock or school or whatever you call it seemed to tumble down on us. Several of the crew putting out fires were knocked out of the rigging as if they'd been hit by bullets. They fell to the deck—I could hear bones breaking—so I grabbed Walter and dragged him back toward Riprash's cabin. Gob was already there, hunkered down in the doorway, watching with wide eyes as the swarm of mummified fish smacked into the sails and deck.

Then, from out of the distance, I heard *The Headless Widow's* cannons fire, a deep roar like sequenced thunder. They were still too far away to reach us, but it was an announcement of sorts: the end was coming, whether sooner or later.

"I have an idea," I shouted to Gob and Walter over the yelling and screaming of the crew, many of whom were barely clinging to the ropes overhead as they dodged the toothy horrors. I asked Gob, "Can you sew?"

He looked at me like I'd asked an earthly teenager if the Macarena was still hip.

"No? Then find me someone who can. Walter, help me find some of these oilskins that are the right size."

"What are you doing?" Walter asked as Gob sped off across the snapping, fishy chaos of the deck.

"They don't want the rest of you, they want me. As long as I'm on this ship, they're going to keep coming. But if I'm off it, well, I think they'll follow me instead."

He looked at the pile of skins collecting beside me. "What? Are you going to make a life raft? They'd catch up with you in an hour."

"No, I'm not going to make a life raft. I'm going to try a little trick. I don't know how much you remember yet about your old life, but on Earth they used to be impressed by someone walking on water."

He stared at me in puzzlement. "You're going to walk on water?"

"Better than that. I'm going to walk *under* the water."

A few moments later Gob returned with what looked like one of the oldest members of the crew, a sailor named Ballcramp whose hell-body seemed to be formed from the least attractive elements of the concepts *spider* and *beef jerky*. The worthy fellow clearly thought I was insane when I told him what I wanted, but saw the benefits of working in the captain's cabin, out of the murderous rain of fish. He arranged himself on the floor and took out a sewing kit wrapped in hide, with needles made of bone and thread made of gut.

I explained what I wanted and left him stitching oilcloths together under the supervision of Walter and Gob while I hurried across the deck with my arms over my head against the continuing flurries of animated fish bones. Riprash was down on the gun deck, trying to get the two workable cannons into firing position nearer the stern.

I told him my plan. Being a demon, Riprash didn't waste any time arguing with me, even though it wasn't very likely I'd survive. It was occasionally almost refreshing how few social niceties there were in Hell, how little time was spent pretending to care about things that nobody really cared about. Riprash had nothing against me, but he loved the *Bitch*, and he probably also thought that I'd just be recycled somehow if my body died. I didn't bother to explain that dying would just be the fastest possible way to deliver myself into the hands of Niloch and the rest of Hell's demon lords. Lameh's instructions had made it very clear: Temuel's arrangements could only get me back into my old body once he'd managed to extract me, and he could only extract me from one particular place, the far side of Nero's forgotten bridge.

"So if it works, Niloch and his men should leave you alone," I finished. "Can't promise, but if they have to choose, I think they'll choose me."

"You'll never make it," Riprash said. "There are necks and black sinkers and a shit-swarm of big fang jellies in this part of the river. Any one of 'em will swallow you like a pickled eyeball."

I didn't even want to be swallowed like a regular eyeball. "Can you get me closer to the shore?"

"Not here. Can't lose the current or they'll be on us. But in a little while we'll be past Bashskull Point where the Styx meets up with the Phlegethon at the edge of the Bay of Tophet. Water's shallower, won't be any fang jellies. Might be some hogsquid, but they're not as bad. You know about them, right?"

To be honest, I didn't really want to know about hogsquid or fang jellies or any of them. Everything already sucked so completely that some new bad information would have just pushed my situation past its current state of Zen-like perfect fuckery into something messy and overdone.

The Headless Widow was gaining on us, and when they fired their guns the white waterspouts of falling shells were now only a few hundred yards behind us. I stopped on the way back to Riprash's cabin and picked up a cannonball of my own to carry off, adding the gunnery sergeant to the list of Hell-denizens who thought I was crazy.

I thumped the heavy iron ball down in a corner of the cabin and did my best to make it secure against the pitch of the ship; it was big enough to break bones if it started rolling. Then I went back to directing old Ballcramp. "Leave a hole here, at the corner," I told the spindly creature.

He shook his shriveled head at this senseless order, but the undead flying fish were cracking against the outside of the cabin, and it was a lot nicer inside, so he said nothing.

"You're both safer with Riprash," I told Walter and little Gob as I strapped myself into the crude oilskin vest I'd had Ballcramp make. Puffed up with the air I'd just blown into it, it made me look a bit like the Michelin Man, but less svelte. A fair wind, one of the few bits of luck I'd had in this whole cursed trip, had kept us ahead of Niloch long enough to reach Bashskull Point, and I was determined to get off the *Bitch* before the commissar destroyed it.

"But they know this ship," Walter said. "They know Gagsnatch's stall, everything. We'll never be able to go back to Cocytus Landing now!"

"Don't matter," said Riprash as he lifted me into the dinghy. "We're not going back."

"What do you mean?" As we talked I hurriedly tested the oilcloth of the vest to see if it was flexible enough, but my main concern was that the seams would give under the pressure: I didn't have a huge amount of faith in the tar we'd used to seal them.

"It's a sign, that's all," said Riprash. "Like I told you, I've been thinking on this, and I see it clear now. I'm to take *Nagging Bitch* and spread the Lifters' word. We'll go where we please, and every port will be our home."

This sounded like a spectacularly bad idea. "The authorities, Eligor and Niloch and Prince Sitri and the rest—they'll stamp on you like ants, Riprash. They'll never let you get away with it."

"Even the Mastema can't be everywhere," he said, surprisingly cheerful. "We'll stop and spread the word, then move on. We'll leave behind those as can keep spreading the word for us. Gob here can say the Lifters' Prayer by heart already! Say it boy. Show him."

The kid looked embarrassed (or fearful, it was hard to tell with Gob) but he stared at the deck and spoke in a quiet, very serious voice.

"Out farther, way up in Heaven,
Hell has took my name
The kind don't come
The will won't come
In Hell as it does in Heaven.
Give us this day our asphodel
And give us our best passes
As we give up on those who passes against us,
And lead us not into time's tortures
But deliver us from our evil . . ."

Again, the lack of tear ducts kept me from making a blubbering fool out of myself. I still wasn't sure whether I'd helped the boy or doomed him by bringing him up out of Abaddon, but it was too late to change anything now. "Keep safe, Gob. Riprash will take good care of you."

The boy nodded. I don't know whether he would have thanked me in any case, but people didn't do much thanking in Hell, as you may have noticed, and we were also surrounded by gouts of white water as Niloch's guns began to find our range, so things were a bit hectic.

"And Walter, I'll get you out of here. Somehow." I felt like an idiot even as I said it—so many promises, so few fulfilled. But Walter was too polite, even as a demon, to tell me how unlikely that was. Instead he just waved like a kid watching his older brother going to the gallows.

Riprash began lowering the dinghy into the water, manning the ropes all by himself. "I put a flask of rum in that vest of yours, Snakestaff. You'll need it, I think. And tell you-know-who back in you-know-where that I'll spread the word all over the Inferno!" he bellowed.

Was that really what Temuel wanted? It didn't matter, because that was what he was going to get. We never know what a gesture or a word will lead to, do we?

"God loves you!" I called. It was what we angels say to the recently deceased. I was pretty sure none of these folks had heard it since then, and some of them like Riprash had probably never heard it at all.

"Bobby!" Walter leaned over the rail, and would have fallen when a

cannonball landed close enough to rock the ship, but Gob caught at his legs and kept him from tumbling. "I just thought of something. The voice! *I remember the voice!*"

"What voice?" I could barely hear him over the wind and the barking of the *Headless Widow*'s guns.

"The voice that asked me about you."

"I don't know what you're talking about!"

"I'm not sure either, but I think it's important. It was a child's voice. A sweet, child's voice . . . !"

My boat splashed hard into the water, and for the next moments I was busy trying not to fall into the river. The waves beaten up by the wind had seemed much smaller from on board the *Bitch* than in the little dinghy. I could hear Riprash bellowing for the rowers to start pulling, and the slave ship began to move away from me. I think the sight of my boat being put into the water had confused Niloch and his crew. *The Widow's* guns fell silent, though the black bulk of the ship continued to bear down on me.

I'm sure the commissar and his crew expected me to start rowing, but in fact I hadn't bothered to bring any oars—no point to it, as you'll see. I watched *Nagging Bitch* pull away, and for the first time I felt how truly alone I was.

Niloch and his crew obviously suspected some kind of bomb or other trap, so when they were thirty or forty yards away from me they disengaged their engines and let the ship drift with the same current pushing my little boat. Many sailors and soldiers looked down through the clouds of steam that drifted from the *Widow's* smokestacks.

Seen this close, Niloch looked even less pleasant than I remembered. A lot of his bone tendrils had simply burned away or broken off, and for the first time I could see that his skeletal head was more like a bird's than a horse's.

"You!" he screeched, "Snakestaff, you miserable turdling! Why do you look so puffed up? Whatever armor you're wearing under that won't save you from me. You destroyed my home."

"Gosh," I called back, "maybe because you were going to torture me and then turn me over to your superiors?"

"Nobody may flout authority," Niloch screeched. "Least of all a speck of dirt like you, a creature with no level, no land, no loyalty . . . !"

"Honestly, I'm not listening," I said. "You're as boring as you are ugly." I looked around to make sure that *Nagging Bitch* was still on the move, that Riprash and the rest were putting distance between themselves and Niloch's larger ship. Then I bent down and picked up the heavy iron sphere from the bottom of the dinghy.

"Do you know what this is?" I asked.

Niloch tittered in surprise. "A cannonball."

"Wrong. Try again."

He scowled, a strange thing to see on such a long, bony face. "A bomb? Go ahead, little traitor. Destroy yourself—you won't hurt us. This ship is iron-plated."

"It's not a bomb, either. It's just a weight." I balanced for a moment with my foot on the boat's rail, just until I could tuck the heavy iron ball into the harness I wore across my belly, then I stepped off the boat and the cannonball yanked me down into the oily, caustic waters of the Phlegethon.

thirty-eight
chained

I'M SURE I would have had to pay extra on any package tour of Hell for the thrill of sinking to the bottom of the Phlegethon River—"swim with the friendly fang jellies!"—but to be honest, I was more intent on surviving than getting the most out of the experience. Actually, surviving probably *was* getting the most out of the experience.

I spent the first few seconds pulling the bone cork out of the air sack on my vest, then getting the opening into my mouth so I could breathe. Shallowly, of course: the air inside had to last until I could reach land, which also meant I had to outlast any pursuit from the *Widow*. I looked up. The eyes of my demon-body were very adaptable to low light and, luckily, the Phlegethon wasn't as dark as the Styx. Even so I could barely make out the hull of Niloch's ship far above me, in a circle of sky. I could see all right, but the Phlegethon wasn't always bursting into flame by accident: its waters made my eyes sting and irritated my nose something fierce. Still, so far so good. The cannonball was heavy enough to keep me on the bottom despite the buoyancy of the oilskin air sack.

Things swam past me in the murk, some of them quite depressingly solid, serpentine forms like huge eels or something fished out of Loch Ness, but others that were scarcely more than dark streaks in the water or cold currents with a definable shape. I didn't see any of Riprash's fang jellies close up, but I saw something large in the dark distance that looked like a floating circus tent trying to fold and unfold itself as it floated along. I didn't waste much time thinking about it or any of the others, because it seemed obvious to me that the bottom of a river in Hell wasn't likely to be a safe place. The only thing I could do to improve my odds was get to land as soon as possible.

As elsewhere in Hell, the animal life was as distorted and depressing as the more complex creatures. As I reached the bottom and began to trudge slowly across the mud in what I believed was the general direction of shore (and if I was wrong I was going to be in serious trouble) I found myself stepping carefully around spiny things that could have been sea urchins if they hadn't been in a river and five feet wide. Flat, disklike crabs with disturbingly human faces skittered in and out of the rocks on the bottom, sending up little puffs of silt as they dodged away from predators that were little more than toothy jaws with fins. Once I stopped, despite my limited amount of air, and waited while a vast shadow passed right over me with a slow flick of its tail. I couldn't see it clearly, but it was covered in bony plates and had a mouth big enough to swallow Bobby Dollar and a few other folk at the same time. I had no illusions that I'd be able to outswim or outfight it—the thing was the size of a school bus—so I just hunkered down. It was a long wait, but at last the living submarine moved on, and I could continue. Later I think I even saw a hogsquid, which truly did look a bit like a my friend Fatback in his pig form, if Fatback was as big as the payload of a tanker truck and had twenty-foot tentacles growing out of his mouth. Fortunately for me, the ugly bastard was too busy rooting up and swallowing doomed creatures from the murky river bottom to notice me.

It was hard to hold myself to small breaths, hard to walk slowly when there were monsters all around, and I could feel the air sack getting smaller and smaller, but I had no idea how long it would take me to reach the shore or whether it would even be safe, at that point, to get out of the water. I was pretty certain Niloch would be watching for me to surface. He might even be waiting when I reached the riverbank, since it didn't take a whole lot of smarts, even by the standards of infernal nobility, to realize what I was trying to do.

I had just kicked away a few larger specimens of the crabs with faces—the bigger ones looked both less human and more expressive, if you can imagine that—and was really beginning to wonder whether I had enough air to make the shore, when I saw another large, long shape coming out of the murk in my general direction. Certain it was another one of the plated monsters or something even worse, I crouched down in the mud and froze in place, trying not to let the bubble of air in my lungs escape and give me away. But what came toward me out of the clouds of silt, heading out toward the deepest part of the river, was not the prehistoric monster I expected, but . . . a parade. Humanoid shapes walked along the river bottom in a line, kicking up the gray ooze so that they seemed to be moving in a fog, like a vision of fairies in the Irish hills. Then I saw that they were walking along the bottom because they were chained together.

Slaves. Somebody's slave ship had been chased by a faster ship, or perhaps merely sunk. Whichever it had been, these poor damned souls had wound up at the bottom of the Phlegethon, too heavy because of their chains to reach the surface. I could only guess how long they had been down here, trudging through the mud, but it had been long enough for the river to take its toll. Several of the slaves were all but gone, only bones and a few rags of skin still tangled in their chains, but many of the others looked almost whole except for the places where fish and other river creatures had gnawed at them. The leader, whose grim determination seemed to have drawn the rest along after him, had lost both eyes, one arm, and most of the fingers from his remaining hand, but still he moved forward through the dark water, one bony, tattered foot in front of another, his fellows stumbling or floating behind him, depending on how much of them remained. When I saw all those empty eye sockets I understood why the poor bastards were headed in the opposite direction from the shore.

I moved toward them as quickly as I could through the slippery ooze, trying to get their attention by waving my arms, but my cannon-ball sinker made me no faster than them, and even though I got closer I couldn't attract the attention of any of them, least of all the blind leader. He marched past me, and the rest of the chained, doomed group followed him. I got close enough to grab at one of them, but the arm came away in my hand and the one who had lost it didn't even seem to notice.

Too far gone, I realized. However long they had been down here, there was not enough left of them, either in body or in thought, to sur-vive on the surface. The kindest thing I could do was leave them marching on as they were, to be pulled apart by fish or to rot gently into pieces and become one with the river.

One of the most profound lessons of Hell was how little an angel could actually accomplish. I had learned that lesson again and again since I'd been here, but never as clearly as this.

The chained slaves hobbled slowly away, vanishing within moments into the floating murk of the river bottom, invisible to my stinging eyes.

If I was a different kind of guy, I could probably spend an entire career studying the life (well, you know what I mean) to be found in the rivers of Hell. But I'm not. All I really wanted to do was just find my way out of the river, off this level of Hell, and down to the Neronian Bridge. Still, it was hard not to notice when I saw something thrashing in the mud and, instead of the fishy monster I expected, discovered two animated corpses, little more than bones, trying to murder each other.

Let me reiterate: I had to step over a pair of skeletons, which were struggling in the silt a couple of dozen feet beneath the surface of the Phlegethon. Both of them were missing most of their lower halves, and their bony hands were wrapped around each other's throats. The throats in question were little more than vertebrae and a few rags of rotting flesh, and they were, I repeat, at the bottom of a river, so it wasn't like one of them was going to suffocate the other. But there they were. I guess that's why it's called Hell.

Anyway, like I said, I could tell you lots more, because there's lots to tell—carnivorous river worms, lobsterlike beasts that vomited out their own sticky stomachs and reeled them back in like fishing nets, things with the bodies of sharks and the heads of insane horses, all teeth and rolling eyes and, of course, more bodies of the humanoid damned in various states of decomposition, not all of whom seemed to be in the river against their will. In fact, more than a few seemed to have chosen lying in the acid mud at the bottom of the Phlegethon, slowly turning to living mush, over whatever they had experienced on land. Hell's version of committing suicide, I guess.

I reached the shallows just as my air ran out. I shed the vest and its weight, saving Riprash's flask, then let myself float to the top. I lay there for long moments, trying to look as much like another suicide as possible until I could take a discreet look around. I spotted the *Headless Widow*, but saw to my relief that it was still some way out in the river, still waiting near the spot I'd gone down, and there was no sign of Riprash's ship at all. So far, so good.

I paddled gently forward until I could touch the bottom, then climbed the bank in the darkest and least visible place I could find, in case somebody on Niloch's boat had a telescope. When I found a comparatively safe spot, I stole a moment's rest and deep breathing, but was roused by the sound of distant voices.

The *Widow* appeared to have given up on its vigil over the spot where I'd sunk and was pulling to shore, fires stoked and oars sweeping like centipede legs. I knew that even in this darkest part of the day there would be eyes on board that could see better than mine, so I unwrapped the pistols Riprash had given me from their protective oilskin bag, slid them and the dagger-sword into my belt, and began to make my way up a low bluff, away from the river. But the bluff quickly proved to be only the base of a larger hill, and I was even more exposed on the slope than I would have been on the riverbank, so I had to keep climbing. As I did so, I could look down on Niloch's ship anchored in the bay, and the landing boats coming ashore. Unlike the *Bitch's* little dinghy, these were good-sized craft with several oarsmen in each and room for soldiers and mounts and even Niloch's hellhounds. It was easy to tell where the hellhounds were, because everyone else was crowded at the other end.

To my dismay, instead of making camp on the shore, the commissar's troops immediately began to follow in roughly the same direction I'd just come, as though they'd already picked up my scent. I did my best to hurry my pace, although it was dangerous climbing in the dark. As I got nearer the top, I could see my pursuers beginning to flag: the horses, or whatever the hell they were riding, were having trouble with the steep, rocky slope. At last they reached a relatively flat spot several hundred feet below me and began scouting for an easier way up.

I took advantage of this pause to find suitable rock where I could rest and also keep an eye on them. I couldn't quite make out what they were saying, but I could tell Niloch was furious. I could hear his shrill tones echo out over the river valley. While he scolded his minions, I watched the hellhounds pace nervously on their chains, each one held by two or three keepers, but I soon wished I had chosen something else to watch.

The hounds were huge, about the length of lions or tigers, with low-slung bodies like medieval pictures of wolves, and pelts that appeared almost flat black. I found out later that they looked that way because they didn't have pelts at all but leathery, scaled hides, something like what you'd find on a Komodo dragon. Then one of them turned toward the place where I was hiding, and its entire pink snout, invisible until that moment, pushed forward out of the rough black sleeve of its face, like a dog's penis emerging from its foreskin. Even in torchlight the pink protrusion glistened, damp and sticky-looking, featureless but for two huge holes that I guessed were its nostrils. Then the end of the snout opened, revealing a mouth full of inward curving teeth like a Conger eel's, and I turned and threw up bile, the only thing in my stomach.

I've seen a lot of nasty things, but I haven't seen too many worse than that, because unlike the horrors in the river, these creatures were expressly after me and me alone. When my stomach had finished spasming, I got up and hurriedly made my way across the hillcrest, looking for a place to climb down on the other side. I was still exhausted, but getting an up close view of the things that were after me was enough to pump a shitload of adrenaline, let me tell you.

To my relief, I could see lights in the valley on the far side of the hill; an array of orange glows that suggested a decent-sized city, twinkling in the mist off the Phlegethon. Closer to me lay a network of roads around the outermost lights, and a winding, torchlit strip along the exterior that looked wide enough to be a highway. I made that my goal and began picking my way down the hill as fast as I could without falling and breaking something important.

It took me what seemed a couple of hours to reach the flats. Once or twice I heard bone-chilling howls from my pursuers in the hills above as they got close. I took more than a few dangerous risks, but I was determined to stay well ahead of them, knowing I had a better chance of losing them in the city than in the wilderness. Also, I needed to find a lifter station, because that was the only way I was going to be able to get down to Abaddon ahead of Niloch and his howling penis-monsters.

The whole time I descended the hill, I saw only four vehicles on the highway: a couple of fancy horse drawn coaches, a simple peddler's wagon, and a big black car which looked like it belonged to one of the infernal nobility. I didn't want to get recaptured, but I didn't want to walk all the way into the city, either, which was miles away, so when I reached the side of the wide road and began following the highway toward the lights, I kept my ears open for possible rides.

I tried to flag down the first one to pass, a coach drawn by a team of horselike creatures (if having human legs can still be considered "horselike") but the driver lashed at me with his whip and sped on. Perhaps half an hour passed without another vehicle as I trudged on, then I heard the chuffing of a steam engine and saw a grotesque thing that looked half-tank, half-bicycle jolting toward me. I waved and, to my relief, it actually slowed as the driver examined me. Then it hissed to a halt and a door opened on the passenger compartment, which was shaped a bit like Cinderella's pumpkin coach. I took this as an invitation and clambered up, only to be greeted with the trumpet bell of a blunderbuss in my face.

I was braced to be robbed or shot (or more likely both), but the gun's owner only surveyed me, then suggested I put my own guns down on the floor of the passenger side. I did as he asked, moving slowly so as not to startle him. Satisfied, the driver engaged his engine again, and we rolled forward.

My rescuer was a wizened, manlike creature with a pockmarked face that sagged on one side and a huge, healing hole in his chest—a hole I could have put my fist through. He saw me staring at his wound and laughed. "Can see why I'm a bit careful, can't you? Last one I gave a ride left me with that. Tried to take this old darling here," he patted the dashboard of his vehicle, "but I blew his head off and left him feeling around for it by the side of the road. Never going to find it, though!" He cackled. "Nothing left!"

I smiled (a bit weakly, perhaps) trying to show how much I approved of decapitating wicked would-be hijackers, because I was of course not that kind of hitchhiker at all. "But you still give rides to people?"

"Gets boring on the run from Poor Meat to Tendon Junction," he said. "Good to have a little company. Keeps a fellow from losing his mind!" He smiled and nodded vigorously.

I couldn't help wondering if a man who kept picking up hitchhikers after one of them tried to blow him to pieces hadn't lost his mind already. In fact, as I learned during the ride, he'd had quite a few near escapes over the years. The hitchhikers had come out of it worse, though.

"And now we are companions," he said. "My name is Joseph. What is yours?"

I made up a name—I didn't want to leave any more of a trail than I had to. "What city is that?" I asked as the lights spread before us.

"That's Blindworm," he said. "Hope you aren't planning on going there to make friends."

"Why's that?" I asked, even though the last thing I wanted to do in any of the cities of Hell was make friends.

"Not from around here? Strange people in Blindworm. City of the Selfish, I call it." He didn't elaborate, but he had lots of other things to talk about. He told me he was in the lock business, like the kind you opened with keys. "Blindworm is my best place for sales. Most of what I make on a trip, I make here. They keep me in business!"

As we approached the outskirts of the city I began to see houses, each one with a neat little yard, like some picture-postcard suburb. But although I could see shapes in some of the windows, nobody was outside. I supposed it was the hour—by my reckoning it was somewhere after midnight in Hell-time—and figured things would be different as we got farther in, but although I spotted a pedestrian or two, they all hurried off the street ahead of us, disappearing into doorways or down alleys as if they feared us.

When I asked Joseph, he shook his head. "You really don't know? I thought you were joking. How could you not know? The folks in Blindworm hate everyone. They keep to themselves."

If they kept to themselves, why had they built a huge city of tall buildings? Judging by the size, it seemed there must be quarter of a million inhabitants or more. But as we approached the city's heart I began to see what Joseph meant. In every dwelling or business we passed, there was never more than one person inside. Even places meant to be used by many people at once, like carriage stops or banks, seemed to be divided into individual stalls, so no matter how many customers there were, they never had to see each other. Half a dozen sat at a bus stop we passed, each cramped in his or her own space like farm animals in a barn. They all looked up at the sound of our motor and watched our passing car with scowling dislike.

Normally I would have examined such a weird thing more closely. I mean, how does a city like that work, full of inhabitants who don't want to see each other? But Joseph was starting to worry me. The closer we got to the center of the city and the towering lifter shaft that dominated the skyline, the more distracted he became, talking to himself and peering at me from the corner of his eye as though I were the one acting strange. I tried to make harmless conversation with him, but that only seemed to make things worse, and by the time we were within a few blocks of the vast square tower of the lifter station, I had fallen completely silent. That didn't help, either. Joseph was murmuring continuously under his breath, and kept reaching out to touch the barrel of his shotgun, which was leaning against the padded dashboard between us. When he saw that I'd noticed, that only seemed to make things worse.

"Ah, yes," he said. "Think you could? But I'd have it first, and then boom! The worse for you!" He chortled, his sagging face as empty as a jack-o-lantern. He was beginning to scare the crap out of me.

"Just let me out here," I said. "This is where I wanted to go. Thanks for the ride."

"Thanks?" Now he looked directly at me, and the wide-eyed expression on one half of his face looked even more severe next to the slack features on the other side. Saliva was dripping from the side of his mouth. "You have the audacity to give me thanks? When you want to murder me?" He slowed the vehicle, fumbling for his gun, which lucky for me was clumsily long for the crowded passenger cab. My pistols were still on the floor, and I knew I'd never reach them before he could shoot me, so I yanked open the door, kicked my guns into the road, then threw myself out after them.

A moment later there was an explosion like thunder. Hot gases leaped over my head as a chunk of the building ahead of me flew into powder and chips. As I went scrambling through the dark in search of my pistols, I heard Joseph get out of the car and cock his gun again. "Try to kill me, eh? Come back to try again, eh? Put another hole in Joseph, eh?" he shouted, but before he fired again the nighttime street was ripped by one of the most fearsome noises I'd ever heard: a howl that made my skin want to crawl right off my body and run away without me. The hellhounds. The hellhounds were inside the city. But I'd left them back in the hills, miles away. How had they caught up so fast?

Joseph may have been crazy, but he wasn't stupid enough to mess with hellhounds. As I recovered my guns, I heard his door slam closed. Then he drove away.

As the noise of his engine dwindled, one of the beasts howled again, an echoing, whooping cry that could stop a healthy heart. Another answered, and it sounded even closer. They were spread out and hunting me, and I was at least half a mile away from the lifter tower in the center of the city. And now I was on foot.

There are times to fight, but this wasn't one of them. This was a time to run.

thirty-nine
isolation row

SELF-PRESERVATION IS the number one rule in Hell, as you've probably already figured out, so you can guess how many people leaped out to help as I sprinted through Blindworm's business district.

Even as I ran, the bizarre sights of what crazy Joseph had called The City of the Selfish jumped out at me, streets and sidewalks as wide as in a fascist capital (so people could avoid each other more easily, I guessed), public spaces segregated by stalls and blinds so that they didn't have to see each other and the clerks and shopkeepers never had to see more than one customer at the same time. Even the tracks of the central train station, which I followed toward the lifter column, had walls between them, presumably so the passengers in their individual compartments didn't have to see riders in other trains. And of course, since it was a big city, even in the middle of the night people were out—cleaners, night-shift workers, coffee shop waitresses and their patrons arranged behind plate glass windows like museum exhibits. And none paid attention to anyone but themselves. Tunnels, walls, boxes, hatches, Blindworm had developed a world-class system of separation. I might as well have been in the middle of the Gobi desert, running across a sand dune, hoping for assistance from the lizards. Not that I was expecting help as I fled down Lonely Street (no shit, that really was the name). The only good thing was, if I didn't get in their way, the citizens of Blindworm weren't likely to get in mine, either. City of Sociopaths might be a better name, I thought.

The hellhounds' bronze claws clattered loudly on the pavement, just half a block behind me now. Even the self-absorbed local citizens were beginning to pay attention, not to me but to the horrible rasp and clang of the pursuit: they disappeared from the street like startled mice as the howls echoed down the lonely corridors between buildings.

I looked back as I turned onto a wide thoroughfare called Isolation Row. The first hound was just turning the corner, mouth jutting from the retracting snout in a complicated snarl of teeth. The beast was almost as high at the shoulder as I was, but I could only run on two feet. It was like being chased by Eligor's *ghallu* all over again—another ancient evil that had wanted to tear me to pieces, that had been bigger and faster than me, too—but this time I had no silver bullets, no Sam or Chico to help me, nothing. I cocked both my pistols, put my head down, and tried to find a little more speed in my exhausted muscles.

I could see the station beneath the massive lifter tunnel at the end of the wide street, and I dug toward it. Several hellhounds were only yards behind me, a rapid-fire clink of claws on asphalt, but I didn't dare look back again.

The station doors were open. I leaped through, nearly knocking myself out on the first of a series of switchback barriers. Instead of a vast open space, like anyone would have expected in such a large public building, the whole thing had been turned into a rabbit run of mazy walls. I had no time to try to puzzle it out, but luckily the walls were only a little higher than I was tall, and I could still see the broad bottom of the lifter tunnel at the center of the concourse. Apparently, Blindworm had been built with a more conventional hellish population in mind and only modified later.

Just like The Infernal Fauna of the River Phlegethon, the sociological peculiarities of Blindworm could occupy a team of scholars for decades, but all I wanted to do was to survive the next minute or two. I sprinted through the maze, committing about thirteen or fourteen Blindworm Cardinal Sins by not only overtaking other citizens from behind but literally knocking them over so I could get past. The hounds were right behind me, and the Blindwormers who got in my way didn't curse me long; I heard an entire train of shrieks and mayhem noises behind me as the locals found out what I was running from.

I burst out of the first set of walls into what had been the center of an old concourse, divided now into a beehive of isolation stalls where the passengers could wait. In a continuation of my run of shitty luck, none of the lifters was signaling, which meant that all the doors were still closed. There were no indicator lights to let me know which ones would be available next, either. For all I knew, the next five lifters to arrive might be on the opposite side of the huge central column.

A deep, reverberating snarl made me leap forward just in time to avoid the hellhound that came barreling out of the passage behind me, an unlucky commuter in his huge jaws. The beast shook the poor, screeching bastard like a terrier with a rat, then dropped the limp body when he spotted me.

I backed toward the lifter column, guns drawn, as the hound came toward me. I had tested Riprash's pistols enough to know I couldn't trust any shot much beyond ten paces, so I waited. But as I tried to keep my gun hand steady and the barrel pointed at its sloping forehead, two more hounds scrambled out behind, one of them chewing contemplatively at the tattered remains of a leg wrapped in a bloody dress.

I might have been able to take out one of the monsters with the bullets I had in the crude revolvers. I was a lot less sure about three. And even if I managed to shoot every hellhound dead without having to reload, I still had to deal with Niloch and his huntsmen who must be close behind. I could only see one chance open to me now, so I backed up a little farther, until I was standing beside a wall of partitioned stalls.

"Ah, yes my dear, *there* you are," said a voice as rotten as week-old fish. Niloch made a whistling noise and the hounds backed off. The commissar shuffled forward out of the entrance maze, something like a long buggy-whip in one hand, a jagged knifelike blade in the other, his bone-frills fractured and charred. "You've led us quite a chase, Snakestaff, but now that silliness is over. I can get on with the important business of making you wish you'd never heard of my beautiful, beautiful Gravejaw House." He turned his bony head toward the soldiers following him out of the maze; they had to kick the torn corpses of several Blindworm citizens aside to force their way onto the open concourse. "Here he is," Niloch told them. "You wouldn't think to look at this puny creature that he could be dangerous, but he is, my sweetlings, oh, yes, he is. So look lively. If he does anything silly, cut him down immediately."

Several of the soldiers had guns, long and impressively trimmed rifles currently pointed at my favorite person in Hell: me. Others had swords and axes. Either way, getting "cut down" was going to be painful.

"And what if I just shoot *you* before anyone can stop me?" I asked, turning my revolver from the nearest hellhound and pointing it at Niloch himself, aiming right between those shiny little red eyes. "I could live with that result."

The commissar laughed, a fluting noise like a breathy, delicate sneeze. "Oh, perhaps you could—"

I didn't bother to let him finish, because I hadn't meant to start a conversation, just make him think that's what I wanted. Like most of these lordlings of Hell, Niloch loved the sound of his own voice. I shot him in the face.

It didn't kill him, of course, or even slow him down much, but I hadn't thought it would. You don't get rid of a major demon that way, even on Earth where the physics are against them. I was more interested in distractions: one of the lifters had chimed its arrival, and I knew it was now or never. As Niloch fell back toward his soldiers, his skeletal head temporarily a blossom of shattered bone, I threw myself at the row of lifter stalls as hard as I could.

I wasn't particularly strong by Hell's rigorous standards—I doubt I could have stood toe-to-toe with Niloch—but I was just strong enough to rock the flimsy, partitioned wall and start it collapsing. Again, I was lucky that Blindworm had been adapted for isolation rather than constructed that way from the beginning. The stalls were little more than the infernal equivalent of plywood. Even as the first soldiers got clear of flailing Niloch and began to fire their guns in my direction, the stall structure wavered and then collapsed sideways like a row of dominos. I took cover behind the wreckage and began firing back at Niloch's troops.

As shocked as the waiting passengers were to have the structure fall on them and then find themselves in the middle of a gunfight, they were even more shocked to find themselves face to face with, or even literally tangled up with, their fellow citizens, the very thing they feared and avoided every waking minute. Needless to say, they shrieked and fought like only the terrified insane can fight, and within a few seconds the fracas was spreading through the terminal as customers were confronted by the twin horrors of hellhounds and their neighbors.

I scrambled along the floor toward the lifter column and then stood up and shoved my way through the panicked crowd until I found the open door. There was only one passenger, a tall, scrawny demon with a face like a depressed mortician, frantically palming the wall to get the door to close. I grabbed him and shoved him out to absorb any random bullets flying around, then called out the name of a lifter stop on a level above Blindworm. I needed to go down many levels to get out of Hell, but I didn't want my pursuers to know that. In fact, since I had no idea if they could trace or even override one of the lifters and imprison me between levels, I didn't even want them to know which one I was riding.

The door began sliding shut, but then clanged to a grinding halt around the broad neck of a nightmare head—one of the hellhounds. The sheath of its face pulled back as the wet pink snout came out. It didn't have regular jaws in that awful jack-in-the-box muzzle, just a round, toothy mouth like a lamprey's. It damn near reached me as I emptied the last of my bullets into it. Foul blood and bits of tissue sprayed back at me, then I put my foot on the beast's chest, doing my best to avoid the ragged, wounded snout, and shoved so hard that I fell back on my ass. That would have been it for me, but the hellhound stumbled back just far enough for the doors to close, and a moment later I felt the lifter car coughing and vibrating into movement as I headed back up toward Pandaemonium.

Panting, forearm bleeding from a bullet wound that I hadn't even noticed, I slapped the wall and called out the name of a nearer stop, then quickly reloaded my gun out of the oilskin bag as the car slowed. When the door opened, I stepped out in as relaxed a manner as I could manage, and several other passengers stepped in, clearly oblivious to what had happened just a couple of levels down. A few of them noticed the bloodstains on the floor and the pair of hellhound teeth in the corner, both as big as my thumb, but this being you-know-where, they didn't seem too upset.

I didn't even look around the new station, but simply got onto the next open lifter, which was also going up, then got out and went down a couple of times, then up again, making sure that I wasn't leaving Niloch and his hunters an easy trail to follow. When I thought I'd mixed it up enough, I jumped into an open, empty lifter in Ragged Armpit station and told it to take me to the Abaddon level, far below.

I was exhausted, of course, and skin-crawlingly nervous every time the lifter stopped and new passengers entered, but after I had traveled downward for a good while unhindered, I began to think I really was going to make it.

Then, at the seventh stop, two of Niloch's soldiers got on.

forty
grey woods

L UCKILY, THE lifter was crowded and the two soldiers were talking
to each other. Also luckily, they were just Murderers Sect and not
the tougher, smarter Purified, the Mastema police. I sank back against
the wall near the door, as much behind them as I could manage, and
tried to look like just another infernal commuter on his way home,
splattered in the blood and dog-brains of an average working day. Because of all my up-and-down trips to confuse the trail, I'd let Niloch's
hunters get past me, which meant I might run into them anywhere
from here on down.

"His lordship is steaming," said one of the soldiers, a bear-headed
fellow with a neck big as my waist and shoulders you could build a
house on.

"And he doesn't look too good, neither," said his companion with a
guttural laugh. He was as big and ugly as his friend, although a little
shorter. Both looked as though they could separate my head from my
body with just a thumb and forefinger. "Did you see the commissar's
yap? Splinters on top of splinters!"

"If the spy hadn't ruined my day with all this running about," said
Ugly Number One. "I'd shake his hand. 'Course I'd still rip it off him
after that."

"From the description, sounds like someone else already did," said
Number Two. His laugh was starting to annoy me already, but he was
looking around the car now so I slouched back even farther and

dropped my eyes. If he saw me, he wasn't really looking at me, because he then said, "Why are we going down to Beggar's End?"

"You dumb shit-hole," said Number One. "Why do you think? The commissar's putting us and a lot more on every level between Tophet and Lower Lethe. This escaped spy can't go below the top Punishment Levels, see? He tried it once, and it made him sick. I heard some Mastema muckamuck was in a lifter with him when it happened, that's how they know. So we start down in the Lethe levels and then we work our way back up, some on the lifters, some on the roads. Commissar's got boats out on the rivers, too, 'case he tries that way again."

It was all I could do not to groan. How was I going to get to the Neronian Bridge if Niloch and his thugs were going to be looking for me all over? For that matter, how was I going to get off this rotten damn elevator?

Well, somebody once said fortune favors the brave. I think it was my buddy Sam, shortly before he drank himself to death. (Well, really, he only drank that particular body to death, but that's another story.) Since I didn't have a plan, or even any hope to speak of, I figured that I might as well do *something*, so I quietly slipped Riprash's huge dagger-sword out of my belt and then, when the lifter lurched to a stop at the next level, I shoved it into Ugly Number One's side as hard as I could, with all the force of my legs, back, and shoulders. As I think I mentioned, I'm pretty strong as a demon, and I was hoping to shove it all the way through both of them at the same time. As it was, by the time I got it all the way through armor and Number One, I only gouged about a three inch hole in Ugly Number Two, but the collapse of his wounded partner knocked him off-balance, which gave me time to get out one of my guns and shoot him in the head.

The door slid open. The customers inside the lifter stared down at the two dead soldiers with wide eyes. The passengers waiting to get on suddenly noticed them, too. Nobody moved for a couple of seconds except for the quiet rattle of scales shivering together. Not many heroes in Hell, thank the Highest.

"Step out," I said to the nearest passenger, a woman with no eyes. Just to make sure she understood, I pressed the barrel of my revolver gently against her forehead. She stepped out. The other passengers quickly followed her. I waved my gun at the passengers outside; they got the idea, moving back from the door. When it closed again and the lifter started down once more, I was alone with the two motionless soldiers, each an ugly, lumpy island in a spreading sea of blood.

I knew they weren't dead in any ordinary sense, although these bodies might never be functional again, but I didn't want to take the risk that they might regenerate on me, so I stopped the car at a random floor, checked to make certain nobody was waiting to get on, then dragged the two semi-corpses out of the car. It wasn't easy—it took me the best part of three minutes to wrestle all that weight by myself, and when I got the door closed and the lifter moving down once more, I looked like I'd just taken a blood shower. I probably didn't smell all that great, either, but I had bigger things to worry about.

You know how when you're trying to think of something really important, these other, much less important ideas keep jumping into your head like bunnies on crystal meth, boing, boing, boing, anything except what you're supposed to be thinking about? You don't? It's just me, huh?

Maybe it was Eligor's crab-demon flexing in my skull, or maybe just exhaustion, but as I was doing my best to figure out what I should do next, I kept getting distracted by ideas that really were not very important right at that moment, like if Hell was no more of a physical location than Heaven was, why was it so much more realistic? Why did people bleed? Why did they eat? Why go to all the trouble of making a permanent torture chamber, then giving it its own ecology and unnecessary shit like that? Was that God's idea or the Devil's? What agreement did they have, exactly?

Then I'd catch myself and try to start thinking about survival again.

I really only had one choice of an escape route. From what the two dead guards had said, Niloch's soldiers were looking for me everywhere from Abaddon on up because they'd learned from that Mastema mud-man who'd commandeered my lifter how badly I'd reacted to the Punishment Levels my first time, when I'd freaked out so badly he'd tossed me out for the Block and his freaks to chew on. It might even have been Eligor who passed the information along to Commissar Niloch, just to torment me in a new and interesting way before having the intracubus in my skull shut me down. But wondering whether Eligor was playing me for a fool or not was a game with no useful ending. What was more important now, Niloch and his thugs thought they had me figured out, so my only hope was to surprise them. If they knew for a fact I couldn't survive the Punishment Levels, well, that's precisely where I had to go—right where they didn't expect me. And if I survived that return visit, I just had to pray that Eligor really wanted that feather back badly enough not to help the ones chasing me, since for all I knew, the intracubus in my head was keeping him informed of everywhere I went and everything I did.

And a great holiday, I thought, *just keeps getting better and better.*

Don't get me wrong. I didn't ask the lifter to take me down to Satan's Parlor or anything, but only a few levels lower than Abaddon. After that I could climb to the level with the Neronian Bridge. After all, I figured, I'd gone a few levels farther below *that* when I experienced the Punishment Levels before, and I'd survived more or less intact.

What I probably should have thought of, though, was that the last time I had descended to the Punishment Levels and escaped, I didn't have an intracubus burrowed into my head like a demonic tick. To say I was astonished when I got down to Itching Stump, still several levels above Abaddon, and the inside of my head began to burn, is probably a bit of an exaggeration—I'm a pessimist by nature and, after all, I was already in Hell—but I was definitely astonished by how much it hurt. It got worse every level down. By the time I was getting close to Abaddon itself, a place I'd already survived quite easily, that red-hot robot tarantula was doing Jazzercise in my cerebellum, and I was twitching like a marionette with its strings caught in a power mower.

Like I said, I probably should have guessed things might be different this time, but what with everybody trying to hack me to pieces or torture me I'd been a bit distracted. So now I had a new crisis: I couldn't afford to get out of the lifter yet, because Niloch's troops were working their way upward from Abaddon. But every second I stayed was making me more and more certain that my head was going to explode in a splatter of flaming nerves and brain goo.

As the levels passed, and my limbs jerked and my nerves sizzled, I kept singing cartoon theme songs over and over in my head just to keep myself from thinking about how much I was hurting, but Spider-Man was already doing me less good than the Flintstones had, and I had a feeling I probably wouldn't even get to start Yogi Bear. Still, I hung on in desperate agony until the lifter sank past the Abaddon stop, then I gasped out the name of the next level. When the lifter ground to a halt and opened, I stumbled out into the deserted little station at Grey Woods and then out into the city beyond the station. Except there was no city.

At that exact moment I was having trouble focusing, what with something inside my head chewing on my neural fibers, but I realized a little later that I was in one of the places I'd actually read about, not in any Camp Zion briefing, but in the words of Dante himself. (We read *The Inferno* for extra credit, even though it's mostly made-up. Surprisingly, old Dante got quite a few things right, including the idea of Hell's vertical arrangement.) If you've read him too, you might remember "The Wood of Thorns," or, more directly, the Forest of Suicides. That's where I was now. The lifter building here was like a remote stop far out on a suburban train line, one of those little places where you think there couldn't possibly be enough passengers to warrant a station.

Not only was the station empty, outside the station was a sort of platform, which was really just the edge of the building, and then . . . nothing. Not literal nothing—although this being Hell, that would have been possible too, I guess—but nothing resembling infernal civilization. The woods stretched as far as I could see and were as gray as reported, a heavy, dripping forest of oak and alder and other ancient European trees tinseled with thick moss. In the spots where you could see ground through the mist, it was covered with grass of such a dark green that it appeared nearly black.

The good part was that I was only one level below Abaddon now. The bad part: I was only one level below Abaddon, and that's where the commissar, his hounds, and his troops would be looking for me, and if they were thorough, they might come looking for me here as well. Then I'd be in Niloch's nasty, rattling hands.

No, I realized, if I was captured, Eligor's crab-grenade was going to go off in the middle of my thinkers, and then my next conscious thought would be, *Oh, shit, I'm in the Infernal Transfer Lounge for Souls and everyone's staring at me.* After that, the *real* pain would begin. Eligor had held back from my utter destruction because he wanted something from me, but the big bosses of Hell wouldn't be so kind. The whole operation here was expressly set up for just the kind of things they'd be doing to me, and they'd do them forever.

So I did the only thing I could do at that point. I pulled up my big boy pants and headed out into the Forest of Suicides.

It would have been an awful, awful place even if it had been right beside some lovely college town, five minutes from great nearby schools and nifty places to walk your dog, but as it was, a real estate agent would have had trouble finding anything cheerful to say. The Grey Woods were halfway to being a swamp, the ground treacherous and squelchy, and the constant mist made it difficult to get any idea of where you were or even where you'd already been. But I knew the way up to the next level would be somewhere on the outskirts, and that fact alone was what gave me any kind of chance of finding my way.

In theory, all I had to do was keep the lifter station behind me, and I'd be heading straight out across the level on a radial track. Problem with that was that once I was a hundred steps from the station, I could no longer look back and see the huge lifter tower through the murk. I'm not joking. The tower was the size of the Empire State Building, a giant cuboid reaching all the way to the roof of this level, and it was already hidden by the dense mist. All I could do was try to maintain my direction by picking an object that I *could* see, then heading toward it, then picking another target by my best guess at the same direction. Efficient *and* fun, especially in a drizzling gray nothingness of skeletal trees and deadly quicksand bogs. And it got worse when I began to encounter the suicides.

In *The Inferno*, written in the days when the Church and other important moral influences still thought suicide was a cheater's way out, the Wood of Thorns was where all of those folks wound up after death, stuck inside the trunks of trees. "Stuck inside a tree forever," you say, "hah, that doesn't sound so bad." But in the poem, there are all these harpies flying around, things that looked like tubby owls with women's breasts—which doesn't sound frightening so much as just plain weird. The harpies would pluck limbs off the trees, which apparently really hurt, and would make the suicide trees weep. All together, a creepy setup. Tip of the hat, Mr. Alighieri. But if you offered every one of the souls in the real version of the Woods their choice, I think they'd have voted unanimously to move to Dante's version, which would have seemed pretty much a romp in the park compared to what they had.

I didn't know that yet. I didn't know that until I stumbled across my first self-murdered soul.

At first I thought he was a large lump of moss dangling from the limb of an ancient, gnarled oak tree, but as I got closer the mist cleared between us, and I could see the whole shape, including the pale feet and hands. Compared to some of the things I'd already seen, that wasn't much. Then as I got a bit closer I saw that the hanging man was alive and struggling.

I really should have figured it out at that point. I mean, Forest of Suicides, right? If killing yourself was a crime—or had been when these people were judged by Heaven—why would they be allowed just to hang around peacefully in Hell, being dead?

As I slogged through the mire toward it, I could see that the corpse was twitching, even clawing weakly at the noose around its neck. Yes, I know, I said "corpse," because that was sure what it looked like, with all the signs of post-mortem lividity (see, I've watched cop shows, too), eyes sunken, tongue black and protruding. But dead or not, this poor bastard was definitely suffering. I pulled out the big knife Riprash had given me, then scrambled up the spider-legged cluster of roots until I could hack through the rope. The first thing the suicide did when he hit the ground was to grab at the noose and loosen it around his throat.

"You shit!" he gasped, his voice as rough as you'd guess with someone who'd spent a good part of forever hanging by his neck. He was on his hands and knees, craning his head around on his lengthened neck so he could glare at me. "What have you done? Why did you interfere? I don't even know you!"

Interfere? I took a step back. The odor of rot that rose off him was so strong that even demon-senses couldn't entirely deal with it.

He struggled to his feet, although he could barely stand, and to my astonishment he began trying to throw his now-shortened rope over the branch so he could hang himself again. I took a breath before stepping closer, then grabbed at him but caught only his decaying clothes, which tore in my hands. His rope had been tied to the tree at one end, and I had halved its length by cutting it. No matter what he did, he couldn't get enough rope over the branch to hoist himself aloft again. When he turned toward me, I saw to my astonishment that he was weeping, viscous tears like snail's tracks edging down his bluish cheeks. "How could you!" he half-shrieked, half-wheezed, then clumsily began to swing his fists at me.

I had only a moment to figure out what was going on and to remind myself that my philanthropic efforts never did me much good even *outside* of Hell, when something dropped out of the fog that surrounded us and attached itself to the struggling corpse like a vampire bat in a Friday night horror movie. The hanged man was screaming in pain as well as weeping now, and although I knew I'd almost certainly regret it, I had to try to help him.

Remember when I mentioned Dante's harpies, the creatures who policed the suicide woods in his literary version of the Inferno? The real ones were a lot less pleasant than owls with tits. They looked more like gobs of phlegm the size of koala bears, with insect wings and faces that were mostly flat, square teeth. And it wasn't just one of them dropping down out of the murk, it was quickly becoming *a lot* of harpies, and they obviously weren't just there to punish the suicide, because another one of those horrid vampire boogers leaped onto my neck, beating its horrid fly's wings in excitement as it tried to gnaw a hole in me. By the time I managed to impale it on my blade, three more were crawling over my body, looking for a way to burrow headfirst into my guts, and I could hear the wings of dozens more as they swarmed toward us through the mist. And while all this nightmare bullshit was going on, my enemies were only getting closer.

forty-one
the pain report

SO THERE I was, being attacked by winged mucus-monsters in the Suicide Forest, wondering what could possibly make my day any worse, when I heard the one thing that unquestionably could: the distant baying of hellhounds. It was like a dagger made of ice right between my shoulder blades.

Not that I could do anything about it right at that moment, because the toothy little snot-harpies were swarming me, experimenting with different ways to get through my skin. The suicide I had tried to help had staved off his own attacker long enough to get his shortened rope over a lower branch. He tied it, then let himself go limp until the noose began to strangle him once more, this time with his feet on the ground. As he choked and struggled, the harpies rose from him like flies off a buffalo's back and headed toward me instead. Unpleasant as they were, there was no way I was going to throttle myself just to get rid of them, and there were far too many to stab or shoot, with more dropping out of the murk every moment. So I ran like a motherfucker.

I'd finally made a good decision. As I got farther from the spot where I'd tried to save the hanging man, the harpies began to drop away. Apparently they were territorial. Either that or lazy.

The farther I ran, the more bodies I saw. And "ran" is a relative term here, because trying to go fast over soppy, muddy ground through tangles of thorns and low-hanging branches was a bit like trying to sprint through barbed-wire bouillabaisse. As with the first suicide, none of these were exactly going quietly. Some were drowning in streams and ponds, often in less than a foot of water; others had blown their own brains out, or slit their own throats, or jumped from the tops of trees onto rocks and lay whimpering quietly as their brains, and other things that should have been inside them, dribbled onto the forest floor. All of them were clearly suffering, but I'd learned my lesson the hard way, and I ignored them. Hundreds of souls in pain, and angelic me just running right past them without a second glance.

Behind me, the howls of the hounds rose in volume, but then faded away again, till I began to hope they had lost my trail. The forest was getting darker and the mists thicker and thicker, until I could scarcely see more than an arm's length in front of me and reduced my pace to a cautious walk. I had gone several minutes without seeing any of the restless dead, so I hoped that meant I was getting close to the edge of the level.

A rock outcropping the size of a small tower loomed out of the tangle before me. No bodies lay beside it, which made me more than ever sure I was getting near the edge of the forest. I climbed it, so tired that my trembling arms and legs barely supported me, but when I got to the top I could finally see a bit of my surroundings past the mist.

Of course the news sucked: the forest looked like it went on forever, in all directions. I couldn't see anything except foggy treetops and the occasional lump of stone sticking up like an ancient skull eroding from the ground. For a brief moment I considered just waiting on top of the rock until the hounds and soldiers arrived, so I could at least take a few of them with me, but then I thought of Caz, of her face as she sat in that horrible, shrieking theater beside Eligor, and knew I couldn't condemn her to be that monster's prisoner forever.

I climbed down and stumbled on in the direction I had been going.

I hadn't seen any bodies for quite a while, until I stumbled over a girl in the stream, facedown in a very shallow pond that had gone largely red. I stopped, still a prisoner of my treacherous angel reflexes. She looked young when I turned her over, scarcely past puberty, her face white as the most determined goth made up for her Facebook profile. Both wrists were cut so deep I could see the tendons, because the blood had mostly run out. She moaned at my touch and shivered. I fought the urge to lift her up, to bandage her and try to heal her. I shouldn't have touched her at all, because I really didn't need any more harpies, but for some reason I couldn't just ignore this one as I had so many others. I didn't recognize her, of course, but she looked like the kind of person I might actually know—some poor soul condemned by God's justice to commit suicide over and over until all the stars burned out. I couldn't remember anymore what it was like when things made sense.

"Why did you do it?" I asked.

Her eyes opened but didn't really focus on my face. I think I must have been something like a dream to her. "Because I could think of nothing else. Because I even dreamed about it. Because I wanted peace."

"But you didn't get it."

She closed her eyes and moaned again, a sound far too deep and dejected for such a slip of a girl. In the real world she would have weighed no more than eighty or ninety pounds, if that. She should have been playing tetherball or studying fractions for a math test. "God hates my sin."

"I can't believe that." And I couldn't. I had never lost a client just for suicide; I think the prosecutors have to prove serious selfishness to get a suicide condemned these days. I asked again. "Why did you do it?"

"Everywhere I went, they stared at me." She shook her head and tried to crawl back toward the crimson water. "No. Don't make me talk. You'll bring the harpies. When it stops hurting so much, they come."

So it wasn't just the act of suicide, it was the pain as well that you had to keep experiencing here. I thought how, in their last moments alive, almost every pathetic soul in these woods must have thought, "At least it's all over now," only to wake up and find out not only wasn't it over, it had barely begun.

My God, my God, I thought. *How could you allow this in Your Name?*

I heard flapping in the mist above us then, so I stood. The wrist-slitter turned over and sank her face back into the pond. I hurried away, but I couldn't unsee what I'd seen.

I hadn't got past the suicides at all, it turned out, I'd merely been crossing a less crowded patch of the forest. As I stumbled on I passed a seemingly endless variety of living corpses, despairing humans who had killed themselves with fire, or water, or poison, or guns, a museum of final moments that would never end. I had learned not to touch them, and after the girl in the pond I didn't want to speak to them either, but I couldn't avoid them. In places they lay on the ground as thick as at Jonestown, other times they remained hidden and almost invisible until I nearly stepped on them, like macabre Easter eggs. And still the suicide forest went on, with nothing changing but the howls and shouts of my trackers growing louder as they began to close in on me once more.

My head was aching with unwanted movement, as though the thing Eligor had put there was excited by the sounds of my pursuers. Even the hardy demon body I wore would run out of strength soon. I had a sword—well, a large knife—but I wasn't going to have much luck fighting off giant hellhounds with the kind of blade they used down at the hoagie shop to slice rolls. I had guns, of course, and enough bullets to shoot a few of my pursuers and still save one slug for myself, but that idea wasn't very appealing either, especially not after spending time in this particular forest. More importantly, though, if I gave up, Caz's last chance was gone. I might not have managed to free her, but at least while I was loose there was still a chance.

I could glimpse my pursuers now only a few hundred yards behind me, dark running shapes that appeared and disappeared in the rolling mist. I wondered if I should go guerilla-style and pick off a few to improve the odds, but I suspected that trying to hide from the hellhounds and their snuffling, wet, pink snouts would be a bad move. No, I was simply going to keep running until I found a good place for a final stand, then make as much of a mess as possible before they took me down.

But plans change. I burst into a clearing and a momentary thinning of the mist, and was startled to find myself only a few steps from a deep ravine. I swayed for a moment on the edge, windmilling my arms to keep from falling in, then began to track sideways along the lip of the canyon looking for a way across. I could see farther here than I had for hours, clear to the other side of the canyon, and I could even make out a deeper shadow beyond the ravine. I tried not to let hope distract me at this crucial instant, but I prayed that farther shadow might turn out to be the outer wall of this level of Hell.

The ruins of an old bridge or causeway lay tumbled on the slope on the far side of the canyon. The near end of the bridge must have rested in the place where I had almost fallen. I started to make my way down the damp, crumbling cliff. Great chunks of earth and stone had fallen when the bridge went, and they provided the handholds I needed. I let myself slide to the ground at the bottom, and lay there in a heap like a sock monkey leaking stuffing. I might even have fallen into helpless, exhausted sleep for a few moments, but the howls of the hellhounds startled me awake again. Worse, either the howls or my sudden movement woke up Eligor's intracubus too, and the little cancer started moving restlessly in the back of my skull, each twitch shooting a bolt of fiery pain right through me. I had been trying to stand but could only drop to my hands and knees and sag there, facedown, hoping it would stop. But it didn't. The intracubus was fidgeting like a frog on a hot stone, and each time it moved it made me want to puke my insides out.

I had to get up. I could hear my pursuers very close now, perhaps moving along the top of the rise just above me. Everything sensible in me was urging me to get up and run to keep that from happening. By now, the nature of Hell was clear to me. Run and run and run or be punished forever. Sanity demanded I get with the program.

But I didn't.

Was the thing in my head really only a failsafe against me giving up Eligor's feather-secret if I was captured? How would it decide that my escape was no longer viable and hit the Destruct button? How was a crab-monster in my head going to judge? And maybe—this was a big one—maybe Eligor had lied to me in the first place. Maybe this was all just some kind of new torture the grand duke had devised, letting me run while all the time the intracubus was transmitting information to Niloch and his hunters as well. The hounds might be following my scent, but the commissar and his gang had certainly found me quickly enough here in the Grey Woods, and now the foreign thing in my head was making it hard for me to escape them again. Could all this be the Horseman's particularly nasty, drawn-out trick? Maybe he'd given up on getting the feather back, or maybe the intracubus was meant to spy on my thoughts and find out where the feather was really hidden, since Eligor had said he didn't find it, *or* my body, in the Walker house.

Once I started thinking this way it was hard to stop, and for some reason it made the intracubus even more fidgety. Nerves and muscles spasmed all over my body as the little ball of hate moved around in my head, and it was all I could do not to cry out and give myself away. One hard clench hurt so badly it knocked me off my all-fours crouch and onto my belly.

No more. I had learned Hell's most important lesson several times over by now: Don't trust anyone, and especially don't trust Eligor. It was time to do something I should have done hours before.

I still had the flask of demon rum Riprash had sent with me, dangling on my belt with the pistols and the swords. I took a long swallow of the godawful stuff and let it burn its way down into my belly like a river of lava, but I didn't take too much. Next I took the knife in my left hand because I didn't trust the misfiring, regenerating nerves in the other, and bent until I could rest my forehead on the damp, muddy ground like a monk at prayer. Then I poured the poisonous swill that Riprash had given me all over the back of my head. I swear it burned as badly as Eligor's crematory flames. I had to shove my face deep into the mud to silence my screams.

Things got worse from that point. My demon hide was healing so quickly that flesh had already grown over the crude stitches, so I had to cut through my own skin just to reach the knots before I sawed them open. Riprash's knife wasn't the sharpest, either, and what I was doing set the intracubus into a panic of claws and teeth. I'll let you imagine the details for yourself.

It's for Caz, I told myself as the worst of the pain shook me like a million volts, but what really kept me going was another, much darker thought: *Fuck you, Eligor. The only good thing about Hell is knowing you're in it forever.*

I kept pouring Riprash's booze over the wound as I worked. I'm happy to say that the intracubus hated the stuff, but that only made it struggle harder. I came close to passing out several times before I finally got my fingers around the horrible, horrible little thing and yanked it out—it felt like I was taking half the insides of my head with it. After that I did go black, but only for a short while.

When I came back to reality, the intracubus was struggling to escape across the muddy bottom of the ravine on its dozen little barbed legs, still trailing several of my nerve fibers. I guess I didn't need any of them too badly, or at least not enough to notice in the midst of so much fucking pain. I poured a last dollop of ogre booze into my breached skull and shook my head from side to side to swirl it around in the baseball-sized wound, then I got up on very shaky legs, found a large rock, and carefully ground Eligor's minion into a scummy smear. Its shrill screams, brief as they were, made little bubbles in the slime.

Oh, but it felt so good to have nothing in my head but my own dubious ideas, I can't tell you. I even licked the knife clean. Hey, it was my own blood, and I couldn't afford to waste any more of it.

Niloch and his lynch mob hadn't waited while I performed self-surgery, of course. Some of the hounds sounded like they'd already found their way down to the bottom of the ravine, which meant they were only a few dozen yards behind me. At least now, when the commissar and his penis-pups caught me, I would have the small pleasure of being able to scream out every secret of Eligor's I knew.

Yes, I was finally beginning to feel at home in Hell.

I clapped a hand over the hole in the back of my skull to keep inside what brains I still had left, then I began to run again.

forty-two
this lousy t-shirt

SO THERE I was, hobbling along, oozing brains and blood, at my lowest ebb, my pursuers closing on me, when a miracle happened.

Well, *I* thought it was a miracle. You unbelievers would probably call it a drainpipe—a big hole gushing water into Suicide Swamp and leading upward.

I probably mentioned before that the rivers of Hell run in and out of the different layers. I couldn't make a model for you if I tried because the physics are impossible, but Hell has holes. Conduits between the levels allow the rivers and their streams to flow through and down to the next level, and I had stumbled onto one of these conduits—a big stone tunnel. Although the water coursing out of it was as foul and disgusting as you'd guess, I thought it was one of the most beautiful things I had ever seen or even smelled, because at the other end, one level up, was the Abaddon level that contained my current number one favorite span, the Neronian Bridge. It felt like the Highest was saying, *"See? You doubt Me, and yet I reach down and give you an escape route. Still feel like busting My balls?"*

No time to celebrate, of course. Niloch and his hunters were sloshing through the undergrowth at the bottom of the ravine not far behind me.

I was lucky it wasn't an actual pipe, but a tunnel scraped by erosion through the raw stone of Hell itself, because there was no way I would have been able to climb through a real, slippery drain pipe with that much water rushing at me. But the rough stone and debris gave me handholds and footholds. All I needed was a little bit of luck and soon my buddies at the Compasses would be wearing souvenirs that read, "My Co-Worker Went To Hell, And All I Got Was This Lousy T-Shirt!"

Of course, nothing really happens "soon" in Hell except the pain reflex, and climbing up that wet tunnel wasn't the piece of cake I thought it would be. There were a few times when only my toe-tips and the fingernails of my one good hand kept me from tumbling back down into the bog of the Grey Woods. But at last I reached the top of the sluice and tumbled out into Abaddon. I stood there for a few seconds, drenched in the stinking, sticky waters of Cocytus, and coughed out some of the sludge I'd swallowed. Coughing really made the hole in my head hurt, of course. I was knee deep in one of several filthy rivulets that came together there, but more importantly, I was back on the same level where I'd found young Gob and begun my journey, so long ago that it seemed like it had happened to a different Bobby Dollar entirely. And, in a way, it had.

I was in a neighborhood that I had passed through before, cramped streets between slumping mud-brick dwellings, a place full of misshapen, shuffling figures, where every breath was full of red dust, and the sounds of violence and suffering never stopped. But Abaddon was the first layer above the Punishment Levels, which made it a place of freedom—at least in comparison with what lay below, starting with the Suicide Forest and getting worse and then even worse and then unimaginably worse the lower down you went. The creatures here in Abaddon were suffering because they were in Hell, but they weren't being actively tortured. These were the creatures the nobility of Hell shanghaied to use as slaves, the workers who performed Hell's most disgusting labors, and served as cannon fodder (sometimes literally!) in Hell's armies. They would have been the lowest of the low in all the universe, except for one thing—they still clung to a tiny bit of freedom, still made lives for themselves in the midst of horror. Some of them, like Riprash, even thought there might be something more for them someday, and dreamed impossible dreams of an end to torment—dreamed, perhaps, of an eventual taste of kindness. The things living here weren't just damned monsters, they were also human souls.

Just when I was in danger of turning maudlin, I heard a horn echoing from the stony walls, along with the distant but still unpleasantly clear baying of hellhounds. The commissar and his men must have retreated when they saw what I'd done and hurried back to the station to climb up to Abaddon in a lifter. Which meant my feelings of relief were bullshit: they were close enough to catch me long before I reached the bridge. Time to run again.

My head felt like a smashed melon, and I could have sworn I was on my last legs. In any other circumstance I would have been, but I didn't have the luxury of collapsing. I tried to recall every single thing Gob had shown me, every trick for getting quickly across Abaddon. I went right through the houses of the damned, I leaped from rooftop to rooftop like a comic book character—well, like an extremely tired, mostly one-handed comic book character—and took every shortcut I could remember, including one where I skittered down a crumbling wall with an immense, fire-belching pit beneath me instead of just the distant ground. Through luck and taking a few crazy chances, I managed to put enough distance between myself and my pursuers that the cries of the hellhounds grew faint, but I knew it wouldn't last.

I finally reached a spot where the streets ended and the dark, empty outer passages began. I had no lantern, but I had been a long time in these lower reaches, and my demon eyes served me well.

I did my best to make the narrow passages behind me difficult for my pursuers, pulling down stone and other debris wherever I could. I'll also confess to running down a few side-tunnels when the pursuit had fallen far enough behind me that I couldn't hear them, then scenting the false trail by sprinkling it with my own piss before dashing back to my chosen path.

One of the problems with being in Hell, I realized as I darted through holes and across open places like a frightened rat, was that you could never really relax, never stop to think about what was going on. I'd learned that lesson the hard way from Vera's house, where I did relax, precisely when I should have been thinking.

I might have chosen to come here, but it certainly hadn't been because I thought it would be fun. Leaving Caz out of the equation for a moment, I tried to make sense of what had happened and what I'd learned, on the *very* off chance that I'd survive to do something about it.

The undead horror Smyler had told me he received his marching orders from Kephas him- or herself. Could that be possible? I'd assumed it was Eligor who so badly wanted me silenced, but now that I thought about it, Kephas had at least as much to lose as the grand duke if the feather that signified a secret deal between important angel and important demon fell into the wrong hands. But would a heavenly VIP like Kephas try to destroy another servant of Heaven, even an unpopular one like yours truly? Then again, I'd wondered for years if a high-ranking somebody had silenced my old mentor Leo, my top-kicker in CU *Lyrae*. How much harder was it to imagine that one of my bosses sent a dead murderer to shut me up?

But Kephas was only a disguise for what I guessed was a fairly powerful angel: I still didn't know who my real enemy might be. What good would it do to escape Hell and save Caz if I promptly got bumped off by my own side? Or even worse, got Sam's whole Third Way thing pinned on me? My record didn't look good: my best friend Sammariel had been working for the Third Way mutiny all along, but when I had a chance to nab Sam, I let him go. Then I'd gone on an illegal jaunt to the actual factual Inferno to rescue my demon girlfriend and had even made a deal with Eligor the Horseman, right in his own demonic palace. I mean, really—how much spin would Kephas need to make me look literally guilty as hell? Not much.

But if this wasn't all some elaborate trick by Eligor (still a possibility) and it really had been Kephas who sent Smyler after me, not just on Earth but all the way to the place of eternal punishment, what could I possibly do about it? Until I knew who the enemy on my own team was, I was an easy target.

As I wearily stumbled through the bleak labyrinth on the edge of Abaddon, breaking occasionally into a desperate sprint when I found the strength, another realization crept over me. A very scary one—yes, even for a man fleeing hellhounds. The mysterious Kephas might very well be one of the five ephors investigating the whole Third Way affair, and also keeping a watchful, disapproving eye on Yours Truly. I wasn't positive that Kephas was one of them, of course—there were literally thousands of angels in the hierarchy above me. But if *I* were a big-time archangel doing something huge and underhanded, I'd want to be on the committee investigating it, not only to interfere with the inquiry in subtle ways but also so that I'd realize if they were getting close to finding me out.

Karael was the toughest and scariest of the Ephorate, at least to me;

he probably still had uniforms spattered with the blood of fallen angels from the Big One. But he also didn't seem like the type to go setting up an angelic daycare center full of socialist ideals like the Third
Way. The other four I didn't really know very well, except for Anaita,
with whom I'd had a brief, slightly strange conversation in the Hall of
Judgement before Karael showed up. Made me wish we'd had a
chance to talk longer. And although I still didn't know why Terentia
had been made leader of the Ephorate over the much better known
Karael, I didn't have any other information about her, bad or good, to
move her up the list of suspects. Chamuel and Reziel I knew even less,
although Reziel was interesting because he/she/it (or "se," as angel
speech put it) appeared to be sexless, just as Kephas had been, at least
according to Sam.

Of course that didn't really mean much, because any one of them
was capable of creating an impenetrable disguise, so I'm sure if Reziel
was the traitor, se could have made hermself appear as feminine as
Tinker Bell or as masculine as . . . well, as Karael.

And now I had another mystery to wonder about: What was angel
Walter Sanders doing in Hell? I couldn't believe it was a coincidence
that he'd been stabbed by the same guy trying to get me, and then just
happened to wind up down here in Hell. Smyler claimed he was taking
his orders from Kephas. Did that include an order to take Walter off the
game board first? Walter had been wanting to talk to me back at the
Compasses that night—was it something to do with all this? Then, of
course, his "death" and banishment to the nether regions had wiped all
that away . . .

It came to me so suddenly and so powerfully that I barely noticed
the mists rising around my feet, which meant I was close to the bridge.
I should have been capering with joy, but a new thought had blos-
somed like a nose-pimple on the morning of senior prom, and it would
not be ignored, even at this triumphant moment.

Walter, in his Krazy Kat form, *had* come up with something just as I
parted from him and Riprash and the rest. *"I remember something about
the voice that asked me about you!"* he'd called as I climbed into the landing boat. I'd had no idea what voice he was talking about, but what if
he'd remembered something from when he was still an angel? What if
that was what got him sent to Hell in the first place?

I was so caught up in these questions I almost brained myself on a low-hanging ceiling, which wouldn't have done my throbbing head any good. I was tired, stumbling, but I couldn't shut off the thoughts.

What had Walter told me? Why hadn't I listened more carefully? Yes, I had been worrying about a lot of other things just then, like fang jellies and hogsquids, but I was furious with myself now. The answer to everything, maybe—or at least the answer to who'd sent Smyler after me—and I'd let a few minor things like hellhounds and self-surgery flush it out of my memory.

I came out of the last stony passage a mere hundred yards or so from the gate and that ugly, glorious bridge. As I hurried toward it I struggled to remember everything from that moment I'd left the *Bitch*—the rotting smell of the Bay of Tophet, Riprash's huge hands passing me the cannonball that was going to weight my descent to the bottom, Gob's interested, skeptical face, and Walter in his damned form, looking like something that could only be found living in trees on Madagascar.

What had he said?

And then it came to me. *"It was a child's voice,"* he'd shouted as I lowered myself into the dinghy, desperate to let me know, to help me, even though I was leaving him stranded in Hell. *"A sweet, child's voice!"*

A hunting horn blared behind me, as startlingly close as a crow screeching on my shoulder. I turned to see the first of the hellhounds plunge forward out of the mist with its two dark, eyeless brothers right behind it, and beyond them the complicated shadow of a company of armed demons.

I sprinted toward the bridge, cursing the usual Bobby Dollar shitty luck. I was really irritated that I was going to be caught just when I finally had the answer to the riddle of Walter's banishment.

Anaita had a voice like that. Anaita, alone among those of Heaven's most powerful angels I knew, often spoke in a voice like a little girl. Wouldn't she disguise it? Not necessarily, not if she didn't realize the sound of her voice would be significant later. Perhaps she had merely asked Walter some questions about me in her normal role as an important heavenly officer, questions that he'd found odd. Perhaps that was what he meant to tell me when Smyler stabbed him. If so, Walter's earthly body had been murdered and his soul sent to Hell just to keep him from telling me that Anaita had been asking about me.

Wow. I knew the higher angels were different than me, but Anaita aka "Kephas"—ephor, Heavenly Principality, and Holy Guardian of Fertility—was evidently fucking *ruthless*.

It didn't matter, though, because I was never going to be able to do anything about it. Niloch and his Ugly Boys' Club were right behind me, and I hadn't even reached the bridge. It looked like my friends weren't going to get those souvenir T-shirts after all.

forty-three
mr. johnson and me

APPROPRIATELY, ROBERT Johnson's infamous blues song kept running through the back of my mind as I raced the last yards toward the bridge.

> *". . . Got to keep movin'*
> *Blues fallin' down like hail*
> *Blues fallin down like hail . . .*
> *And the days keep on worryin' me*
> *There's a hellhound on my trail*
> *Hellhound on my trail . . ."*

One of his very best songs. I don't know anyone who loves the blues who isn't fascinated by Johnson; his strange, short life and his haunted voice. And at the moment it was literal truth for me—hellhounds baying just behind me, Hell-soldiers and ratbat-crazy Commissar Niloch behind them—and that made it an odd time to have *any* song going through one's mind instead of one of the standard variations on *Oh my God I'm going to die run run run fucking run!*

Still, even an angel can have feelings of inferiority, and as I sprinted for my life and soul across the ashy, stony ground of the last inner cavern toward the gate and the Neronian Bridge, a part of me was actually pleased that I could finally consider Johnson without feeling like such a white-guy poseur. At last I could say, without reservation, "Yeah, I know just what you're talking about, Robert—I've had those blues. I know just what you mean."

Stupid, I know, especially at a time like that, but if I hadn't been stupid I wouldn't have been in that situation in the first place, would I?

I plunged through the gate tower, forgetting how close it was to the end of the Bridge. A couple of steps later, when I crashed into the first ashy, Pompeii-victim Purgatory creatures trying to force their way into Hell, I almost slid right off the bridge into that unimaginable abyss. Getting past them was like forcing my way through rotting Styrofoam. The silent shapes created just enough resistance to make things difficult and blocked my vision as well, not to mention that any damage I did to them left their soapy scum on the Bridge itself. Now try to imagine fighting your way through literally dozens and dozens of the things on a bridge less than six feet wide, with nothing beneath you for miles except screams floating up from the deeps.

I still had Riprash's giant knife in my belt, so I yanked it out and began to hack my way through the things. I know I'm an angel, and I'm supposed to be sympathetic by nature, but after having just spent a really long time in Hell, the thought that the only thing these horrible, mindless shapes wanted was to get into the place made me far less patient with them than the first time through. I shredded them like a cluster bomb in the middle of Smurf Village, sending bits flying everywhere like dirty suds. The hellhounds were roaring behind me as they encountered the first of the Purgatory refugees, and I fancied I heard a note of doggie surprise at how difficult it was to get through them.

As the throngs of faceless shapes thinned, I was able to pick up speed, but that meant the hellhounds were able to do the same. I heard their talons clank against the stone behind me, louder and louder, so I pushed my blade back into my belt as carefully as I could while running flat out, then pulled out one of my revolvers.

I still had plenty of loose bullets, but couldn't think of any foreseeable sequence of events where I'd get a chance to reload, so I slowed just enough that I could make sure every chamber of both guns was full, then dumped the remaining shells back into my pocket. Maybe my luck was turning, because that awkward movement caused me to stumble just a little, which saved me. A harpoon flew past my shoulder, trailing rope that burned the side of my neck before it curved away into the abyss.

I had wondered briefly why Niloch and his men hadn't been shooting arrows or guns once they were in range, but I realized now that they didn't want to lose my body off the bridge. They clearly had much more elaborate plans for me than just to shatter me on the rocks impossibly far below, or have me melt away to nothing in a fumarole of molten shit. Thus, the harpoons. Bullied office temps and grumpy commuters, trust me: you haven't really had a bad day until someone's tried to harpoon you.

I was already slowing down, exhausted but with hours yet to go, so I decided I should try to improve the odds a little. When I encountered another of the crawling Purgatory-things grubbing its way across the span, I vaulted over the obstruction, then stopped and crouched behind the humanoid shape and aimed both revolvers back at my pursuers. The grubby, wispy little thing wasn't going to shield me from anything, but I hoped it would at least obstruct my pursuers' view and create a second or two of confusion.

My old boss Leo used to emphasize taking one good shot over three or four bad ones (in most, but not all situations) but the honest truth was I didn't have time to take more than one shot: the lead hellhound was only a dozen yards behind me, its two fellows right on its tail, and the closest of Niloch's harpooners only another ten yards behind them. I braced myself police-style, breathed out, and shot the lead dog right in the face just as its scaly black muzzle retracted, exposing the disgusting pink underneath. I hit it square on and the dog's head unfolded in a red mist. Somehow, even with its snout exploded like an Imogen Cunningham flower made of blood and bone, the hellhound still managed to let out a shrieking yelp of pain and take half a dozen more steps before it stumbled and collapsed. To my further astonishment, it didn't die on the spot but got up, staggering, and looked like it might try to pursue me even with most of its head missing, but one of the other dogs ran helplessly into it from behind; both the bloody-mess hound and the second dog got tangled and tumbled off the bridge together.

I squeezed off another couple of shots, hoping to get the last hellhound while it was skidding and struggling in its doggy-pal's blood, but I missed. Niloch's men hesitated for a moment at the sound of the shot, but then hurried toward me once more, so I scrambled up and sprinted onward.

I caught a break I hadn't expected when the commissar's men tried to get the last hellhound moving again. Looking back, I saw that the ugly beast was refusing to budge, not because it was afraid of me (stop, don't make me laugh) but because it was so busy licking up the blood and brain fragments spilled by the one I'd shot. When one of the handlers tried to urge it forward with a whip, the hound turned on him, snapping at his face with that toothy snout and pulling off what looked like a good chunk of his nose and cheek.

I managed to reload both guns as I hurried on, knowing that the respite was going to be a short one; I could hear Niloch screeching to shoot the dog if it wouldn't get moving again. Unfortunately, I fumbled the rest of the bullets, then missed my grab as they bounced into the abyss. The commissar might have only one hound left, but he had about half a hundred armed followers against my total of twelve bullets.

Running as hard as I could, drawing on reserves of demonic strength that were probably well outside the body's normal factory specs, I managed to put a little distance between myself and the stalled hunters. Hearing Niloch's angry shrieks getting fainter was the sweetest music I'd heard in a long time.

I don't know how long I ran before I heard the sound of talons ringing against the stone again. It seemed like a long time, but I'd slid into a kind of unthinking state where not even old blues songs were running through my brain, only the slap of my own feet like a slowing metronome. I heard the hound crashing along behind me, very close now, then the noise suddenly stopped. I knew better than to assume something had distracted it, so instead of turning to look, I threw myself flat against the stone of the Neronian Bridge. A long shadow passed over me like a shark above a startled diver. It seemed to take a long time. Making the beast miss its killing pounce hadn't really done me a lot of good, however: the hellhound landed and kept its balance. In fact, not only didn't it slide off the bridge, it managed to spin around a few yards ahead of me, like a Mini Cooper making a handbrake turn, cutting off my escape. Any moment now Niloch and his men would be coming up behind, and that would be that. So I did the only thing I could do. I ran at the hellhound.

Okay, now if I were writing a book of advice for young angels, I would probably start it out with "Never, ever, *ever* go to Hell." Then I would add a footnote that said, "However, if for some reason you *do* happen to wind up in Hell, never, ever run directly at a hellhound." But I didn't have any choice, really, since it was now between me and any possibility of escape. I lifted my guns and fired as I went, but the beast was bounding toward *me*, moving so quickly that my two fast shots went right over it without even creasing its weird, leathery hide. It landed on top of me, and that's the last clear thing I remember for a little while except a lot of snarling and screaming (I think I was doing most of the second part). The drooling lamprey mouth darted at my face. The creature's eyeless head followed my every move as though I had filed a plan of action with Hellhound Central ahead of time. I had to use both hands to fend off the crazed hellhound, and while I was fighting I lost one of my guns over the side. Just when I thought I could get my remaining gun free to shoot the four-legged bastard, it struck like a cobra, sinking its teeth into the meat of my hand so that the gun flipped loose, clattering on the bridge. I reached for the blade, which— thank the Highest and all His very nicest archangels—was still in my belt. When I got the chance I shoved it through the hellhound's lower jaw and up into where its brain should have been.

I don't know whether the beast didn't have a brain in there or just didn't use it much, but it clearly wasn't going to die just because I drove a knife the size of a machete through its head. It did, however, seem to get grumpier, and began trying even harder to suck my face into its unpleasantly round, toothy mouth. I used the knife embedded in its jaw to keep it at bay, hanging onto the hilt for dear life as the hound kept forcing itself at my softer, more important bits.

I won't spoil your day by describing what genuine hellhounds smell like up close, by the way. You can thank me later.

It was a stalemate, one that I knew I was going to lose pretty quickly. The thing weighed twice as much as I did, and if a knife in the brain wasn't slowing it down, chances were I wasn't going to outwrestle it either. So I grabbed my last chance: I pulled my feet up under me, put them against the thing's bone-armored chest, and then shoved as hard as I could.

If I thought I'd get lucky twice, and it would fall away and slip off the bridge, I was disappointed. To be honest, I hadn't thought things through that carefully—I just knew the beast was about to eat my head, and that my head was something I shouldn't let it eat. The hound did fall back, and its back legs skidded out from under it, but that only meant it scrambled in place for a moment until it could find its balance and lunge toward me again.

But while that happened, I'd found my gun.

I lay on my back as the monster came toward me, with little chance to aim as carefully as I had at the first dog, so I emptied a couple of rounds into it as quickly as I could pull the trigger. I hit it in the chest, making a big, dripping red hole, and also blew off one of its ears along with a chunk of sloping skull, but although the thing whined and choked a little, it straightened its legs and took another few staggering steps toward me. Cursing like a man who's just seen his hated brother-in-law win the lottery, I shot again. This time I put a round square in its chest and the dog took a strange, awkward sideways step, then another, as if the bridge beneath it had suddenly slanted to one side, then it walked right off the span.

I heard angry shouts from the hunters who had just reached the scene, but I didn't bother looking: I was busy trying to struggle upright. If I'd counted correctly in all the confusion, I had one gun and one bullet, so I wasn't going to outduel Niloch and his boys, but perhaps, since they no longer had the dogs, I could outrun them. I was sure going to try.

Something hit me as I took my first steps—hit me *hard*, like I'd walked in front of a speeding pickup truck. I flew half-a-dozen feet forward through the air, flopped on my belly and slid, ending up with my arm and shoulder hanging off the bridge's edge. It all happened so suddenly that it took a moment to realize I had about a foot of harpoon sticking out of my chest. The fact that the harpoon was attached to one of my pursuers became clear a moment later when something pulled on it from behind and the harpoon slid back until its barbed head caught on my collarbone.

You will not think me too big of a sissy, I hope, when I tell you that despite my lack of tear-ducts, I did my best to weep like a disappointed kindergartener. Well, in between bouts of coughing up blood.

The cable attached to the harpoon yanked tight again, dragging me back from the edge. Through the horrible agony I reached up to grab the rope as I struggled to roll onto my back where I had a chance to defend myself. I had no strategy. All I could think of was that I didn't want anyone to yank on that barbed harpoon ever again until the universe ended.

Niloch was coming toward me past the creature who'd speared me, a squat, troll-like thug wearing a proud if unevenly-toothed grin. The commissar followed the tight, vibrating harpoon line like a child coming down to the tree on Christmas morning. His head had mostly regrown.

"And what do we have here?" Niloch murmured. "Oh, goodness me, oh, look! It is the Snakestaff creature, the one who ruined my beautiful, beautiful Gravejaw. I think that before we bring you back to the Mastema, we must make you answer for *that*, mustn't we? I think all we have to do is bring back a good-sized portion of you to be tortured by the Inquisitorial Board, hmmm? The head and a few dependent bits, perhaps? And after we have played with it, the rest can go into the mortar for rebuilding Gravejaw. That would be appropriate, would it not, my rude little guest?"

It took me a moment to figure it out, because so many parts of me were sending back messages of terrible, overwhelming pain, but I was lying on my gun. I reached under myself as unobtrusively as I could, meanwhile closing my eyes as if I had just given up, trying to get Niloch to move closer. One shot left. It wouldn't save me—there were too many other hunters behind the commissar—but I could at least take Niloch out.

When I thought I was in position to move quickly despite the pain, I tugged the revolver out from under me, aimed, and pulled the trigger. The noise was surprisingly loud for a place with no ceiling, the echoes snapping back off the cylindrical walls, over and over. It hurt a lot to roll and move so violently, so quickly, but it would have all been worth it if I hadn't missed.

Niloch didn't seem disturbed that a bullet had just flown past his bony head. "Tch," he said. "So unpleasant. First you destroy my sweet hounds, now you would attack me, too? For doing my civic duty? Shame on you, Snakestaff, shame."

I think the rattling noise was him laughing, but I was a bit distracted by the glow now hovering in the air just behind him. Several of Niloch's nearest soldiers were also staring. At first it was only a fizzle, no more than the smolder of a road flare, but then that fizzle suddenly dove down toward the ground, leaving an unstable streak of light hanging in the air. Just as Niloch himself realized that something was happening, a glowing hand appeared from the jagged, midair stripe of light; a second later Smyler bounded out of nothingness and onto the bridge beside Niloch. Even as the commissar opened up his bony jaw to shout an order, and well before his astonished soldiers could do anything, Smyler grabbed Niloch and jammed his four-bladed knife into the commissar's neck, then began to twist it around in a way that couldn't have been pleasant even for an arch-demon. Niloch screeched in pain and surprise. His men came crowding in around him, trying to pull loose the scrawny thing, but they couldn't get a decent grip. Smyler was literally climbing around on Niloch, clinging like the commissar was a bunch of bananas and he was some kind bionic-murder monkey.

I realized I was staring at all this with my mouth open when I should be running like crazy. I tried to get up, but the heavy rope still ran from the harpoon in my chest and all the way back into the melee, and now it was wound around several people. Every tug as they fought with Smyler made the harpoon twist in my bloody chest, an agony I won't insult with the weak word "pain."

"*Now it sees!*" Smyler screeched from the middle of the tangle. Niloch's men were fighting desperately to free their master, but they were limited by the narrowness of the bridge and Smyler's astonishing, horrifying quickness. "*It sees now. The reason. You are the reason. That is why you came before you should—it sees!*"

At the edge of the fight, the demon soldier holding my harpoon suddenly grunted, staggered, then tumbled off the bridge in a spray of his own blood. I had only a split-instant to brace myself against being yanked over with him, but to my grateful astonishment the rope lay slack on the bridge, a bloody meat spider still clutching its far end: the harpoonist had gone, but his hand had stayed behind, thanks to Smyler's crazy knifework.

Given a second's reprieve, I did my best to break the rope, because I couldn't run with that thing trailing behind me. It was going to be bad enough with the harpoon still waggling around in there, probably tearing the shit out of my demon lungs and demon heart. As I struggled to free myself, I backed carefully away from the melee. The space left by the harpoon-demon's sudden exit had given Smyler more room to work, and work he did. It was the damnedest thing I've ever seen, and I don't care if you pardon the expression.

Imagine a world-class but spastic ballet dancer. Now run the video in your head about three or four times faster, and try to imagine that ballet dancer carries a long sharp blade, and when it uses that blade on flesh it believes it's praying. I have never seen anything so horribly brutal that I could also call beautiful. I know it sounds weird, but it was art, like the wildest improvised solo you've ever heard spun out, sped up, and then landing at the end with a crash right back on the main riff. Everything happened so quickly it was hard to tell it wasn't planned. But nobody, not even a demon, ever planned to die like that, on the murderous blade of that giggling, rubbery thing.

Two more of Niloch's soldiers staggered bleeding off the bridge into nothingness. The whole pack of them now were converging on my unexpected savior like piranha in a feeding frenzy, but I didn't think it was Smyler's blood I saw fountaining in the air, or Smyler's fingers and ears flying out of the scrimmage.

"Run!" he shouted. "Run, angel!" Then, as if to prove Smyler's kind intent, something else came flying out of the ruckus and rolled to a stop near my feet, blood dribbling from it to join my own good-sized puddle. It was Niloch's long, skull-like head, the jaws snapping at nothing, slow as a dying crab. The wet red eyes rolled up, and it saw me. Somehow, despite no longer being attached to larynx or lungs, it said in a near-whisper, "I . . . will . . . !"

I didn't think, just stomped on it as hard as I could, feeling the bones smash beneath my foot. "Shut up," I said, then kicked the broken, ooz-ing lump off the bridge. "Just. Shut up."

I ran then, although it was more like hobbling, blood and brain mat-ter still oozing out of the back of my skull, clutching the harpoon stuck through my chest in both hands to minimize the horrible pain from its every movement—a picture William Blake might have painted after a really bad Saturday night. I ran until the bellows and squeals of Niloch's soldiers had fallen away behind me, then ran on, through a darkness I can't even remember now. I vaguely recall reaching the el-evator, but I think I kept running even after that, throwing myself blindly against the sides of the coffin-shaped box until I understood I was safe, or at least as safe as I'll ever be in this life, until I could finally say the words Temuel taught me and lay aside my demon body, until I could leave Hell behind me and surrender to blessed, blessed blackness.

I've never seen Smyler again since the Neronian Bridge. I don't know whether he survived. I'm not sure how I feel about that, but I am sure that he saved me when nothing else but God Himself could have done it.

forty-four
body in the trunk

SOMETHING FINALLY pulled the blanket of darkness off me, but I couldn't find the buttons and switches yet to make my muscles work correctly, so I lay there for a little while trying to figure out where I was.

I had left my body hale and well under a sheet in the late Edward Lynes Walker's house, so that was where I should be, but Eligor had told me his people had searched the place without finding it. That could mean anything, not much of it good. I had to be patient, though; this long out of my earthly shell made reintegrating a bit like one of those weird dreams you get when you think you're awake but you aren't, or at least not entirely. You hear noises and sometimes even voices from the real world, but you just don't care.

Not that I heard voices, because I didn't. I could feel my body, though, or at least *some* body: I had the cramped, prickling muscles to prove it, and I seemed to be wrapped in the appropriate sheet I'd left my body in. I decided to hope for the best. I was going to give myself another minute or two to reintegrate properly, then get out from under the bed in the upstairs guest room at the late Edward Walker's house and take a shower for about nine hours straight. If I was *extremely* lucky, Walker's granddaughter Posie and her boyfriend Garcia would be out somewhere, and I'd have the place to myself for a while, but that wasn't crucial. What I really wanted to do after my shower was go somewhere that had good food and alcoholic beverages and consume lots of both, then go home and do some actual sleeping—not that a few drinks and a nap was going to make me forget what I'd just been through. I also needed to check in with Heaven as soon as possible. Since I still had an earthly body to come home to, I assumed I hadn't been cast into the outer darkness quite yet, but it wouldn't hurt to check. At the very least, I'd probably missed a shit-ton of messages.

And, of course, I'd have to debrief with Temuel, but I didn't want to think about that yet. I'll be honest—the thought scared me. Yes, he'd done a lot for me, but I didn't know where he stood with Anaita, and nobody—not even Bobby Dollar, everybody's favorite poster boy for lack of impulse control—just jumps up and accuses a major angel and sitting ephor like Anaita of being a traitor to the Highest. Especially somebody like me, who was already on nineteen kinds of secret probation. Oh, and I had no admissible evidence whatsoever.

In fact, the more I thought, the more certain I was that I should just keep my mouth shut about most of it, even with The Mule, since I didn't know what game he was playing or where he stood vis-à-vis not just Anaita, but also the Third Way and all the rest of this crazy shit I was floundering in. However much he'd helped me, Temuel was clearly up to his halo in secrets and weirdness, and I didn't want to force him to choose between me and whatever else he had going on.

All this was swirling through my brain as I began to feel awake and connected enough to pull the sheet off my face and, Lazarus-like, rise from the tomb. Okay, rise from under the bed in the second guest room, the bed with the catalog coverlets and floral-print pillows, but you get the idea. I had already noted idly that the sheet wrapping me seemed to be a bit rougher and heavier than I remembered (not to mention quite a bit tighter) because of how it lay on my face, but as I tried to rise I realized that my problem was more complicated than that: it wasn't a sheet on me at all, it was a tarp, and it wasn't draped over me, it was wrapped around me from head to foot, so that my arms were pinned at my sides. This was *not* the situation I'd been in when I had last lived in this body. Not to mention that I could feel that something was moving me, bouncing me, even tilting me a bit from time to time, as though I were lying in the palm of a very, very large creature, and was being tilted at different angles while it decided which end to start eating first. (I had definitely been in Hell too long.)

Of course I kept my cool, because I knew the worst thing to do was start freaking out before I knew the facts. I calmly began shouting, "What the Jeezly fucking Christ is going on here? Somebody help me!" loudly and repeatedly. Okay, "calmly" isn't quite the right word, but I didn't only yell, I started pushing and scratching at the heavy tarp big time, inflating my chest and shoving outward with my arms, until I finally made enough space to get my hands up to my face.

Hands, plural. That was the first good news. Whatever else had happened to me, I had the full set of grasping implements in working order again, one attached to each wrist, with lovely bouquets of functioning fingers at the end. I could tell this because I was busily palpating my face, trying to tell if I was Bobby again, or still in the Snakestaff body. There were no stony lumps over my eyebrows or on my cheeks, and my skin felt much less sandpapery than it had in Hell, so I seemed to have returned to being B. Dollar, slightly itinerant angel. A probe of the back of my head found nothing but scalp and hair. No Doctor Teddy surgery scars either, so I was definitely out of the demon body. That calmed me down a little.

As I managed to work the canvas tarp a bit farther from my face and began to hear sounds more clearly, I finally realized that I wasn't just rolled in a tarp, I was rolled in a tarp and riding in the trunk of a car. Okay, I'd survived repeated tortures by various finalists from Hell's Got Talent, and pursuit by honest-to-Blind-Lemon hellhounds, so mere earthly troubles should have been no sweat. Still, I've watched *Goodfellas* and the *Godfather* movies often enough to know that *rolled up in a tarp in somebody's trunk* is usually not a situation you want to be in.

I did everything possible to work the tarp loose so I could use my arms properly, but the thing was thick (and old, and smelly, I might as well mention while I'm feeling sorry for myself) and I could barely pull it down past my forehead. Still, I could see that I was definitely in the trunk of a car, and I could get my hands out far enough to actually try to work the lock open on the inside of the trunk lid, but the vehicle was apparently too old to have one of those emergency-release latches. If I'd had more leverage, I might have been able to rip the entire lock out—I'm pretty strong in my earthbound body—but that wasn't happening, either, so I was left with only one heroic alternative.

As soon as I began pounding on the inside of the trunk lid the car started swerving around. Still, whoever was kidnapping me didn't pull over or anything, so I had to start thinking about what I could try next. I wasn't carrying my gun as far as I knew—I certainly hadn't been when I left the body behind, because who wants to spend days or weeks lying on top of a large foreign-made pistol, even if you're unconscious? At the very least I'd have been coming back to a body with a bunch of painful bruises, if not a few accidental gunshot wounds. So what was I going to do when they came to take me out and finish me off? And who had grabbed me, anyway? Eligor said his people hadn't even found my body, let alone the feather. Was Anaita making sure somebody finished the job she'd originally given to Smyler?

I wouldn't have to wait much longer to find out: the car was slowing down, the jouncing growing less. I redoubled my efforts to get free of the tarp and even the odds a bit, because wrapped in canvas I was about as dangerous as a large burrito.

I had finally worked my upper body free when the car stopped. Someone fumbled with the trunk lid. Disgusted with myself for not having hidden some kind of weapon on my body before leaving it helpless, I braced myself against the floor of the car. When the trunk popped open, I shut my eyes to keep myself from being blinded by the glare, and struck out as hard as I could with my fist. I had the deep satisfaction of hearing somebody gasp in serious discomfort and fall down, so I opened my eyes, kicked my way loose from the canvas, and started climbing out of the trunk, but slowed down a bit when I saw that instead of Luca Brasi or one of Don Corleone's other button-men, I had instead just punched Clarence the Junior Angel right in the nuts.

"What the fuck are *you* doing here?" I shouted. "In fact, what are you doing *period*? Why am I in the trunk of a car?" This might have been a bit unfair to Clarence, who was lying on his back, curled up like a dying insect, moaning with pain and nausea, and not in the best position to answer questions.

I heard the driver's side door slam. A moment later Garcia Windhover, aka "G-Man," aka "World's Most Useless Human" came trotting around the side, dressed in his usual gangster drag, like he'd put together his Young Jeezy outfit during a sale at Hot Topic. He'd added to it this time with a black eye patch, which made him look less like a pirate or Nick Fury than like a fourth-grader being treated for lazy eye. "Whoa!" he said, looking worriedly at Clarence, who was lying in the road next to the car quietly retching and panting like a woman in painful labor. "Bobby, dude, why'd you do that?"

"Why'd I do that? No, why am I in the trunk of a car?" I looked at the gaudiness and unnecessary chrome and winced. "Even worse, *your* car? I don't want even my *dead* body in this car, ever. And what's Clarence doing here, Windhover? He wasn't supposed to know about this."

"I needed some help."

"You're going to. That's a promise. I didn't mean to sock Clarence in the balls, I was just defending myself against kidnappers, but you . . ." I glared at G-Man so direfully that he actually took a couple of steps back. "I'm going to punch you in the manfruit over and over again until you're ringing like the bells of Notre Dame when the hunchback bought caffeinated by mistake."

I actually felt better after I said all that. More like my old self. I sat for a moment on the edge of the open trunk, then bent to help Clarence off the ground. He didn't want to get up at first, but after a moment let himself be coaxed into, if not standing, at least being partially upright.

"Oh, oh, oh," he moaned, still holding his crotch. "Bodies suck. I think one of them *popped*." We were on a side street just off the Camino Real, and a few pedestrians were checking us out, probably wondering whether someone was peddling stolen goods out of the back of their car. Which Clarence and G-Man were, in a sense, since I had stolen myself right out of Niloch's clammy hands. Thanks to Smyler, of course. It felt very weird to think that, I'm sure you can imagine.

"Sorry, Junior," I said. "Honest, I didn't know it was you. All I knew was someone had wrapped me up in a tarp. I figured some bad guys were going to dump me in the baylands or something."

Clarence winced and shook his head. "We were taking you back to Garcia's house."

"You mean Garcia's sort-of-grandfather-in-law's house? The place I already was? Where he was supposed to keep my body safe and sound and *not* put it in the trunk of his godawful embarrassment of a car and drive it around San Judas like I was a bunch of Mexican dress shirts heading to a flea market?"

"You sound pissed, dude," G-Man said.

Always quick on the uptake, that lad. "Just a little. And I'll probably get over it. But right now I'd like to be somewhere other than by the side of a road, so why don't we go back to Posie's granddad's house, Windhover, and you can explain to me what exactly is going on?"

G-Man nodded. "Okay. They probably took the tent down by now."

*   *   *

It turned out that Edward Walker's nice house in the Palo Alto district, where G-Man and Posie had been squatting for the last few months, was going on the market. As part of that process, the real estate agent had informed Posie that the place would have to be tented for termite fumigation. I suppose I should have been grateful that G-Man had the brains at least to figure out that a massive dose of pesticide might be bad for my body, but he handled it in typical idiotic fashion. I was too heavy for him to carry, he said, so he'd recruited Clarence—who, you may remember, I had *intentionally not told about any of this*—to wrap me up in the tarp, carry me out, and drive me in G-Man's car over to the place in Brittan Heights where Clarence rented a room. I'd spent the last few days in a toolshed that Clarence's landlords never used. The Littlest Angel at least had the wit to look embarrassed about this.

"A toolshed? Really? What, just propped up with the spiders and earwigs and whatevers crawling all over me?" I knew I was being unpleasant about it, but I wasn't ready to care yet. Maybe having just spent a massive amount of time undergoing torture in Hell had something to do with that.

"No!" said Clarence. "No, Bobby, I put you on an old pool table. I kind of made a space and then stacked some other stuff on you. You weren't just propped up or anything. And I didn't see any spiders."

"Thanks for that. It's nice to know I was so well cared-for."

Clarence frowned. "You don't have to be so bitchy, Bobby. You already punched me in the testicles."

"True." I nodded, downed the rest of the bottle of pisswater that Garcia kept in the late Edward Walker's refrigerator, some weak-ass hipster beer that used to be drunk by blue-collar guys because it was the only weak-ass crap they could afford, and was now supported almost entirely by nostalgics with tattoos and semi-expensive bicycles. Still, that stuff was better than no beer, although the contest was closer than you might think. "Sorry about that again, Clarence. Really truly. Self-defense, disoriented and confused, probably even PTSD. Put that together and make an excuse out of it you can live with, okay?"

He gave me one of his looks, somewhere between "hurt puppy" and "irritated older brother." I might not have wanted to trust him, although I was going to have to now, at least to an extent, but how could I dislike anyone who was so easy to annoy and so profitable to tease?

"So . . . what were you doing, Bobby?" he asked.

"Crazy shit. Don't try it at home," I said. "Seriously, don't try it anywhere else, either. Let's go find me some real food instead of this box of Triscuits and I'll tell you what I can."

"You want to ride in my whip?" G-Man asked.

"You were not included in the invitation," I said. Because it was going to be hard enough talking to Clarence, who at least knew I was an angel, being one himself. There was no way I was going to include Garcia Windhover in the discussion.

G-Man's expression, though, was so much that of the kid who not only doesn't get picked, but also the team that gets stuck with him then demands compensation, that I felt sorry for him. "Okay, you're right, Garcia, I at least owe you dinner. I mean, you may have carried me around in your trunk like a deer you ran over on the road and were trying to sneak home to make venison jerky, but I survived." I would come up with some sanitized, non-terrifying-to-ordinary-humans version of what had been going on, although I'd need at least another couple of drinks in me before I could imagine what that version might be.

After the explanations-obligations were disposed of, I'd get back to my real job: getting Caz out of Eligor's clutches. I hadn't forgotten that for a second, especially because I was now wearing my jacket again, the one with the secret angel-feather pocket which happened to be in another space/time continuum. Eligor had actually told the truth about not being able to find it, because if he had, there was no way he'd have let me escape Hell. "And then afterward, you, Clarence my man, can drive me back to my charming apartment, assuming my landlord hasn't already rented it to some wife-beating crackhead, and I'll catch you up on company business on the way."

"I'm down wit' that!" said G-Man. "You want to hit the Chinese place down in Whisky Gulch?"

"Sure. But one thing, Windhover. If you're going to hang around with me, you may not wear that eye patch. Not in public." It reminded me too much of the Broken Boy's helper, little Tico. That kid hadn't been covering up to look cool; he had been hiding something ugly and painful.

"But it's a tribute to Slick Rick!"

"And Rick would agree with me. For one thing, Slick is actually missing an eye. You aren't."

The G-Man pouted but agreed to leave his newest accessory behind. I almost told him that, even without it, he would have looked right at home in Pandaemonium, capital of Hell, but he probably would have thought that was a compliment.

forty-five
job creation

IF SOMEONE had asked me what I'd do if I ever escaped from Hell, my first guess would not have been pot stickers and cashew chicken, but that's how it turned out.

My second guess would have been pretty close to the money, though: As soon as I got back to my apartment, which was as dingy and unwelcoming as always, I promptly took a very, very long shower and then slept for the next fourteen hours straight. When I woke up, I was so pleased to find myself back in San Judas and wearing an ordinary (or at least non-demonic) body that I showered all over again, sang Dinah Washington songs at the top of my voice, and finished with a smoking rendition of "Don't Get Around Much Anymore" that caused a tin-eared neighbor to pound on the wall. I ignored the critic. Don't get me wrong, I had plenty of new scars that were never going to heal completely, and nightmare-fodder that would last for centuries, but things were finally moving my way. I was not so much of an idiot that I assumed exchanging the feather for Caz was going to be as straightforward as doing it with someone who *wasn't* a cheating, murdering, psychopathic demon lord, but I knew Eligor and I both wanted what the other guy had, and that was good enough to start with.

I got the main switchboard at Vald Credit and slowly worked my way up the ladder, dropping names and telling lies until I made it all the way to Eligor's own personal assistant. This one had an English accent, which reminded me a bit of Caz and made my heart beat even more impatiently.

"Who are you?" she asked—a bit bluntly, I thought.

"Bobby Dollar. Your boss knows me."

"Does he? I've never heard of you."

She seemed to be trying to piss me off. Well, that might have worked a few weeks ago, but not now—not on The Angel Who Walked Through Hell. I couldn't help wondering if she'd behave any differently if she knew I was the one who shot her predecessor through the face and then helped her out a fortieth-story window. Maybe she'd be grateful to me for that bit of impromptu job creation.

"Doesn't matter what you think," I said. "Just tell your boss. Tell him I'm back, and I'm ready to do the swap."

"Huh." She didn't sound impressed, but she did pause for a second. She might even have been paying attention. "Okay, the swap. Got it."

"Yeah, tell him that he picks the time, I'll pick the place. All nice and cozy and aboveboard."

"Fabulous. I'll pass it along." And then she hung up. Hung up! Some bloody personal assistant, treating Eligor's associates like that. Of course, it hadn't been that long ago that her boss was busy setting all my nerve endings on fire, so I guess it wasn't that rude, given the context. I even wondered a little if it might be the same secretary I'd killed, just re-bodied (and with an English accent this time for extra *zing*).

Now I needed a place to do the exchange. Even if Eligor actually meant to honor the bargain (something I wasn't taking for granted) I was going to need help.

I left a message on the phone number Sam had given me, then got on with my other post-Hell errands. I went down to the Compasses to see my angel friends and made up crazy stories about where I'd been for the last three weeks. (Yep. It turned out I'd only been gone three weeks. Like I said, time runs differently in Hell. They sure could pack a lifetime's misery into twenty-something days.) But I was so pale from lying in a closet all that time that I had an inverse suntan, so I told them I'd gone up to Seattle to visit a friend. Monica, who knew me better than anyone now Sam was gone, treated this fiction with the contempt it deserved, but she didn't press me for the actual details. She probably assumed I'd been shacked up with someone. I had a few questions for her, however, and waited until we had a table to ourselves for a few minutes while Young Elvis and Teddy Nebraska arm-wrestled at the bar and everyone else made fun of them.

"What about Walter Sanders?" I asked. "Has anyone heard from him?" I knew they hadn't because I knew where he still was, which was serving as purser on *The Nagging Bitch*, sailing the seas of Hell and spreading the Lifters' message, but I was curious what people thought about his disappearance.

To her credit, Monica looked worried. "No, nobody has. I asked The Mule, but he says he thinks he's been transferred. It's just shit trying to get information out of the Big House."

"Amen." Which reminded me, I definitely had to talk to Temuel soon. The archangel deserved at least an edited report on what had happened to me, since he'd been more instrumental in getting me there (and back) than anyone else, and I in turn had quite a few questions I needed to ask him. "And you, kiddo. How are you doing?"

I just meant to be affectionate. We'd been through a lot together, Monica and I, and if much of that time I'd been trying to escape having a proper relationship, well, that wasn't her fault. But as soon as I said it, she started looking furtive, even guilty. "Okay, I guess. Why? I mean, you don't usually ask, Bobby."

"Sorry. Didn't mean to break any rules . . ."

I never got to finish my thought, because just that moment, to everybody's surprise (mine even more than the rest) the door of the Compasses swung open, and my dear old friend Sam Riley walked in. I nearly fell out of the booth.

Monica jumped up and ran to hug him. Within moments almost every angel in the place was swarming him like bees come to watch the honey-dance. Sam laughed and shook hands, even accepted some hugs and kisses, which wasn't much like him. At last he shouted to Chico to get him a ginger ale, then let himself be backed against the bar while the rest of his chums threw questions at him.

Chico the bartender looked almost as nonplussed as I was, as if he knew about Sam's real current status with our bosses, but he kept his mouth shut and kept the ginger ales coming. As far as I knew, Clarence was the only other person besides me who knew that Sam was officially a Traitor to Heaven, but I was still so surprised to see him there,

I could hardly speak. What was Sam doing? Was he trying to force our bosses' hands, somehow?

I hung back while Sam spun some crazy tale to the Whole Sick Choir, hinting that he was on some kind of super-secret undercover mission (which raised the question of what he was doing here, in broad tavern-light, but nobody bothered to ask). With a notable lack of interest in his own safety, my old buddy sat in the Compasses for nearly an hour, answering questions (or, to be more honest, pretending to answer questions while lying through his teeth) and acting pretty much like the same old Sammariel that everyone missed so badly. At the end of the performance he finally slid past the others to me, draped one of his large arms over my shoulder, and suggested we go grab a late-night bite.

The residents of the Compasses lined up to say goodbye like Sam was visiting royalty. They made him promise not to be a stranger and reminded him of several upcoming events that, in other times, he would have been part of. Sam laughed and promised he'd do his best to make each and every one. That part was a lie too, but I think most of the angels knew that. They might not have had any idea of the true reason, but Sam's return had the distinct air of someone who had moved on—who was only back for a visit.

As soon as we got outside, I was up in his face. "What are you *doing* here, man? Really? You're just going to waltz in like nothing's wrong? What if Clarence had been there? He would have tried to arrest you again."

"I knew he wasn't there. As for me showing up at all, well, think of it as my plan to keep our bosses guessing."

"What do you mean, '*our* bosses'? You're on the Enemies List, remember?"

Sam looked up and down Main Street. "You know, I wasn't making that up about being hungry. I'm starved. One thing about living in a pocket universe and not wearing a mortal body most of the time, you get really nostalgic for food. Is that Korean place on the edge of Spanishtown still open late?"

"Bee Bim Bop? Yeah, I think so."

We got there and found a small line of hipsters blocking the door, but it didn't take too long to get a table, even on a Friday night. I had rediscovered beer since I had returned from you-know-where—that was one of the things I had been thinking about the whole time, how good a cold beer would taste instead of one of the weird root-based drinks they served up in Hell. Hell-beer might get you shitfaced even quicker than the earthly stuff, but it was about as refreshing as drinking lukewarm bathwater after a fat guy's gotten out of it.

I ordered a bowl of the stuff the restaurant's named after, rice and shredded meat and fried egg. Sam had his usual order of inexplicable soup, followed by several kinds of hot, spicy stuff, and we mostly concentrated on eating and drinking—tea, in Sam's case. By the time I was working on my second beer I finally felt ready to talk, so I started with my meeting at the Museum of Industry with Temuel, then gave him the rest of it—abridged, of course, or we would have been there for days.

"Well, B, I don't want to say 'I told you so,' so I'll just say, 'What a dumbshit,' instead." He shook his head. "I did try to tell you not to go there, though."

"Yeah. And I want a little credit for how hard I had to work to ignore you." I leaned back and signaled for another Sapporo. We were close to the only patrons left in the place now, the hands of the clock reaching for midnight like a stick-up victim's, but I leaned forward and lowered my voice anyway. "I'm gonna tell you something, Sammy-boy." I was definitely feeling all those beers. My body had gotten out of practice while I had been filtering Inferno-booze through demonic kidneys. "Yeah, it was probably stupid, but that's not what's bugging me. It's the whole setup. Hell. Heaven. I mean, you should have seen it. It was horrible, but they were alive, Sam. They were doing things, making plans, struggling to get by. Shit, in some ways it wasn't that different from San Judas."

"I could have told you that, and I've only been to Jude."

"I'm not joking."

Sam smiled. "I know you're not. And I know tomorrow morning you'll think you were telling me really important stuff, BD. But just remember this when you've pissed all that beer out of your system: I already figured this shit out."

"Huh?"

"Why do you think I parted company with our original corporate sponsors? Why do you think I'm living in exile in a hole in reality that both Heaven and Hell will be happy to disintegrate back into the ether as soon as they find out where it is? Because I can't put up with this shit anymore. Who knows, maybe our bosses are right." He frowned. "Maybe they're telling the truth about everything, and maybe sheer nastiness really is the only way that Good will ever defeat Evil. Maybe by bowing out of the Cold War I've just doomed you and the rest of my friends when the Last Trump starts blowing and the dead get up and salute." He looked flushed, as if he'd been drinking something other than rice tea, but after a moment I realized it was something else, a deep, deep anger. "But you know what? I couldn't do it. I couldn't just keep pushing an agenda I didn't believe in. And if you ever get to feeling the same way, Bobby . . . well, just let me know."

I stared at him. It was strange, seeing this Sam. I knew about his change of heart, his decision to act on his principles and join the Third Way—hell, I'd had it rubbed in my face on that night at Shoreline Park—but somewhere deep down I'd never quite let myself believe it, as if all this political stuff was just a lark for him, like a pop musician who suddenly wanted to play real roots music. It wasn't just a lark, though. And if I thought about it long enough, it began to make sense.

I couldn't afford to think about it that long.

"Yeah, but what I need from you now is something a bit more specific, pal." I picked up the check and looked it over, then put a couple of twenties and a ten on top of it and set it back down on the little tray. "Yes, I'm buying. That's why you're going to earn your meal. I need a place to make the exchange. Any suggestions?"

"With Eligor?" He shook his head. "Of course with Eligor. Right." He drew circles with rice tea on the tabletop as he considered. "I'd say you have to pick a public place, for safety's sake, but the more I think about that the less certain I am."

"Why?"

"Because someone might recognize you. You're already walking a tightrope with the Big House folk. All they'd need is a report that you've been meeting up with Eligor the Horseman, and you'd be headed for a Deep Audit." Which was a way of saying I'd have my soul taken apart by Fixers, fleck by fleck, and everything I'd ever felt, thought, said, or done would be delivered to people like the Ephorate, at least one of whom was probably my sworn and deadly enemy. From the rumors I've heard, Heaven's interrogators are as thorough as the torturers of Hell, just a bit more subtle. "Well, where then?"

"I don't know. I'll figure it out and call you. I've got a few things to take care of while I'm here in town, but I'll be thinking about it."

"Things?"

"Jeez, Dollar, you're not the only friend I have in the real world, you know." He picked a toothpick out of the bowl on the front counter. "You might be the only one who'll go out to Korean at eleven o'clock at night, though, so I'll do my best to come up with a location that will improve your chances of surviving. Fact is, I think I better come with you on this little mission."

I finished the last of the beer in the bottle, then caught up to him as he went through the door. "Last couple of times you've come along to help me we almost died. Almost died *ugly*, too. Let's try to do better next time."

He saluted me with an imaginary glass. "Confusion to our enemies, sport!"

"Yeah." I walked out beside him, but he held up his hand.

"Don't worry about me," he said. "Like I said, I've got some other stuff to do tonight. I'll call you. Tomorrow at the latest."

I watched him saunter off, hands in his pockets and big shoulders rounded. It had gone cold, especially for a July night, and I was just considering whether I wanted to stop back in at the Compasses or head home when someone softly cleared her throat just behind me.

I spun around. Standing in the garish light of the Korean restaurant's window was an old Hispanic-looking woman, a stranger. She extended a hand toward me, and I saw she was holding a slightly ratty bunch of carnations with a rubber band around them.

"No thanks," I said out of reflex, but even as I did so I realized I had done a dangerous thing, walking out into the night with my guard down. And just as I realized this, I realized I had seen this woman before, but not as a woman. Something in the face was familiar, but I couldn't quite put my finger on it.

"You're not going to buy a flower from a nice old lady, Bobby?" She smiled, showing me some authentic-looking, small-town Mexican dentistry. "How about taking a stroll with me, then?"

I had my hand inside my coat, groping for the butt of my FN, before I realized who it was. "Temuel?" I whispered. "Is that you?"

The archangel nodded and rearranged her headscarf. "And I really would like to take a little walk."

forty-six

the funniest racist i know

IT WAS about midnight, but the Camino Real was still pretty busy. We walked south, past the clubs and liquor stores of the mixed-up neighborhood that had grown between Spanishtown and the rich, might-as-well-be-private streets of the Atherton District. We walked more than a few blocks, and Temuel didn't seem in any hurry to start talking.

Meanwhile I was doing my best to figure out where my archangel and I stood. There were some things I was definitely going to tell him, including how I delivered his message in Hell, and what happened because of it. There was some other stuff I thought I should mention, but carefully, like the fact that Walter Sanders was now working as an accountant on a religious missionary's pirate ship in Hell. But there were other things I felt much less comfortable discussing: Caz was one of them, of course, but so was a lot of the stuff about Smyler, most definitely including the fact that I now felt pretty sure the crazy little monster was sent by Anaita, a high-ranking angel who just happened to be one of Temuel's own superiors.

Someday I'd love to be able to have a conversation with somebody who has no secrets or subtext, just to see what it's like. I bet it would be fun. At the very least, it would be less exhausting than what I usually have to go through.

It was probably only coincidence, but as we passed an Episcopalian church, Temuel finally began to talk. I could see the lights inside, but since there was a janitorial service van parked in front, and I could hear the loud moan of a vacuum cleaner, I guessed the church was open for cleaning rather than for a late-night spiritual crisis.

"I'm glad to see you back, Bobby," Temuel said. "I was worried about you."

"Thanks. I was worried about me, too."

"Were you able to deliver my message?"

"Yes, as a matter of fact." I told him the whole story of my time with Riprash—well, most of it: I hadn't mentioned Walter Sanders yet, and I didn't go into a lot of detail about my own itinerary before and after delivering Temuel's message, but I'd been strangely touched by the Lifters and felt he deserved to hear about it. "Am I right in thinking you've traveled there yourself?" I asked.

"Yes, but I'm not free to talk about it." That was unusual right there—a higher angel who didn't give you the truth wrapped up in a lot of fortune-cookie vagueness. "Now, let me ask you a question, Bobby. The ideas these Lifters have—do you think Riprash will be able to spread the message?"

I had no idea whether the missionary work was a project of Temuel's own conscience or whether it was part of a larger heavenly strategy, but I answered him as truthfully as I could. "The system is so weighted against him and his message that I can't be real optimistic. But if anyone down there's able to do something with it, Riprash is the guy. He's strong as an ox, smarter than most of the other folk, and has a pretty good heart for someone condemned to an eternity in Hell."

Temuel nodded, then looked down at his phone, which I realized he'd done several times. "Are you expecting a call?" I asked.

He gave a little laugh. "I'm just looking for cell phone signatures from Heaven-issued phones. I keep getting a ping from one pretty close by."

I wasn't used to this side of Temuel. It was like watching your sweet old grandpa turn into Q from the James Bond movies. And I'm guessing about that since I didn't know my own grandfather any more than I knew Alexander the Great. "Do you think you're being followed?" I asked him. "Watched?"

"I'm not worried about that so much as about bumping into one of your co-workers."

I looked at him and tried not to laugh. "Um, but you look like some lady who runs a corner bodega. How are any of them going to recognize you?"

He gave me a slightly disappointed look, as though I'd failed a test. "It can't hurt to be careful."

It occurred to me that other than the occasional visit to Hell, and this, his second offsite with me, The Mule might not get out of Heaven very often. "Okay. You know best. But now I've got to talk to you about some other stuff."

I gave him the rundown about how I'd met Walter Sanders in Hell. Temuel listened without comment, except to ask me what Walter, who the Mule called by his angel name, Vatriel, had remembered of his transition from off-duty advocate to infernal accountant.

"Nothing, really." I was leaving out my interactions in Hell with Smyler and any suspicion of Anaita's involvement, of course, which was a lot to leave out. There was a perfectly good chance Temuel was on my side—a mere archangel wasn't supposed to be personally messing with Hell anymore than I was, so he certainly had secrets from our bosses—but angelic politics were too murky for me at the best of times, and the last few months had made them even freakier. "The whole thing's pretty much a mystery. Someone tried to stick a knife in me outside the Compasses, as far as I can tell, but Walter got stabbed instead. Next thing you know, Walter's in Hell with amnesia."

"Vatriel was talking to you when it happened," Temuel said shrewdly. "Maybe someone was trying to send you there instead."

Which was pretty much what I'd thought myself, until Walter told me the last little bit he remembered, the sweet, angelic voice asking him about Bobby Dollar. The first attack might very well have been *about* me, but I was pretty sure now Walter really had been the target. Again, I kept this from Temuel. Damn, it was frustrating to have this kind of open access to a higher angel and not be able to take advantage of it. Still, those who know me would probably say whatever keeps me from rushing in headfirst is a good thing, and I really was trying to learn how to keep my mouth shut and my ears and eyes open.

"So, after all this, where are we?" I asked by way of changing the subject.

Temuel looked up from his phone and glanced around. "I think we're coming up to Oakwood Road."

"No, I mean where are *we*? This is crazy stuff, and obviously there's a lot we're not even discussing, like how you know what you know and why I wanted to go there in the first place."

"I trust you, Bobby. And I hope you trust me."

"Of course." I trusted nobody.

"Good." He put his arm through mine. We continued walking, me and the tiny little Hispanic lady with the invisible halo. "I think we should leave everything just like this for now," Temuel began, just as a car pulled up alongside us and screeched to a halt.

This time I did have the butt of my Belgian automatic in my hand and halfway out of my jacket when I recognized the vintage blue Camaro; a moment later I saw the driver's head and the insane, expansive crest of hair that clinched the deal.

"Hey, Bobby!" yelled Young Elvis. "Who's your girlfriend?"

He gunned the engine, which rumbled like a drug dealer's powerboat. It was a pretty car, even I had to admit, with twin racing stripes down the front. Young E. may be kind of a twit, but he's the only angel I know who really gets cars.

"What the hell are you doing in this part of the world?" I asked him, discreetly letting go of Temuel.

Young Elvis looked the archangel's human disguise up and down and made an amused face. "Seriously, Dollar," he said as I reached the curb, "are you dating your cleaning lady or something?"

"You're the funniest racist I know." I leaned into the open passenger side window. "Got a client?"

"Just finished with one. Nice enough guy. Fell off a roof. Half the neighborhood was standing around crying. What are you doing here? And, really, who is that?"

"The woman? She's just some poor old homeless lady who started talking to me."

"Seriously?" Young E. grinned. "You weren't hitting on her? You two look close."

Normally when he got this annoying I'd have spent some time explaining to him why he was a serious candidate for Heaven's Biggest Asshole, but right now I just wanted him to leave. "Yeah, right. I reminded her of her son, or that's what she said. I'm being *nice*. You might want to look that up in the official handbook. I believe that's what angels are supposed to be."

"Angels who are pussies, maybe." He shook his impressive quiff of hair and revved his engine. "Well, didn't mean to interrupt your good works. I'll tell everybody back at the Compasses we may not see you for a while, since you're busy ministering to the poor, fat, and horny."

He roared away, waving. He's not as bad as he seems, honest. Well, he is, but he doesn't really mean to be such a dick, God just drew him that way.

By the time I got back to Temuel I could tell he was a bit nervous. He told me we'd talk again soon, and that we should never discuss any of this stuff in Heaven, only here, and only when we were sure nobody could hear us. Then he just kind of slipped away.

It wasn't until I got back to my apartment that I realized my phone had been off all this time. A voicemail had come in from Sam, suggesting where we should set up the exchange with Eligor. By the time I finished listening to it, my phone was ringing again. The number was blocked, so I answered and said, "Yeah, I got your message."

"That's pretty impressive," said Eligor, Grand Duke of Hell. "Especially since I didn't leave one. Do you have what I need?"

Stopped me dead. The last time I'd heard that voice, its owner had just finished torturing me in pretty much every conceivable way, and was throwing me out to run for my life from Niloch and his hellhounds. You won't be surprised to learn that my heart sped up a bit, and I could taste blood in the back of my mouth. "Yeah, I have what you need. I already told your secretary. When do you want to meet?"

"What is it, one in the morning? I'll meet you an hour from now. Just tell me where."

"An hour?" As much as I was aching to get Caz away from him, I didn't know if I could get hold of Sam in time, and I couldn't retrieve the feather without him. "That's going to be difficult."

"Really? I'd have thought you'd be in more of a hurry to get your hands on the . . ." he paused for effect, ". . . merchandise." He laughed. I wanted so badly to reach through the phone and hit him in the face. "Well, you're the boss, Dollar, if you want to wait . . ."

"Never mind. I'll be ready. Meet me on the top floor of the parking structure opposite Pier 40. That's the one—"

"Next to the ferry port, yes, I know. I'll be waiting. Ciao!"

Yes, I know I let myself get hustled, but other than getting hold of

Sam, I didn't really have anything else to do to get ready. See, I was hoping that if I let Eligor think he had the upper hand, it would make things easier.

What's that you say? That Eligor really *did* have the upper hand, and I was a fucking idiot to let him hurry me? Sorry, I didn't catch any of that. You'd better tell me later when I'm not ignoring you so hard.

To my massive relief, Sam picked up when I called him, and he was still on my side of the funhouse mirror, so I wouldn't have to cancel the meet. He promised he'd be there.

"Are you really sure Pier 40's a good place to do it?" I asked.

"How could anyone be sure about something like this? But I think it's our best bet. Just think clean thoughts and I'll meet you in the parking lot down the street by Wimpy's Steamers about ten minutes to two."

"Right," I said and hung up. I was so nervous I really needed to piss. *What a piece of work is Man*, my ass. Brain too big, bladder too small, and only the most boring bits are immortal.

But even before I hit the bathroom, I filled my pockets with speedloaders full of silver bullets in case shit went south at the exchange. Not that they'd do me much good against the grand duke himself. In fact, if the swap did go fuckity-boom somehow, the only thing that might save me from Eligor would be if he started laughing at me so hard that he gave himself a rupture.

Still, there was just a chance, the tiniest, most unlikely chance, that it would all work and in a few hours I'd be bringing Caz back here to my apartment.

I remember wishing I had time to tidy up the place a little.

forty-seven
almost on the waterfront

BY THE time I made it to Wimpy's Steamers, a hamburger fetish restaurant in an old-fashioned silver diner car on Parade Street, Sam was just coming out with a bag full of tiny burgers. The burgers didn't bother me so much—even angels have to eat, at least on Earth—but he had Clarence the Junior Angel with him, which bothered me a lot.

"Oh, come on! Does everybody talk to everybody behind my back?"

Clarence smiled a little, but he had the good grace to look embarrassed. "Pretty much, Bobby."

"Pardon me for being difficult," I asked Sam, "but didn't *he*," I pointed to Clarence, "try to arrest *you*? And isn't he still supposed to?"

"Don't be so black and white about everything, B." Sam took a cupcake-sized burger out of the bag and pretty much inhaled it. "Yes, in other circumstances, our friend here might think it was his duty to turn me over to his superiors, my ex-bosses." He licked his fingers and then wiped them on the leg of his pants. I always hated when he did that. Dogs used to follow him in the park. "But like any sensible angel, he's capable of understanding that sometimes changing circumstances require more *flexibility*."

"What he's saying is that I'm here for you, Bobby," Clarence told me, sincere as someone delivering the wrap-up on an Afterschool Special. "I don't care what you might have done, you're still an angel, and we're still on the same side. No way I'm going to let some pitchforking high-hat take you out without a scuffle."

I groaned. "Jesus, Sam, that sounds like something you'd say. This sucks." My problem wasn't with a potential skirmish; I thought the kid would probably do okay. He'd had some training, and he could shoot pretty well. My problem was what Clarence would do if we all survived the night. "I can't risk it, Junior, sorry," I said at last. "Can't take you along. Can't risk you learning too much about my personal business."

"Why? I already know pretty much everything," he said. "I mean, I know all about your girlfriend from Hell. I've known that for a while and didn't tell anyone, so what's the problem now?"

"You *know*?" I turned to Sam. I could feel a vein in my temple throbbing like it was going to pop loose and start spraying high-pressure blood everywhere, like a fire hose. "He *knows*?"

"Don't blame me," said my best friend, absorbing another tiny burger. "Man, these are good. He already knew about Caz. Didn't have anything to do with me."

"Come on, Bobby!" the kid said. "What was I supposed to believe? That you left your body behind for three weeks so you could holiday at Sandals in Puerto Vallarta? Or, what did you actually come up with? Seattle? Yo, man—Hendrix museum and the Space Needle!"

I glared at him, and I pretty much meant it. "I liked you better when you were the village idiot. Okay, you can hang around, I guess. And I guess I appreciate it. But you *don't* get to do the jokes."

He didn't look particularly chastened. "Right, Bobby. Whatever you say."

It was just turning two o'clock as we walked down Parade toward Pier 40. I told them what I thought might happen and what I wanted them to do, whether things went as expected or not. When we reached the parking structure across from the pier, we found the chain, usually stretched across the entrance ramp at night, had been cut and left in two tangled piles like a pair of really depressed snakes.

It was a cool night, and the wind off the bay made it seem more like February than July, but I had hope to keep me warm. We made our way up to the top floor, talking quietly but making no other effort to disguise our arrival. Two figures were waiting in the far corner, next to Kenneth Vald's long black car, no doubt an armor job of Orban quality. Hell, the ancient Hungarian bastard might have actually customized Vald's car, for all I knew.

One of the pair was extremely tall, and the other was Eligor himself. I had to suppress a sudden flood of anger and panic. Where was Caz? Was she in the car? Was she even here?

Eligor's companion was more than just lengthy, he was also pretty strange: nearly seven feet tall and reasonably muscular, but his hands and feet were way too big for the rest of his body, and his head was too small, giving him the look of (I really can't find a nicer way to say it) a titanic pinhead. But the eyes in that sloping skull were sharp and focused, and I was quite sure those serving-plate hands were as strong as they looked.

"Mr. Dollar." Eligor wore his Kenneth Vald body and his most earnest leisure clothes, as if about to go yachting with his old prep-school chums. He looked at Sam, pausing just long enough to show that he recognized him, then flicked a glance to Clarence before turning back to me. "So we meet again! Congratulations on escaping. Oh, and those of us who find Commissar Niloch rather tedious would like to thank you for dropping his head down the Outer Gorge. It should take him a few thousand years to tongue his way back up."

"Where's the Countess?" It was all I could do not to shout.

Eligor shook his head. "No appreciation for the art of conversation. That's the problem with this tough-guy model of yours, Dollar—it's all terse quips and sour replies. What's wrong with Holmes or Hercule Poirot, heroes who could string a few words together?" He lifted an eyebrow at the involuntary growl that escaped me. "Oh, very well then, if you insist." He waved to the tall guy. "He wants to see the Countess, Fiddlescrape. Would you do the honors, please?"

The bodyguard opened the back door of the long car and bent over. He helped Caz get out, although "helped" isn't really the word I'd use unless fishermen "help" gaffed fish onto a boat. She was not her usual graceful self because her hands were tied behind her back. She was also gagged. I forced myself to take deep breaths so I didn't just shoot somebody.

"Now let her go, and you'll get the feather," I told the grand duke.

"This is the part Sam didn't really explain," said Clarence into my ear. "What's he want the feather for . . . ?"

"Shut up," I advised him. "Send her over, Eligor."

Eligor chuckled. "Oh, no, no. Feather first, then I promise you get the woman. You have my word."

"Great! I was so hoping I could get the sworn promise of one of Hell's biggest fixers," I said. "Because then I'd feel really secure." But I knew that he couldn't just cheat me. The lords of Hell have a curious love-hate relationship with the truth, and if you're smart enough, you can take advantage of that. "Go ahead, Sam. Get it."

Sam took out the thing he called the God Glove, the powerful article Kephas had given him when Sam first agreed to work for the Third Way. It was going to be pretty damned ironic that the glove Anaita had given Sam was going to help me again, I thought—my only cheerful reflection at that moment. The wispy nothingness flared white in the dark garage, bright as a road flare but with more colors. Once Sam had pulled it over his hand, he reached into my pocket and produced the feather. Clarence gaped, so fascinated by this display of heavenly magic that I was very glad I didn't need anything from him at that moment. Caz stared at me helplessly from behind the gag. I did my best not to get lost looking at her, but just seeing her out of the corner of my eye was like something sharp poking me in one of my ventricles.

Eligor eyed Sam's incandescent fingers. "My, you have been a busy little bee, Sammariel. Doloriel told me you could do that, but I didn't entirely believe him."

Sam gave him the fish-eye. "There's lots of things you don't know about, Your Grace. What do you want me to do with the feather, Bobby?"

"Give it to Clarence."

The kid looked at me like I'd just started speaking in tongues. "Huh? Why me?"

"To hold onto it," I said and eased my gun out of my pocket. "Because in a second things are going to start getting complicated. Take it."

Clarence did, wide-eyed. I could tell that just holding the thing was making him nervous. To be fair, if you ever saw it yourself, you'd be nervous too. Even an idiot would have known that it was a feather from a powerful angel. It was just . . . obvious.

"Now, go check Caz to see if she's all right, Sam," I said. He and I had discussed this, but that didn't make it any less dangerous. I flipped the safety on my pistol.

"Really, Dollar, this is insulting," said Eligor, but he was still grinning. "That's the problem with you Heaven people, you think you're the only honorable ones."

I met Caz's eye as Sam approached her. She looked strangely flat and hopeless, an expression I hoped would soon be explained. Sam passed his glowing hand over her head and in front of her, hovering for just a moment above the bodice of her white minidress. Caz stared at Sam's hand in what almost looked like terror.

"Not real, Bobby." Sam put his God Glove hand in his pocket. "She's an illusion."

I leveled my gun at Eligor's face. I was about fifteen feet from him and felt confident I could put at least two or three silver slugs into his earthly body before he could get me, no matter how fast he was. That ought to at least change the equation a bit, give me time to decide what to do next. I had assumed he'd play games, so I wasn't too surprised. "So, that's how it is, huh? Really?"

Eligor rolled his eyes. "Oh, please. Just having a little fun. You cloud-huffers need to lighten up a little." He gestured offhandedly and the false Caz vanished, leaving Fiddlescrape standing by himself in front of the open limo door. There was nobody else to be seen inside.

"You said you wanted an exchange, Eligor. I came to deal fairly. Now are you going to produce the Countess or am I going to turn your face into ground chuck? I owe you that and a whole lot more."

For the briefest moment the Kenneth Vald face shimmered and ran like water sheeting down a rock. Beneath it was something much, much worse, a mask of dark rage, a head shaggy with snaky hair and a pair of curving horns, one long, one oddly dwarfish and misshapen, like something that had melted in great heat. Then the genuinely terrifying anger-face dissolved back into the Vald smirk again. "Really, little angel?" he said. "You'd draw down on *me*?"

The grand duke didn't give any visual signal, but I heard Clarence gasp as Fiddlescrape shook a sawed-off shotgun out of his wide sleeve and into his hand, then pointed it at my head. It looked like a derringer in his massive fist. "Drop it or I'll drop you," the pinhead suggested.

Click. Click-click-click. Now Sam and a far-too-excited Clarence had their weapons out and cocked too, both of them sighted on Fiddlescrape. That added up to all of us except Eligor with our guns drawn, in a small, confined area. A lot depended on what the Horseman did next. I stared at him.

"Well?" I asked.

"Well, what?" Eligor was enjoying himself, or at least that's how it looked. "Are you doing Phillip Marlowe? Because if so, you'll have to make sure and end up sadder but wiser at the close of this evening."

"Just get on with it," I said. "I want Caz, like you promised back at Flesh Horse. I want her released, I want her healthy, and no reprisals, like you promised. For that, you get the feather. After that, you and Kephas can work out your own arrangements. I don't care about any of this political bullshit."

"Fine, fine. You're quite a whiner, aren't you? 'I want, I want . . .' Where *did* they find someone like you?" Eligor made a sarcastic show of sticking his hands in his pockets and looking around like he was really thinking things over. "All right, you win. Enough time wasted on this." He reached out to the side and suddenly there was a Zipper there, or at least the hellish version, a red glare traced like a vertical slash wound in the air. He reached through the red glare and pulled out another Caz, bound and gagged like the last one, but where the previous model had been strangely passive, this one was fighting to get free.

Eligor held her by the collar at arm's reach, as if she weighed no more than a polo sweater. Her kicking feet hung six full inches above the ground. "Take the bitch," he said. "All she ever does is complain, anyway."

"And this is really her, this time? You swear by the authority of the Highest?"

He rolled his eyes like a bored teenager. "Yes, just like I told you back in Flesh Horse. I showed her to you, and you said you'd give me the feather, remember? This is her, I promise. No, as you wish, I *swear by the Tartarean Convention, the authority of the Highest, and my own existence*. That's what you want, isn't it? To hear one of the lords of Hell give his solemn word? Then listen—*I swear by all those things that this is the same woman*."

Sam was slowly moving the God Glove over her head and above her breast. "This one is real, B."

Eligor set her down. She almost fell, but Sam caught her elbow and helped her find her balance. She ran to me, still gagged, arms still tied, and threw herself against me. I wrapped an arm around her, thrilled beyond anything I can say by the feeling of her heartbeat so close to mine.

"Give him the feather," I said.

"Are you sure?" Sam was looking at Eligor, who stood with arms folded. Fiddlescrape still had his shotgun pointed at us, but didn't look quite as eager to pull the trigger as he had a few moments earlier.

"Yeah. Give it to him."

Sam held it out, but being Sam he stayed where he was and made Eligor take a step toward him to get it. The grand duke took the feather between his fingers, then lifted it up to the weak yellow glow of the garage's ceiling lights. "It's a beautiful thing, really," the Horseman said. "Rather special, too, when you think about what it represents: Heaven and Hell working together. It's a pity you and the other small-minded folk can't think of anything better to do with that symbol than blackmail me."

I wasn't going to dignify this kind of bullshit with a reply. I kept my temper, concentrating instead on the slender, shivering woman pressed against me. She looked up, eyes pleading. I undid the gag, then bent and kissed her cheek, just a touch, before turning back to Eligor. She tasted of salt. I thought it was because she was crying.

"Oh, Bobby . . . !" she said. She definitely did not sound happy.

"Anything else? Last pithy one-liner? No? Well, you and your friends enjoy your evening, Dollar." The grand duke sauntered to his big car and climbed into the back. Fiddlescrape closed the door behind him. As the big freak got into the driver's seat and revved the engine, I realized it had been running quietly the whole time. Why should Eligor be ready for a quick getaway? He couldn't have believed that I was going to fall for his doppelganger, could he?

Eligor rolled down the backseat window. "I suspect we'll see each other again," he said as the car backed up and then turned to face the exit. "That's the way it is with annoying people, you just keep running into them over and over and over . . ."

And then the big car bumped down the ramp. Clarence let out a little breath of relief—it sounded like someone stepping on a hamster—and sat down on the oily cement floor of the parking garage. Obviously it had all been a bit much for him. But it had all been worth it, because I was holding Caz again.

I had been waiting until that bastard was gone to kiss her properly, but before I could lower my face to hers I realized that my arm felt wet where I was holding her. For an irrational moment I thought she'd been shot, even though no gun had been fired, and I was terrified.

She was crying, harder than I'd ever seen anyone cry, the tears just sheeting down her cheeks. Then her face began to waver, as if I was seeing it through deep water. A moment later everything that was Caz about her just washed away, like wet paint hosed off a wall, and I was staring down into the haunted, filmy eyes of Marmora, the drowned social secretary of Flesh House.

"I'm . . . I'm so sorry . . . Bobby . . . Dollar." Her voice was her own now, her body her own too, long and thin and weedy. The puddle around her feet was growing by the second as I stared in helpless terror. "She cares . . . so much." She coughed, bubbled a little. "I'm sorry. He made me . . . trick you," she murmured, her words fast becoming a gurgle. "And sorry . . . for me, too. I could have . . . lived here . . . and been happy, I think." Her head lolled on her long, pale neck and her poached-egg eyes took in the parking garage, the skid marks on the ground and the exhaust stains on the concrete walls. Her mouth twitched in an unsteady but radiant smile. "Here is . . . so . . . *beautiful* . . ."

And then she simply collapsed into liquid and color, running out of my arms and onto the hard floor in splashing rivulets. The water ran in all directions until one edge found the exit ramp, and then it all flowed that way, down into the lower level.

forty-eight
accessories after the fact

SOMEBODY WAS pounding on my door in a very determined manner. Really thumping away. Every impact seemed to crash through
my head like one of those super-slow-mo videos of someone shooting
an apple to pieces. I groaned and fumbled around on the floor next to
my bed for my automatic and clutched it against my chest. If the
pounding didn't stop soon, I was going to use it, either on the idiot at
the door or on myself, whichever would end the suffering quickest. I
didn't feel that way because I was hung over, either. I mean I *was*, like
a motherfucker, but the drinking and the aftereffects were just byprod-
ucts of how little I gave a shit about anything.

Thump, thump, thump. "Bobby! Open the door or I'll kick it in!" It
was Sam.

"Fuck you a hundred times for making so much noise," I shouted,
but that made my head hurt as much as the pounding had. I swear,
even for someone who'd recently dug into his own brainbox to remove
an angry intracubus, this was bad. "Go away, or I'll shoot you in the
dick."

"What's-his-name was right—you *are* a whiny little putz. Come on,
get up and let me in."

I realized that if I pulled the trigger in my present, rather impaired
condition, my aim might not be good enough to get off a fatal shot. It
would, however, go *BLAM* really loud right next to my ear. Then Sam
would kick in the door, *BANG BANG CRUNCH.* Might as well set my

own nervous system on fire and try to put it out with a tenderizing mallet. I started to crawl toward the door, got stuck behind the cheap sofa, then finally levered myself onto my feet and staggered to where I could let the noisy, heartless bastard in.

I still had the gun in my hand. Sam looked down, raised an eyebrow, and said, "Happy to see me?"

"Shut up. Never speak again. Come in if you have to."

"Can't. I'm waiting for Clarence. He's parking the car."

"Clarence?" I groaned and stumbled to the couch. "You brought him here? *Et* fucking *tu, Brute*?" Just thinking about the rookie's cheerful, boyish questions made me want to throw up inside my skull. "Just go away. Both of you." I closed my eyes and wished I would die faster.

"Not going to happen." I smelled something and opened them again. Sam was waving some kind of huge venti-trenti-giganti coffee under my nose. "Drink this. You've been locked in here for six days, B. It's bad, I know, but you can't just give up."

I laughed, but even I didn't like the way it sounded. "I can't? Just watch me, baby, and you'll get a master class in total surrender."

Clarence came stomping into the room like a mastodon in steel-toed boots. "Man, it stinks in here!" was the first thing he said.

"Nice to see you too, kid." I swirled a little of the hot coffee around in my mouth. I knew if I swallowed I was agreeing to live for at least a few more hours, and I wasn't in any hurry to sign that deal. Still, it tasted good. Well, it tasted hot and it tasted like coffee. Same thing. "Now why don't you both just fuck on off?"

"Because we're not going to let you drink yourself to death, Bobby," Clarence explained.

"Then you're too late. Because I'm already dead, remember? Now that *that's* solved, it really is fucking-off time for both of you. Drop by again soon. Early twenty-second century would be good."

Sam stood looking around the room. "And this, Clarence my young friend, is a perfect example of the power of self-pity. You can see it, you can hear it in his voice, and the Highest knows, you can smell it."

"Bite me, Sam. Seriously."

"Honestly, we know you're upset. We completely understand." Clarence came closer, stepping through the empties and the food bags as carefully as a minesweeper. I was terrified that he might sit near me and try to be helpful, but he stopped a few feet away so I didn't have to shoot him in the foot or anything. "But don't give up, Bobby. You know what they say—it's better . . ."

"If any of the next words out of your mouth are 'loved and lost,' kid," I told him, "I will hit you in the face so hard that your eyes and ears and all your other facial features will run around to the back of your head to hide and never come back. Never ever. You'll spend the rest of your angel life looking like a Mister Potato Head someone dropped from a tall building."

"See! You're still funny."

I closed my eyes again. "I've *been* to Hell already. Why are you doing this to me?"

"Because we want to get you out of here," said Clarence. "You need to get cleaned up. You need some air."

"What I really need—well, you'll know it's happening about the time you realize that screaming isn't helping you any."

Clarence sighed and rolled his eyes. "Sam, can you get through to him?"

Sam laughed. "Shit, he never listens to me. He wouldn't be in this situation if he did."

"What's that supposed to mean?" But I was still keeping my eyes closed. I hadn't entirely given up hope that these people talking so loudly in my apartment were just another nightmare of the kind I'd been having plenty of. "Seriously, you give the worst advice since someone suggested Lincoln take in a play on his night off."

"That's an old one, you pathetic lush." He turned to the kid. "You can tell he's perking up when he starts thinking he's amusing again. Don't tell him the truth or he might panic. Let's get him into the shower."

It wouldn't have been so bad if I'd remembered to pay my utilities. There would have been hot water.

We went to Oyster Bill's, on the waterfront.

I wasn't really going to be revived that easily, but I'd run out of mixers a couple of days earlier and the combination of straight booze and leftover bits of congealed fast food was killing me. Since I'd been in no condition to find my car, I'd started cutting the vodka with things like maraschino cherry juice. I made White Russians with little tubs of coffee creamer. After all that, I was more than ready to have a few drinks mixed by a professional. (Actually, this is slightly overstating the skills of the bartender at Oyster Bill's. Both he and the cook are obviously either relatives of Bill's or his old prison buddies, and both know just enough not to kill any of their customers. But on the plus side, the place also has a jukebox full of agonizingly horrible seventies and eighties pop music.)

Getting clean and leaving the house had definitely been a step forward, but if I was going to live, I'd need to find something worth living for, which meant finding something about *myself* worth living for. The failure side of the ledger was pretty impressive, and all I could come up with on the other side was Gob. I hadn't managed anything a real hero should have, like getting the poor kid out of Hell, but I'd at least helped him out of a terrible situation and into a slightly better one, with Riprash. That might count for something. Yeah, Bobby Dollar, demi-mini-quasi-hero.

Every time I tried to think of good things I'd accomplished, the rest of my failures wailed out at me like cartoon ghosts. The latest and biggest failure of all was Caz, of course. Even the idea of her was a scorched, radioactive hole in the middle of my thoughts—I couldn't ignore it, but I had to stay as far away as possible or I'd go crazy. But not thinking about her was really just another way of thinking about her, and then it all started over again.

Like I said, the failure side of the ledger was pretty impressive, maybe even spectacular. Case in point: I'd gone through everything Hell could throw at me and somehow managed to survive, but I'd lost the one thing I should have held onto at any cost—lost her because I was arrogant and careless, because I trusted my own ability to anticipate Eligor's tricks. Orpheus went all the way to Hades for his girlfriend, then lost her when he looked at her too soon. I lost my love because I hadn't looked carefully enough.

"I should have known," I said for what must have been the three hundredth time since the parking garage. "I should have never left Hell without her. He was setting me up way back in Flesh Horse—showing me a fake Caz and telling me he'd release her. He was already planning it then! He hands the fake over, and he's not breaking his word. He didn't even need to, but he had one last chance to torture me, and he took it."

My stomach felt curdled. I looked down at my Bloody Mary. Now that I was drinking one—well, my second, to be completely honest—I wondered if I really wanted any more alcohol. Oblivion was the only thing that had allowed me to survive the first few days, but even drinking wasn't helping much anymore. Unless I seriously intended to nosedive into the big black, I had to start thinking about other strategies. Tomorrow. I decided I would definitely start being alive again tomorrow. Or the next day. No, maybe I could do tomorrow.

Trying to care sucked.

"The thing is," said Clarence, "I still don't get what was so important about that feather. I mean, even if it was from one of our bosses, why should Eligor care? Is there something he can use it for? And why would he want it so much he'd give up the demon woman? Well, I guess not give her up, but at least pretend he was going to." He saw my face. "Sorry, Bobby."

Even with all the crazy stuff that had happened to me since I went to Hell, I'd continued to be selective about what information I'd share. Even Sam didn't know *everything*, because I'd kept from him what Walter Sanders had remembered. Even if Sam's Kephas really *was* Anaita, and she had sent Smyler to extort the whereabouts of the feather from me to protect her secrets, I didn't want to put Sam in the position of having to choose loyalties before I had better evidence. I didn't think he'd sell me out, but our friendship had changed in ways I didn't entirely understand yet, and I wanted to be fair to both of us. I could only hope I wasn't putting him in danger by holding out.

And Clarence knew even less, of course. He knew a lot more now than I would have liked, but he still didn't suspect how crazy this stuff really was, that a power as important as Anaita, a Heavenly Principality, could be revivifying serial killers and sending innocent angels like Walter to Hell. If I didn't completely trust Sam on the subject, I sure as holy harmony wasn't going to open it all up for the kid.

"The simplest version," I said, "is that Eligor made a deal with someone in Heaven, someone pretty important. The deal was about creating Sam's Third Way, a spot outside Heaven, Hell, and Earth. But Eligor wanted protection, especially against his own side's finding out, so he took the feather from the Heavenly Someone to use as—what? Blackmail fodder, I guess. The idea being that if the Heavenly Someone didn't uphold their end of the bargain, or things went bad, Eligor would have that feather to keep the angel honest, because it's basically a signed confession that says, 'I made an unauthorized deal with Hell.' Both of them had to keep their bargain secret. They couldn't let either side find out." I was suddenly, and rather surprisingly, hit with a hunger pang. Probably because I hadn't eaten in a day or so. "And now the bastard has the angel's marker back."

"So what does the important angel have?" Clarence asked.

"I don't know. Regrets, probably. Like all of us." Maybe I *would* get a little food, I decided. Nothing too dramatic, because my stomach wasn't up to it.

"Are you going to order something, B?" asked Sam. "Good plan. Get a stack of big old pancakes. Soak up some of that booze." He leaned back and sipped on his ginger ale. "Maybe I'll get some calamari. Even Bill's cook can't fuck something up too badly if it's deep-fried."

"You forget that time you found a double A battery in your fish and chips," I said, squinting at the menu. I waved for the waitress and sat back. Then, as if a fuse had been burning and finally reached the barrel of gunpowder, something went *"boom!"* in my brain. "Hang on a second—what did you say?"

"Calamari."

"Not you, you big asshole. Clarence."

The kid had to think for a moment. "I asked what the angel has."

"What the angel has . . . ?"

"Well, if the feather was a marker for a deal they had, what was the other marker? If the demon gets the feather, what does the angel get in case Grand Duke Eligor needs to be blackmailed some day?"

The waitress finally arrived, but I was too stunned to speak. At last Sam took pity and ordered pancakes and more coffee for me, as well as some crispy artery-clog for himself.

After the waitress wandered off, I was still thinking hard. I must have looked like I'd had a stroke, because Clarence leaned forward and said, "Are you all right, Bobby?"

"Kid, if I wasn't slightly insecure about my masculinity, and if I didn't know for a fact that Sam would never let me forget it, I'd kiss you right now."

"Huh?"

"You're right, you're right, you're so fucking right." I shook my head, amazed by my own epic stupidity. "I've been obsessing over this feather for months, but I never stopped to wonder what Eligor had to trade for it. But, of course, he must have swapped something. You don't swear blood brotherhood without both sides bleeding! And I know what it was."

"Can you summarize this shit before my calamari gets here?" Sam asked.

"Simple. I noticed something the other night."

"The other night, and several on either side of it, you were drinking heavily, listening to blues records, crying, and vomiting into your wastebasket," said Sam. "Occasionally all at the same time. Are you talking about *last week*, in the parking garage?"

"Whatever. The last time I saw Eligor he showed a little of his true face, just for a moment. Not that it's anything like a 'true' face," I explained to Clarence. "Because Eligor and the other fallen angels are . . . well, they're older than faces, actually. But he lost control, and I saw a little of his seriously-angry-demon face. I should have wondered why he always looked like Vald, even in Hell." I felt my heart beating. I wouldn't say I was feeling better, because I was still missing Caz so badly it was all I could do to talk and move around, but for the first time since Marmora turned to sludge in my arms, I felt there might still be something I could do. "But I didn't think about it. When his disguise slipped in the parking garage, one of his horns was . . . well, kind of crumpled and pathetic. Like when a goat or some other farm animal gets a horn sawed off, then it starts to grow back."

"So, you're saying . . ." Sam began.

"That when they made their deal, and our important angel gave Eligor a feather to hold onto, it's likely that Eligor gave the angel something, too—that horn, which still hasn't grown all the way back. That's why he's been hiding his real Hell-head."

Sam made an impressed face. "Huh."

"But knowing that still doesn't do you much good, does it?" asked Clarence. "I mean, if one of the big angels has Eligor's horn, how are you going to get hold of it?"

"You mean how are *we* going to get hold of it," I said. "Because I can't do it alone. I've tried and I've tried, and it's not working. I need both of you to help me."

Sam laughed, but it was one of his hollower efforts. "You dick. You're joking, right?"

"I can't afford to joke about this, Sam. It's too important. Eligor has the only woman I've ever cared about, and he also cheated me out of the feather—something I risked my life a dozen times for, at least. If I get hold of that horn, then I've got something on *him*! A bargaining chip!"

Clarence had finally figured out I was serious. "No. No way, Bobby. It's bad enough that I'm off meeting up with important demons in my off-hours, and covering up secrets that will get me in a lot of trouble if it ever comes up . . ."

Actually, secrets that will get you sent to Hell—or worse, I thought but was sensible enough not to say out loud.

". . . but I can't do this! Stealing from one of our bosses! So that you can get back together with your girlfriend from Hell!"

My pancakes arrived. I doused them in syrup and got to work. Suddenly, I really was hungry. "No, you can't afford to do that, Clarence. You're right. But you can't afford *not* to, either."

"Damn it, will you quit calling me Clarence!" He said this so loudly that people at other tables turned to look. He blushed—how come my Earth body never does that?—and leaned close to the table, as if he was only going to talk to the catsup bottle and the napkin dispenser from now on. "What do you mean, can't afford not to?"

"Because I'm going to go after it no matter what. And although I promise I would never voluntarily rat on either of you, if and when I get busted trying to do this, Heaven will probably squeeze every bit of information about the last few months out of me. Who knows what they can do to find things out? And that means they're going to know that you should have blown the whistle on both me *and* Sam a long, long time ago."

The kid was shocked. "Are you blackmailing me, Bobby?"

"No. Really, no. I'm just being a realist. You can't play this game both ways, Clarence—or 'Harrison,' if you really, honestly like that better. Personally, I think that name sounds like someone should be arranging playdates for you after your Suzuki Method violin classes." I poured some more syrup. "Clarence is way cooler."

He seemed stunned, although whether it was what I was saying or the fact that I'd actually remembered his name, I couldn't say. "I don't know. I have to think." A moment later he got up, fumbled out some money and dropped it on the table. "I have to go. I'm on call. I'll . . . I'll talk to you later."

"There goes your ride," I said as he left.

Sam snorted. "Are you kidding? I drove. Don't you remember?"

"That was your car we came in? How do you have a car, living in a funhouse mirror?"

"Borrowed it from Orban. He sympathizes with people who are kind of stuck between the two sides."

"Yeah, I guess he would." I finished off the rest of my pancakes and downed my coffee. "You wanna drop me back at my place? I've got to start thinking about what I'm going to do next."

"Aren't you worried about the kid?" Sam stood up, jingling his car keys. "That he's going to go drop a dime on you or something? Go right to your bosses?"

"Clarence? Yeah, right. That's why he left five bucks on the table for his cup of coffee. He's such an idealist, and he wants to hang out with us big boys so badly, that I'll probably have to hold him back when he decides to storm Heaven itself with guns blazing—for *Justice!*"

"That's a very scary thought," said Sam as we walked out to the parking lot, headed back to my place. "You're not really planning something like that, are you? I mean, even us Third Way folks don't actually want Heaven to collapse. Shit, we don't really even want Hell to collapse—there's a lot of scary motherfuckers locked up there, and I can't think of a better place for them."

"Oh, yeah," I said. "I agree. I think I met most of them. No, I don't want to tear anything down. I'm just tired of being kicked around, that's all. I want the truth."

Sam flicked away the toothpick he'd been using to work the calamari out from between his incisors. "You know that's exactly what people always say just before the *really* bad shit starts happening."

A bit of a wind came in off the bay, fresh but surprisingly cold.

"I want answers, Sam. I just want a fair shake. I don't want a revolution."

He spat something onto the asphalt. "From your mouth to the Highest's ear, B. Hope He's listening."

"Amen, buddy," I said. "Amen."

Then, believe it or not, I went home and cleaned my apartment. Because you've got to start somewhere.

epilogue
queen of the snows

I WAS THIRSTY. *I found a little bottle of bitter lemon in Caz's refrigerator and brought it back to bed. She was dozing, the sheet pulled up only to her thighs, and I stopped in the bedroom doorway, suddenly unable to breathe. So beautiful. I know I keep saying it, but it's because I'm not good with words, not about things like that, anyway. She was a small woman, slender, but the curve of her haunch still made weird things happen in the pit of my stomach (and other places). I can't explain it, but something about that wonderful slope between hip and ribs that you see when a woman's lying on her side . . . well, it's a lot like poetry, I guess: If you analyze it too much, you miss the most important part.*

And her hair, so long, so straight, so pale, like Caz herself. The longing was already so strong in me that I couldn't help wondering whether I'd been snared by one of those famous infernal snares. But I hadn't. It was her, and the things I felt were real. I'd been suckered by Hell more than once. I knew the difference.

She rolled over and peered at me out of one eye. "What are you staring at? Haven't you ever seen a fallen woman before?"

"Never seen one who fell this far."

"You mean to San Judas, or to you?"

"Either way." I sat down on the edge of the bed because I wanted to look at her, and I knew if I got too close I'd get distracted again by all the fascinating novelty of touch and smell and taste.

I know it sounds crazy, but right at the moment I was thinking of a picture I'd once seen of this '60s actress, Jean Seberg, wearing armor to play Joan of

Arc. Unlike Caz, she had her hair cut really short, and, of course, she was wearing a couple of dozen pounds of metal to Caz's absolutely-nothing-but-half-a-bedsheet. But there was still something compellingly similar—the delicacy of her face, maybe, the fragility of that slender body set against a big, dangerous world. I don't think that actress had a much better time of things than Joan, so maybe it wasn't a very healthy comparison.

"You're still staring."

Caught, I laughed. "Sorry. You're . . . I was just thinking about Joan of Arc."

"Why, are you planning to set me on fire?"

"Only with mah love."

Caz laughed, which was nice of her. On her back now, she pulled the sheet up to her navel, which didn't really solve the problem of me staring or being distracted. "I remember when she was executed."

"Wow. Were you there?"

"Me?" She shook her head. "No, of course not. You're such an American! I was in what's now Poland, at least a thousand miles away. But the word of it spread all over Europe. My husband, may his soul never rest, heard about it when he was traveling and couldn't wait to come home and tell me about it. He thought it was—I don't know. Fascinating. Exciting." She was silent again. "When my own time came, I thought of her. Not of her faith, though. I had none of my own left at that point."

I was about to ask a question, but the look on her face stopped me.

"I thought of her because the horror was not in dying, but in the hatred of the crowd. There must have been at least a few watching in Rouen who thought she was innocent, after all, or at least not worth hating—someone gave her a cross made of sticks, so she wouldn't have to face the end without God. But I don't think there was a single person in that crowd in our city square, not even my own children, who didn't think I deserved to die in agony."

At that moment, for the first time, I really felt the difference between her and me, or rather, between her memories and mine. I shuddered, imagining the avid, hostile faces of the medieval crowd.

"Don't," I said. "It's over. You're here—I'm here."

She turned to me. For a moment I thought she was angry. I'm still not quite sure what the expression on her face meant, but all she said was, "It's never over, Bobby darling. Hell doesn't work that way."

I climbed in next to her and put my arms around her, and she turned until her rear was against my groin. I did my best to ignore the distracting nearness of her, her warmth against me, the feeling of her breasts moving against my forearms as she breathed.

"I can't get over how pale your hair is," I said as I kissed the back of her neck. I spent a lot of our night together doing that. "It's amazing—nearly white. Do you have Vikings in your family history?" I guess it could have been dyed, although it matched the rest of her coloring, but I had learned enough in my years on Earth to know that, "Do you dye your hair?" is only a marginally more acceptable thing to ask a woman than "When are you expecting?"

She shrugged in my arms. "Vikings? Possibly. But my people were a mixture of so many things: Slav, German, Goth, even Mongols." She slid back against me, pressing firmly, not in a sexual way but like someone seeking comfort. "There's an old story about where the golden-haired people come from. A Gypsy story."

"Gypsy? You have Gypsies in your blood, too?"

"No, I don't think so." Her voice had slowed a little; I wondered if she was getting sleepy again. "They had only been in the kingdom for a few generations. But we had a Gypsy servant when I was a girl, and she would sometimes tell me stories while she worked."

I waited. "And the story? About the people with golden hair?"

It took Caz a moment to get started again. "Yes. She said that once upon a time, a tribe of Gypsies had camped at the base of a mountain. They didn't go up it, because it was always misty and cold, and at night they could hear voices howling in the wind. The only man who was brave enough to climb it at all was a fellow named Korkoro the Lonely, a young man who had no family of his own. But even he wasn't foolish enough to climb too high, because he would have been trapped there when the sun went down.

"Then one night there was a terrible, terrible storm, with thunder and lightning. The whole top of the mountain was covered in mist, so that the peak was invisible. A woman appeared near the Gypsy camp—a beautiful but very strange young woman with white hair and blue eyes—"

"Like you," I said.

"Shut up, Wings, I'm telling a story." She reached back and stroked me with her hand in such a way that I became very distracted. It worked though: I stopped interrupting. Of course, it did make it a little difficult to concentrate on her Gypsy story.

"Anyway, the first person who met her was Korkoro the Lonely, who liked

to roam far from the camp, hunting. He brought her back and the people of the camp fed her and gave her wine to drink, but they were still frightened because she looked so strange. All the Gypsy folk were dark, with hair and eyes like night, but she was like something from another world.

"They asked her where she had come from and who her people were, and the pale-haired woman told them the she was the Queen of the Snows, and that she lived atop the cold mountain with her father, the King of Fog, but that she had escaped from his court because she had heard that humans knew how to love and that was what she wished to learn more than anything else.

"She fell in love with Korkoro, who had found her, and he fell in love with her, and at last the tribe of Gypsies came to trust her, although she was always strange to them. She and Korkoro—who was no longer called 'the Lonely'—had twenty children, and each one had hair the color of light, like the mother. And that is where golden-haired people came from, according to the Gypsies."

"And is that the end of the story?"

She stiffened a little in my arms. "Not entirely. I mean, not the version I learned."

"So what happened?"

"I don't remember. I'm tired, Bobby. Let me sleep for just a little while."

And I should have. But I wanted every moment we had, and I also wanted to know why she'd left off the end of the story. "Is it one of those where one of the kids grows up to be some hero?"

"No." She sighed. "No. Her father, the Fog King, was jealous of her living among humans and especially of her being married to one. So he ordered her to come back or he would destroy the Gypsies. A mist surrounded the Gypsy camp, and it was full of the Fog King's soldiers. Their eyes gleamed like cats' eyes. Korkoro wanted to fight, but the Queen of the Snows knew that the Gypsies couldn't defeat the Fog King, so when it was dark she walked away into the mist and disappeared. But she left her children behind, and they all lived to grow up and marry and bear children of their own, and all of their descendants had the same pale hair, and so ever after in Poland there were people with hair like mine." She curled herself up a little smaller. "Now let's sleep. Please."

"But what did Korky do?"

"What?"

"Korky, Korko, Korkodorko, whatever his name was. Her husband. The one who found her and fell in love with her. What did he do when she vanished back to the Fog Kingdom?"

"Nothing. There was nothing he could do. No living man could reach the top of the mountain where the Fog King lived. Korkoro raised his children. He remembered her. That's the end of the story."

"That's stupid," I said, and rolled onto my back.

For a moment Caz just lay where she was, but then she gave in and rolled over so that she was facing me, or at least facing my side. Me, I was staring up at the ceiling.

"Stupid? It's just an old story, Bobby."

"I don't care. I want stories to make sense. I would never have let you . . . if I was that Korkadoodledoo guy, I would never have just let her go. I would have gone after her."

"But he couldn't." She said it patiently, as though I could see it too if I just tried hard enough. "There was nothing he could do. She was gone. He had to learn to live without her."

"No way," I said. "He should have climbed that mountain."

"He would have been killed." She stroked my head as though I were a feverish child. "And then the children wouldn't have had a mother or a father."

"Doesn't matter. He should have gone after her."

She stared at me—I could feel it more than see it from the corner of my eyes. Then she levered herself up a bit and lay her head on my chest. "Sometimes there's just nothing to be done, Bobby."

"Bullshit, Caz. There's always something you can do."

"It's a fairy tale. Why are you angry?"

She was right, and I didn't really know why I was angry. I didn't then. I do now, of course, and I suspect you do, too.

"All the same, he should never have let her go." I wrapped my arms around her as though to keep her with me when the fog rolled in. "Never."

"Sometimes it's more complicated than that," she told me.